Swallows   12
+
House Martin

2 Swifts

Woodpecker   14·3

thrush   15·5.

Goldfinches — jackdaws —
wood pidgeon — lots of sparrows
+ blackbirds
  first bat of the year

    the Dairy at Hoff.

LOTHARINGIA

ACKNOWLEDGEMENTS

This book would not have been the same without the honesty, passion, generosity, and attention to detail of my editors, David Imrie, Sam Clarke and Johanna Craven. A huge thank you for your patience, kindness, and support.

Special thanks to my cover designer Jenny at Historical Fiction Book Covers for turning my vision into reality.

LOTHARINGIA
Charlemagne's Heir

Lara Byrne

Let your women keep silence in the churches: for it is not permitted unto them to speak; but they are commanded to be under obedience, as also saith the law.

St Paul, Corinthians 14:34, King James Translation

NOTE FOR READERS

The cast of this novel is multicultural and multilingual. I have called the characters what they would have called themselves in the language of the land they lived in. I felt it was fitting to acknowledge them as human being, as well as historical characters.

CAST OF CHARACTERS

The Canossa-Lotharingia household

Matilde Attoni, Countess of Canossa, soon-to-be Margravine of Tuscany
Beatrice, Margravine of Tuscany, Princess of the Holy Roman Empire, Matilde's mother
Gottfried, former Duke of Lower Lotharingia, Matilde's stepfather and Beatrice's husband
Vinicia, Matilde's personal maid
Rolando, captain in the service of Margravine Beatrice
Godefroy, Matilde's stepbrother and betrothed, soon-to-be Duke of Lower Lotharingia
Albert, German pilgrim living in Mantova

The royal court of the German Kingdom

Heinrich, third ruler of the Salian dynasty, King of Germany, Italy and Burgundy, designated Holy Roman Emperor, Matilde's overlord
Adalbert, Archbishop of Bremen, Heinrich's former regent, now advisor
Agnes, Dowager Empress, King Heinrich's estranged mother
Anno, Archbishop of Cologne, Arch-chancellor for the Italian Kingdom
Berta, Heinrich's wife, Queen of Germany, Italy and Burgundy, designated Holy Roman Empress
Siegfried, Archbishop of Mainz, Arch-chancellor for the German Kingdom
Rudolph of Rheinfelden, Duke of Swabia, Heinrich's brother-in-law

Adelheid, Abbess of Quedlinburg, Heinrich's sister
Guiberto, Archbishop of Ravenna, former Chancellor of the
Italian Kingdom, Matilde's cousin
Otto of Nordheim, Duke of Bavaria
Cuno, Heinrich's childhood teacher, now his chamberlain

The papacy

Pope Alexander, formerly Bishop of Lucca and confessor to
Matilde and Beatrice
Pier Damiani, Cardinal, former hermit, chief papal advisor,
friend of Gottfried
Ildebrando di Soana, chief papal advisor, head of Roman
diplomacy
Hugh of Cluny, head of the most powerful monastic order,
godfather to King Heinrich, technically Ildebrando's superior

HOLY ROMAN EMPIRE c.a. 1062

Hildesheim
Goslar
Quedlinburg
Aachen
Trier
Mainz
Worms
Nurnberg
Speyer
Regensburg
Ulm
Augsburg
Cluny
Reichenau
Basel
Mantova
Canossa
Lucca
Rome

PROLOGUE

Mantova Royal Palace, March 1048

'My name is Albert,' said the blind man in rags kneeling on the uneven mosaic floor of the great hall.

'I live in the pilgrims' shelter of Santa Maria Maddalena.' He spoke with a strong German accent.

Margravine Beatrice of Tuscany examined him from her throne on the dais. 'How do you make a living?'

His head dropped lower. 'I beg.'

The unease jarred with the poverty of his clothes. Long silver hair, slightly receding, framed a face made striking by a refined, straight nose and solid cheekbones. He must have been a handsome knight in his youth – before his sight and his life had been wrenched from him. His dignity was all he had left.

She reached out. 'We can speak in German. It is the tongue of my childhood. What brings you to me?'

He lifted his chin, facing her with his empty gaze. 'An angel appeared to me and ordered me to dig in the vegetable gardens of Santa Maria Maddalena. The monks will not allow it.' 'They cannot let people root their food out on a fancy—'

'But it is there!'

'What is there?'

'Our Saviour's blood, brought here by the soldier.'

The story was well known in Mantova. The legionnaire Longinus, serving in Palestine under Pontius Pilate, was going blind. Ordered to carry out the Crucifixion, he had pierced Jesus's chest with his spear. Blood drops had gushed out of the wound, spraying his eyes and restoring his sight.

Humbled by the Saviour's mercy, Longinus had converted and collected the blood-soaked sand at the foot of the cross, becoming its custodian.

At the end of his service, he had retired to Mantova. The locals,

i

though, were not ready for his new God. The vegetable gardens of Santa Maria Maddalena stood on the spot where he had suffered martyrdom, or so the stories said.

According to other stories, eight centuries later, Saint Andrew had appeared to a man from Mantova in a dream, ordering him to dig in the gardens.

The man had unearthed two iron coffers. One contained the bones of Longinus and his spear. The other was full of sand the colour of dried blood, covered with a red-stained sponge, used by the legionnaire to wipe the Lord's blood from his eyes.

The relics had attracted swathes of pilgrims from nearby areas, and the attention of Charlemagne. A century afterwards, during the Hungarian siege of Mantova, the holy objects had vanished, as if swallowed by the earth.

Beatrice challenged the beggar. 'What proof do you have?'

'The angel visited my dreams, three times, with the same message.'

She addressed the captain of her bodyguards. 'Find two soldiers and excavate where this man tells you.'

The small squad returned in the late afternoon, shoving the beggar in. The captain gave his account. 'We dug up the whole orchard and the herb garden—'

Albert clenched his fist. 'We gave up too soon! It is there!'

'Perhaps your dream's meaning is not literal,' she said in German to shelter him from the soldiers' judgement. 'Why would different people bury the relics in the same place?'

She placed a silver coin in his hand and waited for the reaction. Charlatans would conjure the most amazing stories to get her to loosen the strings of her purse. The old man felt the metal with his fingertips, and all he could muster was a polite thank you: he did not care about the coin.

She chose words that would not be too hurtful. 'God speaks to us in mysterious ways. Your faith will guide you to the meaning of His message.'

His hands joined in prayer. 'I beg you to heed the angel's call.'

One guard touched him to indicate he should leave. He refused all help and felt his way out of the throne room.

§

Protected by her bodyguards, Beatrice left the chapel of San Michele after daily Mass. The veil was her shield, preventing eye contact as she hurried onwards, past the dissonant choir of supplicants scrambling to get near her. Her secretary was handing out coins and collecting requests written on sheepskin parchment, each action turning a loud voice into a grateful murmur, or silence.

A voice reached her from the back of the small crowd. 'It is in the vegetable patch, by the garden wall, in the corner.'

Few people in Mantova spoke German.

The crowd stilled, following her gaze. Albert was tall, so she identified him easily.

'Let the blind man come forward.'

They parted like the sea, steering him towards her. Albert dropped to his knees and his hand felt the air, looking for hers to kiss.

'I have had another vision, Margravine,' he whispered on her fingers. 'I beg you for one last chance.'

She turned to her captain. 'Go with him. Dig where he said and nowhere else.'

She pressed on, wondering how she would feel if she lost the gift of sight, and if that loss alone could breed a need for visions. Hopefully, a last search would give old Albert the peace he needed.

The guards found her in her chamber, singing songs about the spring rain with her one-year-old daughter, Matilde, and the girl's nurse.

They were carrying a plain, earth-encrusted chest. Albert was not with them. She handed the girl back to the nurse.

'What is inside?'

'The beggar said only you should open it, Margravine.'

'Do it for me.'

The wooden chest looked ancient, with rusty hinges. It may have been locked at some point, but the mechanism had rusted too, so it opened easily. It revealed two caskets: one silver and one gold, lying side by side.

She felt dizzy. 'Open the silver one.'

'Sand, Madonna, with brown... streaks.'

Beatrice seized the sides of the coffer and peered inside the silver box. She did not dare touch the sand. 'Open the golden casket.'

The lifted lid revealed a threadbare sponge and a piece of parchment, probably ripped in haste from a manuscript. She unrolled the frayed vellum. Just a few sentences in basic Latin.

On this precious cloth is the blood of He, who gave His life for us.

Longinus ended his mortal life in Mantova. Before his martyrdom, he asked to be buried with his Spear, and the cloth he had wiped our Lord's wounds with, and the earth on which the Saviour's blood had dripped.

The Hungarians are climbing our city walls. Death will be upon us all. The bishop is taking care of the Spear. In this coffer, I am interring the Holy Blood, to protect it from the barbarian rage.

Through these relics, the Lord anointed Charlemagne king of kings. May a new Charlemagne one day reclaim the Blood and the Spear and restore peace and justice to Christendom. Amen.

Romualdo, Canon of Santa Maria Maddalena
A.D. 924

Memories of the Hungarians' savagery still persisted in Mantova, so the message between her fingertips was surely the brave canon's testament. A tear made the characters more vivid as she whispered a prayer to his soul.

Albert's faith had protected the memory of the canon's courage, ensuring his sacrifice had not been in vain. Extricating herself from the sorrow, she absorbed the implications of the discovery, for the world and for her life.

The canon's message corroborated the truthfulness of another text, a prophecy she had been secretly guarding for ten years, the last words of her ancestor Charlemagne.

iv

Since his death, the world had been out of joint. It was time to restore it to greatness. And she would be the instrument of that restoration.

Longinus's Spear was now in the hands of the Holy Roman Emperor, the heir of Charlemagne's mantle. God had picked the actors in the contest that would decide the future of Christendom, anointing her bloodline.

Emperor Heinz only had daughters, whereas she had the Blood, and a son. The Lord's perfect symmetry. With honour, though, came danger. The emperor did not know, should never know, that she was the custodian of Charlemagne's prophecy.

'What shall we do with the coffer, Madonna?'

'Leave it here.' Best to keep the relics away from prying eyes, while she decided what to reveal, and to whom. In the meantime, she had a debt of gratitude. God had sent a German beggar as His angel.

'Fetch Albert,' she said. 'I need to bow to his faith.'

CONTENTS

A.D. 1062

I.

Bay of Ostia, 25 April 1062

Being sixteen and a woman, Countess Matilde had never set foot on a warship, or even travelled by sea. Yet here she was, on her fifth day aboard the admiral galley, a few miles from the fleet's destination. The previous week, the German troops of Antipope Cadalus had breached the *Civitas Leonina*. Saint Peter had fallen, and Cadalus had recited Mass over the tomb of the Apostle.

Holed up in the walled hilltop monastery of Santa Maria in Aracoeli, the legitimate pope, Alexander, could not hold out forever.

Dawn was spreading across the water when she joined the commander on the stern. She was dressed to blend in, in black hose and tunic, light leather armour protecting her chest and back.

'Not long.' The commander's eyes scouted the shore, silhouetted by dark woods. 'The south-westerly blew us all the way.'

Gottfried, her stepfather, arrived, helmet in hand, with the defiant grin of a warrior before battle. 'The hard part begins now.'

He had agreed a truce with Cadalus to escort the Holy Father out of Rome. A squad of his best fighters was waiting on the starboard side.

She looked him in the eye. 'I am ready to play *my* part.'

'You are untested in battle.'

'You made a promise to my mother.'

'Follow me.' He descended the command platform. Even before they were out of earshot, he waved an admonishing finger at her. 'Do not question my orders. Do you know what the punishment for insubordination at sea is?'

'I only ask that you keep your promise—'

His chest heaved under the armour. 'I made *two* promises to your mother: you will play a role in this, and you will be safe.'

'What role do I play sitting here?'

He rolled his eyes. 'Would you rather take charge of the fleet?'

- 2 -

'Of course, I would.'

He studied her, both eyebrows raised. 'The fleet is yours then – until I come back.'

Nerves made her feel sick, but she would not have it any other way. In charge, despite her sex. 'What are your orders?'

'Avoid interception. If intercepted, flee. Preserve the ships at all costs. No fleet, no journey back.' He put the helmet on. 'Marco, the commander, stays with you. Rely on his knowledge. No-one sails like a Pisan.'

He climbed back onto the command platform as the ship prepared to anchor. Sailors lowered the square sails, and below deck the oarsmen slowed their pace to the rhythm of the rolling waves.

Gottfried was talking to Marco, presumably about her being in charge; the commander received the news expressionless.

They had reached the mouth of the Tiber, the contours of the riverbanks hazy in the early morning light. The fleet scattered around the admiral. Rowers locked their oars and sailors dropped the anchor. Ropes lowered launches into the water.

Gottfried patted her on the shoulder. 'May God be with you.'

'And with you.'

From the bulwark he slipped into the launch on the starboard side. Four of his men joined him, with another five lowering themselves down the port side to fill the second launch.

Similar operations took place on all galleys, and soon a swarm of small vessels rowed off, disappearing past a bend in the river. Local henchmen waited there, ready to let them into Rome for handsome pay.

Matilde scanned the deck. She had to assert her authority at once, or they would question her abilities. 'Place lookouts along the bulwark and up in the crow's nest. Everyone else on standby.'

Marco shouted the command to the deputy at the bow, who repeated it across the water. The watchmen took their positions.

The silence amplified the murmur of the waves. All twelve galleys, sails furled, lay waiting in half sleep. Twelve galleys, twelve like the apostles – a good omen, according to her stepfather. She tried not to think of Judas.

Gottfried expected the mission to last most of the day, even provided things went to plan both inside the city, and there, on the

Tiber.

The fleet's presence would not go unnoticed; German silver made easy friends; the Normans ventured along the coastline and upstream, in search of ransom; as for the Saracens, she could not afford to worry about ending up a slave in Cordoba or North Africa.

Her mother had not let fear deter her when, two months earlier, Antipope Cadalus's army had crossed the Alps in the melting snow. While the subalpine lords, torn between their oath to the child king Heinrich of Germany and their oath to the Holy Roman Church, had laid low, she alone had stood in his way.

'God will be with us,' she had said, ordering her soldiers to dig a trench across the Roman road between Verona and Modena, forcing the Germans to a temporary but humiliating halt.

Trust God, not fear, Matilde reminded herself, slipping into the commander's seat.

Blinding sunshine flooded the deck, conferring on the events that had led a young woman to lead a fleet in the Tyrrhenian Sea the texture of a strange dream.

Her father, Margrave Bonifacio of Tuscany, the most feared warrior of his generation, killed when she was six... Her brother and sister's deaths... She becoming her father's unlikely successor, unless her overlord King Heinrich objected... Her mother who saw herself as equal to men and taught her to do the same... Her confessor Anselmo da Baggio, who had strengthened her faith in God and in herself with the love of a father for a daughter, before being called to Rome and becoming Pope Alexander.

She was here because could not bear to lose him. 'Trust God, not fear.'

The lookouts were intent on their jobs. If they were uncomfortable with the idea of a woman in charge, they were careful not to show it. Marco was checking the horizon.

'Time for fresh men?'

He went off to execute her order, and she sat, cross-legged, staring into the blue.

Marco re-joined her. Still no news. Peaking, the sun started its descent into the sea. Neither spoke, and she was grateful for the silence.

'They are coming!' One lookout pointed his tanned forefinger towards the bend of the river.

The rowers were spitting their lungs out, as if they had enemies on their tail. Gottfried, on the first vessel, was slamming an oar. He was sharing his seat with another man, wrapped in a dark hooded cloak. It had to be *him*. The launches pushed closer, and the sailors threw rope ladders to help the men onboard. Hands grabbed hands.

The *anulus piscatoris*, the pope's ring, caught the pink light on top of the bulwark. Gottfried's solid frame helped the Holy Father onto the deck.

Matilde kissed the ring and Pope Alexander lifted her face to his. 'God will not forget your courage, daughter.'

Gottfried tugged his cloak. 'Let's lift anchor. I don't trust that snake. Your Holiness, let me show you to my cabin. You and I need rest.' He winked at her. 'Matilde and Marco, sail us back to Pisa.'

'Yes, sir.'

Her face was neutral, but her heart was singing. She had won Gottfried's trust as a leader of men.

The sun was fanning flames, low on the water. On the platform, the air was heavy with the living smell of the sea, and foam wetted her plaited tresses and sprayed her face.

She did not wipe it off; it would dry on her skin. A few drops of it slipped through her lips and she tasted salt on her tongue; the taste of adulthood, the taste of freedom.

II.

Greetings between Pope Alexander and Margravine Beatrice were always awkward. As the Holy Father, he was her and Matilde's shepherd, with the power to judge and excommunicate. As the Bishop of Lucca, he was their subject. 'This is not feudal homage,' he said, kissing her mother's ring. 'I owe you my life.'

In return, Beatrice's lips brushed the *anulus piscatoris*. 'You will repay me by saving my soul.'

'I am also indebted to Matilde, our distinguished admiral, and to our brave Duke Gottfried.'

Her mother squeezed her hand.

'After dispensing all this praise and gratitude, you will need to protect me from the sin of vanity, Holy Father,' Gottfried joked. 'Thank you for calling me duke, though.'

'When this struggle is over, I will back your claim to your ancestral title in Lotharingia.'

Smugness spread over Gottfried's face. 'You would make me the happiest man.'

Beatrice cleared her throat. 'I have news from Germany.'

Gottfried eyed her. 'Good news, I hope?'

He and Matilde arranged four chairs to form a small circle in the middle of the hall.

'Significant. King Heinrich has been snatched from his mother and is now in the custody of Archbishop Anno of Cologne.'

Pope Alexander voiced Matilde's thoughts. 'The poor child.'

Gottfried raised an eyebrow.

The pope noticed it. 'I cannot condone kidnapping an eleven-year-old. The boy was barely five when they placed him on that throne. He deserves compassion.'

Gottfried scratched his beard at the light rebuke. 'Beatrice, where is Empress Agnes?' Although the king's mother, Agnes was his regent, and politics seemed to be all that mattered to Godefroy.

Her mother replied in turn. 'Her whereabouts are unknown.'

Gottfried rubbed his hands. 'So, Empress Agnes, the architect of Cadalus's election, is consigned to history!'

Pope Alexander made his nod slow. 'Being the Crown's Archchancellor for Italy, I hope Anno appreciates the disadvantages of her policy.'

Beatrice pursed her lips. 'I would not be so sure.' Regardless of his theoretical loyalty to Rome, Anno had not prevented the empress from backing Cadalus.

Gottfried shrugged off her pessimism. 'He is minor nobility but fancies himself a cardinal. This could play into our hands.'

'On the subject of cardinals, any news of Ildebrando?'

'My son sent word to me in Pisa,' said Gottfried. 'They are on the Via Cassia; they should be here soon.'

At his words, Matilde froze. In their time at sea, Gottfried had never mentioned that his son, her betrothed, was in Italy, involved in the mission. The bars of her cage were closing in, and after the freedom and hope she had known at sea, she could not bear it.

In Beatrice's chamber, maids armed with needles and silk threads were at work on a tapestry portraying her ancestors.

Matilde often thought that needlework was an apt expression of her mother's true self: a weaver in the fashion of Athena, a warrior of the mind.

Beatrice's pale blonde tresses and slight frame disguised a sharpness of wit and an indomitable spirit.

Femininity had prevented her from leading armies on the battlefield and maybe from seizing the crown of Germany. But when it came to diplomacy, she would outdo any prince of the empire.

She waved. 'Join us, Matilde.'

'I am useless a needlework.'

Beatrice handed silky threads of vibrant colours to her women. 'I did not know about Godefroy either.'

'Is Gottfried trying to put pressure on me?'

Beatrice drew away from the tapestry, out of earshot. 'It could put ideas in his head if I asked.'

'I do not need a husband.' She meant it.

'I know. But I am a woman, regent for another woman. This has never happened in the history of the Holy Roman Empire. The

Lotharingians are our allies. We need to bide time for now, at least until King Heinrich comes of age and confirms you as your father's successor.'

'Too much time, perhaps. 'Heinrich is eleven.'

'Right now, his age is a positive, Matilde. For the sake of peace, your marriage should receive your overlord's approval – when he comes of age.' Beatrice smiled briefly. 'Gottfried can press as much as he likes; Pope Alexander will stand firm; he has promised.'

The joy of her time at sea returned for a moment. Matilde hugged her mother.

There was a commotion in the palazzo courtyard. Below their window, next to a Benedictine monk, a cloaked man with a hunched back was handing his horse to a guard.

Technically, Matilde's betrothed and stepbrother, Duke Godefroy, was not a duke. His father had been stripped of his ducal lands in Lotharingia before marrying Beatrice. But he demanded to be addressed by the title.

A full-grown man, of average height and strong built, six years older than her; apart from his hunch, he was not unsightly. But she wanted nothing to do with him; he scared her. She had heard stories of his cruelty in battle, unnecessary cruelty: burning harvests, starving villages, torture.

Next to him, the smaller and angular Ildebrando di Soana, in his grey Benedictine cassock, was holding the reins of his mount. A little stable boy came forward to help.

'Faster!' Godefroy shouted at him.

Ildebrando placed the bridles in the child's hand and set off across the courtyard. The little helper began to pull the horse towards the stables.

'Look at me when I speak to you.' Godefroy snatched the whip from him.

Trembling, the boy stopped.

Ildebrando, on the opposite end of the courtyard, stopped in his tracks.

Grabbing the boy's collar, Godefroy slapped him across the face.

Ildebrando shook his head but dashed off.

Godefroy let go, and the child fell to the ground, face forward. He was not moving. Her betrothed kicked him a few times.

'No-one keeps the Duke of Lotharingia waiting, piece of scum. I will use the whip on your face next.'

Matilde's gaze met her mother's. Horror mirrored horror.

Beatrice called a maid away from the tapestry. 'A boy in the courtyard needs help.' She had tears in her eyes.

III.

Reading Ildebrando's motives was impossible, but passions would fleetingly colour his coal-dark gaze. He was pleased to see Beatrice.

'Madonna.' The archdeacon lay his quill aside, pointing to a seat. A sheet of parchment was open on the table, and he placed weights at both ends to let the ink dry. 'So thoughtful of you, furnishing me with fresh vellum before my arrival.'

'I knew you would be aching to resume the work of God.' She smiled. 'Especially considering the developments in Germany.'

'Before we delve into that discussion, I finally have the opportunity to thank you for the trench. In bravery, you tower above all the great lords of the empire.'

Interesting language. The great lords of Germany, Burgundy and Italy, be it dukes, margraves or archbishops, called themselves *princes* of the Holy Roman Empire. Ildebrando's choice of words highlighted that the only princes, for him, were the archbishops – subject to an imperial pope.

'I just answered God's call.'

He rolled the sleeves of his grey cassock. 'Now, Germany. Have you heard from the empress?'

'No,' she lied. Agnes had asked for help, but Ildebrando did not need to know. 'I have... my sources.'

He tapped his finger on the table. 'Is the boy unharmed?'

'Physically, yes.'

'Still in Anno's custody?'

'As far as I know, yes. Although I imagine Anno will look for partners in the regency. I would, in his shoes. Sharing power could shield him from future blame, be it from other factions, from the empress, from the boy when he comes of age...'

'He might also fancy proving to the lords that he can reconcile with Rome at the stroke of his quill.'

'What do you make of those troubling reports – that he secretly encouraged the empress to back the antipope?'

'I believe them. But every crown bishop has a price. Anno's currency is power. If I put on the scale our willingness to acknowledge him as regent... he may trade us Cadalus for that.'

Changing his mind on Anno was not her priority. 'The tide is changing in Germany. Whether through Anno or otherwise, I am confident we will defeat Cadalus. Whilst you take care of such negotiations, I am drawing up plans for the Holy Father's protection.'

'What are your plans?'

'A half of my knights and footmen will remain at his disposal here in Lucca.'

He was not the smiling kind, but his gaze brightened. 'The Highest will reward you.'

'Actually, I dare to hope for a small reward from the Holy Father.'

Surprise on his face. 'What exactly?'

'I have been steady in my loyalty to Rome.' Defying King Heinrich, risking a second charge of treason, after the one she had suffered for rising against his father the emperor, paid for with exile and the death of her son...

'You do not need to remind me of that.'

'The moment we defeat Cadalus, Rome will finally secure the room it needs to reform the Church. The king will be controlled by regents for a little while longer, and when he comes of age, he will need time to assert his power.'

'What are you planning to request of the Holy Father?'

She threw down the gauntlet. 'A stronger Rome and a weaker Germany; this scenario opens an opportunity to review my daughter's future.'

His gaze speared her. 'Your daughter's future is decided.'

She made her tone more submissive than the actual meaning of her words. 'There is a betrothal, but a marriage has not happened.'

'It needs to happen.'

'Have I ever failed Rome? The alliance between Tuscany and Lotharingia will continue, thanks to my marriage to Gottfried.'

'What does he say about this?'

'A discussion with him is premature, but I can bring him around. He loves his son, but he cares for Matilde too.'

Something in his countenance whispered: 'stupid woman.' The dark coals of his eyes darted at her. 'Matilde needs a warrior husband at her side, to protect the exceptional claim of a woman to her father's lands.'

She snapped. 'It is in Rome's interest to support her claim, to avoid Germans at the gates.'

He lifted his seal as if it were a weapon, their breathing the only noise in the room. 'Let us speak plainly. Matilde's inheritance includes her lands, her titles and the Holy Blood relics.' Ildebrando had been Pope Leo's assistant when Beatrice had uncovered them.

'Another reason to oppose that marriage. I do not trust my stepson near the relics any more than I trust him near Matilde.'

'God has chosen you, and your bloodline, to fulfil the prophecy of Charlemagne.'

It was the first time he had admitted he was aware of the prophecy. Thankfully, the pope, or popes, who had confided in him, could not know – no-one knew – that she had the text.

She raised the obvious hurdle. 'Should we be ruled by words whispered down the generations, from emperor to emperor, when we have nothing in writing to prove Charlemagne even spoke them?'

He glared at her as if she had questioned a verse of the Bible. 'I prefer not to take risks. The Carolingian bloodline is a few withering branches; Godefroy is the safest option. Your daughter cannot marry a Salian.'

The Salians, King Heinrich's dynasty, were Charlemagne's descendants, and had the Holy Spear. A union between the bloodline that held the Spear and the bloodline that owned the Blood would go an uncomfortable way towards the fulfilment of the prophecy.

After Emperor Heinz had instigated her first husband's and her son's deaths, Beatrice had refused the alliance, as he knew.

'We are agreed on that,' she said. 'But she would rather not marry at all.'

'Rome needs a protector, and it cannot be a woman. Young Godefroy will be the sword of Saint Peter like his father.'

'You saw him with that stableboy yesterday; he is violent to innocents.'

'That was beneath him. But he would not lift a finger against your daughter.'

'You are willing to risk her life!'

'I never said that, Madonna. You raised an issue; I am trying to find solutions.'

'I have offered you a solution: undo the betrothal.'

Another patronising gaze, and tone to match. 'I will insert a clause of non-consummation in the marriage contract.'

She wished she could strangle him. She did not kiss his cardinal ring as she rose.

'Insert that clause. But this fight is not over, Ildebrando.'

IV.

A tapestry of the Resurrection on the opposite wall, elegantly carved chairs, two ivory writing boxes, a display of silver quills, golden volume bindings encrusted with sapphires, Venetian glass jars, and cups... The magnificence of the chambers clashed with their owner's professions of asceticism.

Anno of Cologne welcomed Adalbert of Bremen with an unctuous smile. 'My fellow archbishop.'

He pointed to a seat by the hearth, where a spent fire hissed. Another one of his tricks: Anno did not like being towered upon, and Adalbert was taller.

He waved a scroll with the papal chancery seal. 'The power behind Saint Peter's throne has graced us with a message.'

There was commotion in a nearby room. Bangs? Thudding? Screams? The sounds were muffled and hard to read.

Anno did not flinch, so Adalbert unrolled the vellum and begrudgingly glanced over the content.

He re-read the crucial passage aloud. *'I urge you to persuade the German court to acknowledge the pope chosen by the Roman cardinals: a man with the power of the meek, a charisma that no earthly power can tarnish.'*

Adalbert had been one of only two German bishops to vote against the election, but it was not the time to remind his colleague. 'We are being offered an olive branch, Anno.'

'We cannot un-elect Cadalus. If only the empress had not backed him—'

'If only she had not been advised to back him.'

The allusion hung in the air. The Archbishop of Cologne let out a deep sigh. 'The real problem, my friend, is that now she is tainted in the eyes of Rome.'

That was a bit rich, coming from Anno. After persuading her to back Cadalus, he had excused himself from the synod convened to elect him; he had set her up while keeping himself clean.

'There are still three years until our king comes of age. We need to redress that.'

'Three more years with a woman behind the throne?'

'Is that troubling you?'

'It is despicable!' Anno had a bull's frame as well as a bull's tendency to anger. His nostrils flared. 'We are the joke of Christendom!'

Adalbert faced away from his colleague, hoping he would find his lack of reply unsettling. The silence was broken by a distant scream.

Anno continued unperturbed. 'I am the first archbishop in the German Church, I crown kings. How can I watch a woman investing bishops? It pains me!'

'Why have you summoned me?'

'Because it is time the German crown regains its credibility.'

The door clattered open. A secretary let in Otto of Nordheim. The Duke of Bavaria, as tall as Adalbert and with the broad-shouldered frame of a warrior, was in hunting attire.

He placed a large sack made of plain brown cloth on Anno's table, and a satisfied grin spread across his face – until he saw Adalbert. He mumbled an acknowledgement.

Anno was captivated by the brown sack. 'Is that it?'

'Yes, my lord.'

'Follow me.' Anno turned towards Adalbert. 'If you will excuse us, my friend.'

On the way out, Otto was too puffed-up to stop talking. 'When he saw himself trapped, he jumped into the Rhine – and he cannot swim!'

Had he been a hunting dog, Anno would be going for the jugular. 'Idiot! We need him alive!' He slammed the door closed.

Otto's muffled words were still audible through the thick oak slab. 'He is alive. We jumped in after him.'

Their steps died down and Adalbert could not hear Anno's reply.

The brown sack lay on Anno's table. Adalbert talked himself out of inspecting the content. But he was unnerved by the conversation he had heard. Had Otto and Anno apprehended someone? Who? The silence was broken by a scream, this time Adalbert was sure.

He untied the cord of the sack. The object inside felt cold to the touch. As he parted the cloth a large reliquary cross emerged. It was encrusted with pearls and gemstones.

It was a treasure, even for someone with Anno's means, and not the kind of object a duke would carry around in a sack.

His fingers felt something else inside the sack, a leathery texture this time. It was a sheath. He loosened the strings to reveal a spearhead.

His gaze travelled from the spear back to the golden cross. It was, now he was sure, the imperial cross. And the spearhead was the Holy Spear, the most precious relic in the crown treasury, made by melting the nails of the Crucifixion.

How did Otto lay his hands on these objects? And why had he delivered them to Anno?

Ignoring the bitter taste in his mouth, he placed them both back in the sack and sat in his chair.

He did not have to wait long. 'Perhaps I should know what is going on?'

Anno closed the door. 'I convinced your empress to let the king travel to Kaiserwerth to see the fleet.' He grinned, his eyes reducing to tiny slits amongst the fat folds on his face. 'She fell right into my trap. Otto was waiting aboard the admiral ship and seized him for us.'

'For... us? You two... kidnapped our king?'

'Someone needed to take action, Adalbert.' He smirked. 'We need the pretty regent out of the way, so this kingdom can be ruled in a reasonable manner.'

Reaching for a Venetian glass jug on the trestle, Adalbert poured himself a cup of white wine from Speyer – not his favourite Burgundian, but it would do.

Anno lowered the sides of the sack to unveil the golden cross and the sheath. 'The emblems of power. Otto has done his job well.'

'Can you trust that man?'

'He is a henchman. He will need remission for his sins, and as acting head of the German Church I am best placed to grant it.'

'One needs important friends, when treading the fine line between treachery and treason.'

'Speaking of friends...' Anno stroked the spear delicately, as if it were the skin of a lover. 'I admire you, Adalbert. You are intelligent, ambitious, you are trying to create a patriarchate of Scandinavia and be the lord of the North—'

He did not need flattery. 'Tell me rather why you kidnapped God's anointed!'

'Do you want to be ruled by the whims of the empress and her beaus, Bishop Augsburg and Duke Rudolph?'

Adalbert's cheekbones contracted slightly. Allegations in such bad taste were not worth a reply. He would not let Anno poison his thoughts. 'This is not about the empress's conduct. You resent being ruled by a woman.'

'A feeling I share with most of the princes, who would outdo each other to be my co-regent. But I want you.'

'I refuse to have anything to do with the kidnapping of our king!'

Anno's chubby fingers traced the outline of the imperial cross. 'Have you forgotten the king's father, Emperor Heinz? He raised us from obscurity – made us who we are.'

'How could I?'

'On his deathbed, you promised to him that you would guard his little boy.' He kissed the cross. 'What happened to your loyalty, Adalbert?'

'Taking a child from his mother is not what I call loyalty.'

Anno's tone became soothing, as he tried to suck him into his web of intrigue. 'Handing to the child a solid kingdom, at peace with Rome and its neighbours, so his path for the imperial coronation is clear – would you not call that loyalty?'

He made to speak but Anno preceded him, circling him like a vulture. 'I will bear the brunt – be the villain who sends the pretty regent packing.'

'And what would I be?'

'The boy's educator. Eleven is such an impressionable age... The King of Germany will be clay in your hands.'

V.

Empress Agnes's cheeks were greyed with the opaque halo of tears. Adalbert kissed her cameo ring, realising as he did so that his homage was now purely personal. The coronet over her red silk veil had become meaningless. 'I am sorry.'

'Have you seen my son?' Somehow, pain made her even more beautiful.

'Physically he is safe and sound.' He could not vouch for the boy's mental state.

Her aquamarine gaze skewered him. 'Make sure it stays that way if you care about the Lord you claim to serve.'

At least she had not lost the will to fight.

As she ended the sentence, she began to weep.

He passed her a silk handkerchief, and she patted her eyes and cheeks dry.

'For me, this is not a political game, Adalbert. He is my son, the son I swore to raise to the empire as my husband lay dying.'

'We will honour that promise.' He squeezed her hand. 'This is why I am playing along. I have agreed to take responsibility for his education.'

She was barely listening. 'How could Otto do this to me? After I raised him to the Duchy of Bavaria!'

'I preach sermons against people like Otto – princes whose true God is their bellies.'

'I was blind to his greed.' Her Aquitanian accent was stronger when she was upset. 'And to Anno's dishonesty. He set me up.'

'If I can offer my view, Anno is not the only culprit.'

She glared at him. 'How many times has he thrown my femininity in my face, claiming it made me unable to rule?'

'Several times... Because he knew he could count on the princes' cowardice.'

For a moment she stared. 'You are right, I have Gottfried of Lotharingia to thank for this, indirectly.'

'Gottfried shamefully disregarded his oath to you and your son, but at least he has the courage of his actions. Whenever we hit a new crisis with Rome, the princes were the ones who—'

'They cowered, like lambs,' she hissed, anger curling her rosebud lips.

'They must be ashamed on some level; Anno pandered to their insecurities. Blaming your nature, he makes you the scapegoat for their cowardice.'

'If they had backed me against Gottfried from the start, we would never have got to Cadalus.' She controlled the wobble in her chin. 'We would not be here... an innocent child wrenched from his mother.'

Practicalities might help – would make her feel she still played a part in her son's life. 'Amongst his current teachers, is there anyone he is close to?'

'Cuno. They have a bond.'

'Could you arrange for Cuno to join my household? He could ride back to Cologne with me this afternoon and be with Heinrich by nightfall.'

She rubbed her cheeks and rose. 'I will see to it immediately.'

'I shall wait in the courtyard.'

'Before you go, I need another promise from you. Anno has snatched the imperial cross, and the Holy Spear.'

'Only until Heinrich comes of age.'

'Heinrich has lost his father, now he is losing his mother. Make sure he does not lose his right to a glorious destiny.'

She was alluding to Charlemagne's prophecy. Whenever that unproven utterance was referred to, Adalbert felt a strong affinity with the apostle Thomas. But this was not the time and place to remind Agnes. Her Carolingian blood was all she had left.

'The treasure will be safe.'

'Watch over it like an archangel of justice. My husband, from heaven, counts on you.'

Was her husband in heaven? Emperor Heinz had a few sins to expiate before passing through those gates.

But the boy was innocent, and scared. The sun was approaching noon. Time to find the teacher.

Cuno did not smile. If he was concerned for his charge, that was a good sign. Medium built, late twenties, a broad and gentle face, clearly of humble origins – not that it mattered.

What he needed for Heinrich was a caring and gifted *magister*, and Agnes's judgement on that could be trusted. She had taken great pride in the education of her children.

The thick walls of the island castle of Kaiserwerth faded into the distance, as they settled their animals into a canter on the Roman road along the Rhine, lined by cherry trees in bloom.

Adalbert let his thoughts roam, as he often did on horseback, but they kept coming back to Agnes, to an earlier version of Agnes, the dreamy Aquitanian girl of their first meeting, after her wedding in Ingelheim.

Life had been gilded with the halo of hope in those days, when she was the beautiful bride of a dashing if ruthless young emperor who had married her for duty but had grown to love her for who she was – a love that been reciprocated.

Her husband had stood by her, crowning her empress when she still had only daughters to her name, unable or unwilling to break a bond of souls. Their love had engendered trust, and the trust a will to defy fate.

That will, his old master's will, had refused to be buried with Emperor Heinz's body in the crypt at Speyer and to ascend with his soul, and they were still living in the shadow of its consequences – a woman robbed of the fruit of her womb for daring to rule on behalf of her child over Germany and beyond.

Agnes was probably crying right now, begging her husband's soul for forgiveness. Had she failed? They all had.

A year into her regency, when the youthful and gentle Pope Victor had been killed by a sudden illness, the German princes had taken to the sidelines, oblivious to their oath of loyalty, while the Roman cardinals denied little King Heinrich his customary right to nominate the pope.

Had Agnes's femininity triggered the cardinals' snub? Possible, but also convenient, the shield behind which Gottfried of Lotharingia and Ildebrando di Soana, the puppet masters of the College of Cardinals, concealed the depth of their ambitions.

The German princes had either looked the other way or named their price for the change of overlord, as it became apparent that Gottfried was exploiting the king's minority to undermine the Salian power and lay claim to the imperial crown.

In the years that followed, the Pandora's box of papal election had been opened a few more times, as Gottfried and Ildebrando, like wolves who had tried human flesh, had kept returning to the taste of pope-making.

Backing Cadalus had been Agnes's attempt to break their stronghold and reaffirm her son's rights in the papal election. Even the great Roman families had taken her side, sending representatives to kneel at the feet of the child king.

Had Adalbert failed her, then? He had voted against Cadalus, in good faith. The Bishop of Parma was an unsavoury character, who would have undermined the credibility of the Holy Seat, and despite his sins Adalbert was a man of the cloth.

Meagre consolation as it might be, he had failed her by standing for his beliefs; others, such as Anno, had failed her to protect their own interests.

The victim of all this, the pawn, was the child. The previous day, alone and scared in the hands of Anno's henchmen, he had seized a knife and made himself bleed.

Cuno, behind him, was keeping his eyes on the road and his thoughts to himself. Adalbert spurred his horse. He needed to get the teacher to the boy before night fell and fear seeped deeper into the king's soul.

A.D. 1064

VI.

Canossa Castle, late April 1064

Matilde removed her helmet and shook her tresses free, grateful for this first day of warm spring sun after such a long, bone-gnawing winter. Grinning, she reached a gloved hand down to help Rolando, her master of arms, to his feet.

'That hurt!'

'You taught me the move; you only have yourself to blame.'

His smile turned into a grimace as he rubbed his hip. 'True. I didn't realise you had been practising it all week though.'

'Aha! The element of surprise is vital in an ambush situation, especially when physically outmatched by your opponent. You have drilled the concept into me, have you not?'

'I should have waited another week for the ground to thaw before doing this,' he muttered. He was trying to keep up the pretence of grumpiness, but she could see the pride in his pupil shining through.

'I won't tell anyone that you got injured fighting with a girl...'

'There is no shame in being floored by you.' He collected daggers and arrows from the ground. 'I do not remember a time when you were not practising fencing, or archery, or javelin...'

'My father wanted all of his children, both boys and girls, to know how to defend themselves.' She took her gloves off and placed them in her upturned helmet.

'Federico taught you how to hold a sword... Maybe you were too small to remember.'

'I remember.' Federico, her brother... It had been ten years since his death on the road to Lucca, and she never spoke of him these days, other than in her prayers.

He offered to carry her helmet. 'When I teach you, I feel like he is watching us from heaven, and sometimes when we practice, like he is fighting with you.'

He lowered his gaze, as if he had said too much. Rolando had been Federico's sparring partner and had loved him like a brother.

He kept nursing her helmet between his strong warrior hands. 'He would be proud of you today.'

'Thank you.' Her heart filled with gratitude that he still treasured Federico's memory like she did.

'Lanfranco!' Rolando shouted to her other master of arms, who was practising on another stretch of flat terrain further down the mountain with her bodyguards. 'We are done for today.'

A cragged path wound its way up the rocky flank of the mountain to the main gate of Canossa Castle. She led the way; the rest of the group, saddled with the weaponry, climbed a bit slower.

The faint breeze carried their roar of laughter, but it would be pointless to turn. Her companions had got used to sparring with a woman, but they would run a mile rather than subject her delicate ear to their rowdy jokes.

Still, they seemed drunk with spring, and their contagious cheerfulness pulled her back to the present. Drawing a rebel strand of hair away from her face, she turned towards Rolando. 'Now that I can catch you by surprise... how do I beat you on the battlefield?'

His dark eyes twinkled. 'On the battlefield? That is a step too far for a woman. Let's get a spade. I can show how to dig trenches to stop armies.'

Despite a fleeting desire to punch him, she found herself laughing so hard that he was soon infected too. No-one cracked jokes involving her mother in her presence. And Rolando of all people; he had led one of the wings when her mother's army had stopped Cadalus. She loved that he could laugh at his own bravery.

'But seriously, Rolando, you always say my hands are too delicate for manual labour and now you want me to dig trenches?'

He brushed his thick curls with his palm. 'Can you beat Lanfranco?'

Was he assessing her physical strength? Her cheeks caught fire when she felt his gaze on her. 'You have told me his weaknesses many times; I can see how they might let me get the better of him.'

'If you beat Lanfranco, you will almost be a match for me. Train with him over the next few days.' He answered the question in her eyes. 'I am travelling to Lucca with Lord Gottfried.'

His words swept the sunshine away. So that was the plan: Rolando was going to escort Pope Alexander to Mantova.

His valour, and her mother's desire to keep things simple,

justified the choice, but two years earlier she had sailed the pope back from a siege situation, and now she could not even take him through their lands on horseback.

'You clearly have my mother's trust,' she said.

'The order came from Lord Gottfried.'

She darted a look at him. 'He may be the lord of these lands by marriage, but my mother would not have left this decision to anyone else. So well done to you.' She was trembling with frustration. 'She has not forgotten your past deeds like she has mine.'

Surprise and confusion mixed on Rolando's face. He looked around, uneasy. A subject could not criticise his lord. 'Why is escorting the pope so important to you?'

'Anselmo da Baggio is the noblest soul in Christendom. And the closest thing I have to a father.'

'You worry I would not look after him as well as you would?'

Could she trust Rolando with her deepest fears? Pope Alexander held the keys to her future. If he lost the papacy, she would be packed off to Lotharingia like some precious cloth, to adorn the castles of her stepbrother and spend each day praying that he feared God and his marriage contract enough to treat her with respect.

Her thoughts were sucking her in like a whirlwind. Explaining her reasons would expose her emotions, and what would Rolando make of them? All she could come up with was a vague answer. 'Nothing should happen to Pope Alexander. Nothing.'

The path took the last turn amongst chestnut trees and revealed the pearly white castle, an eagle nest watching over the Apennines.

Canossa had three rings of walls. The watchmen lifted the portcullis, to admit them into the outer ring. Their companions caught up with them. At Lanfranco's signal, the watchmen sealed the outer gate and lifted the portcullis of the middle ring.

The archway felt like a dragon's mouth, ready to swallow her. She could let her fears devour her or fight them back.

'You are dismissed,' she said to her troop.

They headed for the armoury, apart from Rolando, who followed her into the inner courtyard. Why had she got defensive with him? He did not have a vicious bone in his body. He was only obeying orders.

She took her helmet and gloves from him. 'I am sorry.'

'Matilde, I am their soldier. I cannot change their choices. But I will defend Pope Alexander with my life, I promise you that.'

'I count on you,' she said, struggling with an emotion that she could not name. 'I will see you in Mantova in three weeks.'

VII.

Matilde stepped into the great hall of the royal palace. The news of her father's murder, twelve years earlier, had reached her between these same walls. She pushed the painful memories away. Too much was at stake today to linger on the past.

The royal chamberlains had just finished hanging above the dais the standards of the great families and archbishops in attendance. Most of the seats were already full. They were all men – apart from her mother, seated in the front row with Gottfried.

At Matilde's arrival, a few heads turned in acknowledgement and others with curiosity. Her naval exploit two years earlier had been on everyone's lips, and for the German princes this was the chance to see the strange girl admiral in the flesh.

Pretending not to notice the gazes, she took her seat in the third row. Never look weak, she reminded herself. But she felt weak – and exposed. The magnificent blue silk gown she had been forced to wear was making her woman's body more conspicuous than her coronet.

She should get used to that kind of attention, and be superior to it, like her mother, if she could ever learn.

These were thoughts for another day. She had moved heaven and earth to be in this room.

Holding her head high she directed her gaze towards the front row. Wearing a plain white mitre, symbol of purity and a power bestowed by God, Pope Alexander was seated between Ildebrando and Pier Damiani, the charismatic former hermit who had organised the synod with Anno. His hair had greyed, an inescapable reminder of his mortal fragility.

If only she could be nearer, to support him through his ordeal and help him to victory. But that would have placed her into her overlord's line of sight, probably the last thing she needed. The throne was empty, for now.

Matilde used to play with Prince Heinrich, as he was called then, during her exile in Germany; what felt like a lifetime ago she had attended his coronation in Aachen, taking her oath of fealty.

How his personality had developed in these eight years, and how the kidnapping had affected him, she did not know. Her only certainty was that Tuscany and the German crown had not been best friends of late, especially after the trench. Heinrich had penned a letter to Beatrice, using the word "treason."

If he were still furious towards her mother, how did he view Matilde for her expedition to Rome? The synod was the perfect opportunity to denounce them for betraying their oath to him, if that was his intention. She could take that in her stride. What she could not afford was him using their alleged treason to accuse Pope Alexander.

The noise abated. Preceded by an archbishop, presumably Anno, Heinrich walked in. She kept gazing at the hem of her gown, her breath caught in her throat. Her red-blonde tresses, barely covered by a translucent silk veil, would be hard to miss. Hopefully, the king had more pressing concerns than making an example of her, but she could not take that for granted.

The blue of her gown reminded her of another shade of blue, the sea, the memories of her "treason" lapping her like waves.

In the eerie silence, Heinrich's steps resonated past her, softening with the increasing distance. Dreams of ships gathering wind and snapping their sails vanished from her mind.

She shot a quick glance towards the dais. He was on his throne. Thanks to the regents' choreography he was seated higher than the pope, a powerful visual metaphor for his hierarchical position in the great scheme of the universe. The Holy Father would have to stand when invited to speak and still not be level with the King of Germany.

Heinrich was staring blankly ahead, so she found the courage to look on. From a distance, under the weight of the diadem, he bore no resemblance to the stern but cherubic five-year-old who used to play in her lap. The lankiness of late boyhood was weighed by clothes devised to make him look like an adult and the straw colouring of his curls had turned into a darker bronze.

For a moment, she was reunited with a distant version of herself. During her exile at the German court, Heinrich's elder sister Adelheid had been her best friend, filling the emptiness left by the deaths in her family with games, song and caring silences.

Now, Adelheid was the abbess at Quedlinburg, and for Matilde the golden haze of childhood had been swept away by the turns that life had taken.

Surely for Heinrich too. The kidnapping must have been harrowing. But today she could not feel sorry for him. He could destroy her, her mother, and Pope Alexander with one word.

'Cardinal Anselmo da Baggio, come forward.' Anno, next to the throne, was ominously addressing the pope by his former name.

The Holy Father rose; the plain habit of Cardinal Pier Damiani rose like his shadow, handing him a large volume bound in gilded leather. Matilde whispered a prayer under her breath.

Anno addressed the pope. 'Cardinal Anselmo da Baggio, do you own up to betraying our emperor, by entering into an alliance with the Normans?'

Heinrich still had to be crowned emperor, but Pope Alexander ignored the debatable choice of words. He lifted the book high above his head, so everyone could see it was a Bible.

'I swear, by the God I have served all my life, that I have never betrayed this king.' With his back to the dais, he made eye contact with the princes in the front row, one by one. 'I was lawfully elected by the Cardinals of the Holy Roman Church, while the Holy Seat was vacant.'

'Long live the pope!' shouted Gottfried in the front row. Everyone knew which candidate he was backing, so his rallying cry did not shift the mood.

Another voice reverberated from the back of the room. 'Long live Alexander, the pope chosen by God!'

An imposing man of about forty years, clad in the austere grey habit of a Cluny monk made it to the centre of the hall. After a nod at Pier Damiani, he stopped next to the Holy Father. Matilde had never seen him before, but only one person could walk into a room and command that kind of attention.

'Venerable Hugh, Abbot of Cluny, welcome. Would you like to address the synod?' The irritation was palpable in Anno's voice.

Thanks to his height, Hugh did not need to step on the dais to be seen by everyone in the room.

'Vassals of my godson King Heinrich, I come from Cluny, invited by Pier Damiani. Being an abbot, I do not depend on the support of king or pope, so I offer a view based solely on the virtue of the two men aspiring to follow in the footsteps of Saint Peter, and on the legality of their election.'

'We are eager to hear your view on the legality of the respective elections,' goaded Anno.

Hugh avoided his trap. 'Cadalus has refused to travel to the synod, whereas Anselmo has put his faith in God and offered himself to your judgement today.'

Matilde's heart was racing as he proceeded with his argument.

'Christian blood has been spilled in vain. Let us stop the infighting amongst brothers. Let us make this the day we search our hearts for the truth. Only truth leads to God and salvation, in this life and the next.' He walked from one end of the front row to the other, before returning to the middle. 'Raise your hand if you believe in Pope Alexander's innocence.'

Matilde raised hers and a crowd of hands sprung up around her. The war was over, and Pope Alexander had retained his seat – and the power to save her from a marriage worse than death.

'It is approaching Vespers. I propose we reconvene tomorrow to reach a decision.'

Anno was not giving up without a fight, but her mother's reassuring glance said the victory was theirs.

Taking his regent's cue, Heinrich rose to his feet. As he approached Matilde's row, he slowed and glanced towards her. His eyes were a deeper blue than in her memories, but she could not read his expression. Was he going to greet her, or accuse her?

In the joy for Pope Alexander's triumph, she had forgotten her fears. There was nowhere to run – not that she wanted to. The king was too young to understand that whatever he decreed against her would pale into insignificance compared to the torture of marriage to Godefroy of Lotharingia. *Breathe*, she reminded herself, *so he does not sense your nerves.* She held his gaze.

He seemed surprised by her daring. He looked the other way and hurried past, joining one of his archbishops at the back of the room.

VIII.

Leaving her guards outside, Beatrice stepped into the dark interior of the church of Sant'Andrea, outside the Roman walls. She slipped into the front pew and knelt, without lowering her hood.

The burnished golden vessels of the Holy Blood sparkled like stars on the main altar. A familiar knot formed in her stomach at the sight of the vases.

Bonifacio, her first husband, beaming under his dark beard when she had shown him her discovery, a treasure more valuable than anything in the emperor's coffers – the proof that God had chosen her, above all people, as the guardian of the blood spilled by Jesus on the cross.

Pride melted into longing. Bonifacio had been murdered before the goldsmiths had finished their work. He had never seen the relics displayed in all their glory in Sant'Andrea.

The soft swish of fine silk broke the silence of the church. A tall well-proportioned man knelt next to her and cast his mantle onto the pew. As was customary of German bishops, he was wearing princely robes, with only the pendant cross and the ring to mark his status of man of God.

'I hoped to find you here,' he whispered in German, making the sign of the cross, 'in the company of your relics.'

Beatrice did not need to turn to recognise Adalbert's voice. But she did.

Their paths had not crossed since young Heinrich's coronation, and she had only seen him from afar earlier at the synod. Time had been kind to the Archbishop of Bremen. His perfect features were crowned by a mane of blond hair that age had streaked with grey but not yet thinned.

The only change was the wrinkles around his piercing blue eyes. Perhaps the responsibilities of regency, taking the art of intrigue to the highest level, had taken its toll.

She redirected her attention to the reliquaries. 'Unlike your august colleague, you do not mind a woman opening her mouth in church?' she teased him.

'Where is your husband the pope-maker?'

'Paying homage to your royal charge at the banquet.'

'That man has nerve. Is your daughter with him?'

'Matilde is not comfortable at banquets as she is at war.'

He turned towards her. 'I was surprised to find her and you at the synod, after the letter my lord wrote to you...' His blue gaze dissected her nonchalant expression, 'surprised but extremely pleased. Although digging that trench was not your best idea.'

Of course, he would mention that. She had shown them what she was made of, and what her daughter would be made of, when the time came to hand over her power. She gave him an amused smile that he reciprocated. 'We are not here to talk about the trench, are we?'

'You should trust me a bit more, Madonna Beatrice.'

He was too intelligent not to appreciate the magnitude of his request. His master Emperor Heinz had instigated Bonifacio's murder.

Probably sensing the struggle in her heart, he let his invitation sink in, his gaze lost in the golden vessels.

Sometimes the best defence was attack. 'What do you gain from supporting Pope Alexander?'

A smile flashed on his lips. 'I am not supporting him. That would jeopardise my position at court.' Outside, steps approached. His gaze shifted to the entrance until the footsteps continued further away. 'Let us just say I am delighted that this synod has turned into a personal victory for you.'

'The synod is a victory for the kingdom too, it removes the largest obstacle to the imperial coronation. If we work together, you may be able to secure another victory.'

'I am listening.'

Time to test his loyalties. 'The empress praises your discretion. I need your word that this conversation will remain between me and you.'

'Before our Saviour's blood, I swear.'

Her voice dropped to a whisper. 'Pope Alexander may be willing to entertain a different option for my daughter.'

Silence. She had surprised him – pleasantly, she hoped.

'I take it your husband is not aware of our conversation.'

'Correct.'

'Similarly, you may not be aware of your husband's conversations with Anno.'

'Thank you for this precious piece of information.'

His archiepiscopal ring caught the light of the chandeliers, as he placed his hand on the front of the pew. 'I have no desire to advance your husband's dynasty, given his disloyalty to the Salians. However, given the entanglement I mentioned, Anno and I might not be on the same page.'

She cast him a complicitous glance. 'You have always been smarter than Anno, Adalbert.'

'I trust the confidentiality clause goes both ways.'

'Of course.'

'Watch your papal friend closely tomorrow. The likely outcome of the synod may... ignite some of his enemies.'

That was a surprise. 'Thank you for your trust.'

Footsteps entered the church. Beatrice and Adalbert shifted away from each other and lowered their heads, worshippers collected in their Compline prayers. Ildebrando and Anno would place spies everywhere.

'I shall go,' she said in a hushed voice. 'With regard to my daughter...'

His gaze lingered on the golden vessels, his hands joined. He was a man of taste, someone who could appreciate the goldsmith's exquisite craftsmanship.

'If Pope Alexander decides to release beautiful Matilde from her commitment, I will convey to the king and princes that it is a blessing for the crown.' He made the sign of the cross and stood up. 'We shall leave from different doors.'

§

A full moon shone over the belltower of Sant'Andrea, whitening the city walls. The watchmen checked Adalbert's safe-conduct and waved him through the gate back into town.

A cat fight nearby made him smile. The day had been muggy, and the night breeze was pleasant on his face. It brought a smell of flowers and ripe wheat, the promise of high summer. His footsteps thudded on the worn paving of the Roman road. He struggled to name the tension in his body. Not excitement; possibly admiration.

No matter how hard he tried, he could never get the full measure of Beatrice. He had accepted that a long time ago, when she was the flower of Emperor Conrad's court. There had always been steel under the grace.

The trench had been nothing for her. Here was a woman who believed herself superior to the Salians – a widow who had defied Emperor Heinz knowing the odds were stacked against her. She had married her cousin Gottfried without their overlord's permission – a rebellion that had cost her her freedom.

God had rewarded her courage; exploiting the power vacuum after Emperor Heinz's death, she had clawed back every bit of her power. Like a phoenix she had risen from the ashes, and she would do so over and over if life threw her fresh challenges. The image of a queen-like young Beatrice dancing with him in the imperial palace of Nijmegen flickered in his mind.

He was glad he had tipped her off. She could make decisions quickly, like a king, and normally they were the right ones.

There had been too many whispers and hints, too many veiled hints. The boy, he hoped, was not privy to the plot, but the suspicion could be enough to damn him. Even a crowned Holy Roman Emperor would not get away with murdering a pope. The conspiracy had to be stopped.

Beatrice would take care of things, preserve her pope at whatever cost, brave, competent, cunning. She would do anything for her daughter.

Beautiful Matilde had inherited her mother's eyes. Had she also inherited her mother's spirit? Her intriguing stab at admiralship suggested so. More reason to deplore the failure of the empress's old plan to marry her to her son – the girl deserved better than being Ildebrando's pawn.

IX.

Vinicia, Matilde's personal maid, stopped braiding her mistress's hair. 'What is going on?'

Her question was barely audible, drowned by the screaming and clattering outside. They opened the shutter. The opposite side of the piazza was full of armed men, fighting. Daggers, swords, even arrows were flying. In the middle of the improvised battlefield, Pope Alexander, brandishing a shield, surrounded by German troops clashing with other German troops.

Matilde's breath stopped. It was impossible to tell if the people around him were trying to protect him or kidnap him – or worse. An ambush. Unable to legally remove Pope Alexander, they were trying to kill him.

'Get my jerkin and my armour.'

'You cannot go,' said Vinicia, with the practical wisdom of a woman in her fortieth year.

'Quick!'

Invoking the protection of the Mother of God, Vinicia fetched her armour. Matilde slipped her helmet on as she ran downstairs, holding a dagger as she had no sword. Her heart was throbbing as if it wanted to jump out of her chest.

'Open the door.'

The soldiers guarding the main entrance of the palazzo exchanged a glance. 'You will have to be quick, Madonna.'

The door slammed closed behind her.

Reading the events was easier from the square. The battleground was shifting from the middle towards the bishop's palace. A good sign, as Pope Alexander would be safe inside it.

The coat of arms of the German soldiers closer to the Holy Father was unknown to her, but they were helping Tuscany's troops fend off a plain-clothed squad with no standard.

The stones under her feet were splashed with blood. Limbs and bodies were scattered on the ground. She had never smelled human organs before. She managed not to retch.

'Matilde! Stay away! Please!' Rolando was standing before Pope Alexander, a sword in one hand and a dagger in the other.

She did not fear her own death. But losing him and Pope Alexander in one go was too much to contemplate. Please God.

Rolando kept hitting right and left. 'I will keep him safe! Please go back inside!'

Transfixed by Rolando's sword, a man fell to his knees, crashing in a pool of his own blood, not even the time for a prayer.

Someone pulled her from behind. She lifted her dagger, ready to spin and attack.

'Come with me – to your mother.' It was Lanfranco's voice.

'She should rather worry about the pope.'

'She has a plan.'

Sliding along the wall, holding their weapons, they sneaked back inside. Soldiers reinforced the closed door with logs. There was an archer by every window of the ground floor, and probably more on the roof. Lanfranco pointed to the staircase.

'No, I will stay down here; our soldiers need reinforcements.'

'Your mother is waiting.' He placed a hand on her shoulder, in an unusual gesture of camaraderie. 'Have faith in our troops. You have seen how well they fight.'

The lives of women. The two most important men in her life were fighting to survive and all she could do was wait and pray.

Her mother rushed to embrace her. 'God be thanked!'

'Do you know what is going on, Mamma?'

'Someone advised me to meet the Abbot of Niederalteich.'

Her mother and her sources. 'And?'

'The good abbot knew of a plot to strike Pope Alexander after morning mass. We joined forces.'

'Will we foil it?'

'Rolando and Niederalteich are outstanding fighters.'

For a moment, if felt like the battle had moved inside. A heavy door slammed closed downstairs, and the whole chamber fell silent, their maids ashen-faced. But the steps climbing the stairs were orderly, not rushed. Her breathing eased, even before the voice behind the door spoke.

'We have won, Madonna Beatrice.' It was Rolando. 'The pope is in the bishop's palace, and Lord Gottfried's troops are watching over him.'

Beatrice opened the door herself. 'And the synod?'

'Pope Alexander wants it to go ahead.'

Matilde joined them in the doorway. 'His bloodied tunic will speak louder than words, proving how low his enemies were willing to go.'

Rolando smiled at her, fleetingly. He was still holding his sword.

'Any prisoners?' asked Beatrice.

'I am sorry. They fought to the death – it was us or them.' He paused. 'We lost four men.'

Matilde made the sign of the cross. Her mother would arrange for the families of the soldiers to be looked after, but there would still be children missing their fathers, wives missing husbands they loved, and men going to heaven in the flower of their years. She noticed the red blot on Rolando's ripped sleeve. 'You are bleeding!'

'Nothing serious.'

'See my physician, Rolando,' said her mother. 'We cannot afford to lose the bravest of my soldiers.'

Off he went, and Matilde hoped he had not downplayed the seriousness of his wound.

Beatrice read the worry on her face. 'He will be fine. Others, just as brave, were less fortunate. It is meagre consolation but at least their sacrifice was not in vain.'

'How can we be sure? We have no idea of who is behind the plot. They could strike again.'

'The instigators will need to cover their tracks now. And the best way to do that is to back Pope Alexander.'

The weight on her shoulders reminded Matilde that she was still in her armour. 'I need to get changed for the synod.'

'Go. We will enter the hall together. I – we – have proven that women have the brains to win wars.'

'We do not need warrior husbands.'

Beatrice stroked her daughter's cheek. 'It is fitting that all this is happening in Mantova, under the spell of the Holy Blood. Ildebrando will be thinking of that.'

X.

The synod had ended triumphally for Pope Alexander, but Matilde, nagged by her worry for Rolando, had struggled to enjoy his victory. The moment she had returned to her chamber, she had sent for him.

'A couple of stitches and some balm; the physician says I should live.' He winked.

She joined him under the architrave. 'Sure?'

'Sure.' His eyes shone with gentle pride. 'I promised I would defend Pope Alexander. You should trust my word next time.'

'I do trust your word. He could not have been in better hands.'

They were so close she could hear his breathing. 'Is the synod over?'

'He won.' Her heart filled with pride. 'You have changed history, Rolando.'

A smile took over his face. 'I did my duty.' He lowered his voice. 'Thank God nothing happened to you this morning.'

Her cheeks caught fire and she prayed he would not notice. 'I could not just watch while you and Pope Alexander risked your life.'

'And I could not concentrate on protecting Pope Alexander while I was worrying about you.' He was the one blushing now. 'Next time leave the battles to me, please. Your duty is to stay alive and rule.'

'I cannot rule if I cannot fight. When is our next lesson?'

'It will be a while. I am escorting Pope Alexander back to Rome with Lord Gottfried.'

'As long as there is another lesson.'

He placed his hand on his heart. 'There will be.'

Vinicia arrived from Beatrice's room, carrying a red silk gown. 'The lady needs to prepare for the banquet.'

'I will leave her to enjoy her triumph.' He kissed her hand and was off.

§

Guido, Pope Alexander's chamberlain, put on the dour tone he reserved for importunate visitors. 'The Holy Father is the midst of his evening prayers.'

'Please, tell him that Countess Matilde needs Confession.'

'Let her in,' said the pope from within.

Huffing, Guido showed her past the guards.

The Holy Father was on his knees, in prayer before the icon of Mary he carried with him on his travels, painted on wood from the olive trees in Getsemani. He took her hand in his.

'Pray with me.' At barely fifty, he was a vigorous man, but the wrinkles on his forehead had deepened since their last meeting. He bowed to the icon. 'Mother of God, welcome in your arms the men who gave their life for mine; may their faith, selflessness and courage be of comfort to their families.'

Her lips trembled as she echoed his words. Rolando could have been amongst those men, his father left with nothing but words about his bravery and the hope of a place in heaven.

Pope Alexander's words pulled her from her thoughts. 'I saw you in the square this morning.'

'I could not lose you. You are not injured?'

His hazel eyes shone as he smiled. 'Just a few scratches. I owe your mother my life, once again.'

'We will always stand by you.'

'Soon, I should be in a position to repay your sacrifices. Cadalus will not recover from this.'

Mentioning her betrothal would be inappropriate, but he read her mind, as he often did.

'Officially, my position on your marriage is unchanged. Nothing will happen until King Heinrich begins independent rule and can approve it. Ildebrando is under instructions to discourage Gottfried from pressuring your mother.'

'I am grateful that you are even thinking of me at such a

moment.'

'A broken heart can damage the most beautiful soul.'

She kissed his ring, overwhelmed with tears of gratitude.

He placed his palm on her head, as if to bless her. 'Your path to freedom depends on the imperial coronation. I need Lotharingia's military support until Heinrich becomes the sword of Saint Peter. When he comes to Rome to be crowned emperor, I will agree with him a new alliance for you.'

'This is the best I could hope for. I can start to imagine a future where I don't have to live in fear.'

XI.

The greatest mind in the service of God was wearing a plain grey cassock with no ornaments; a wooden cross hung from his neck.

When, thirteen years earlier, the then-pope had offered him a cardinal's hat and the title of chief advisor, Pier Damiani had accepted on one condition: he would remain morally independent, hence outside the official edifice of the Church.

Independence had increased Pier's reputation as a living saint, later transforming him into the ideal negotiator between the pope and antipope's fields.

That morning, the cardinal had approached Anno for an audience with the king, a request impossible to refuse, and, in different circumstances, very welcome. Not today. Niederalteich was adamant that the conspiracy had support at the highest level. What if Pier knew something that could ruin Anno or Heinrich, or both?

'My son, you are Christendom's greatest hope.' At least he had struck a positive opening note.

'Father, through your teachings and the example of your holy life you are a guiding light for me and so many others.' The boy was handling himself well.

The hermit waited before replying. Pride was a sin. 'If through my *exemplum* God can steer you towards Him, I am grateful,' he said. His gaze, framed by bushy eyebrows, firmed on the king, as intense as his words. 'In this day of jubilation, I am here to urge our future Holy Roman Emperor to reflect on his duty to the Highest.'

Sweat gathered on Adalbert's brow.

'In my prayers and my action, I will heed your teachings.' Thank God the boy was an excellent speaker.

'Your reply delights me, my son. Here is my thought for you. At the synod, one person was notable for their absence...'

Cadalus. He had refused to attend. Adalbert held his breath.

Pier's next words both relieved him and stunned him: 'The empress your mother has paid a high price for her sin. You and your regents should know that our daughter Agnes has made penitence and the Holy Father has forgiven her.'

With the corner of his eye, Adalbert saw Anno recoil. For a few moments, the room stilled. Heinrich lowered his gaze until he spoke. 'I will follow the Holy Father on the path of forgiveness.'

Placing his hand on the king's head, Pier blessed him. 'You have pleased God, son. Peace in Christendom begins with peace in our hearts.' He turned to Anno. 'My friend, will you join me in prayer, to thank God for what we have achieved today?'

Never before had Heinrich diverged from Anno. If only Agnes could have been there to see it.

The moment they left, Heinrich turned to him. 'This day has been full of lessons.'

'You have experienced the power, the intrigue, and the purity of Rome, all in one sitting.'

The boy never smiled, but there was a hint of satisfaction in his dark blue gaze. 'How many times has Anno changed his skin in this battle for the Holy Seat?'

'More than I can remember,' and he was glad Heinrich had noticed. Where was he going with this?

'You taught me that a king's advisers need to be steady – in their views and their loyalty. Anno is neither.'

A.D. 1065

XII.

'Why the urgency?' Gottfried came in from outside, in wolfskins.

'Changes at court,' said Beatrice. 'Heinrich has dispensed with Anno's services.'

Matilde made room for her stepfather by the fireside. He shook the snow off his clothes and rubbed his hands. 'Any sensible king coming of age rids himself of his regents. Will Anno retain his archbishopric?'

'That, and the arch-chancellorship for Italy.'

'Ildebrando will be pleased.'

The mention of the cardinal alarmed Matilde, who fixed her gaze on Gottfried.

Beatrice confronted him mildly. 'I thought you did not like Anno.'

'He has his uses.'

'As in weaknesses that can be exploited?'

He winked. 'In the service of God, as Ildebrando would say. Is the boy getting rid of Adalbert too?'

'Not for now,' said Beatrice.

'Hmm, bad news. The Saxon is the true danger.'

'You are about to warm up to "the Saxon," Gottfried,' she said. 'He is asking you to take part in the king's coming-of-age celebration.'

'Like all the princes.'

'Not as a guest – Adalbert offers you the honour of being Heinrich's shield bearer.'

He clapped, smug. 'The cub needs allies.'

'The cub is willing to reward his allies.' She paused. 'Adalbert signals that he intends to restore you to the duchy of Lotharingia.'

He lifted her in his arms, happy as a child. 'When are we leaving?' He grabbed Matilde's hand. 'You are coming too, as the soon-to-be Duchess of Lotharingia.'

Her daughter went as white as the snow outside. 'No. Matilde and I will stay behind – rule the lands.'

Still holding his stepdaughter's hand, Gottfried insisted. 'Why? Her betrothed will be in Worms.'

Desperate glances from Matilde. 'I need her here. She is receiving the homage of our vassals at Easter.'

He let go of her hand. 'Beatrice, my son can be... difficult: tough with his troops, harsh with his enemies. But he will treat Matilde with respect.'

'It is too late to cancel our Easter engagements.'

He frowned. 'Fine. She can use the time to plan her wedding. As soon as I receive my duchy back, we can set things in motion.'

'We will not have a repeat of the crisis our marriage caused, Gottfried,' she said, more firmly than she had intended. 'I am sure Ildebrando mentioned to you that the Holy Father wants nothing to trouble the harmony between Germany and Rome until Heinrich's imperial coronation.'

'It is a stupid idea! As stupid as that consummation clause you insisted on!' Now Gottfried looked like a bear in his wolfskins – an angry bear. 'You used to dream of your daughter becoming empress, of fulfilling Charlemagne's prophecy through her. What happened to your ambition? The lioness of Canossa has become a dove!'

'How many years have you waited to get your duchy back, Gottfried? The Holy Father has used his influence to secure this outcome for you. Following his wishes for Matilde is the least you can do.'

§

Matilde pulled the heavy chest out from under her bed. The conversation between her mother and Gottfried had ended in a truce, but it could be another year before the young king came to Rome – and before her betrothal could be undone. And that was provided everything went to plan. She could not avoid Godefroy forever. His attack on her stableboy, still etched in her memory, filled her with dread.

She unlocked the chest. The sword in it had belonged to her father. She held it between her hands.

How many battles had he won with it? Burgundians, Lombards, Normans, Byzantines had fallen at his feet. Until he too had fallen, dispatched to the Lord by a treasonous arrow in his chest.

The sword had been passed to her brother. The day he had died, before burying him, her mother had handed it to little Matilde. Even now that she was fully grown, and tall for a woman, it was too heavy for her to use in battle.

Her finger traced the sheathed blade, and her lips brushed the silver-coated hilt before her hand closed around it.

She needed her own sword, a weapon the right size, to defend herself. Hiding the weapon in the folds of her cloak, she made her way to the armoury.

The blacksmith was not there. A tall soldier, with his back to her, was choosing a bow and arrow. He turned, and the smile filled his face. 'Matilde!'

Rolando kissed her hand, held it between his.

'You are back.' He had been in the pope's service since Mantova.

'I came with Lord Gottfried from Arezzo. The Holy Father says he is returning me to my rightful master – or mistress.'

She blushed at the words, although he had clearly meant her mother, his feudal mistress, and not a lover.

'What is a lady doing in the armoury?'

She pulled the sword out from under the cloak. 'Do you recognise this?'

'Your father's sword.'

'It is too heavy for me. I need a smaller copy, but identical, so I can feel like my father is watching over me when I fight.'

'I will speak to the blacksmith for you.'

She handed him the weapon. 'Thank you.'

'Your mother has placed me at your service between now and Easter.'

'I am so happy you are back.'

'I am happy to be back. With my family, with my friends, protecting you.'

XIII.

With its pink-hued stone drenched in light, the castle of Rossena, overlooking fertile rolling hills and the olive-green waters of the Enza River, was a different world from the nearby wind-battered towers of Canossa. Easter was falling early, and Rossena's mild climate made it the most suitable setting for the Holy Week celebrations and the banquet of Resurrection Sunday.

Matilde, in hose and tunic, bade farewell to the chaplain and dashed down the front steps of the church.

Being in charge of the Easter festivities meant the freedom to move between Canossa and Rossena without the watch of servants and guards – two weeks outside her unmarried noblewoman's gilded cage. She would make the most of it. Climbing up the battlement, she hummed a minstrel's song.

Rolando was waiting, her folded cloak on his arm. 'It took you a while!'

'We planned the Holy Week ceremonies, the alm-giving, and I gave the chaplain the relic.' Her mother had enshrined a tiny amount of the Holy Blood sand in a precious rock crystal vase, to be placed on the altar during Easter Mass.

'All done then?'

'Oh no, the banquet has to meet my mother's standards!'

'I shall not keep you. I am done with Lent food!' He winked.

In her life, jokes were rarer than precious pearls. People showed her deference and concern; Rolando was the only one who tried to make her laugh. She teased him back. 'You should have come back sooner, then...'

'I could not refuse your friend Pope Alexander!' He helped her put her cloak on. 'Besides, I cannot say I missed being beaten by a woman!'

'I thought you would be over that by now...'

'It hurts more than battle wounds.' Another wink. 'I'll get the horses.'

Down below the battlements, children were throwing pebbles in the river, cheering as they splashed, without a care for what tomorrow held in store. The sun warming her hands, forced her to live in the present, filling her heart. *God, thank you for giving me this day.*

Rolando checked the saddle of her mare, as he always did, before handing her the reins. Suddenly, he turned. 'Swallows!'

Black wings were fluttering over the chestnut tree. A Latin poet had called swallows the harbingers of hope. 'Winter is over!' A smile ripened on her lips. 'Oh, they are beautiful!'

Rolando kept looking upwards, spellbound. 'If only I could be one of them.'

'You... a bird?'

'I could fly wherever I want.'

'And where would that be? The Holy Land?' Pilgrimages had just resumed.

His dark eyes shone like deep pools. 'Just to a good place... where swords are not needed.'

'Why would the warrior give up war?'

'To be with... the woman I love.'

Her pulse quickened. Was he referring to her?

He picked a daisy from amongst the grass and offered it to her. When she took it, he retracted his hand swiftly, as if it had been burnt. Fire spread from his cheeks to hers.

Matilde hid the flower in her tunic's pocket. 'I also wish I were a bird, and free.'

His broad smile enveloped her like the sunshine.

They climbed on their horses and rode back, racing each other. She arrived first in the courtyard.

He held her gaze a moment longer than normal, and she wished she could run her fingers through his hair. But that could never be. He set out for the stables with the horses, and she walked up to her room.

Vinicia was not there. She curled up in her bed, and her fingers reached for the yellow token of Rolando's love, deep in the pocket of her tunic. Her lips kissed the daisy and her thumb and index finger played delicately with the petals.

Her life, her freedom, were as fragile as the flower she was holding. The salt of tears spread in her mouth. Hopefully, she could be rid of Godefroy and marry someone kinder and more respectful. But even with Pope Alexander's help she remained an heiress of the Holy Roman Empire, preserved for an alliance, or the convent, never for love.

XIV.

Rolando was a lone figure by the armoury's door, sacks full of weapons lying at his feet.

'Where are Lanfranco and the squad?' Matilde asked.

'On their way. We can practise here in the meantime.'

He had acted strangely since the day she had accepted his flower. She probably had too. Unsheathing it and examining the blade, he chose a sword for himself, before dragging the heavy sack towards her. 'Pick your weapon.'

Inside, there were three swords, but two were longer than Rolando's, unsuitable for someone her height. She drew the last one out of its sheath and gasped. 'The blacksmith did it!'

She wanted to hug him but knew she could not.

He read it on her face and just gave a beaming nod. 'It is a perfect replica, to the finest detail.'

'Oh, Rolando! You have no idea what this means to me!'

'Let's test it. Tighten your armour.' He positioned himself for a duel. At the last moment, he passed the sword from his right hand to his left.

'I don't want an advantage.'

'We are testing a new weapon. I do not want to hurt you.'

'Rolando, please.'

He switched back. 'Go.'

The silver hilt was cold in her palm. She breathed to focus. The first half of a fight was all about trying to learn your opponent's style, and the second half about trying to hit him. She chose a reasonable distance, from which she could tap the end of his sword with hers.

'Good move.' He still intercepted. 'Try again.'

She traced a wider and faster arc, but he blocked her again, blade against blade. She had noticed when he practised against Lanfranco that reflexes were Rolando's strength.

She paused, breathing hard. He was taller, faster, stronger; her best hope was surprise.

She lunged forward, waiting for his deflection, and dropped her sword under his, attacking from the other side.

His blade was far away, he could not respond. The tip of her sword was close to his ear now, and she did not want to harm him. She withdrew. 'I am sorry.'

'You do not need to be. Keep going.'

'No, not with you. I cannot... hurt you.'

He lowered his sword. 'I cannot hurt you either.'

Other words were lurking behind the ones they were uttering, words they could never speak to each other.

He stared into her soul. 'You are a wonderful warrior.'

His fingers clasped a strand of his hair and he passed the blade through it. 'For your courage,' he said.

She had never felt like this before, honey melting inside her, vanishing as she tasted it and constantly renewing itself, streaked with the pain of impossibility.

She did not blush this time. She placed his hair in her pocket and pulled her silk handkerchief out. 'For everything you are doing for me.'

He stroked it gently between his hands, before slipping it away. He waved. 'Lanfranco! You are late!'

At the end of her training, Matilde hurried past the library and the monastery, to the crypt of Sant'Apollinare. She knelt by a simple plain stone, bearing only a name and dates, placing her new sword on the floor.

In the half light, her finger traced the letters engraved on the soft travertine. Her sister had been called Beatrice after their mother, but to Matilde she would always be Bebe. She had missed her for years, clinging to her nurse for comfort in the large oak bed they had shared.

A flower cut before its time, the bishop had said at her funeral. A flower that would not be crushed or wilt. Had she lived, she would have been destined for marriage to Godefroy – and even death was better than that.

Bebe was buried at the feet of Adalberto Atto, their paternal great-grandfather – he who had built the church of Sant'Apollinare as the resting place of their dynasty.

In his days, his legendary endeavours in the service of Emperor Otto had dazzled many a lady into sin, and the Church had surely looked the other way.

The contrast between the fates of men and women of the same blood was engraved in those stones. Popes and kings might allow her to inherit Adalberto Atto's feudal rights, ruling over half of Italy. But when it came to love, the men in Rome who made the rules, even the holy soul of Pope Alexander, would always see her as a daughter of Eve, with only two choices: faithfulness to her husband or damnation.

Bebe had escaped that trap. She could love whomever she wanted in heaven.

'We need to talk.' Her mother's voice resonated in the low vault.

The glowing hilt of her new sword darkened as they climbed up the winding stairs of the mast.

'Gottfried wrote. He is being restored to Lotharingia and intends to stay there until the autumn. There is serious talk of Heinrich coming to Rome next year.'

Such good news, yet the words were spoken neutrally. Beatrice sat at her writing table, straight and regal like when she was administering justice in the great hall. A silk handkerchief appeared out of a pouch and her mother placed it on the table between them. 'How could you?'

The words cut like a sharp knife. How could they, rather. Someone must have seen her with Rolando and informed Beatrice. She held her mother's piercing glance. She was not going to apologise for her feelings.

'He has been brought into my presence and confessed.'

A nail hammered through her heart would have hurt less. Had he been beaten, or tortured, to confess to a crime he had not committed? 'Have you harmed him? If you have I shall...'

'You shall what, exactly?'

She was not going to let go. 'What have you done to him?'

'The more pertinent question is what has he done to you?'

Her cheeks were on fire. 'I would never bring dishonour to my family.'

Beatrice's back relaxed slightly. 'I am inclined to believe you. He swears he has not attempted to take your honour.'

'He speaks the truth, and you know it. He has a noble heart, he is your best warrior, the one who fought for you in Modena, who saved the pope—'

'I have not forgotten his deeds. But your mutual attraction is evident. You have betrayed my trust.'

'We are innocent!'

'You are also naïve. This feeling will grow until it is no longer innocent. I need to preserve your honour.'

Sure, she did. Had she been a son, Beatrice would have looked the other way, maybe with the occasional reminder to be careful and not to father too many bastards. But a daughter could not even exchange gifts and words with a man who had proved willing to give his life for their family.

Her hand gripped the hilt of her sword. 'If a stain on my honour is what it takes to undo that wretched contract, let it be.'

She jerked backwards and her cheek was burning. It took her a moment to understand why: her mother had hit her.

'He is intelligent and valiant. He impressed the pope. I have recommended his services to Count Guido of Florence. He is to leave in the morning.'

Did she have to say thank you? She was not going to. She made for the door.

'You think I am cruel,' Beatrice said. 'One day you will thank me for this. You are your father's heir, Charlemagne's heir, the heir to the Holy Blood. You cannot destroy your life with a simple soldier, no matter how brave he is.'

Matilde turned to face her. 'You'd much rather have me destroy my life with your stepson.'

She ran off along the corridor, without waiting for a reply. She did not want her mother to see her cry.

Her chemise was already on the bed, ready for the night, and Vinicia was sprinkling the floor with lavender seeds. She stopped when Matilde entered.

'He is leaving at sunrise,' she whispered.

Of course, Vinicia knew; she would have been the first person that Beatrice questioned. 'You are not allowed at the gate. But we could climb up the battlement of the outer walls.' She did not seem disappointed in her. She drew her into her arms, patting her hair. 'You will get through this, my child.'

If anyone had a right to find her plight trivial, it was Vinicia. In her youth, a harsh winter had killed her husband and young child. She had ended up a kitchen servant in a nunnery in Lucca, where she had tried to get over her loss by working hard and praying. But she had preserved the warmth that ambition had drained out of her power-obsessed mother, who lived for her relics and her titles.

'I am next door if you need me,' Vinicia said, with a kiss on the cheek. 'I will knock before dawn when the monks rise for Lauds.'

Matilde slipped her jerkin off and threw herself on the bed. Rolando's strand of hair was tucked at the bottom of her chemise's inner pocket, against her breast. She held it in her palm, wishing the universe could disappear, leaving only her and Rolando, and the purity of their love.

The hours drained fast, like water in the summer heat. When the cockerels sang, Vinicia and a guard came to take her to the battlement of the outer ring of walls. That whole sleepless night she had tried to think of ways to change Rolando's unjust sentence.

Down in the courtyard, the man she loved was embracing his father and mother, the stillness of dawn muffling their words, if they were even speaking. The woman did not want to let go of the son who had been her pride. His stallion, the meek Bruno, was grazing peacefully. At least he had been allowed to take his horse.

Pulling away from his mother, he took a few steps towards his mount. He was limping, and his back was not straight. He had been beaten, for giving her a flower.

If her mother truly expected her to one day give thanks for this, then she did not know her at all.

XV.

Agnes always brought radiance to a room, and the whizz of rose oil. After Pier Damiani's plea, Heinrich had gradually re-admitted her to court, and her name had found its way back onto the royal diplomas. She could barely conceal her excitement. 'What happened with Anno?'

'News travel fast. He left after the Epiphany.'

'And his departure is... permanent?'

'He remains Archbishop of Cologne and arch-chancellor for Italy but has no future as an advisor. Heinrich made it clear that there is a trust issue.'

'The scars of Kaiserwerth.' She read his thoughts. 'Does he trust you, Adalbert?'

'I have not spent three years enriching my family like Anno has,' he sneered. 'But things are in flux. Your son is finding his feet as a ruler, and advisors are expendable.'

'I hear you will hand him the sword at the ceremony?'

He smiled. 'That pleases me more than I care to admit.' In the knighthood ritual, the sword was handed from father to son.

She placed her hand on his forearm. 'He would not bestow such an honour on someone he does not trust. And you have earned it, with your selfless dedication.'

'Thank you. God has chosen an interesting day to send you to me.' Opening the coffer marked with Anno's coat of arms, he lifted the imperial cross out of it. 'I have kept my promise.'

'Adalbert!' Happiness suited her. She snatched it from his hands, placed it on the table and lifted one of the gold plaques covering the openings. In its interior, lined with dark red fabric, lay the Holy Spear. 'Did Anno put up any resistance?'

'Heinrich needs the emblems of power for the coming-of-age ceremony.' He grasped the bronze tip and studied it against the sunlight streaming from the window. 'I was fascinated by its legend as a child. Constantine melting the Crucifixion's nails to make a weapon that would protect him in battle, like a pagan talisman. This is actually the first time I hold it in my hand.'

Her delicate fingers pointed to some little marks upon the head of the spear. 'These little crosses used to be the nails.'

'Aesthetically, it is unremarkable. Would you believe that Heinrich the Fowler risked bankruptcy to buy it?' He had funded his purchase by selling a large chunk of the duchy of Swabia.

'A wise investment. It became the cornerstone – the foundation of his dynasty's power.'

Minstrels at court still sang of the battles of the emperors of his Saxon dynasty: Otto, the Fowler's son, carrying the spearhead in front of his troops, and defeating his internal enemies at Andernach, and then the Hungarians on the Lech.

The spear had transformed Otto the First into Otto the Great. And his grandson had conquered Rome with it...

'I see your point. There is the object, and the power of the object, as it reflects in the eye of the beholder. Whether the Holy Spear is or is not what it is purported to be, that does not tarnish its halo.'

'You question the authenticity of the relic?' She shook her head. 'My husband was right to call you his personal Saint Thomas!'

'I have seen enough fingers of the apostles, and pieces of Mary's veil to fill the royal treasury. They are valuable, in that they add prestige to an abbey or a city, enabling them to live off the revenue brought by pilgrimages. Or, in the case of the Holy Spear, they anoint a ruler, and his dynasty.'

'This is why I needed you to preserve it for my son. The princes would never challenge its holder.'

He placed the spearhead back in the imperial cross. 'Unless they own the Holy Blood.'

'Do you believe in Charlemagne's prophecy now, Saint Thomas?'

'Its text has never been found, why should I trust a whisper? I am persuaded that your father-in-law, Emperor Conrad, fabricated it – to scare Rome into submission.'

'For once, you are wrong on Conrad's integrity. He did believe in Charlemagne's prophecy, and the proof is in front of you. He commissioned the imperial cross.'

'An apt reliquary for the Holy Spear.'

'Not just for the Spear.' She lifted another one of the gold plaques covering the openings in the cross. 'Here is a piece of the True Cross. And can you guess what these smaller rectangular openings were meant for?'

'The Holy Blood? Didn't Beatrice only discover it after his death?'

'Which proves my point. Conrad believed in the prophecy so deeply he started looking for the Blood.'

'Interesting.'

'Am I closer to turning you into a believer?'

'You have persuaded me that, no matter what I believe, Heinrich should be told about the prophecy.'

'When the time is right, I will tell him. In the meantime, we need to create opportunities for him to fulfil it, Adalbert.'

'If only Beatrice's aversion to your husband's bloodline did not run so deep.'

'She blames her son's death on my husband; reason will never prevail over that kind of pain. So, I am looking for another relic that may enable Heinrich to fulfil the prophecy. You are aware that Siegfried of Mainz has left for Jerusalem?'

'It is Anno's only joy right now.' There was an old rivalry between the archbishoprics of Cologne and Mainz, over the right to crown kings.

'In return for my financial support for his mission, he will look for something Charlemagne himself may have concealed in Jerusalem.'

'What gave you the idea?'

'My family are Carolingians. We have documents, proof of donations made by Charlemagne to build a library in Jerusalem.'

'Does anyone else know about this library?'

'Beatrice, of course. But she has not told Gottfried. Let's say it is two noblewomen's idle gossip. You will keep it to yourself.'

XVI.

The banquet was over. The few remaining princes knelt by their overlord and renewed their oath, or what they remembered of it, before making for the doors, unsteady on their legs. Their singing died down along the corridors and the great hall was plunged into silence.

Outside, the city of Worms was wrapped in its night cloak. The Easter full moon whitewashed the stone of the cathedral. The two guards at the entrance could no longer fight the urge to yawn.

Heinrich was still seated at the head table, studying what was left of his wine. 'It was a magnificent day, Adalbert. You took care of all the details to perfection.'

'It is the least I could do. I will treasure forever the moment I handed you the sword.'

'Gottfried was a happy shield bearer.'

'And chuffed to be getting Lotharingia back. You know my views on him...'

'Keep him busy this side of the Alps until I am crowned in Rome.'

'Indeed. Also, your coronation as Holy Roman Emperor should take place before his son marries Matilde of Canossa, just in case the union goes to the Lotharingians' head.'

'Are you saying I should hold off acknowledging her as her father's heir?'

'Absolutely not. It is in your interest to keep the Canossa ladies happy. The Lotharingia-Canossa alliance is a threat to your power and recognising Matilde's rights might embolden the heiress to consider other options, with the pope's blessing.'

'Good advice. I agree.'

Placing his coronet on the table, Heinrich reached for a message from Pier Damiani that the empress had delivered to him earlier, insisting it was important.

His fingers played with the reddish cord attached to the wax, as if he were in no rush to open it in Adalbert's presence. There had been other moments like this recently. Was he about to be dismissed? With a king, like with a dog, you could never allow your fear to show. Adalbert waited.

Eventually, the seal was broken, and Heinrich pulled a candle nearer to examine the content, his face golden in the light. He handed the note across the table.

The royal and the priestly dignity are bound together with the Christian people by a reciprocal treaty. Each must make use of the other. For the king is girded with the sword so he may be armed to resist the enemies of the Church and the priest devotes himself to prayers and vigils so as to make God well-disposed towards king and people.

Agnes was right. 'You should hold this letter dear. It is a theological gift.' Reaching for a jug, he refilled their goblets with a tasty but young red from Burgundy. 'Pier echoes the words of Charlemagne: that the emperor's role is to defend the Church against pagans and heretics and promote the faith with his conquests.'

Heinrich's shadow wavered as he swirled the contents of the cup. 'And what would the pope's job be?'

'The pope's role is to lead prayers for the emperor's success.'

The king took a swig from his chalice. 'Once, you said to me that, after crowning Charlemagne, the pope prostrated himself at his feet. Anno got angry at you. Why?'

'It is a contentious event, uncomfortable for some.'

'Not for Pier?'

'Pier honours you as God's anointed.'

'Even though he serves Rome?'

'You can drag Pier into the deepest mud of the Roman Church, he will still emerge pure. He has no master but God.'

Heinrich emptied his cup. 'Who is your master, Adalbert?'

If that was his test, he was not going to be found wanting. 'While I tread the land of the living, my first loyalty has to be to my earthly overlord.'

The candlelight caught a glimmer in Heinrich's eyes, which could have been interest or provocation. 'If I am earth, by following me, you look after the bodies in your diocese. What about the souls?'

Adalbert gathered his thoughts. 'When your father invested me, he entrusted bodies and souls into my care. To quote Charlemagne, the pope is priest; the emperor is priest *and* king.'

Heinrich's face was momentarily in darkness. 'Would you like to elaborate?'

'My lord, I am not a bishop in the latest fashion. Concepts such as a king owing obedience to the pope in all things... you will not be hearing that from me.'

'What will I hear?'

'That God anointed you; He chose you to succeed Charlemagne when you were a five-year-old. Rome exploited the weakness of your position as a child king to rob you of your God-given rights. But by His will, you will ascend the steps of Saint Peter's and seize the noblest crown. You will rule over Christendom, *Vicar Christi*, second only to Christ.'

Heinrich's face emerged from the darkness. 'It is time I reclaim what is mine.'

It was time, but his grin made Adalbert uneasy. It reminded him of the undecipherable smiles of Heinrich's grandfather Conrad, the emperor rumoured to have made a pact with the devil.

XVII.

Island of Reichenau, 29 May 1065

It was unusual for Cuno not to be in Heinrich's private chamber at this time of the morning. The reason became apparent when Adalbert parted the bed hangings.

The king was asleep next to a half-naked maid the archbishop had never seen before. The girl gave a light scream, slipped off her side of the bed and grabbed her clothes from the floor to cover her nudity.

From the quick glimpse Adalbert caught of her, she was slightly older than the king. Her haste suggested she might be married. But he had no time to study her face. She was off before Heinrich, disturbed by the noise, opened his eyes. 'What is it?'

Adalbert rummaged through one of the coffers and handed fresh clothes to the king. Then he sat by the hearth and gazed into the dying flames, giving him some privacy to get dressed. 'I have some developments to discuss with you – unless you would like me to wait.'

'I am ready if you are.' Heinrich had slipped his embroidered tunic on and was sitting on the side of the bed. His ashen face hinted at the aftermath of heavy drinking.

Adalbert poured a cup of water. Heinrich grabbed it and took a sip. 'Thank you.'

Unusual for him to show gratitude, he must have been hurting. 'Who is the lucky lady?'

Heinrich blushed, strengthening his suspicions.

Adalbert stoked the embers. 'Your Majesty, your secrets are safe with me. Yet, a king should be careful in the choice of his female friends and keep away from married ladies – unless you can afford to compromise the crown's relationship with their husband.'

'She offered herself to me.'

Adalbert said nothing.

The content of his cup spilled on the bed. Heinrich dropped it and rushed to the garderobe. He resurfaced, looking even more ill, and slouched in a chair.

Adalbert rose. 'I shall come back tomorrow when you are recovered.'

He was in the doorway when Heinrich spoke. 'I do not want to marry, Adalbert. Not yet, and not Berta.'

Such openness was very unlike the king. 'Is it about that girl?'

Heinrich shook his head. 'I will not see her again. She is cheap. It is about me.' He blushed, the redness of his cheeks contrasting with his greyish complexion. 'I want to give my heart to someone.'

Never before had the young king showed such a tender streak. Adalbert retraced his steps, recognising, in Heinrich's plight, the echo of another, buried deep within his hardened churchman's heart.

Ermelinde, the young girl from Halberstadt that Adalbert had taken as a mistress when he was slightly older than the king. Her hair was the colour of honey and her lips a rosebud. Then Goseck, his father, had summoned him, his countenance as stern as ever. The dust of time had never settled on that memory.

'You are about to take your vows. Priests may keep concubines; you are not a country priest; you are the son of a palatine count,' the old man had sentenced. 'Your conduct should be irreprehensible. You will go places,' he had added, in his only effort to soften the blow.

Adalbert knew he had been wasting his talent. Leaving Ermelinde had been the price to pay to break away from the curse of cadet sons. She had understood, of course, because she had loved him more than she had loved herself. He had left with her blessing, his hands covered in the tears of when he had last held her face.

Adalbert of Bremen had gone places indeed, far further than his older brothers.

Ermelinde had been married off the moment he had left. Whispers that her first daughter had come too early had tempted him to ask questions. But questions would only renew her pain and his. She had died a few years later, in childbirth, while Adalbert was evangelising Scandinavia for Heinrich's father.

He hated going back to Halberstadt. The whole place was a garland of images of her; the wind carried her voice and the flowers her smell. His wound had never healed.

Perhaps the Roman sunshine gleaming on the cheeks of a southern girl would have worked a miracle. But when years later Heinrich's father had invited him to stay on in Rome, it had been as his pope. He had declined as he knew his inability to keep the vow of celibacy. Anyway, it was too late for that.

Heinrich's gaze was still in his, a desperate plea in it. Adalbert mustered a smile, the smile he had never received from his father, when his fate had been spoken. He patted him on the shoulder.

'Life can be harsh. I will do my utmost to help you. But assume I fail until I succeed. I do not want to make you false promises.'

He moved the pewter jug from the trestle to a coffer by the king's side, so he could have more water. Heinrich drank directly from the jug. 'Do you think Mother could help?'

'You need a champion in Rome.'

'Pier Damiani?'

Adalbert weighed the idea. 'Despite the purity of his motives, I doubt he would persuade his superior.'

The king wiped his mouth with his sleeve. 'Pope Alexander is a decent man. He should be able to see the justice of my claim.'

'I believe he would. But Ildebrando di Soana would not. Sadly, you are a pawn in his chess game.'

Heinrich kept nursing the empty jug. 'How do I thwart him?'

'First you need to extricate yourself from the double bind you are caught in. To lord over the Roman Church, you need to be crowned emperor; and to be crowned emperor you need the Church to bless your marriage.'

§

The empress's arrival was a pleasant surprise and Adalbert invited her to walk along the shore. It was sunset and a pink gold light was reflecting the abbey's majestic walls onto the calm waters of the Constance Lake.

The air was scented with fresh grass. Unusually, Empress Agnes did not seem interested in the miracle of the summer about to break. 'I am here to thank you.'

'Will you dine with me?' A few hours in her company, talking about poetry and beauty, would be delightful. 'We could toast with wine from Aquitaine,' he tempted her.

She shook her head, and her eyes caught the blue-green hue of the lake. 'Pier Damiani says my son has evil counsellors who lead him astray.'

He tried to lighten her mood. 'If you refer to the appreciation of good wine, I own up to that.'

'You know what Pier is referring to.' She gave him a shrewd look.

'If our ascetic friend refers to the king's decision to delay his journey to Italy, I own up to that too.'

Her jaw hardened. 'Heinrich needs to receive the imperial crown.'

He caught the hint of reproach in her voice. He stopped and admired the late afternoon light gleaming on the lake, hoping she would do the same, but she kept looking at him, as if her gaze could bend his will. 'That will have to wait a bit longer.'

Agnes eyed him with a mixture of mistrust and exasperation. 'Why, Adalbert? Pope Alexander, Ildebrando, and Anno are furious about this—'

'Since when do you care for Anno's opinion?'

'Just tell me the reason.'

He resumed walking. 'Heinrich would be delighted to receive the imperial crown if his betrothal could be undone.'

She stopped in her tracks. 'That is insane! Ildebrando will never agree to that!'

'You and I know that. But he is a young king testing the boundaries of his power.'

They were staring at each other. 'You know I was against this betrothal.' She went on to shatter his briefly-held hope. 'But now we need to accept reality and work with it.'

'Might it be time to discuss... things... with your son?'

'Are you referring to the prophecy?' She glared, incredulous. 'He is not exactly ready, is he?'

'That would be for you to decide.'

'How ready can he be if he cannot take the truth when it is given to him plainly?'

'May I ask what you are referring to?'

'I have reminded him of the political reasons that would make undoing his betrothal unpalatable to the Church.'

'How did he react?'

Her chin trembled. 'He banished me from court.'

Adalbert was lost for words, an unfamiliar, unpleasant feeling. He had not seen that coming – at all. Somehow, pain made her even more beautiful. The late spring light gilded her white veil, making her look like a painted Madonna. At least Mary had lost her son to God. Agnes had lost him to Ildebrando's schemes.

Their eyes met. It was the end of the road, in so many ways. The deathbed of a dying emperor, and all those oaths sworn, felt like a memory from another life. He had not felt so sorry and so old in a long time.

He redirected his energy towards a rational analysis of the situation. Regardless of her protestations, she still had a slim chance of victory.

'Perhaps it is time Heinrich knows Ildebrando's real motives. It will put your actions in a different light. It may help him—'

She controlled the wobble in her chin. 'There is only one way to help my son. Tell him to stop playing with fire!'

She had given up. He nodded, slowly, accepting it. 'Where will you go?'

'On pilgrimage to Rome. I used to go with my father as a child. It may help my soul.'

'Now I envy your lot!' The image of a rosy-cheeked young Agnes kneeling on the altar steps of Saint Peter to be crowned empress, all those years ago, flickered in his memory, with the golden taste of what could have been. He tried to snap out of the melancholy. 'Will you seek the pope's forgiveness? That may help your son – from afar.'

She did not reply. She bent her neck, so the veil covered her face.

The shadows were longer on the lake shore. Adalbert picked a primrose from a bush on the edge of the lake and offered it to her. 'You will be missed.'

He was glad he had made her smile.

XVIII.

Trier's grandest ancient buildings had been quarried for stone to build the cathedral and the royal palace, but the sun-drenched, hill-strewn bend of the Moselle bore the marks of Trier's Roman origin.

The road leading to the amphitheatre, whose stone paving had withstood the ravages of time, cut through fields of grapevines, another gift of the Romans, the gold green nectar of forgotten gods still as effective. Adalbert could have done with a cup of the liquid to steady his nerves before his conversation with the king.

Heinrich had his own news to relate. 'Gottfried of Lotharingia's son came to pay homage. We went hunting.'

'I am glad you had a chance to acquaint yourself with him.' The Lotharingians has been on their best behaviour since getting their duchy back but remained a threat to the crown. As Gottfried was not getting any younger, the relationship with his son Godefroy was of increasing importance. 'First impressions?'

'Devious but can be controlled. He sounds eager to get married, unlike me.'

'I would be eager to lay hands on Tuscany too.'

Heinrich looked at him strangely.

'I mean the land, not the heiress – although the lady Matilde is charming.'

'He sounds more interested in the relics his fiancée is bringing him in dowry than in the lady herself.'

'I am not surprised.' If only he could broach the subject of the prophecy with Heinrich, but he had given Agnes his word.

Heinrich eyed him interrogatively. 'Speaking of marriages...'

Time to relate the unpleasant outcome of his conversations. 'The majority of the princes are not averse, as long as you negotiate an alliance of the same standing or higher than that with Savoy – perhaps a foreign princess, like your father's brides.'

'But?'

'You are facing opposition from two parties.' He braced himself for the reaction. 'The first is the Duke of Swabia.'

'The snake who married my sister and buried her within six months!' Heinrich kicked a stone off the road. 'He is greed personified. What is his price?'

'He is not making it a matter of price. Being betrothed to Lady Berta's sister, he wants the Burgundian lands that come with her dowry.'

'I welcome his marriage plan – if anything, it should limit the damage to our relationship with Berta's mother.'

'I took the liberty of mentioning that to him, but to no avail. He wants two things from his marriage: the Savoy dowry and re-joining the royal family. If you do not wed his future wife's sister, the latter will not happen.'

Heinrich's eyes darted at him. 'So I have to marry to make his marriage worthwhile? Pure Rudolph!'

Emotions always ran deep when the Duke of Swabia was involved. The short-lived but unsavoury marriage to Heinrich's sister, and later the rumours of an attraction between him and Agnes, which Adalbert refused to believe but Anno had stirred... He let the king's anger settle.

Adalbert could hear the birds in the trees around the amphitheatre. Eventually Heinrich turned and spoke. 'I can guess who the second opponent is.'

Adalbert nodded. 'I offered him Kornelimunster, Malmedy and even Filike.'

'And?'

'Anno replied he remains the arch-chancellor for Italy and he cannot jeopardise his standing in Rome for a marriage alliance agreed long ago.'

'Lame excuse. Is he trying to take revenge for being dismissed by me?'

'That may well be. He may have friends to keep happy in Rome too.'

'Ildebrando?'

'I suspect so.' They would never know; Ildebrando was skilled at covering his tracks, and Anno, who hated coming across as someone else's puppet, would deny it.

The silence became heavy, and Adalbert waited for Heinrich to break it.

'There must be something you can do.'

'It pains me to admit to this. I think I have hit a wall. Berta's mother is a formidable woman and controls strategic Alpine lands. She has the ear of the pope–'

'Do not waste your breath on things I know.'

'If Anno were willing to canvass your case with Pope Alexander, we could dangle an alliance with a foreign power in front of him, maybe Byzantium or France. As things stand...'

'Finish.'

'I lack the authority to undo the contract your father signed with Berta's mother. Anno plans to use his journey to Rome to secure the pope's approval for your marriage. Once the pope has signed the papers, you can consider the marriage done. The wedding will be an addendum, a feast to celebrate the alliance with your princes.'

Heinrich's jaw contracted. 'Anno can tell Rome to use the Lotharingians as swords of Saint Peter for a while longer, then. Delay my imperial coronation.'

'You should be crowned before Godefroy and Countess Matilde are married.'

'Gottfried has not asked me to approve the union yet, so there is time. Next year I will marry Savoy and be crowned. For now, let Rome suffer – let the Normans breath down their necks for a few months. They are making my life hell – give them a taste of their own medicine. Excuse me.'

He disappeared along the side of the amphitheatre. Adalbert did not follow him. He could not recall Heinrich apologising to him ever. He clearly needed space to cry.

Adalbert descended towards Trier. The cathedral built out of Roman stones would be a magnificent setting for the royal wedding. Adalbert's own marriage – to the Church – had taken place in a similarly magnificent setting, the cathedral at Halberstadt. But the beauty of the surroundings is small consolation for a life you have not chosen.

He had carried out the will of his old master, the king's father. But he had failed Heinrich, and by doing that, he had failed his old self.

A.D. 1069

XIX.

Rome, June 1069

Pier Damiani and Ildebrando were facing each other in the middle of Pope Alexander's chamber in the Lateran. The humid heat might have been increasing his irritation, but Pier Damiani's real issue had to be with the task.

'Why me?'

'Why not you?' replied Ildebrando.

Pope Alexander, by a lectern, was watching them.

King Heinrich had postponed his travel to Rome, and hence his imperial coronation, multiple times. Now, Archbishop Siegfried of Mainz's plea for help proved that the Salian king had no qualms about plunging the relationship with Rome into deep trouble, unless it happened on his terms.

Sidelining Anno of Cologne, the monarch had approached Siegfried, asking for a divorce, claiming he had not consummated the marriage in three years.

Just when the Normans were planning an attack on Rome, the king was suddenly failing the conditions for being crowned emperor and becoming the sword of Saint Peter. Someone needed to go to Germany to deal with the matter immediately.

'Why not you, Ildebrando?' objected Pier. 'You are a holy version of the devil, and this is how you serve the Church. I follow the laws of love I learnt from Jesus, and there is often a blatant clash between those laws and papal policies.'

Ildebrando's chest puffed up as he unleashed his attack, his coal-black eyes shining with anger. 'You are more entangled in politics than I am. You are the confessor of the king's mother!'

Pier did not take his bait. 'Has it ever occurred to you, Ildebrando, that my closeness to Agnes may actually be an obstacle in this matter, as it may cloud my judgement?'

Pope Alexander raised his hand to silence Ildebrando. 'Let Pier finish.'

The hermit seized his chance to speak uninterrupted.

'Considering the Church is not benefitting from his marriage, is it worth keeping Heinrich married against his wish?'

Ildebrando's voice crept up behind him. 'I detect some intellectual arrogance in your question, Brother Pier. Who are we to separate what God has united?'

Pope Alexander took the opportunity to make a point dear to his heart. 'The royal marriage has troubled my conscience in the past, just like the impending Tuscany-Lotharingia union.'

Ildebrando cast a dark look at him and made to speak but Pier preceded him.

'This type of marriage is an offence to the purity of the sacraments.'

Ildebrando leaned towards Pope Alexander, trying to create a physical barrier between him and Pier.

'Holy Father, I have reminded our allies amongst the German princes of the assassination attempt you suffered in Mantova, and that we know the Salian is still in contact with his beloved antipope.'

'I am sure you have.' Pier sighed, exasperated. Having a practical streak, he accepted that someone had to be in charge of the Church's diplomacy, but Ildebrando's willingness to spin webs of intrigue often angered him. He eyed Pope Alexander. 'In Mantova, Heinrich was thirteen and controlled by regents; there is no proof of his involvement.'

The archdeacon ignored him. 'I ask both of you, why would the king deliberately risk his own imperial coronation? Is it part of some plot? Maybe he wants Cadalus to crown him!'

The argument was weak, thought Pope Alexander. 'He is still a boy, Ildebrando. Maybe it is something much simpler.'

'Such as?'

'He may not want Berta crowned. It would add legal complexities to his divorce.'

Ildebrando did not appreciate having his conjectures dismantled. 'His envoys Otto and Anno have met Cadalus!'

Pier glanced in the pope's direction and sighed before making his point, as calmly as he could. 'Gottfried attended that meeting. Would you doubt his loyalty to the Church?'

Ildebrando gritted his teeth. 'This is not about Gottfried. It is about Heinrich. He is an agent of evil. The boy's grandfather made a pact with the devil, and his father was born on Judas's day—'

'Who is being childish now, Ildebrando?' He frowned.

The archdeacon insisted. 'You and Pier are blinded by his youth. But he is a Salian, a son of the devil, and he has the Holy Spear—'

'It is not relevant.' He had had enough, and Pier shared his feeling: his eyes darted upwards.

'Perhaps you will consider another argument,' replied Ildebrando. 'The Salian's crazy request is a golden opportunity for the Church to undo his credibility.' His voice was warming up to the prospect. 'He is showing an authoritarian streak. Turn this divorce into an opportunity for the princes – to unseat him. It is written nowhere that the empire has to be hereditary.'

Pier spread his arms in exasperation. 'What is the Christian point of all this?'

Pope Alexander agreed. 'This is what troubles my conscience.'

'Christian point? Is there anything Christian about the Salian's behaviour? He refuses to bed his wife, and yet he keeps a collection of concubines!'

'Most kings do,' said Pier, matter-of-factly. 'Maybe you should try to administer Confession from time to time.'

'I wanted to spare your holy ears the details, Pier,' shrieked Ildebrando, 'as you are so close to the empress. But he is beyond lustful, he is depraved. He sees three concubines in one night.' Satisfaction was palpable in his voice. 'Is that the behaviour of a king, of the alleged head of the German Church?'

The pope and Pier exchanged silent glances.

Ildebrando mustered a smile. 'To get back to your point, Pier, the Christian point of all this is that marriage is a sacrament.'

Pier advanced towards Ildebrando. 'Do you ever look at the mosaic in the Triclinium on your way here?'

'Of course.'

'Saint Peter gives the pope power over the souls of men, and Charlemagne over the Earth. Perhaps you should meditate on its meaning.'

The reminder was received with silence.

Pier carried on. 'The Church should look at the king's marriage with one purpose only: the salvation of his soul. Are we, Ildebrando?'

With an irritated shrug, the archdeacon turned away from the hermit, towards his superior. 'How long have we striven to free the Roman Church from subservience to the German crown?'

That was too much for Pier. He snapped. 'I have always been on the frontline of that struggle.'

Pope Alexander backed him. 'This is undeniable.'

Pier continued. 'There is a vast difference between fighting for the independence of the Church and unsettling the order of Christendom. You are asking us to forego our duty of compassion and put the Church on a collision course with the crown, for selfish political considerations.'

He had to stop him there. 'Pier, you raise a lot of valid points.'

'Thank you.'

'Do not thank me yet.' Pope Alexander was not looking forward to delivering his conclusion. 'It is difficult, in this instance, to disentangle the spiritual and the political. We should have had this conversation four summers ago, before I gave my approval. As things stand, the marriage has been celebrated. The king was of age when he took his vows.'

Pier looked taken aback. He probably wished he were back with his fellow hermits in Fonte Avellana, with only the skies and the trees for company, and God filling his heart with His silent blessing.

'It is so hard at times to believe in purity.' He kissed the papal ring. 'This is why I never wanted to become a cardinal. Rome of all places always ends up making me feel soiled.'

'Will you carry out my order?' He spoke softly as he shared the hermit's pain.

'I will. At least I will be out of this city soon enough.'

XX.

The princes fell silent as Pier Damiani stepped onto the platform in the great hall.

Adalbert would have made his excuses if it had not been for Agnes. She had beseeched him to attend the proceedings and do whatever he could to stop Heinrich from behaving foolishly, an order he doubted he could fulfil.

It had been almost three years since that fateful January evening when Heinrich had urged him to leave court in the middle of a snowstorm. Dukes Otto and Rudolph, and Archbishops Anno and Siegfried were about to accuse him of treason, and it would be safer for him to go before they lodged their demands, the king had said.

Since that snowstorm, despite his protestations of affection, the king had kept their contact to a minimum, as if he held a grudge against him.

If his dismissal had any positive, it was that Adalbert would not have to preside over this doomed synod. Let Siegfried take the blame this time.

Pier Damiani had not changed for the occasion. He was known for detesting his cardinal garments, the corruption stitched into their sumptuous fabric by gold threads and precious stones. The coarse cloth of his cassock rubbing against his ageing skin kept him grounded in humility, he had said to Adalbert years ago, in Rome.

'It reminds me that no matter how many nights I spend in contemplation of the face of God, I am still a sinner,' he had said.

They were all sinners, in that room, including the king on his throne, a young soul fluctuating between the darkness of political intrigue and the purity of hope.

He was wearing a simple gold circle, as if he resented his crown, and the obligations connected with it.

'I am not here to cast the first stone,' Pier said to the congregation as his gaze met the king's. 'Like you, I do have desires.' Once embarked on the path of honesty, Pier was the kind who travelled it to the end. 'In my dreams I am tempted to fornicate by young women whose skin is whiter than snow, and with nipples as pink as cherries.'

The startled faces of some of the princes, and the blushing cheeks of the younger ones... They had not expected that language from a living saint with a mane of wispy white hair.

Pier slowed his utterance, presumably for clarity's sake. 'I control these desires. This is a lesson we all have to learn, sooner or later.'

His words were greeted by a murmur of approval.

The princes' moods were easy to read. Resentment for the Church's interference in the king's personal life mixed with a belief that Heinrich had brought this debacle upon himself. Why he would not just beget a couple of heirs on his wife and keep his concubines on the side like they all did, was beyond their understanding.

Siegfried called to the dais a man dressed in a red silk tunic embroidered in gold, as ostentatious as those of a cardinal.

'Eminent scholar, from Bologna,' whispered Bishop Benno of Osnabruck, the fellow Saxon seated next to Adalbert.

Bologna was the most renowned law school in Christendom; Heinrich must have covered the lawyer in silver to persuade him to take up his case.

The man in red was probably acquainted with Pier, who hailed from the same area. He addressed him in his elegant Latin. 'Cardinal Pier Damiani, I bow to you, as you are a martyr in the literal sense of the word – a man who bears witness to his faith, living by the same values that he preaches. I am reverentially laying the plain facts in front of you, as they are eloquent enough.'

Pier nodded for him to continue.

'The king swears that he has not consummated the marriage, which the queen has confirmed. Therefore, the bride's family's ability to negotiate another prestigious marriage for her is intact. As everyone in this room knows, the king was betrothed as a toddler, without a say in the matter. How can Rome deem valid a marriage that was never consummated and was forced upon the husband?'

Pier Damiani crossed the platform to address the Bolognese. 'Legally, your points are valid. On a personal level, I am saddened by the pain of a young man who has failed to find the consolation

of love in his marriage.' He directed his gaze upon the princes.
'But this young man is a king and needs to make decisions for the common good rather than his own. History books are full of kings who have married women chosen for them and striven to honour them, including the king's own father.'

Heinrich's blank gaze was a wall hiding the depth of his pain.

Pier walked off the platform, so he could be level with the princes. 'This young man is not just any monarch. He is God's anointed. How can a prince unwilling to put the political good of his subjects before his personal pleasure be crowned Holy Roman Emperor?'

More murmurs came from the audience.

'God has chosen your overlord to succeed his father as defender of the freedom of the Holy Roman Church.' Pier stepped back on the platform, to deliver his conclusion. 'The right arm of the Church cannot be impure.'

'God's wisdom has spoken,' thundered Gottfried of Lotharingia, from his seat in the front row.

He would surely rush to get his son and the Lady Matilde married now, to profit from the king's tarnished reputation and see if it opened an opportunity for them to challenge the Salians for the imperial title.

The rest of the room remained tensely quiet, so quiet that you could hear the rain hitting the roof.

On the king's nod, Siegfried of Mainz closed the synod. Heinrich's steps and the swish of his red mantle filled the silence.

Pier watched him disappear along the corridor. The princes started chatting to each other softly. For all that Heinrich might seem to submit to the will of the council, Adalbert was sure this was not the end of it.

'Brother Adalbert.' Pier had come over to greet him.

Sadness suffused the features of the cardinal hermit. His was the face of someone who knew that he had done the will of the Church, not the will of God.

XXI.

The barge was moving slowly across the rain-swollen waters of the river Po, but the contours of the towers of the Ford of Guastalla were losing their solidity with the increasing distance. Beyond the poplars on the riverbank, the Apennines had been swallowed by fog.

It was the end.

Matilde had fought with everything she had, leaving no stone unturned. When Gottfried, feeling near death, had summoned her mother to Lotharingia, she had ridden the opposite way to Rome.

The attendants in the Lateran had frowned at her riding attire and her demands, but Pope Alexander had agreed to see her. He had not asked the reason for her visit. His precious icon of Mary, painted over wood from an olive tree in Getsemani, had been their witness.

'I will go to a convent of your choice, anywhere you see fit,' she had offered, on her knees.

'A convent is not a place for you.'

'If by renouncing love I am spared the horror of this marriage, I am gladly doing so.'

'The problem is not you. It is your overlord's divorce madness. I cannot release you before King Heinrich is crowned emperor and becomes the sword of Saint Peter.'

'Gottfried wants me to marry before he dies!'

He had reached for her hand and held it between his. 'The Normans are at the southern gates. I need Lotharingia's soldiers.'

The salt of her tears had bathed the back of his palms.

'I will do everything in my power to make your suffering bearable.'

'Prayers will not make my lot bearable.'

'Please, put your faith in our Saviour.' His hazel gaze had silently spoken his sorrow, his guilt. 'And please return to Tuscany. It will not be safe here for you when the Normans arrive. I need to organise the city's defence.'

In that he had succeeded. At the last minute, thank God, Rome had been spared. But her summons had come, and without the pope's backing her only choices were disgrace or obedience.

Her hand reached for her sword, the copy of her father's. Margrave Bonifacio had loved hunting on those riverbanks, and if his soul sometimes revisited the places where he had been happy, perhaps he would hear her.

He would most certainly have been unforgiving with Rolando, and he would have married her to an ally, she was not so naïve to expect it any different, but he would never have signed her away to a man who terrified her. 'Please Papa, help me.'

Vinicia squeezed her hand, in her firm but caring way. Maybe she had heard her.

Even the Romans had given up building bridges on that stretch of the Po, as the opposite riverbanks were too distant. The only way across was by tying a string of barges together in a line.

Ahead of her, the barges were bursting with wagons and people – the men, carts and packhorses travelling with her to Lotharingia – where she was to be sacrificed at the altar of political interest and greed. 'I wish I were poor,' she muttered.

'Don't be silly,' Vinicia said.

'Poor women look forward to their wedding... to spending their life with a man they love.'

'Poor women watch their children and husbands die. Is that the lot you want for yourself?'

She felt a pang of shame. Vinicia never mentioned the family she had lost to poverty.

The towers of the monastery of San Benedetto were rising from the north bank of the Po, ahead of them. 'Where are we going after this?' asked Vinicia.

'I need to collect part of my dowry from Mantova.'

Everything Beatrice cherished – her daughter, her relics, a half of her jewels – was being taken to Verdun in payment for the military protection of Godefroy of Lotharingia.

'My future husband is cruel. We should not be bringing him holy relics,' she hissed. 'I think it may displease the Lord.'

- 78 -

A.D. 1070

XXII.

Heinrich had gone for a ride outside the city walls to clear his thoughts. Countess Matilde of Canossa had not changed much since the Mantova council of five years earlier, so despite her riding garments, he recognised her from a distance. He was surprised to find her in Bavaria. Then he remembered that Welf of Este, a local lord, was her cousin.

Her horse was grazing next to her, under a majestic oak tree. But why was she alone? He spurred his mount in her direction. It would be rude not to congratulate her on her recent wedding.

She did not move as he edged closer. He tethered his stallion to a tree trunk. She recognised him and curtseyed, but her movements were rattled. As he drew nearer, he understood.

She had a cut under her eye, and various bruises. The blood had coagulated but still looked fresh. Her cheeks were streaked with grey lines of drying tears. 'What happened to you, Matilde?'

She lowered her gaze as if she wanted to be swallowed by the forest floor. 'He had sworn.' Her breath was rapid and shallow. She burst into sobs, shaking.

'What did he swear? Who?'

She gazed upwards and then down at her feet again. 'The marriage...' She swallowed. 'They said it was going to be just on paper. That I... he...'

His unease grew. 'Did you not intend to perform your bridal duties?'

Her gaze transfixed him, and he felt stupid for asking.

'I am sorry.' He was not used to comforting women. But the sadness of forced marriages was too familiar. He wrapped his arms around her, careful not to hurt her. She stiffened, like an injured animal scared of physical contact.

'Our families have been enemies, but that is in the past. I will not hurt you.'

She nodded but could not be still. She kept looking over her shoulder, her eyes scouting the forest for dangers.

'Where is he?' he asked.

The question must have re-awakened her memories. Her chin, her shoulders were shaking. 'We were in Ulm, on our way back from my cousin's in Ravensburg. He is either still there or looking for me.'

A light, cold February rain started to fall, painting the leafless trees a darker shade of grey. Realising that she was not wearing a mantle, he took his off and wrapped it around her shoulders to keep her warm.

He had to get the facts. 'Did he do all this?' he asked, delicately moving a strand of red-blonde hair away from her face and pointing to her bruises.

'The real scars are in my soul.' Fresh tears mixed with raindrops on her face.

This was a young lady who could command fleets and troops, and that animal had broken her.

Heinrich was not sure how to handle it. Drawing her to him, making her rest her head on his chest, holding her as gently as possible, to make her feel safe – it seemed to help.

He pulled his mantle over the top of her head, to prevent her hair from becoming completely soaked. For a while, they both listened to the rain falling softly, relentlessly on the barren late-winter fields.

§

Matilde's right cheek leaned against Heinrich's chest. It hurt every time he breathed. She was afraid of speaking to him, and afraid of moving away. She swallowed her sobs.

The soft fur lining of his mantle made her feel safe. At the same time, she wished she could feel the rain on her hair again, washing away the dirt, the horror, the memories... She had to stay in the present. Heinrich seemed concerned. It sounded like he remembered her from childhood; perhaps he could help.

He adjusted the cloak around her shoulders. 'I am sorry.'

Her gaze crept upwards, a flicker of hope in her heart.

'I cannot punish him, Matilde. A good half of my princes probably abuse their wives.'

The breath died in her lungs. That was all he could muster: a king's cynical analysis of her situation.

The corner of her eye found the sword Rolando had had made for her, hanging from the side saddle of her mount. She pulled away and grabbed the silver hilt, unsheathing the sword. Gottfried had forced her to surrender it, said it was offensive for her to keep weapons in their chamber, and the next night he had forced himself on her.

When he had left to go drinking and hunting to celebrate his deed, leaving her like a lump of flesh on the floor, somehow, despite her terror, she had known she could not run away without it; her sword was more than a weapon for protection; her sword was her dignity.

The rain made the hilt colder. She handed it to Heinrich.

Dumbfounded, he grasped it.

Hopefully, it would do its job quickly. She dropped to her knees, her fear gone. 'If you cannot save me, finish me. Please. Here, now. I would rather die than go back to him.'

In a moment, she would join her father, her brother, her sister and be free. She was grateful for the rain across her face. Her last memories would be the touch and sound of water, cleansing her soul, just like it was renewing the dripping woods around them. It was a decent way to go.

Heinrich was clutching the sword, his gaze blank like a statue. Then he placed it on the grass and knelt next to her.

'I cannot do that.' His voice was low, reassuring in her ear. 'Come with me to Augsburg. You will be safe for a few days.'

That had been her destination, before meeting him, in the hope that someone in the city, maybe an abbess, could take her in.

His hands on her shoulders, Heinrich made her rise with him.

Godefroy had punched her in her ribcage when she had tried to sneak away from under him, and the movement was painful, but she was too ashamed to mention it. Besides, he had just thrown her a lifeline.

'Thank you,' she said.

He helped her onto her mount, Lampo, adjusted himself on the saddle and spurred his horse to a canter. The piercing pain in her ribs was forcing her to take shallow breaths. She prayed that he would not turn and see her features twisting in pain. Thankfully, he did not, and, somehow, she handled the pace.

They arrived at a castle on the outskirts of the city. The portcullis was lowered, and sentinels came forward, ready to take care of their horses. The cloak pulled over her face concealed her wounds.

'I will send you my physician,' Heinrich whispered as he helped her off Lampo, before addressing a chamberlain who had dashed out of the main building. 'Cuno, prepare suitable accommodation for the Countess of Canossa.'

Countess, her old title, avoiding painful references to her husband. She had not expected that kind of attention from someone with Heinrich's reputation for selfishness and womanising. When your body and soul are hurting, you hold onto little things like that.

She set off after Cuno, but Heinrich called after her.

'Countess, as I prepare for my imperial coronation, I would benefit from expert advice on Italian politics. I trust a couple of weeks will suffice. I will inform the duke.' He was the last person she would have expected to come to her help, and yet he had. 'What is the name of your personal maid? I will have her brought here from Ulm.'

He was watching her, as if his gaze could shield her from more pain, or perhaps she was reading too much into it.

'Her name is Vinicia, my lord. I cannot thank you enough.'

XXIII.

Framed by the doorway, despite his riding attire, Heinrich looked like a king in an illuminated manuscript.

Empress Agnes had been a beauty in her youth, and he had inherited her high cheekbones. Also, his eyes, though different in colour, glinted in the same way when he smiled.

His physician had called on Matilde every day, administering balms for her bruises and remedies to help her sleep, but this was Heinrich's first visit since he had brought her to court.

He stopped her curtsey halfway. 'I am here just to see how you are settling in. No formalities.' The concern, and the lack of royal arrogance, as his bodyguards were witnesses to their meeting, were pleasant surprises.

'I am deeply indebted for your kindness.'

She could not mean it more. Even the shortest delay he could steal for her, before she faced the horror of her marriage again, was precious.

He was showing no signs of coming in, so she fetched his embroidered mantle, neatly folded on a coffer. 'I need to return this.'

'Put it on. We are going for a ride.'

Did he need time alone to break the news that he had gone as far as he could go to help her? His expression was unreadable. Draping the garment over her shoulders, she followed him and the bodyguards to the stables in silence, fighting to keep her lucidity, as she knew she might need it.

She prayed for a gentle gait, because she was unsure if her ribcage had healed sufficiently – and she could not bring herself to mention it, as if the attack had been her fault.

He pushed the stable doors open. 'The attendant will show you to your mount.'

There was no need. Lampo's gentle eyes recognised her immediately; he neighed with delight. She caressed his long gentle face and let him eat a couple of apples from her hand, while a stableboy put a saddle on him.

Heinrich turned to the bodyguards by the door. 'Your services are not needed.'

His pace towards the gate was a slow trot, and her chest coped well. But as they crossed the portcullis, he spurred his mount and whizzed through the large, tree-scattered expanse in front of the palace.

Only a gallop at full speed would let her catch up with him. There was a dull ache in her rib, but it was bearable. On the edge of the nearby forest, she caught up with him. He nodded, seemingly pleased, before steering his stallion to a path in the thick of it. She did the same with Lampo.

He turned, smiling. 'Do you always ride astride, like a man?'

'Like a warrior,' she corrected him. 'I detest side saddles.' They meant a slower pace and a groom on the ground leading your horse. 'My father taught all his children how to ride. Male or female, we had to ride like warriors.'

She regretted her words the moment she had spoken them. Heinrich had been a toddler when her father had been murdered but discussing him with a member of the Salian dynasty felt like an insult to his memory.

Heinrich seemed concentrated on the path ahead, or on his own thoughts. As her overlord he must be finding the situation unpleasantly awkward – she would, in his place. Yet, the silence unnerved her, stirring her fear. In the silence of her mind, she found herself praying that he was not just about to announce that her time at court was over.

Lampo's hooves crackled on the crust of light ice that sheeted parts of the muddy forest floor. Eventually, he turned.

'My mother had a soft spot for you when we were little...'

The reference to Agnes rang alarm bells. After Heinrich's coming-of-age, something serious had happened between mother and son. The empress had moved to Rome and soon rekindled her friendship with Beatrice. Was Heinrich annoyed about that? She had to tread carefully. Taking sides between mother and son would be a diplomatic faux pas.

She waited for him to finish the sentence, but he did not. With patches of snow everywhere, it was hard to make out the trail. He focused on the task and she followed in his wake. When they got out of the forest, he spurred his stallion again.

Could he be testing her horsemanship? She kept up with him, ignoring the ache in her ribcage, concentrating on bouncing in the saddle and refusing to think beyond that moment to what his silence might be heralding.

They were riding low hills, partly forested. The weak late-winter light held a mirror up to her fear. She felt like a ghost. Actually, she would rather be a ghost, so Godefroy's dirty hands could not touch her.

Heinrich halted his horse and helped her dismount. Despite the courtesy, he looked stern. She fought down her anguish.

'Countess, you have been hurt deeply,' he said. His back was turned as he fiddled with the reins, tethering the animals.

The use of her title warned her that he had switched from relaxed to formal, from friend to overlord. She waited, shivering in the cold. He met her anxious gaze. 'My father was against your betrothal, and I am too. Your alliance is a threat to the Salians. The problem is that he is one of my dukes.'

She knew what was coming. Heinrich could not escape the rules of power, just like she could not escape them. Of course, he could not begin to imagine what it had felt like when Godefroy had beaten her body into surrender. A wave of nausea surged through her at the memory.

He was still fiddling with the reins. 'My marriage was also arranged, as the whole of Christendom knows.' There was no compassion in his tone. 'We all do what we have to do here.'

He may as well have spelled her death sentence. A film of tears spread over her pupils, and then trickled along her cheeks.

Heinrich stopped fiddling. As a king, he must be used to seeing people cry, either out of fear of him, or because of his decisions. But he raised his hand, hesitated for a moment, and then wiped her tears.

'I said that you should go back to him; I did not say that you will,' he whispered.

Had she misheard? Hope was a luxury she could not afford. She searched his face for clues.

'I will find a way to protect you,' he said, his features taut.

He handed her the reins of her mount. 'I cannot afford to lose

Tuscany's support.' He sounded as if trying to persuade himself that he was doing the right thing.

'You will never lose Tuscany's support, not after this.'

She attempted a smile, and he did not reciprocate it, clearly worried at what he was getting himself into. 'Time to ride back.'

In the courtyard, he checked the time on the stone sundial.

'I need to dash off. Thank you for the company,' he said. 'I am staying behind to meet your cousin Welf. But you shall join the court's journey to Saxony.'

XXIV.

Queen Berta was perhaps not striking in her looks, but she was undeniably pretty. Her skin had the radiance of late pregnancy; her smile was open and there was endearing warmth about her. At first impression, it was hard to fathom that Heinrich might have gone to such lengths to divorce her.

Matilde was not looking forward to the meeting. She had not even contemplated the possibility that her ordeal might become a topic of conversation between Heinrich and his wife, or that he might think she needed a female shoulder to cry on.

Reliving the horror of Godefroy's attack, and the feelings of dirt and shame that came with it, were the last things she needed. But she had to put on a brave face.

The queen took her seat by the hearth. 'I am delighted to meet you, Countess. I have learnt about your presence at court this very morning, from Cuno!'

A weight fell off her shoulders. If Berta had found out from the chamberlain, she could not know what had brought Matilde to Nurnberg.

But she might still guess it. What would she make of the scar under Matilde's eye? The afternoon light was dim, but probably not enough to conceal it if one wanted to see it. She seized the moment when Vinicia served them spiced wine to move her chair further back from the hearth, so the glow of the fire would not shine on her face.

Wine was a debatable choice during Lent, but still seemed more appropriate than bland penitential water. While her maid poured it into silver goblets, Matilde studied her visitor.

She had the straight back and the calm demeanour expected of her role, and her coronet was placed on a veil of the purest silk, probably Calabrian. But she tended to lower her eyes. The humiliation of her husband's public rejection was still fresh, and it would certainly take more than a baby to heal it.

They sipped the warm clove-laced drink, and the conversation flowed easily.

'I remember you as a little girl in the empress's lap,' Matilde said to break the ice.

'Have we met before?'

'When Emperor Heinz took my mother and I to Germany, he stopped in Zurich to fetch you, so we spent a few months together in the imperial nursery.'

'I have no recollection, I have to admit.'

'Oh, you were so small! But I could never forget Countess Adelaide's daughter!' She had spoken from the heart. In those dark days, Berta's mother had stood by Matilde and Beatrice, shielding them from Emperor Heinz's wrath.

Berta did not reply, other than with a polite nod. That simple gesture corroborated the reports on the queen's personality that had trickled through over the last few years.

Berta's goodness shone strongly through her honest eyes, but there was a quietness to her. She had not inherited her mother's spirit, or if she had inherited it, it had been squeezed out of her a long time ago.

Separated from her family as a two-year-old, after the coup against Agnes she had ended up a pawn in the regents' game, treated purely as the wooden doll who would one day sit on the throne. Her education had been neglected, so she had not attained a level of culture that could engage Heinrich on an intellectual level. Matilde felt sorry for the young couple.

She changed the subject. 'You must look forward to becoming a mother.'

Berta stared into her cup. 'A high-born woman is nothing but a well-dressed breeding tool.'

Her words awoke a fear that for weeks Matilde had been trying to bury in the recesses of her mind: that she might be pregnant with Godefroy's child. 'I could not agree more.'

'Thank you for your sympathy. Kindness is a luxury in my household,' Berta lashed out. 'My husband is too busy praying that I deliver daughters so he can try for an annulment.'

Saying anything against Heinrich, who had done so much to protect her, was out of the question. Matilde was still thinking of a suitable reply when the queen's eyes lit up.

'I almost forgot!' Berta asked the guard outside to bring in a volume she had left with him. 'My mother sent me some poetry.' She flicked through the illuminated pages of manuscript. 'We shall have a jolly afternoon.'

They continued to read until well after the sun set. The poems of unrequited love brought bittersweet memories of Rolando, but at least they rescued Matilde from her dark mood and her fear of Godefroy. With a bit of help from the wine, she also found the courage to inquire about his whereabouts.

'Heinrich mentions him in his most recent letter. There are unsettled disputes in the lands around Bouillon, which require sorting before the Easter court.' Berta hesitated, as if worried about causing offence. 'Apparently Godefroy is a good warrior, but when it comes to legal cases, he struggles a bit.'

Matilde was so relieved she struggled not hug Berta. Easter was almost four weeks away. She might be spared facing Godefroy until then.

XXV.

The royal train's next destination was the abbey at Hildesheim. Drawing the leather curtain of her litter open, Matilde saw that they were travelling across a plain, and that forests had given way to pastures and ploughland. The yellow banners with the black eagle of the king's guards were striking against the backdrop of the windswept road.

Heinrich, on a white mount, was in the midst of them, talking to a knight. His finger was pointing to the small hamlet ahead of them, a few wooden huts surrounded by chestnut trees, interspersed with vegetable patches and some animal pens. To the east side of it was a slightly grander hut with a cross on top.

The knight rode away, and an order reverberated through the train, reaching her litter. 'On the king's order, we shall take our Sunday Mass with the Hildesheim farmers,' said a guard, helping her and Vinicia out.

Matilde was glad to stretch her legs, and of the opportunity to see how Heinrich handled himself in his role as head of the German Church.

Judging by their vacant expressions, the other princes were not enthusiastic about mingling with the local peasants. Her mother had taught her to value such gatherings. Often these accidental appearances were an overlord's only way to check how his vassals treated the serfs entrusted to them.

The wind had stopped blowing in her face, making the short walk pleasant. The sun was casting a warmer light on the fields, still barren but swollen by the recent rain, full of promise. Something in the air was beginning to thaw.

Here and there, flowers had burst through the ground, and the children had been celebrating spring's arrival, picking blossoms, and turning them into wreaths; some of them were decorating the little church and some were hanging off the trees' branches.

She handed a coin to a small scruffy girl who was nursing her baby brother, maybe an orphan, before joining Berta and her women.

At the end of mass, Heinrich addressed the whole community in the clearing in front of the church. 'I thank you all for your hard work through the seasons of the year, which makes these fields so prosperous and beautiful. I pray to the Lord and His Mother to preserve you and your families in health.' He scanned the faces of the serfs. 'Who is the village elder?'

'Martin,' said a choir of voices.

An old man with wisps of white hair and a thick beard came forward and knelt at the king's feet. Heinrich bid him rise and Cuno drew a small leather pouch out of the folds of his cloak and handed it to Martin.

'These coins are for the whole hamlet,' Heinrich explained in a crisp tone. With the entire community as witness, the old farmer would not fall into the temptation of keeping the money for himself. 'I know the difference between hunger and fasting for Lent,' he added as the old man, on his knees again, kissed the hem of his cloak. 'With this money, you can get yourself through the next months, until the first vegetables of the new season are ready to harvest.'

There was something spontaneous and thoughtful about Heinrich's gesture. He had not thrown some coins at them, jovially but thoughtlessly, like Gottfried would have done. His speech, his clarity, had turned a mere display of royal largesse into an actual enactment of royal justice.

The vacuous puppet watching as Anno bared his teeth at Pope Alexander in Mantova had grown into a true king.

Heinrich blessed Martin in the name of God and a pretty rosy-cheeked girl came forward and offered one of the flower wreaths to the king, on behalf of the hamlet.

Heinrich did not seem to notice the fire on her cheeks. But Berta, standing next to Matilde, did notice.

'If you ever wondered how he learns all this noble stuff about the needs of the poor... He cannot resist relieving the plight of low-born girls.' She lowered her veil, close to tears.

To Matilde, the exchange between king and maid had seemed innocent, but she held her tongue. Berta clearly felt humiliated.

Even though her suspicions may have been unfounded on this

occasion, she must have had her share of bad experiences.

At least he was not a violent husband, she felt like saying, to comfort her. She would have swapped lots with her any day. But that would be of no consolation to the queen, who only demanded to be treated with respect.

An elegantly cloaked man rode in on a sturdy gelding. The serfs made way for him. 'Our lord bishop is eager to welcome you to Hildesheim.'

'We shall follow you in a moment,' Heinrich said.

The serfs gathered before their king, on their knees, to wave goodbye. He blessed as many as he could. For a moment, he looked like a splendid Byzantine Christ in an Ascension icon, golden and serene.

XXVI.

Hildesheim, 15 March 1070

A fine tapestry of the Annunciation, probably the gift of a wealthy noblewoman, decorated one of the walls of Matilde's room, and to the touch her plain bedsheets felt like soft cotton. A well-stocked fire blazed in the hearth, and while sweets were not allowed because of Lent, the trestle was laden with warm bread laced with pepper. All discreet little touches that reminded the guests of the prestige of the monastery.

She had just made herself comfortable on a bench, warming her extremities by the fireside and nibbling the spicy bread with warm milk, when Cuno arrived.

'My lady, I bring orders from the king.' He bowed. 'The court remains in Hildesheim for two weeks, until Easter. But the queen's household travels onwards to Goslar for her confinement. His Majesty would like you to join her.'

'Please tell His Majesty I am grateful for this great honour.'

It was much more than that. Godefroy was due to attend the Easter court, to be acknowledged as his father's successor. By attaching her to Berta's household, Heinrich was delaying yet again the day she would be returned to his claws.

Her relief vanished when Cuno left. She had gained a couple of weeks but was still living on borrowed time. His steps fading down the corridor reminded her that at Easter time Godefroy would tread those same floors. The knowledge made her stomach churn in fear.

Memories engulfed her, their nightmarish quality accentuated by the soft evening light. The way Godefroy had entered her chamber and lowered the latch before chasing her around the room, while the guards outside – his guards – had stood by, oblivious to her screams.

She would rather die than go through that horror again. But she did not want to die. She wanted to rid herself of him for good.

Her writing box on the table by the window, caught her eye. Godefroy had crushed her through brute force, but she retained the power of her eloquence, and it would matter, in some corners. Reaching for a quill and inkpot, she unrolled a parchment sheet and contemplated its clean surface. Time to take her destiny into her own hands.

She started a letter to her confessor, Langerio. Tears were falling on the fresh ink, but fighting through the shame, she described Godefroy's attack.

The Church powers would not be swayed by the feelings and rights of a woman, so she framed her plea within an argument they might find harder to ignore. She questioned the validity of a marriage in which the husband breached the terms of the contract and disrespected his father's will.

She poured wax and sealed the scroll. Her quill was standing tall in the inkpot. There was another letter she needed to write. She had already tried and failed in Augsburg, paralysed by the mixture of longing and resentment she always felt when she thought of her mother.

When she found out what Godefroy had done to her, Beatrice would be devoured by heartbreak and guilt. Yet, fifteen years had not been sufficient for this woman who had risen against emperors, kings, antipopes, to disentangle her daughter from a betrothal that she knew could destroy her.

Of course, Matilde's marriage was part of a chessboard of alliances larger than her own need, and the Holy Blood, and her Carolingian ancestry, demanded a suitable union. But had her mother tried hard enough?

'One day you'll thank me for this,' she had said, disposing of Rolando in less than a day. There was nothing to thank her for.

She wiped the quill dry, placed it back in the box, grabbed her fur-lined mantle from the coffer and walked out.

The path from her lodgings to the church was uphill. Saint Michael's was one of the great cathedrals of the kingdom, lavished with precious gifts from Emperor Otto and his father.

Evening services were about to end when she slipped through one of the bronze doors and settled into one of the nearest pews, so as not to disturb the monks' prayers.

She took in the grace and strength of the building; grace and strength she needed so desperately in her life. For too long, she had had no option other than wait, for too long she had depended on someone else's strength; her mother's, Rome's, now Heinrich's.

Her gaze ran along the line of alternating pillars and columns to the altar, where, in the centre of a circle of candle offerings, stood the statue of the archangel Michael, with his sword lifted.

She had escaped her room to avoid writing to her mother, and yet Beatrice's presence was haunting her. The small wooden statue of Saint Michael she took everywhere; her choice to lay Bonifacio to rest in Mantova, in a chapel dedicated to the archangel, and that image of her mother on her knees before Saint Michael's statue, after receiving the news of Emperor Heinz's death... 'Thank you for delivering justice,' Beatrice had said, sealing her prayer with a kiss on the tip of his sword.

Forming an orderly line, the monks left through one of the side doors. As Matilde made her way across the nave, the image of her mother's wooden Saint Michael vanished, replaced by the cold stone features of the Hildesheim archangel in front of her.

His soft marble curls and graceful wings contrasted with his stern expression of avenger and his drawn sword. She found strange comfort in his empty, unforgiving gaze. Could grace be merciless?

The candles around the statue brightened the depth of her soul. Time to shrug off fear, time to rise. Enthralled by the archangel's promise, by his sword, she prayed to him for justice for what she had suffered from Godefroy.

XXVII.

Goslar, 8 April 1070

Matilde patted Lampo's coat, fed him a ripe apple as a reward, and handed him to a stableboy. With the queen in confinement, everyone was free to spend their days as they wished, so she had reverted to morning rides, like in her old life in Italy. In the courtyard of the Kaiserpfalz she slowed to take in her surroundings, feeling, for the first time in months, at home.

During her mother's German exile, Matilde had spent happy months in Goslar, sharing teachers with the Salian children, under the care of Empress Agnes.

Playing with Adelheid, Heinrich's eldest sister, on the pale stone floors of the great hall, their laughter echoing in the vaulted ceilings; practising her Latin in the nursery with little Heinrich; following the siblings through a gallery on the upper floor of the palace to join Agnes and Beatrice in the women's chapel of Saint Mary to sing Christmas songs; learning to hunt with her new friends in the forests covering the low hills of the Harz, rosy cheeks warmed by campfires...

It had all ended suddenly, one autumn day. A stern-faced canon had been waiting for the small party right there in the courtyard. The Salian siblings had followed him, swallowed by the gloomy winter shadows of the minster towers, and Matilde had been gripped by a hunch that there would be no more playing.

The next day, death had taken the emperor, sweeping away what was left of Adelheid's, Heinrich's, and her childhood like an unforgiving wind. But Goslar would remain etched forever in her memories, as a haven of safety and happiness.

At night, even the peace of Goslar could not crush her demons. Often, she would wake at her own screams, so terrified that her body was hurting in the places Godefroy had wounded her.

Breaking into a royal residence would amount to treason, and surely he would not be that stupid. But without Heinrich and his soldiers she felt vulnerable.

The days when she had pleaded with Rolando to join him in battle seemed part of someone else's life. That was what she hated the most. Godefroy had not just taken her body; he had taken her soul.

She arrived at her lodgings, and pushed the door open, and her memories back into a corner of her mind. She was removing her cloak and riding gloves when she noticed the folded strip of parchment on the table.

'That Cuno chamberlain came.' Vinicia, with a needle in her hand and a ripped gown under her arm, appeared and then disappeared again into the connecting room.

Matilde broke the seal with trembling hands. Had Godefroy cornered his overlord and demanded her back? She rushed through the content. It was only a couple of lines. *The Duke has returned to Lotharingia. I would be honoured by your presence at the royal banquet this evening.*

She clutched the note and let out a sigh of relief. She was safe for a few more weeks, as safe as she could be. Her eyes sought out her sword and she secretly smiled at it.

She would enjoy the music, the food, and the poetry. That monster of a husband was not going to rob her of the joys of life.

'Vinicia! I need to dress for a banquet.'

'Good, my lady is finally getting out of her riding garments!'

Vinicia's words made her realise that Heinrich had never seen her in anything else. She needed to make the right impression. 'I need to look... elegant – good but not ostentatiously so.'

'You mean beautiful.'

'Yes, I want to look beautiful.' For years she had been trying to efface herself and become invisible, to avoid catching her husband's attention.

Rummaging through her coffers, Vinicia produced a burgundy gown, the lines of which brought out Matilde's slender figure, the wide-rimmed sleeves embroidered with small pearls.

'The king and his guests will not believe their eyes.'

Next, she had to choose a veil. As a married woman, she was expected to cover her head, and she hated wearing a reminder of Godefroy's rights to her. Even the one she picked, the most delicate Calabrian silk, felt heavy on her brow, making her feel pinned down, trapped.

Vinicia read her thoughts. 'Let's choose some jewels to go with this dress,' she said soothingly, passing her a small casket.

Matilde poured the contents into her lap and settled for a cameo necklace.

'My lady will look like a queen this evening.'

When Vinicia passed her the mirror, she saw that the cut under her eye had finally healed.

§

Although the princes invited to the Easter court had all left, Heinrich's banquet turned out to be a lavish affair. Jesters made jokes during the first courses, their voices filling the hall, until the first of three minstrels took over. The food was festive, a triumph of the meats that had been forbidden during Lent; the local beer and the wine from the royal cellars were flowing freely. Berta was still in confinement, and it was impossible not to notice the unusual number of pretty girls.

Instead of sitting at the head table, Heinrich moved around to talk to his advisors and guests. The mood became sombre as the second minstrel sang stories about the gold of the Rhine, and the great warriors of old.

Matilde had heard whispers that the Easter court had been tense and that someone had been murdered. But Heinrich looked unperturbed when he stopped by her.

'I apologise for the quality of the wines and food. It is probably not up to Italian standards,' he said with the carefree elegance of a consummate courtier.

'Everything is lovely, Your Majesty. The songs are elegant and deeply moving.'

He sat opposite her, his back against his chair, sipping from his silver cup. 'I am glad you enjoy my choice of poetry.' He turned towards the minstrel to hear the rest of the song.

'You must be relieved to be in Goslar in time for the birth,' she said tentatively, as the singer took a pause.

He ignored her comment. 'What is the most beautiful song that was ever dedicated to you?'

He had put on the spot, and she decided frankness was the best way to handle it. 'I was betrothed at eight and officially engaged at twelve. Nobody ever dared to dedicate a song to me.'

He took another swig from his cup. 'If the countess honours us with her presence at court a little more often, she will find plenty of knights wishing to dedicate songs to her.'

For a moment, she imagined him dedicating a poem to her. What would he choose?

His voice brought her back to reality. 'We need to talk. I will come and play chess in your apartment tomorrow afternoon.'

XXVIII.

The following morning, while Matilde was out riding, servants installed Heinrich's favourite chess table in her chamber. He arrived as the afternoon light was starting to abate.

Matilde had always seen him either in sumptuous royal robes, or in his riding garments, but he was wearing a simple white tunic, calfskin boots, and a woollen cloak, which he casually threw onto a chair next to him.

Had it not been for the ring on his index finger, a Roman cameo representing an eagle, the symbol of the empire of Rome and of the Salian family, he could have easily been mistaken for one of his courtiers.

He did not seem surprised that she was not wearing a veil. After pouring spiced wine for both of them, he checked the pieces on the chessboard.

'As we finally have no witnesses, let me tell you where I am with your situation.'

Matilde looked up from the chessboard, dreading his words, yet glad he would not keep her wondering much longer.

'In Hildesheim, Godefroy and I had a private audience. I told him that, given your closeness to the pope, I need you to remain at court to assist me in smoothing diplomatic relations with Rome. He insisted on joining us, but I ordered him to go to Antwerp as my representative, to administer justice. That should buy you about a month.'

She could not have asked for more. He had pushed as far as he could without endangering the crown's relationship with Lotharingia. 'Thank you, Your Majesty.'

'You can call me Heinrich when we are alone. Like when we were little. Or maybe you do not remember?'

She smiled. 'Oh, I do. I remember a lot of things... For example, the first time you rode a horse—'

'That was a good day!' He picked up the horse chess piece, his expression one of amusement. 'What about when you appeared in my mother's room in Aachen, with Margravine Beatrice... My little brother was alive... He was crying and begged you to be her champion and you—'

'I beat you at sword fighting!'

He placed the ivory horse back on the chessboard. 'A five-year-old boy against a ten-year-old girl! I had not yet realised that size matters. You taught your king an important military lesson that day!'

They were both silent for a few minutes, reminiscing on that day of thirteen years ago.

She was the first to speak. 'My fighting instinct just got the better of me. My mother knew I would not hold back, I could read the fear on her face. She dreaded your father might take offence, and our situation was bad enough as it was; you know the history...'

'It takes bravery to say this to me, and I appreciate bravery.' He sipped some wine. 'My father was Beatrice's enemy indeed. But my mother, God only knows why, always stood by the ladies of Canossa.'

Feeling more relaxed in his presence, she could not resist a cheeky remark. 'Are you heeding the empress's advice?'

'Only because it agrees with mine.'

His sudden coldness made it clear it had been a faux pas. 'Can I tempt you with some food?' she asked, to defuse the tension.

'I shall have some meat and cheese, and some of that vinegar sauce we get every year from Canossa.'

She summoned Vinicia from the next room and imparted her orders in Tuscan. The maid walked down to the palace kitchens.

Heinrich adjusted the wolfskin on his back to make the chair more comfortable and turned his attention to the chessboard. 'Now, Countess, do you know how to play chess?'

Matilde had been taught but had not played in years. Heinrich had spent long nights learning from Adalbert of Bremen and was an accomplished player.

He taught her patiently for a while, correcting her moves and giving her hints, and then they tried a proper game. He won quite easily but insisted on giving her a second chance.

Vinicia, announced by the unmistakable smell of honey loaves, deposited a food-laden tray on the trestle and refilled their goblets.

Outside their window, the sun was setting on the beech forests of the Harz, and the outlines of the hills were shining against the impeding darkness.

'There are places like this in central Italy,' she said, 'although a bit warmer. At this time of year, the countryside is dotted with small flowers, and a bit later it fills with sunflowers. They bring happiness.'

'When I embark on my progress through Italy, you shall show me these places.' His whole face lit up with expectation. 'I was three the last time I went to Florence. I do not remember it at all.'

She chased away her own memories of his visit to Florence. They had just buried her brother on the Apennines and her mother was on trial. 'It was the first of the many times I had to pay homage to you.'

'I would take it as a sign that your loyalty is valued, lady of Tuscany,' he chuckled.

'I am flattered.'

Vinicia cleared the trestle, leaving just the cheese and dates and the wine flagon, and closed the shutters to keep the room warm. Matilde was conscious that the maid had been up since dawn. 'You must be exhausted,' she told her in Tuscan. 'You can retire to your room.'

Vinicia scratched her chin, hesitant. 'Will you be all right?'

'Of course.' She was more than all right, she was safe – a feeling she had forgotten since her marriage vows. 'Sleep well.'

Heinrich called her attention to the chessboard. 'Now, shall we see if white will beat black any time soon?'

It was a challenge, and she had forgotten how much she relished challenges. In a few moves, she found a way for her queen to trap Heinrich's king.

'Checkmate!' Her cheeks were glowing with the heat, the wine, and the excitement of the game.

'Checkmate indeed. You have won the king.' He picked up his black king and making him bow to Matilde's white queen.

Her smile froze on her lips.

'Do you understand what I am saying, Matilde?' The black king was still bowing on the chessboard.

'I am not sure, my lord.'

He leaned back in his chair, letting the black king go. 'Stop calling me my lord and Your Majesty. You are the only woman who can call me Heinrich.'

The flames from the hearth were reflecting on his bronze curls. His eyes were glowing.

'Do you know why I let you call me by my name?'

'No, Heinrich.'

'Because you are the only beautiful woman who understands me.' He reached for her hand. She did not feel scared or horrified as she had felt when her husband had touched her. He brought her fingers to his mouth and kissed them one by one. 'I should go.'

He got to his feet and made for the door. She stood up to bid him goodnight but hesitated. The crackling fire was the only noise in the room.

Heinrich let go of the door handle and retraced his steps. He traced the contours of her face, and then, gently, drew her into his arms. His lips brushed her neck and travelled up her face to meet hers.

'I am not doing this to swing you away from your alliance with the pope. Politics is out of this room tonight. There is only a man and a woman. Let me love you.'

She surrendered without hesitation. She had never faked her feelings with Heinrich; she was not going to start now. She was scared, but she needed to feel what love could be like after Godefroy's brutality.

He lifted her in his arms and carried her to the big walnut bed, then went back to bolt the door. He flung his tunic off and guided her hands and her lips over his body, teaching her where he wanted to be touched, then he removed her gown and camisole and admired her, in complete stillness, for a few minutes.

She felt his fingers slide over her hips and his lips on her breasts. 'We will take all the time we need, Matilde. This is not rape. This is love. You will enjoy it as much as I will.'

He guided her hand so she could feel he was ready. He rolled on top of her and penetrated her gently, kissing her tears away at the same time. What had felt utterly wrong when Godefroy had pinned her down, was now a shining light towards which she rushed eagerly. It hurt, but she treasured the moment, its startling glow burning away the memory of evil, and her body knew the difference.

Heinrich moved away slightly and stared at her. She sensed he wanted more. His lips glided over her neck until his mouth found hers. He did not let her go until she started to relax and return his kisses. 'Trust me,' he whispered as he nuzzled her ear. 'You just have to trust me.'

The second time, there was no pain. Instead, her body tingled with a happiness she had never known. She watched as he reached his climax, grateful for the joy her body was giving his. He gave her another long kiss and drew out of her. But he made her curl up to him and continued to hold her in his arms.

'You are not going anywhere,' he whispered on her eyelids, with such intensity that she felt another wave of desire.

'Thank you.' She kissed his chest.

He was still holding her when the candle went out and they fell asleep.

§

When she woke up, Heinrich was gone. For a moment, she wondered if it had all been a dream. But the mess of sheets in her bed told a different story. Curly hair was trapped in the fabric of her pillows. She could not afford to hope that it had meant anything to him. But she was still grateful.

Vinicia knocked at the door.

'One moment,' she shouted, hurriedly adjusting the bed sheets, fluffing the cushions, and throwing some lavender seeds into the fire.

Hopefully, Heinrich had sneaked out when Vinicia had left for Prime mass. And hopefully no-one else had seen him.

Her maid was staunchly loyal, but other servants or guards would not be. Adultery between the wife of a duke and his overlord was not only a mortal sin – it could destabilise the kingdom.

Vinicia knocked again. 'A message for you.' She handed her a piece of folded vellum before dashing off to the kitchens.

Matilde spread it out. It was a poem, in the *langue d'oc*, Empress Agnes's language. She did not know Heinrich could speak it.

The Church frowned upon poetry, which had arrived in Europe via the Moors, but it had become popular in recent years, especially in Aquitaine.

Had it been read at a banquet in Canossa, she would have blushed, but in her room in Goslar it just rekindled her desire.

When the nightingale sings,
And day follows night,
I am with my love
We are covered in flowers.
Then the watchman shouts
From the tower: 'Rise, lovers,'
As dawn is here, and the bright day.

XXIX.

Heinrich came back in the evening, straight from his court duties, still wearing a golden coronet and the royal mantle.

'I missed you all day.' He drew her to him for a kiss. 'I need to see Berta,' he whispered, caressing the nape of her neck. 'I will be quick.' He dashed off.

Berta. She could feel no guilt towards Godefroy, after what he had done to her; in her heart, she was not married to him. But Berta had suffered enough, and she had no desire to hurt her.

Heinrich returned, happy, like a carefree child. Grabbing an apple from the fruit bowl, he took a bite, then dropped the rest of the fruit on the trestle and pushed her hair away from her face.

'Last night, I felt like Adam must have felt with Eve,' he whispered into her ear. He kissed her hungrily.

She wanted him more than the night before, if that was possible. But she could not shrug off her guilt. 'Heinrich, how do you feel towards your wife?'

'I feel nothing.' His lips explored her neck and started slowly making their way down.

She pulled herself together. 'We have sinned, against God, and against Berta.'

'I was married against my will, like you. You do not have to justify yourself; I do not have to justify myself.'

That did not ease her guilt. She put some physical distance between them. 'You are right about us. But Berta is innocent.'

He stiffened. 'Innocence has nothing to do with this. When I look at Berta, all I see is myself back in a church in Trier, lying to God, saying words I did not mean... Or in that room in Frankfurt, trapped by Pier Damiani. She could have gone gracefully, and she did not.'

'She is a pawn, like us. Her family probably forced her to save the marriage.'

'They probably did. Does it change how I feel? No, and she

knows that. She knows her job is to be the mother of my children and appear on the royal diplomas.'

'Are you trying to relieve my conscience?'

'I did not realise I had come to a trial tonight!' he snapped. 'Surely, given all the time you have spent with your mother and the pope, you know that I am a selfish bastard.'

His bitter half smile spoke of sadness and loneliness. He poured himself some wine from a flagon.

'You have not been selfish with me,' she said to his back.

He pushed the cup aside, edged closer, and started undoing the brooches of her gown. 'I am always selfish with you, even now. I want you.'

'But you started to protect me well before this.' She lifted his hand away from the brooches.

He seemed intrigued by her behaviour. 'I often wondered what happened to the girl who beat me at sword fighting.' He leaned against the mantelpiece, watching her, and Matilde felt like prey facing a supremely confident hunter. 'Five years ago, I saw her again in Mantova. She had become an admiral – and a beautiful lady...'

'I was scared you would punish me for the expedition to Rome.'

'I should have.' His gaze lingered on the curves of her body. 'But I could not confront you, or the whole assembly would have seen me blush. That is the only reason you escaped your king's wrath.'

His smooth talk proved that Heinrich's reputation as a seducer was fully justified. Yet her body struggled to agree with her brain.

Probably sensing a weakness to exploit, he edged closer. 'You were always grown-up and independent. You were beyond my reach.' He grabbed her hand and brought it to his lips. 'It all changed the other week when you cried in my arms under that tree. For the first time, you needed me. For the first time you were seeing me as a man.' His hand was playing with the brooches again. The first one came off.

'You are sending me astray, Heinrich. We were talking about your marriage.'

'To hell with my marriage – and yours. They are political treaties.'

'The Church—'

He pulled her dangerously close. 'Our feelings have never

- 108 -

mattered to anybody – not to our families, not to the Church.'

'Most certainly not to the Church,' she agreed, and realised she had taken a step towards his trap.

His lips were brushing hers. 'You and I are alike. You are about to rule lands like a man. You know the loneliness of power.'

'I do know the loneliness.' She pulled a couple of inches away to look into his eyes. 'Our feelings will not save us if we are caught.'

He gave the slightest of shrugs. 'They will excommunicate us. Godefroy will get my lands, and either he or Rudolph of Swabia will get the imperial crown.'

'Are you willing to risk that?'

A glint of defiance in his eyes. 'Of course not. The puppets will outsmart the puppet masters. We will be careful.' He drew her to him and kissed her ravenously. 'Did I hurt you last night?'

Her cheeks heated up. 'Only the first time, a bit.'

'I love making you blush.' He lifted her in his arms and carried her to the bed. 'Tonight, it will not hurt. I promise.'

When the morning light woke her, Heinrich was getting dressed. She stretched under the sheet, and admired his pale, muscular body, framed by the window. 'Will people not notice that you are wearing the same clothes as last night?'

'Cuno may notice but will not ask. Anyway, a few details are different.' He pointed to the table by the bed where his coronet lay. 'You will look after it for today, will you not?' He stole a last kiss. 'The queen who defeated me at chess can look after my coronet until the next match. Good day, my love.'

XXX.

Goslar, 12 May 1070

Heinrich lay asleep in Matilde's bed, by the light of a candle they had forgotten to put out. She thought of the story of Eros and Psyche, the tale of a woman who loses her beloved because she looks at him. Heinrich's pale skin, his messy curls, his lips slightly parted by his soft breathing, the defined muscles on his chest, there was nothing about him that she did not desire.

Desiderium, the longing for someone even as they are present, she thought in Latin, thinking of a book about love she had secretly read in the Canossa library.

She had never spoken to any woman who had fallen in love. Her sister had died too young, and other than Adelheid, she had never had a confidante. Yet when she looked at Heinrich or heard him speak or felt his skin against hers, even the memory of Rolando that she had treasured in her heart all these years faded at the edges.

Heinrich was the son of the man who had instigated the deaths of her father and brother, and even that could not change her feelings for him.

The prospect of being returned to Godefroy was all the more dreadful now that she had experienced the joy of falling asleep in the arms of someone whose simple existence shook every fibre of her being. She had no desire to take Confession, because she could not call her actions a sin, and she doubted God would either.

If she could choose her fate again tomorrow, she would rather be shamed and excommunicated, after having experienced love with Heinrich, than retain a façade of dignity while being raped by her husband.

What Heinrich would choose, what he truly felt, she did not know. Taking his words, the honey-dripping claims of someone taught the art of persuasion from the cradle, at face value was a luxury she could not afford.

Had he simply wanted to add her to his collection of lovers?

Possible. Yet, he had sneaked into her apartment almost every evening, as she had kept hoping he would.

That night, though, before falling asleep, he had told her he had to go first to Quedlinburg, and then on to Merseburg for Whitsun, and she had been kept awake by a fear that his trip was going to mark the natural end of their liaison. Judging by his reputation, Heinrich was not the kind to keep the same lover for long; besides, she was not a village girl, and their relationship was a threat to his power.

'My absences are starting be noted,' and 'tongues are wagging,' he had admitted on a couple of occasions, urging her to pay heed to the smallest sign of being watched.

'You are Rome's darling princess – the one they have sacrificed to a hunchback on the altar of their greed. They would never suspect you of anything sinful. But they watch me all the time,' he had said over dinner.

If they were caught, he would be in so much trouble with Rome and the princes that his failed attempt to divorce would look like child's play.

The Whitsun court at Merseburg would also mark Heinrich's next meeting with Godefroy, who had been relentless in demanding his wife back, so that he could work on the succession to the duchy of Lotharingia. Sooner or later, Heinrich would be cornered to return her. Her sword, hanging above her fireplace, reflected the light of her candle.

What would she do then? Run away again? Where? Italy was too distant and riding there without an escort too dangerous. Before Merseburg, Heinrich was going to visit his sister, her old friend Adelheid, now abbess at Quedlinburg. She could pass her a letter through him, making an enquiry about a temporary spiritual retreat. Yes, Adelheid was her best hope.

His soft, regular breathing helped her relax, and she finally fell into a deep slumber. But it did not last long. For the first time since Heinrich had started sleeping with her, she had a nightmare of Godefroy lurking in the shadows, breathing down her neck.

She opened her eyes, wondering if she had screamed aloud. Heinrich was not in the bed. Wiping the tears lining her cheeks, she parted the hangings.

He was lying on warm sheepskins by the hearth, staring into the flames. 'Is something wrong?'

She sat next to him. He wrapped his arms around her shoulders and kissed her on the neck. He was naked, and she could see that he wanted her. But he searched her face instead, concerned. 'Is it about Godefroy?'

'You said he will be in Merseburg.'

He kissed her hand and then held it reassuringly. 'I will deal with that. You stay here with the queen's court and wait for me.'

She felt only partially relieved. She did not want to see Godefroy's twisted face ever again, but she did not want Heinrich to fight her battles for her. And he did not know Godefroy like she did.

'What if he figures out what's been going on between us?'

Heinrich laughed. 'He is not smart enough.'

'What if he vents his frustration with Ildebrando? He is smart enough – his spies could catch us.' She had to know how he framed their relationship in the great scheme of things.

He gave a light shrug. 'I was doing some thinking before you woke up. If Rome catches and excommunicates us, let them.' His calm tone contrasted with the raw anger in his gaze. 'I will turn the whole of Germany against Ildebrando di Soana.'

'Excommunication is serious, even for a king. You could lose your power.'

He looked as if he did not care. But then a different thought crossed his mind. 'If I lose power, it will stop me from controlling Godefroy. We cannot have that.'

He kissed her fingers softly, one by one, in a gesture that was starting to become familiar, but that did not stop her from feeling like she was melting inside. 'Do not worry. I know how to deal with dogs like Godefroy. That animal will not touch you again.'

XXXI.

Abbess Adelheid of Quedlinburg had inherited her mother's rosebud lips, the kind of beauty even a nun's veil could not erase, and the steel gaze of her mighty grandmother Gisela, the two-time widow of political genius and Carolingian blood who had made Conrad the Salian emperor material.

'I trust my brother will not keep you waiting too long,' Adelheid said, before leaving Adalbert with a jug of Aquitanian white and some delicate almond biscuits. She had given him a warm welcome, delighted to meet him again for the first time since childhood.

He swirled the wine in his silver cup. Heinrich's summons had been unexpected. Why, and why now? He revisited their last conversation of Epiphany 1066, when, between pauses in the minstrels' singing, Heinrich had stunned him with the revelation that Otto of Nordheim had brought serious allegations against him.

'I hate Otto, and he lies,' Heinrich had admitted. 'But he has the backing of Duke Rudolph, Anno, and Siegfried of Mainz. Go this very night, Adalbert, before I hear their demands, so I can protect your titles and your lands.'

Adalbert had bowed to the inevitable. 'I will make things easy for you, my lord,'

Had the plot been the only reason for his dismissal, or had Heinrich cooled on him when he had failed to undo the royal betrothal? Adalbert would never know. Kings should keep the rationale for their decisions to themselves, he had taught Heinrich that.

All he could tell was that Heinrich sounded sorry to let him go.

'Everything I know, you taught me, Adalbert.' He filled their goblets. 'As a thank you for your services, I have signed deeds to grant you fertile land around Speyer, where you will be able to grow your own grapes. I will send for your wines once a year.'

After he had left, there had been no letters from the king other than through his clerks at the royal chancery. Occasionally they had met at synods, such as the dramatic one to debate the royal divorce, but conversations had barely progressed beyond polite greetings. Until now.

'This is more of a pleasure than you imagine,' Heinrich said on his way in.

'The pleasure is mine, Your Majesty.'

'I have enjoyed your wines.'

'Speyer is not Burgundy, but the quality is improving.'

Heinrich sampled his sister's wine, dipping one of the almond biscuits in it. 'You are a talented wine-maker, and the greatest trader amongst my bishops. Your archdiocese is growing ever richer, as your ships crisscross the Baltics in all directions.'

'Hungry souls are not good Christians. I try to keep my subjects well fed.'

'Most princes of the Church would not agree on your priorities, Adalbert. I do.'

'I am glad to hear it.'

Heinrich's gaze steadied on him, as if he was weighing his odds. 'Things have changed, at court. The anxiety towards you is receding.'

Life could be amusing, if one managed to look at it with a degree of detachment. 'You mean that the principal actors are making fresh enemies – and new friends?'

'Both,' he said. 'I have strengthened my power, but there is a lot more to accomplish. I am surrounded by snakes, and I need someone trustworthy at my side.'

Adalbert sipped from his cup. 'The princes will not like it.'

'It will not be an outright restoration. Your role will be... discreet. You will be my Ildebrando.'

XXXII.

Beatrice had spent a month in San Benedetto, the island abbey outside Mantova, on the river Po. After leaving her daughter across the Alps, her soul needed penitence, comfort, and prayer, and the routine of the monastery had helped.

Letters had arrived from across the Alps, from her cousin Arnould, the Count of Chiny, and from Bishop Theodoric of Verdun. But nothing from Matilde.

Arnould's letter had troubled her. Godefroy had never thought much of the monastery she had started building in Orval, on her cousin's land, while she was nursing his father last autumn.

She had drawn plans with Bishop Theodoric, and the Calabrian monks she had brought with her had dug foundations around the simple Merovingian chapel, turning it into a much grander building, the centre of which a new abbey would radiate from. She had visited one last time in late winter, with Arnould and Theodoric. Pleased with the sturdiness of the external wall, they had agreed to proceed with the second part of their plan.

Beatrice, Matilde and Godefroy were due to travel south to Bavaria, to visit their kinsman Welf, before she set off for Italy. Their absence gave Theodoric and Arnould the opportunity to act, moving the relics of the Holy Blood from the cathedral of Verdun to the new abbey at Orval.

Godefroy was due to attend the Easter court and by the time he returned to Verdun and realised that the relics had been moved it would be too late for him to act. Orval's charter stipulated that the monastic foundation reported directly to Rome, bypassing the local duke.

Ildebrando, informed of the plan, had given it his personal blessing and would deal with Godefroy's likely grievances.

The relics' transfer to Orval honoured the letter, if not the spirit, of Matilde's marriage contract, while keeping the Holy Blood under Beatrice's jurisdiction and protecting Matilde's right to be its next custodian.

She had hesitated, in the beginning, out of fear that Godefroy might take his anger out on Matilde. But Ildebrando's involvement had given her the reassurance she needed.

The slightest breach of her daughter's marriage contract, just like any attempt to seize the relics from Orval, would put the new duke on a collision course with his protector in Rome, at a time when his relationship with his overlord in Germany was still in its infancy.

She re-opened Arnould's letter.

Cousin Beatrice,

God has watched kindly upon our efforts, but I need to relate events that require immediate attention.

Your son-in-law returned to Lotharingia sooner than expected and visited the cathedral. Bishop Theodoric could not conceal that the relics had been moved to Orval, although he stressed that an order had come from Rome in that respect.

Before the next dawn, while the monks were asleep in their wooden cells, Lotharingian troops surrounded Orval. Threatening to torch the foundation, Godefroy forced himself inside the grounds. Thankfully, Theodoric had sent word after their meeting, and thankfully we had built a small barracks on the inside.

When I arrived, the duke was holding the abbot at sword point by the main altar. I spelled out that the order to move the Blood had been issued by Archdeacon Ildebrando, and that stunned him.

He gave up searching the abbey, although he kept shouting that he would continue to patrol all the roads out of Orval and would seize the Sacred Vessels the moment we try to move them.

I hope I have impressed on him that he should leave these brave men of God alone, but I urge you, like Bishop Theodoric, to alert the archdeacon to the danger.

Arnould

God had clearly watched over the relics, and she would raise the alarm with Ildebrando. But what on earth could have caused Godefroy to return to Lotharingia before the Easter court, when he was due to be confirmed as his father's successor?

She prayed that these events had nothing to do with Matilde's silence.

XXXIII.

Mantova, 9 May 1070

After Count Arnould's letter, a similar one had arrived from Theodoric. Beatrice had taken it as a sign that it was time to cross the river. As Mantova was better connected through the Roman road network, there was a small possibility that a letter from Matilde may mistakenly have ended up in her study there, together with the political correspondence that she had asked her secretary to let pile up on her table during her retreat.

She rushed through the pile of scrolls. Nothing.

Her heart felt heavy. The way Matilde had looked and acted when she had said goodbye was haunting her. Instead of the outburst of anger or desperation Beatrice had braced herself for, her daughter had barely uttered a word, as if the past no longer mattered because the future was too unbearable to behold and go through with.

Fear was what she had seen in Matilde's gaze on that last morning in Bavaria. That fear had seeped into the fabric of her being, devouring, questioning, accusing. She would never shake it off until she knew that Matilde was safe.

'Madonna, Ildebrando is waiting for you in the great hall.'

She rushed to meet him.

'The monks of San Benedetto said I would find you here.'

'I only just left the abbey. I needed to make penance for sacrificing my daughter. What can I do for you?'

'I detect some hostility in your words, Madonna. I thought we were working together.'

They were and they were not. But she was not going to discuss her anxiety about Matilde with him, after his stubborn opposition to undoing the betrothal. 'You must be here to find out if I managed to protect the Holy Blood.'

'Bishop Theodoric of Verdun wrote to me while I was in Milan – he says he wrote to you too.'

'He did, and so did my cousin. Saying Godefroy is not pleased is an understatement.'

'You should not worry about your daughter, Madonna, I hear she is at court, attached to the queen's household.'

She was about to voice her relief, but something, a hunch, held her back. If she was safe at court, why had Matilde not written?

Taking her silence for encouragement, he continued. 'Theodoric says that Godefroy tried to seize the Holy Blood from Orval.'

'Already last week I have committed additional funds to the Count of Chiny. That abbey will become a fortress.'

'I knew I could count on you. For my part, I will write to Godefroy. The sooner he makes peace with the fact that the relics are not his property the better. Perhaps you should write too.'

She shook her head. 'If anyone can instil the fear of God in my son-in-law, it is you, Ildebrando. And for Matilde's safety, he should be put in his place while she is away at court.'

'Of course.'

During his last illness, Gottfried had revealed to her that for years Ildebrando had filled his son's mind with promises he would champion his right to the empire, behind the Holy Father and Pier Damiani's back. Now he was discarding him like an old boot, to keep his claws on the relics.

'Thank God Matilde is at court. Hopefully, she will stay until Berta is churched. By then, your message should have worked its effect on Godefroy.'

§

Swallows circled the belltower as Beatrice walked the short distance from the palace to the church of San Michele. Ildebrando had left for Rome in the morning. The heavy wooden door swung behind her, and she made for the small crypt, permanently lit by a myriad of candles. She dropped to her knees on Bonifacio's tombstone. Matilde's silence continued to haunt her, and she needed the comfort of his presence.

In all these years, she had never managed to pray for his soul without feeling regret for things that could have been said and done, on that day that had changed her family's life forever, condemning her children to pain and death.

Her fingers ran over the marble slab at the feet of the archangel, the way she had once traced the outline of his cheekbone. So many of her dreams had died with him.

'I have not broken my oath to you,' she whispered, as it was true.

She had remarried, but there had been no consummation. She had never told Gottfried that she was the secret custodian of Charlemagne's prophecy, and to that day his son had no proof of the truth of the prophecy and the meaning of the Holy Blood.

She had been so close to telling the truth to her daughter before leaving Lotharingia, and perhaps she should have. It may have helped Matilde make sense of the loveless life she was condemned to live. But Bonifacio's death had taught Beatrice the hard way that some truths were better left untold.

'Watch over Matilde for me, for us,' she prayed to him. 'Help her fulfil her destiny.'

Time to say goodbye and go back to Canossa. Hopefully, there would be a letter waiting for her there. She finger-kissed his tombstone, made the sign of the cross and rose. The scent of beeswax carried some comfort as she made her way upstairs.

XXXIV.

Canossa, 18 May 1070

Shaking, Beatrice consigned Matilde's letter to the flames of the nearest brazier. She struggled even to name what Godefroy had done to her daughter.

Betrayed his promise in the most violent manner, she had written. *Every day I fear for my life.*

Nausea surged through her as the flames swallowed what was left of the parchment. Her heart was close to breaking. That fear in Matilde's eyes the day they had parted now felt like foreboding.

On the unfinished tapestry on the opposite wall, the Queen of Sheba was serenely receiving King Solomon's gifts. The contrast with her daughter's fate could not have been starker.

Loose green threads hung from the left side of the cloth. She had not touched the tapestry for years. The day she had started it, in this very room, had also been a bright day, spring sunlight warming the stone floor. Her children had been playing noisily in the courtyard, blissfully unaware of what lay around the corner. She had been about to leave for Mantova with Bonifacio on that last fateful journey.

Praying for his forgiveness, she promised she would never settle until she rescued her daughter from Godefroy's claws.

'Analyse the facts, look for solutions,' she said to herself; it would help her stay sane.

Matilde had found unlikely support in Heinrich, but that support was not going to last forever. He may be overlord to both, but he would not tread on Lotharingia's rights lightly. So, they could not rely on him for long. Unless... Unless.

Another sentence from the letter she had fed to the flames had struck her as ominous in a different way. *I find my opinion of Heinrich is changing.* What exactly had she meant by these words? Only one person could help her find the answer.

Agnes had just arrived in Canossa. She was sitting at a table in the scriptorium with Brother Aesculapius, one of the monastery

- 121 -

librarians. A Greek from Calabria, he was one of the few men of God in Italy with good knowledge of Hebrew.

A pleasant smell of parchment rose from the scroll spread in front of them, permeating the air. They were immersed in their work, trying to establish if some relics of the Virgin Agnes had recently purchased were what they were purported to be.

Lifting her head to the approaching steps, the empress smiled in Beatrice's direction, but her expression changed upon seeing her grim face. 'I shall re-join you shortly, Brother Aesculapius.'

Agnes followed her down the few steps of the library onto the esplanade. 'What is wrong?'

Beatrice stopped at the bottom of the stairs. 'I have received a distressing letter from Matilde.'

'Distressing in what way?'

'She is still at court.'

'So?'

Her chin trembled. 'She is there because... Godefroy... attacked her.'

'How could he!'

Sheer horror spread over Agnes's face, and it melted Beatrice into tears. 'I married her off to fulfil my ambition. God is punishing me through her.'

Agnes embraced her. 'We cannot read God's design. Please do not blame yourself. Rather, use your energy to help her.'

Beatrice pulled away, trying to regain her composure. 'She cannot stay at court forever.'

'Unless Heinrich intervenes.'

'There is not much he can do...'

Agnes sat on a bench in the courtyard. Her expression was neutral. 'Does she say anything about Heinrich in her letter?'

It was an unexpected question. 'She says strange things.'

'He wrote to me as I was leaving Rome. It was a pleasant surprise, the first time he had done that in years.'

'What did he say?'

'Strange things, I suppose. He told me that Matilde was at court, he praised her intelligence...' Her friend's fingers moved nervously across her necklace. 'He asked *me* to help him change the pope's mind – and yours – about his divorce.'

For a moment, Beatrice could not breathe. 'What do you read

into his request?'

Agnes's gaze was open. 'He acknowledges that the circumstances are stacked against him even more than last year. His marriage has been consummated and although Berta may have failed to deliver a boy, she has proved she can have children. I started being at risk of repudiation only after three girls in a row...'

'So?'

'So if knowing all this he is still pleading with me...'

She could not bear to hear it, there had to be another explanation.

Agnes seemed to hesitate before delivering her final blow. 'He has feelings for her... And his actions are so out of character that he must be sure of her feelings too.'

Fear was dragging Beatrice lower and lower into the abyss of her guilt. 'I pray that you are wrong. If you are right, we need to stop them.'

An enigmatic smile crossed Agnes's face. 'Stop them or protect them. Maybe God is showing us the way, Beatrice. The Spear and the Blood, two heirs of Charlemagne.'

'The prophecy may be a hoax. No-one has found its text,' she attempted.

Agnes pulled her shawl tight around her shoulders. 'If it is fulfilled, what does it matter if we have a text for it or not?'

XXXV.

Symbol of the imperial crown, the octagon was a recurring feature of the architecture of Goslar, from the minster to the main residence, to the palatine chapel. On his deathbed Heinrich's father had even asked Agnes to have his heart sealed in an octagonal gold capsule and enshrined in Saint Ulrich's.

Matilde was yet to set foot inside the chapel. The soul of the man who had ordered the destruction of the male line of her family lingered too strongly within those walls. Yet she had welcomed that man's son into her life and into her body and could not bring herself to regret it for a moment. Short-lived as their relationship might be, it had taught her beauty.

She could not wait to see Heinrich again. But the distance had given her the opportunity to reflect on the risk that their relationship represented for him. Politically, he could not afford a showdown with Rome, and Godefroy was a liability. Grateful as she was for everything that he had done for her, for both of their sakes, it was time she took her fate into her own hands.

Pieter, the papal envoy, was a man in his early forties with a piercing gaze and a thin face, well-groomed but spartan in his clothing and habits – a blue-eyed younger Saxon version of Pope Alexander. His allegiance, though, was to Ildebrando, whom he had met in Cologne during the archdeacon's time there.

His message, asking for a meeting, had come as a surprise. Apart from Berta and Heinrich's inner circle, and her mother in Italy, no-one knew she was in Goslar. But Ildebrando had his way of finding everything out. Servants could be bribed, and princes would share snippets of court gossip in their letters to Rome.

She had to tread carefully. If she conducted herself well, this could be her first opportunity in a year to make her own decisions.

Pieter accepted some water but declined food or wine. It was not just a reflection of his ascetic character. Since Heinrich's divorce attempt, Ildebrando had been lashing out at the corrupt and lax ways of the German court, and such vehement accusations made it crucial for papal envoys to act beyond reproach.

'I pass greetings from the Holy Father,' he said.

'Please reciprocate them.' Since last year's meeting in Rome, she was yet to write to him; the wound of his inability to help was still too deep and fresh for her to confront. But the envoy could not know that.

'He will be glad to receive them. And he will surely be glad to hear how you are adjusting to married life.'

Matilde turned frosty. 'What else does Pope Alexander expect of me? The Normans have spared Rome, I hear.'

He looked stunned for a moment. 'It is, alas, but one of many assaults upon Rome's territory.'

'Indeed.'

He recovered his poise. 'Doubtless you are aware of the king's stubborn refusal to acknowledge that the right to nominate bishops extends from God and must be the exclusive preserve of the Church.'

Unsurprisingly, it was not phrased as a question. He was cast from the same mould as his master Ildebrando: self-righteous and intimidating.

Nodding politely, she held back the denunciation Pieter would be expecting.

He carried on, quoting anyone from Humbert of Silva Candida to Pope Leo. 'The king is surrounded by advisors who refuse to see that the Church should have its own government and be free of the earthly constraints of imperial influence,' he concluded in a pompous style clearly influenced by Latin oratory.

Only then she concurred, and blandly. 'You know my mother's position on this issue.'

'Perhaps he fails to appreciate the risk that a clash with Rome would entail for his rule. Yet, surely, he should be concerned at least about the salvation of his soul.'

She had enough of Pieter's honey-coated arrogance. Her mother had served Rome's cause for as long as she remembered, Matilde had risked her life and inheritance for Rome, but Rome had not been there for her when it had mattered the most. Only Heinrich had.

'I am not part of the crown council,' she replied coldly. 'All I can offer are prayers for the king's soul.'

'Speaking of his soul... What do you make of the queen?'

She had to be as tactful as possible. 'She is kind and caring. I can only speak warmly of her.'

'You have also become acquainted with the king...'

Hopefully, Pieter would attribute the sudden redness of her cheeks to the warmth spreading from the braziers. 'He is a clever man. It is hard to make him out.'

A nod of agreement. 'And that spells trouble. Our king enjoys playing with fire a bit too much. Perhaps you could put your time at court to good use and persuade him to reconsider his attitude towards Rome?'

She had no patience for patronisation. 'Pieter, you have been looking after the relationships between Church and kingdom for years. You have seen King Heinrich grow. You know it is impossible to change his mind unless he decides to change it. I need to use my limited influence on him sparingly – or risk losing his trust.'

'The Holy Father would have given up on him long ago, if it were not for Hugh of Cluny.'

'Really?' Challenging him might be reckless, but there had been no major political developments in recent months, and Pieter's claims were mere reflections of Ildebrando's personal opinions. Although Pope Alexander might change his mind if he found out about her and Heinrich.

His lack of reaction betrayed his surprise.

She seized the initiative. 'Will Archdeacon Ildebrando and the Holy Father ever give up on me?'

'I am not sure what you mean, Countess.'

'Focusing on imperial politics is hard while I live in fear for my life.'

He gaped at the strength of her words.

Summoning all her strength, she firmed her gaze on him. 'The Holy Father knows that my marriage contract stipulates terms to protect me, including a clause of non-consummation.' The words came out, dignified. 'Such a contract was breached, as my confessor knows.'

'I am sorry to hear about your... problem.' For once, he seemed uneasy. 'Would you like me to relate it to Rome?'

'I would be grateful if you shared my denunciation with Pope Alexander.'

'You have my word. In the meantime, Rome would be ever so grateful if you could use every opportunity to bring the king to reason.'

'As things stand, I am merely the wife of one of his dukes. My influence on him would grow if I were granted a divorce.'

XXXVI.

The queen's chamber was vastly different to what Agnes's had been in her days. There were tapestries, embellishments, mirrors, and prayer books, an icon of the Mother of God, pots of unguents and perfumes, needles, and piles of fine cloth to embroider. There were elegantly carved chairs and silver chalices. But there was no writing table. The queen's seal was probably locked away in the royal chancery. That room was the gilded cage of a woman of high birth and no power.

It was Matilde's first visit after Berta had given birth, and she had been dreading it. As she had said to Heinrich after their first night together, his wife did not deserve what had been going on behind her back.

Physically, the queen, sitting in the solar, looked well. The midwives had praised her courage during the delivery. The wet nurse helped her adjust little Adelheid in her lap. But at her first scream, Berta handed her swaddled baby back to the nurse and reached for her embroidery.

'I was distraught when they showed her to me,' she admitted between stitches. 'Each girl condemns me to one more pregnancy, to risking my life for someone who does not care.'

'I understand.'

Berta's needle kept going through the fabric, angrily. 'His first duty is to the kingdom, of course. But why celebrate Whitsun in Merseburg? It was a ruse, to avoid being around for the birth.'

Thinking about Heinrich's reaction when she had mentioned the queen's pregnancy at the banquet after Easter, she could not rule it out herself. 'I am sorry.'

Berta's fingers stilled. She passed the fine cloth and needle to one of her women. 'Leave us,' she ordered.

The royal maids disappeared into the anti-chamber. Berta sighed and twisted her mouth to stop her chin from wobbling. 'My chamberlain notified him of the sex of the baby. I could not bring myself to do it.'

Her pain was so raw that Matilde hugged her, but she felt devious for doing so.

The queen was sobbing lightly on her chest. 'If I deliver another girl, he will have a case for repudiation.'

'Has he said so?' Despite her feelings for Heinrich, Matilde could not stop caring for the young queen and wished she could help her out of her misery.

Berta dried her cheeks. 'I should not burden you with my worries. You have yours.'

She mustered a smile. 'It may be a small comfort, but a first-born royal heir would be handed over to tutors from the cradle. With a girl, you will be able to bring her up close to you for a while longer.'

Berta nodded. 'She is a good baby. I think I may grow fond of her, unless Heinrich decides to marry her off too soon, like my parents did with me.' Her eyes wandered around the chamber and she squeezed Matilde's hand. 'I am so grateful for your concern. I will light a candle for you at Mass this evening.' She fetched a large leather-bound volume from a lectern. 'I need some light-heartedness now. My mother has sent another manuscript.'

She pushed her chair closer to Matilde's and started going through the beautifully illustrated pages, reading the verses aloud. They were poems of knights and ladies, of love and devotion, a devotion Berta had never known, a devotion Berta's husband would rather bestow on Matilde.

It had been easy to forget her sins in Heinrich's arms in her apartment, but here in his wife's rooms, soaking up her pain, guilt was staring her in the face.

Berta pushed the volume aside and squeezed Matilde's hand again. 'I am glad he left you behind with me when your husband must be in Merseburg.'

'I am relieved too.' She welcomed the opportunity to be honest. 'We have both been unlucky in our marriages.'

Bringing her palms to her face, Berta chided herself for her own forgetfulness. 'Duke Rudolph tells me that Heinrich is giving private audiences to Godefroy. Do you know what the matter is?'

Clearly, Rudolph was taking advantage of being her brother-in-law to prod the queen, directly and through her sister. Did Berta realise it? If she did, it might not bother her, given his motive was so plain to see – fear of being overlooked for the new Duke of Lotharingia.

Matilde tried to defuse the concern. 'It must be something personal, perhaps Godefroy's inheritance?'

'That has been settled swiftly, I hear. Oh well, Rudolph will find out soon enough.' Berta's sigh signalled that her mind had wandered back to her own worries. 'The Whitsun court at Merseburg must be a cover-up, so Heinrich can spend time with his new lover.'

Was Berta suspecting something, and trying to force her into an error? Matilde kept her nerves under control. 'He has political meetings in Merseburg, such as the one with my husband that Duke Rudolph mentioned.'

The queen assessed her words. 'You are right. But I have never seen Heinrich so infatuated before. Either he has truly fallen in love or his new beloved practises the black arts – or both.'

Slowing her breathing for calm, Matilde hung on to the facts. Berta had just come out of confinement and she and Heinrich had always been careful, seeing each other at night when the court was asleep or going for separate rides before meeting in the woods. There was no way she could know.

'Heinrich will do some work in Merseburg, that is true,' the queen concluded. But her expression was still downcast. She placed a hand over Matilde's arm. 'He sent me orders that I hate to share with you.'

'What orders?'

'My household and I are leaving Goslar next week, after I have been churched. But he wants you and the bishops to travel to Berstadt, his next stop, tomorrow. Apparently, there is a meeting you need to attend?'

Every muscle in Matilde's body stiffened with fear. Had Heinrich been cornered? She had to know what lay waiting for her. 'Is my husband going to be in Berstadt?'

'I believe he has gone back to Lotharingia.'

So, he had left court. But what if he was just hovering around, to reappear in Berstadt and claim her? Never before had Heinrich sent his orders through the queen. Was his unusual behaviour a sign of guilt? Her head was spinning.

Berta placed her hand on Matilde's arm. 'I am so sorry, and I will miss your friendship. But I am expecting a visitor.'

'Of course.'

She almost collided with Pieter in the doorway. So, he was the visitor. She had to hope Berta kept her suspicions to herself. Any negative detail about Heinrich, even his queen's slightest doubt, would make its way to Ildebrando's ears.

Matilde's thoughts were pulled back towards the order she had just received. Heinrich had promised to look after her, but Godefroy's dream to lay stake to the imperial title rested on his marriage and he would not give up on that. Had he managed to corner the king in some way?

By now, Heinrich would have passed her letter to his sister, the Abbess of Quedlinburg. But what would happen if Heinrich were forced to agree to her return to Godefroy? Would Abbess Adelheid be able and willing to protect her, if that meant defying an order from her own brother and overlord?

Her mind ran through other potential allies she could enlist. An archbishop would have been the best.

Adalbert of Bremen, whom her mother trusted, had retired to his lands.

Siegfried of Mainz was the second-best option. Last year, he had deferred Heinrich's divorce request to Rome. Would he be willing to do the same with her and offer her protection while a decision was being reached? Perhaps.

But unless he happened to be in Berstadt, she needed to devise a way to get to Mainz undetected, and to keep Vinicia safe.

XXXVII.

Berstadt, 7 June 1070

An attendant helped Matilde dismount Lampo and took him to the stables. Another showed her to her lodgings.

'Do not unpack, wait for me,' she told Vinicia, before following Cuno along the corridor to the king's chamber.

She was trembling as he lifted the latch. Her sword was hanging from her belt, just in case Godefroy was waiting inside, that leer she would never forget distorting his face. Neither Cuno nor the guards at the door tried to disarm her, probably doubting her ability to handle the weapon.

As the door opened, she caught a glimpse of Heinrich. He was wearing a mail shirt, and his helmet was on the trestle next to him. He must have just finished sword training and was having wine with a guest, possibly a foreign ambassador.

'He is still with Denmark.' Confirming her guess, Cuno gestured for her to sit on the bench by the door.

Not that she wanted to listen. All she could think of was her future. Godefroy was not with Heinrich but could still be somewhere else in the palace or waiting for her to be dispatched to him in one of his castles.

To ignore the leaps of her heart in her ribcage, she fixed her gaze on the elegant stone engravings of the architrave. The steps of the Danish ambassador behind her startled her. He was introducing himself when Cuno stuck his head out, inviting her in.

Heinrich was going through some documents and nodded for her to join him on the dais.

'My sister Adelheid sends greetings,' he said as she drew nearer. 'She was thrilled to receive your letter and says you are welcome to Quedlinburg at any time.'

He did not look, or act, as if he were about to deliver bad news. His smile was open.

'I hope she is faring well.'

He picked up his seal from the table. 'She has no master, apart from her annoying little brother from time to time. I see that as faring very well.' He impressed his seal on the letter he had been reading. Only then did he notice her strained smile.

'He will leave you alone, Matilde.' His tone was warm, reassuring.

'He is not lurking in the woods around here?'

'I thought there was trust between us.' He frowned. 'Would I summon you just to hand you over to him? This is actually offensive!'

'You sent orders through Berta. That was so out of character. It worried me.'

His tone softened. 'I am trying to keep our communication to a minimum, to make life harder for the papal spies.'

That was some relief, but not enough. 'What did you say to Godefroy?'

He locked the scrolls he had just sealed in his writing box. 'I have been ruling an empire since I was fourteen. I have learnt a few things. Sometimes it is better to pre-empt an enemy's suspicion.'

'You did not answer my question.'

'I said I did not have a chance to claim the first night, but I am now exercising my feudal rights with his wife.'

It was an ancient custom that no-one would dare to contest. The overlord had first right to his subject's woman, if he so wished. But it would be deeply insulting for Godefroy, one of the most powerful princes in the empire. 'What did he say?'

Heinrich contracted his jaw. 'He made a vulgar boast about how many ways he took you on your wedding night.'

Her knees started to rattle; her chin trembled. How could she feel ashamed of having been raped? She did not know, but she did. She prayed that Godefroy's claims had not affected Heinrich's view of her.

His expression was stern. 'I punched him so hard he fell to the ground. He will be richly compensated for being a husband just in name, but I warned him I could crush him like a worm any time I want.'

He was not judging her; he was simply trying to spare her the details. Reassuring as Heinrich's scorn for Godefroy was, she had to make sure it did not cause lasting damage. 'You cannot speak to him like that. You need him politically.'

'He has just inherited his dukedom. He has too much to lose.'

He did not have the measure of Godefroy. You can lose a chess game by attacking too much or too early, she wanted to say, but she held her tongue. After what he had done for her, she could not hurt his feelings. By now, the Heinrich described by Ildebrando and his envoys would be dispatching her back to Godefroy to move on to his next prey. This Heinrich she had met was different: he cared.

She cast her pride aside. 'Thank you for protecting me.'

Heinrich downplayed his actions. 'As your overlord, I have a duty to keep you safe.' He took her veil off and she felt as if he was freeing her from Godefroy's hold. He kissed a strand of her hair.

'You are his overlord too. Your other princes would expect you to take his side.'

'Protecting you is more rewarding.' The courtier jocularity of his replies barely masked his warmth. He traced her lips with his finger. 'I missed your smile. It is beautiful.' He put his hand behind her neck and drew her mouth to his. His hands explored every inch of her body through her light summer gown. 'I missed everything about you.'

She stroked him passionately, relishing the bliss of being reunited. Without letting go of her, he turned her towards the open window.

The wind was scattering flower petals in the fields. They both admired the magic of late spring for a while, to the sound of their heartbeats, his body leaning firmly against hers.

'It is time for some serious talk,' he said.

'On Rome?'

'No. We know how to play Rome, by being careful, like I was today, even though it caused so much concern.'

'I am sorry.' She felt naïve. Yet, he had not suffered what she had suffered. 'I will trust you next time.'

He moved a strand of hair away from her face. 'I want to talk about us. What do you feel for me?'

His skill with words again – she had to be careful. 'It has been... the most wonderful couple of months.' She glanced upwards to check his expression. 'What do you feel?' She feared the answer but had to ask.

His gaze followed some windswept petal. 'When I was little, I met a big girl. She was brave and beautiful, a skilled sword fighter.'

His tone dropped to a warm whisper in her ear. 'When she left, I thought she might have been just a child's dream.'

His hands tightened around her waist. 'Years later, I heard reports that she had been leading fleets. Then, I travelled to Italy and saw her again. She had turned into the most amazing woman and this time I knew she was real.'

His words touched the core of her being. 'Thank you.'

'I do not need a thank you. What do you think of me?'

'Your reputation has preceded you—'

'You judge me on my reputation rather than on my actions?'

She spun around and gave him a kiss. 'What I have learnt of you in the last few weeks does not agree with your reputation. I owe my life to you.'

He smiled nervously. 'I am still no clearer as to what you think of me.'

'What I feel for you.'

His hands ran along her back. 'What you feel for me.'

She blushed. Could she take the leap of saying that she loved him? Or would it make her look weak? 'I am afraid of what I feel for you.'

There was a triumphant smile on his lips. 'It will do. For now.'

He pushed her gently against the wall. He loosened her gown and pulled it off her shoulders, his lips savouring the smoothness of her bare skin, all the way down to her breasts. There was a knock at the door.

'This must be Cuno with Duke Rudolph,' he said aloud, while rearranging her gown. 'One minute,' he shouted through the closed door. He passed her veil to her with a quick kiss. 'I am not finished with you.'

He sat back in his carved chair and watched her walk out.

XXXVIII.

Berstadt, 7 June 1070

Heinrich had gone from meeting Duke Rudolph to meeting Pieter. He looked like he needed a drink.

'It was the usual: a good grilling, a lecture on the marital duties of a king, and a long digression on my dissolute life,' he sneered, slouching in a chair. 'I should have mentioned that I am spending my nights with their holy Countess of Tuscany, to make it a bit more interesting. By the way, he asked me what I think of your marriage.'

Matilde stopped in the middle of the room. 'What did you say?'

'That I am not as opposed to it as my father was.' He laughed, presumably at the shock on her face. 'I know their little games. If I am happy with something, they may decide to be against it. So, I said I know Godefroy will lend me his support, should the need arise. I also reminded Pieter that, as your husband, *he* rules your lands now.'

She was stunned, for a moment. Then she understood. 'If you tell them that through Godefroy you control my lands, my marriage becomes a problem for them.' Devious as it might be, his approach was clever, and might help with her request to Pope Alexander, of which he knew nothing. 'You are amazing.'

Cup in hand, and a twinkle in his eye, his index finger traced her lips. 'You are amazing too. Berta would have just fainted with shock, but you see that they are likely to do what I appear not to want. You are different from any woman I know.'

'I confess you surprised me for an instant.'

'But you recovered.' With a kiss of her fingers, he drew her against him. His lips brushed hers. 'We should play chess again, rather than our usual evening activities – you can hold your own against me.'

'I may take you up on that.'

He sat down and gestured for her to sit in his lap. He kissed her on the neck and behind the ear. 'You never told me what it was like.'

'What what was like?'

He nibbled at her right lobe. 'Leading the fleet.'

She could still taste the salt on her tongue at the memory. She snatched his wine cup from the table and sipped from it. 'Oh, it was one of the best moments of my life.'

His hand closed over hers. 'Why?'

She thought for a moment. 'I felt free.'

He gave her a long kiss and then offered her another sip of his wine. 'Would you do it again?'

'Tomorrow.'

He put the cup away. 'You would challenge your overlord again tomorrow?'

'Of course.' She whispered in his ear, 'Or we could both sail away from all this.'

'Maybe.' His index finger traced the profile of her face. 'Have you heard from your friend the pope?'

'I have not. But even if I had... some of the things he discusses should not reach your imperial ears.'

He raised his eyebrow, either puzzled or annoyed. 'You and your mother are ruling Italy in my name. Why can we not discuss things openly?'

It was a flattering overture. But she had a debt of loyalty to her old confessor, despite his inability to protect her from Godefroy. 'I need you to trust me on the pope.'

Rising, he pulled away. 'I need *you* to trust *me* on the Church!'

'I do trust you.' She tried to defuse his sudden anger.

'If you did, you would give me a chance to explain my ideas.' He kicked the chair. 'Instead, you are letting bloody Ildebrando and the pope tell *you* what *they* think *I* think.'

'Pope Alexander deserves your respect.'

'Your father would have agreed with me,' he snapped.

'You know nothing about my father. You were a baby when he died.'

'So?' he insisted, a grin on his face. 'Adalbert told me what my father thought of Count Bonifacio.'

The grin was too much to bear. 'What does Adalbert know? Let me tell you what your father thought of my father. He killed him—' She drew breath. '—and then he killed my brother.'

For a moment there was surprise in Heinrich's eyes. 'There is no proof. It could be just rumours—'

Matilde lashed out. 'Oh, really? Well, let me tell you something that is not a rumour. We would be dead without those "bloody" cardinals.'

The silence, for a few minutes, was absolute. She regretted her outburst, but it was too late. She had heard a few tales about Heinrich's fits of anger. She braced herself.

His jaw hardened. 'There is no proof,' he repeated, and a shadow crossed his face. 'Is that why you cannot bring yourself to speak the words "I love you?" Because of what my father allegedly did to your family?'

She had no answer. Her feelings for her family and his were too complex to express in words.

He read her silence the wrong way. 'If my father's alleged crimes so strongly overpower any feeling you might have for me, you could have had the decency to mention it!' Something in his eyes shifted. 'Unless revenge was your plan all along.' He clapped mockingly. 'In that case, well done to you.'

'Revenge? No, Heinrich.'

'I don't want to hear your lies, on Rome, on your family, on anything. Why the hell did I ever think you could be different?'

Was he drunk and had she not realised? She could not believe the change. 'Heinrich.'

'Shut up!'

On the doorstep he stopped. 'I keep my word. Your husband will not trouble you again.' He lifted the latch. '"Poor Berta" has just arrived. I guess I should pay her a visit tonight.'

XXXIX.

Berstadt, 8 June 1070

The rising sun was tracing a golden stripe on the stone floor. Matilde accepted she could not sleep, slipped her riding clothes on, and tiptoed through the anteroom so Vinicia would not wake up. The precinct was deserted, and the attendants in the stables did not take notice of her beyond a polite nod.

She saddled Lampo and walked him to the gate, crossed the moat and spurred him into a vigorous trot across the plain. The animal's body was taut and hungry for freedom. She needed time alone with her horse and the morning breeze. Heeling his flanks, she released him into a gallop.

She was still reeling from her fight with Heinrich and struggling to make any sense of it. All she knew was that in the space of two months, she had gone from the horror of her marriage to the beauty of Heinrich's love, to losing him.

As if that were not painful enough, if anger made Heinrich thirsty for revenge, how low would he be willing to go? Her fear kept on conjuring images of royal butlers packing her belongings and dispatching her back to Godefroy. Even at the peak of his anger, he had promised to continue protecting her; she clung on to the hope that he had meant it.

Drying her cheeks, she rode back. She had to attend a banquet that afternoon, in honour of the Archbishop of Bremen. The contrast with the excitement of her preparation for that other banquet, after he had returned from Hildesheim, could not have been starker.

She chose a demure pale blue and white silk gown. Her braids, plaited with strings of pearls, were completely covered by the veil. Keeping a low profile seemed the best course of action.

Seated between Berta and his guest of honour, Heinrich spent most of the evening talking to the archbishop. He was drinking heavily, and Berta, familiar with what Heinrich could be like when in a bad mood, kept sending miserable glances in her direction.

The meats on Matilde's plate were delicious, but she had no appetite. When, halfway through the evening Berta politely took leave of the archbishop, she wished she could follow her.

Instead, as an ordinary guest, she felt obliged to stay until the royal chef served the strawberry cake, which was claimed to be his spring specialty. After sampling the dessert, she drew her strength and requested permission to retire.

He emptied his cup. 'Is the countess bored with our company?'

Ignoring the sarcasm, she tried to sound firm but not confrontational. 'The countess humbly requests Your Majesty's permission to deal with urgent work.'

'Your king grants you freedom...' Heinrich let the words hang in the air before adding, 'to leave. Goodnight.'

Adalbert, next to him, looked puzzled by the exchange, but soon he turned his attention to the precious goblet that his former pupil was filling to the brim with Tuscan wine.

There was only one candle burning when she arrived in her room, and Vinicia was already asleep in the antechamber. The pale pile of parchment waiting on her table glared at her in the semi-darkness. Thank God for work. It had always helped her cope with pain.

She picked two more candles from her stash and lit them, to have sufficient light to read.

Heinrich would be too drunk to make a decision on her fate that evening, so she immersed herself in a report on the income of the city of Mantova, although occasionally a tear smudged the ink of a parchment sheet.

Well past midnight there was a knock at the door of her apartment.

'Open up.'

She had to stop Heinrich from waking up Vinicia, and the rest of the castle. She hurried through the antechamber.

The moment she unlocked the door, he staggered in, past her maid's cubicle and into her bedroom. Bolting the door behind him, he stopped in the centre of the room.

His gaze seemed unfocused. In the bright light of the candles, he looked even drunker than at the banquet.

Was he about to spell out her punishment? With bated breath she waited.

'I fucked the prettiest maid I saw in the hall.' The wine was making his words slightly slurred. 'But you are the only woman I want.'

Determined not to show him her pain, she spun to face the wall. He forced her to turn, felt one of the tears on her cheek with his fingertip and grinned. Then he pushed her against the wall and kissed her, leaning against her.

At least he did not seem about to send her back to Godefroy. She gently moved his hand from her breast and tried to pull away. 'You are not yourself tonight. Please.'

'I have not been myself since you rejected me.'

His self-pity gave away his drunkenness. From her mother's diplomatic dealings with him, she knew that he was unforgiving and that this could be her only chance to make things right. 'I did not reject you.'

He let go of her. 'You led me to believe you loved me, just to humiliate me – to settle scores in our families' feud.'

'I swear to God, revenge never crossed my mind.'

'I did not kill your father, or your brother.' He spoke so loudly he could certainly be heard from the anteroom. Vinicia's German was basic, but the presence of a drunken king in her mistress's bedroom would be hard to explain.

She re-focused on the immediate priority – soothing him. 'I never said you did. Your father killed them. And your mother saved us.'

Her words startled him. 'And does that balance out my father's alleged actions?'

His insistence on "alleged" was annoying, although he had a right to believe his father's innocence.

'I suppose it does. Anyhow, the truth is that I judge you on your behaviour towards me, not on the behaviour of your parents.'

He blinked, assessing her words. 'And how do you view my behaviour?'

'You saved me from a fate worse than death,' she whispered, hoping it would drive him to lower his tone. 'You are the best thing that has ever happened to me.'

He was gentler this time. His finger traced her cheek. His breath smelled of wine, but there were tears in his eyes. She had never seen Heinrich cry before, not even as a child. He dropped to his knees, maybe because he did not want her to see his tears. He kissed her hand, his voice a hush.

'Tell me that you love me. I am so drunk I will not remember it tomorrow.'

She knelt next to him and squeezed his hand. 'I love you.'

He kissed her hair and then her lips, squeezing her so tight it almost hurt. 'I love you. You are my Eve.'

He rose as steadily as he could, grasped her hand and led her towards the bed, stumbling into a chest. He struggled with the hangings. When he managed to part them, he lay down and drew her to him.

'Do not leave me,' he whispered.

He fell asleep immediately.

XL.

Berstadt, 9 June 1070

Heinrich guzzled the contents of the jug of water on the trestle, wiped his lips, and slouched in a chair, nursing his head. After a brief pause, his left hand searched the floor for his undergarments, and he slipped them on with laboured movements.

Matilde got out of bed to help him look for his tunic. 'It's well past sunrise, your household will notice you are missing.'

'It's not the first time I've gone... missing. Besides, the entire court saw me drink myself into oblivion. My household would not expect me to be up early.'

'Vinicia will be here soon.'

'You should tell her what is going on. Cuno knows. We need the people we trust to watch out for us, cover for us.'

Although he was right, she was not looking forward to the conversation. It was easy for Heinrich to appraise Cuno on his conquests; the woman would always be judged the sinner, even by her own servants.

He was admiring her naked body. 'I have not forgotten what you said to me last night.' He drew her onto his lap and gave her a lingering kiss.

'I meant it.'

The admission felt like a liberation. No matter what Emperor Heinz had done to her family, these were her feelings, and they were true even if sinful in the eyes of others, and she would no longer fight them.

He scratched his head. 'Actually, I'll go. Yesterday Pieter gave me a letter from Ildebrando. The snake hints that I have a new paramour. Adalbert is drafting my reply. I need to see it.'

'Really? That is... strange. We need to take even more care than normal.'

'Why strange?'

'Last time I saw Berta, she was convinced you had met someone new. She must have shared her fears with Pieter. But the timings do not add up. How could Ildebrando have known before Pieter's letter had even been written? He must have spies.'

'Of course, plenty of spies. We need to bait them with contradictory trails, so he doubts their reports.'

She helped him slip his tunic on. 'Maybe I caused more harm than good...'

'Why?'

Her face emerged from her chemise. 'By next week Pieter will have shared my request with the Holy Father – and Ildebrando, no doubt.'

'What request?'

'I asked to be divorced from Godefroy.'

'What?'

Unwillingly, she blushed. 'I should have told you sooner. I was hoping to surprise you with a good outcome.'

He kissed a strand of her hair, still plaited from the banquet. 'It would be wonderful news indeed. Although for now we need your marriage as a cover.'

'A cover?'

He looked surprised by her question. 'Sure. In case you get pregnant.'

Dread rose within her, the dread that had not left her since Augsburg. The question could no longer wait. 'What if Godefroy made me pregnant?'

His expression darkened. 'I assumed you were not. If you had any concern, you should have mentioned it to me.'

Perhaps he should have asked before making love to her, but she did not dare say that. 'Between the day you saved me and our first time, I bled once. But Vinicia says some women bleed when already pregnant.'

He drew her face closer. 'Everything is possible, but it is very unlikely.' He kissed her on the eyelids, suddenly tender. 'He has failed, Matilde. Please put the horror behind you now.'

'I will try.'

Heinrich lifted her chin to meet her gaze. 'So, it is only between you and I, now. If you get pregnant, I am the father.'

Excitement was fighting apprehension in her stomach. 'Do you mean—'

'My actions speak for themselves. I never...' She could feel the tension in his fingertips, read it in his eyes. 'I always make love to you like a husband to a wife.'

Perhaps he should have asked her permission, but he was a king and used to having his way. 'And you are not afraid of... the implications?'

'You are the most precious thing in my life. I want to own you completely. If it happens, we will deal with it.'

He kept searching her eyes as if he could find her soul in them. 'If you want me to be careful while you wait for a reply from Rome, you need to tell me.'

Like every girl, every day of her life she had been warned that one day she would face childbirth. Was she ready to risk her life for the man she loved? In her heart, the answer was yes. But an adulterous pregnancy could ruin her. Could she afford to jeopardise her standing with Rome, and the threats that came with that?

The Matilde sitting on a deck, staring into the Tyrrhenian Sea was still within her. Godefroy had not killed her completely. 'It may take ages for them to reply—'

He silenced her with a kiss. 'I don't trust myself to behave for that long.'

XLI.

Mainz, 13 June 1070

The rain brought the smell of fresh grass from the other bank of the Rhine through the open shutters. Attendants were serving local wine, cold meats and thirst-quenching fresh radishes to the princes in attendance, gathered at a long table in the great hall for their first meeting since Whitsun.

Adalbert had chosen a seat at the left end, an unassuming place best suited to his discreet re-admission to the rooms of power.

The local lord, Archbishop Siegfried of Mainz, was compiling the list of items for discussion, helped by the royal brother-in-law Duke Rudolph.

Heinrich was toasting his cousin Bertholdt of Carinthia, his sparring partner in that morning's sword practice.

To the immediate left of the king were the Saxon powers, lay and religious, with Duke Otto in their midst.

A few places to Heinrich's right, talking to the charming bishop of Wurzburg, was none other than Anno – aged, perhaps thinner, but looking strong, somehow tempered by his recent difficulties.

Siegfried rang a bell. 'I declare the proceedings open.'

Adalbert brought the cup to his nose, a crisp white. It would go well with the radishes.

As the room fell silent, the door swung open. One of Heinrich's new advisors, the chubby and plainly dressed Liutpold of Merseburg, crossed the floor to address his master with a deep and nervous bow.

'I apologise for the interruption, Your Majesty. The noble Egeno von Konradsburg is in the anteroom. He says he has important revelations to make.'

Heinrich's gaze darted up towards the ceiling. 'Can it wait?'

Restrained smiles appeared on a few of the dukes' faces.

Liutpold, a bookish former novice who never seemed to put a foot wrong as far as the king was concerned, was the epitome of the king's penchant for advancing bright Goslar monks over the dukes' protégés. If he were about to get a dressing down from his master, that alone would make their journey to Mainz worthwhile.

'He says it cannot, my lord.'

'Send him in.'

Egeno von Konradsburg was young and handsome, with long blond hair, a straight nose, and the lean frame of a wingless angel, clad in a tunic of light blue silk a bit too expensive for a simple courtier. The entire room watched him, fascinated, as he knelt before the king and kissed his ring, until his words broke the spell.

'Your Majesty, I have pleaded to be admitted into your presence, to unburden my conscience of my sins.'

Strange preamble, intriguing even, thought Adalbert. Even stranger that Heinrich was not dismissing him.

'Why would your sins matter to me?' he was asking, handing his goblet to a servant to refill.

'Because of their nature.'

Someone laughed at the double entendre.

'Too much information,' shouted a lone voice.

Heinrich exchanged glances with Liutpold before redirecting his attention to the new arrival. 'Have we met before?'

Egeno was still on his knees. 'In Bavaria last summer. I was... invited to court.'

'Why?'

The young man uttered a deep sigh, joining his hands, as if to stop them from shaking. 'My family's fortunes have taken a turn for the worse, and I was offered... a great sum of gold to—'

'Your illicit liaisons are of no interest to the crown,' sneered Heinrich, taking a swig of his wine.

The room roared with nervous laughter. It would be no surprise if one of the dukes' oft-neglected wives had found Egeno's charm impossible to resist. They just had to hope it was someone else's; or that the wingless angel had agreed to warm up the bed of one of the bishops.

Egeno glanced up towards the king. 'I was not offered money in return for my body, Your Majesty. I was paid to gain access to your apartment.'

Duke Rudolph left his place at the table to address the young man. 'Access... to what purpose?' His tone suggested incredulity.

The room fell silent.

Egeno unsheathed the sword hanging from his belt and laid it on the floor. 'I was asked to kill you, my lord king, with this weapon.'

At Liutpold's nod, the two guards by the door seized him, tying his hands behind him. Still on his knees, he made no resistance.

One of the sentinels handed the sword to Heinrich, who placed it on the table for all the princes to see. The dukes were keeping their gazes on the weapon and their fears well-guarded.

Heinrich's steps resonated in the quiet room. He bent as if to whisper in Egeno's ear, his crowned head blocking the sight of the delator's face from the princes at the table.

'I may execute you for treason, Egeno von Konradsburg.' He spoke loudly so everyone could hear.

The young nobleman's hand grasped the king's. 'I am at Your Majesty's mercy. I am not the one who betrayed you.' His cheeks were streaked with tears.

'Who is the traitor? I may spare you if you tell me.' Heinrich lifted his chin up. 'Who is it?'

Egeno turned to his right, where Otto of Nordheim was seated. He opened and closed his mouth repeatedly, as if to gain strength, before pointing at him. 'He is.'

The duke burst into laughter. 'Why should anyone believe you, insolent little hanger-on?'

Guards moved swiftly but discretely alongside Otto.

Suddenly, Adalbert wished he were elsewhere. Otto held Bavaria, the richest duchy; he had risen in power in the last three years; despite the wounds of Kaiserwerth he had even re-joined the crown council. Why would he plot the king's murder?

'You will speak when your turn comes, Duke,' said Heinrich and he turned to Egeno. 'Give me the facts – everything.'

The die cast, the nobleman's features relaxed, as a penitent after he had finished confessing his sins. 'Duke Otto hosted the court last summer. We agreed I was going to join a banquet and seize my chance.' He wiped his cheeks. 'You left early. I waited, then followed you. But Cuno was in the antechamber.'

'He always is,' said Heinrich.

'I had not expected that. I unsheathed that sword—'

Heinrich lifted his chin again, applying pressure. 'You tried to kill Cuno?'

'When I saw it was him, I could not bring myself to do it.' Egeno's voice wavered. 'I have known him for years. He is a good man.'

Heinrich let go. 'Did Cuno realise your intentions?'

'I said I had drunk too much, and he believed me.'

There was another swift glance between the king and Liutpold, who stepped out, presumably to get Cuno.

Heinrich turned towards Otto. 'Your turn, Duke.'

'My lord, if I may.' Duke Rudolph picked up the sword. 'Young Egeno has brought us the alleged weapon. It is a sign from God, is it not?'

The faces of the other princes were stony across the table.

Rudolph pressed on. 'We will never get to the bottom of this. Duke Otto will deny the allegations and Egeno will stand by them.'

'These are treasonous accusations, Duke,' Heinrich replied darkly. 'I cannot dismiss them.'

'I was not going to suggest that, Your Majesty. My point is that the case can only be solved by ordeal.'

Adalbert was stunned. Otto was a couple of decades older than Egeno. He was a strong warrior, but no longer in his prime. The odds were against him. Why was Rudolph proposing the ordeal? Was he creating an opportunity for himself – thinking that Otto's death might increase his standing at court?

Liutpold, who had just returned with Cuno, stopped in his tracks.

Heinrich did not seem to like the suggestion either. He stared coldly at Rudolph.

Siegfried and Anno were exchanging glances, just as puzzled as Adalbert was.

Who was trying to frame who? Had Rudolph just scuppered a poorly conceived royal plan to frame Otto? If that was the calibre of Liutpold's advice, the king was better off on his own. But that was not going to be an easy message to convey.

XLII.

Mainz, 14 June 1070

'This wine is a gift from my good friend the Archbishop of Wurzburg. He paid me a visit yesterday.'

Adalbert poured it into the two precious rock crystal goblets he always took with him on his travels. Heinrich had just returned from a morning ride. It was promising to be another stuffy day, and a cool drink would be welcome.

'I am glad you enjoyed your time with Wurzburg.' Heinrich swirled the liquid in the translucent cup to catch its reflections.

'The taste, for a new vineyard, is decent.'

Heinrich sniffed it and lifted the chalice against the sun. 'Have you had a chance to investigate von Konradsburg's claims?'

Adalbert took a sip. 'Sifting through all the allegations about Liutpold's infatuation for our handsome Egeno takes more than a day.'

The king laughed. 'Adalbert, I need your appraisal of von Konradsburg's allegations.'

He took his time to enjoy the wine on his tongue, fresh as a Mediterranean lemon. 'I utterly detest Otto of Nordheim: for kidnapping you, for engineering my expulsion from court—'

'And for plotting to take lands from the Church of Bremen.'

'That too.'

'But?'

'I would be interested in Liutpold's sources. Personally, I have found no evidence of Otto's wrongdoing. Besides, I struggle to see his motive. No-one commits treason lightly, and, after my banishment, his influence was on the rise.'

'Thank you for your view on that,' replied Heinrich, without agreeing with his assessment.

The bitter taste of doubt spread in Adalbert's mouth. The possibility that Liutpold might have made the whole Egeno drama up, or that Heinrich might have asked him to make it up, remained.

'Let us talk about Rome now,' the king said.

Adalbert was glad of the opportunity to discuss something constructive. 'Shall we give Pope Alexander a date for your coronation?'

'Before we commit to anything with him...' Heinrich scratched his chin pensively. 'Is there a possibility that the tide may be changing?'

He hoped to be wrong.

'I still need my marriage undone, Adalbert.'

The goblet lay by Heinrich's side, untouched, building the pressure.

Adalbert prepared his ground. 'Pope Alexander is on good terms with your godfather, your mother, and her confessor—'

Heinrich's gaze fastened on him. 'Is there hope?'

'That is difficult to say.' He fetched a platter of cheese and dates from the trestle. 'He is a genuinely compassionate man.'

Heinrich accepted some dates. 'The Countess of Tuscany said the same things.'

'Speaking of the countess, is her presence in Berstadt connected to an attempt to smooth the diplomatic relationship between the Church and Germany?'

Heinrich nodded. 'She holds the keys to the Holy Father's heart, does she not?'

'Yes and no. The pope's affection did not save her from an awful marriage – an undeserved fate for such a brave and attractive young woman.'

'Indeed.'

'If you are looking for influence, I would focus energies on Pier.'

'Pier Damiani?' He may as well have evoked the devil.

Adalbert clarified his advice. 'Last year Pier did the job he had been asked to do. But he is a man of integrity who sees you as *Vicar Christi*.'

Heinrich finally took a sip of the wine. 'Have any conversations you feel appropriate. You have full liberty in this matter.' He placed the cup back on the table. 'I should be going.'

'My lord—'

Heinrich stopped in the middle of the room. 'Are you about to remind me of the existence of Ildebrando di Soana?'

'He remains... a challenge.'

Heinrich sat down again. 'Tell me what happened between you two.'

'You are aware of Sutri?'

A smile upturned the king's lips. 'The town close to Rome where my father deposed three unworthy popes and appointed a worthy one?'

Adalbert's heart warmed at the memories. 'It was your father's triumph. Pier Damiani hailed him as the saviour of the Church.'

. Heinrich started fidgeting with some chess pieces. 'What has it got to do with Ildebrando?'

'After Sutri, we went to Rome. Your father was crowned emperor, and we were there for weeks. I became acquainted with Giovanni Graziano – one of the deposed popes.'

'A dangerous friendship?'

'His sins were not as dark as the others', and your father liked him. He sentenced him to a dignified exile in the Rhineland, which meant he travelled to Germany with us.'

His hand stilled on the board, around a horse chess piece. 'What was so interesting about him?'

'He was one of a kind. Greek, Hebrew, there was nothing he could not read. We enjoyed his company.'

'So?' Heinrich turned away from the chessboard.

'Giovanni was followed in exile by his former chaplain, a small olive-skinned monk—'

'Ildebrando!'

Adalbert's forehead creased. 'He insinuated himself in your father's trust, constantly seeking private audiences, interfering with his advisors—'

'So, in those days he was not hostile to my father?'

'He was, in a subtler way, by trying to manipulate him.'

'Did he succeed?'

'He secured one important victory: your betrothal.'

Heinrich looked startled, maybe even disappointed. 'Why are you only telling me now?'

As ever, a raised voice held no sway over Adalbert. He remained collected. 'Your mother and I have no proof. But twice your mother and I persuaded your father to negotiate a certain marriage for you, and twice Ildebrando appeared at court, only for your father to change his mind and resume his conversations with the

- 152 -

house of Savoy.'

'What are Ildebrando's motives – if you are right?'

If only he could tell him. 'I understand the empress is coming. She is best placed to answer that.'

Heinrich rose. The revelation had stunned him, and he looked dejected. On the doorstep, he turned. 'Out of curiosity, what match had you and my mother recommended instead of Berta?'

'The Countess of Canossa.'

'She would have been a good match.'

XLIII.

Matilde had asked Heinrich to be lodged away from the court. Her appearances without Godefroy were becoming too frequent, and Mainz was a particularly risky location. Archbishop Siegfried was close to Pier Damiani and Ildebrando; news could travel uncomfortably fast.

She had spent the last few days in a small fortress a couple of hours' ride from town, which Heinrich had inherited from his grandfather. She had made the most of the cool summer mornings, riding Lampo through the nearby countryside, trotting along the beech-lined Rhine path, with the breeze on her face.

The time alone with Vinicia had given her the opportunity to reveal the truth to her. Heinrich was right. The longer the relationship continued, the more important it was for them to have allies who could pick up on gossip or notice if they were being followed. Besides, Vinicia had stood by her through the pain of losing Rolando, and, regardless of how she would judge her sins, she deserved her honesty.

'I do not expect you to condone my actions. I just need to know I can count on your loyalty,' she had said, blushing to the roots of her hair.

Vinicia had squeezed her hand. 'Of course you have my loyalty. I am worried, but also happy for you.'

The next morning Heinrich had arrived, but he had disappeared into the tower with Cuno and his new aid Gottschalk. The moon was rising when he joined her.

'Thank you for staying up for me. I know it is late. I am working on something important.'

She pointed to the food on the trestle.

He tore a piece off a honey loaf. 'I am spending a lot of silver. We are building new castles.'

'So I have heard. I would love to hear what your plan is.' She meant it. Royal castle-building was one of the sharpest weapons in

Ildebrando's propaganda arsenal; proof, he argued, of Heinrich's being unfit to rule. She passed him a wine cup.

'My regents assigned plenty of crown lands to the princes. Technically they are mine to dispose of.'

She sat on a coffer by the window to catch the night breeze. 'The law is clear. When a vassal dies, you can reallocate them as you wish.'

'So, every time the opportunity arises, I transfer them back to the crown.'

'It must be causing grumbles aplenty.'

The moonlight whitened his features as he sat next to her. 'It is a new world, Matilde.'

'Maybe it is.' He had chosen a dangerous path, and she owed him honesty. She leaned against his side and spoke softly, not wanting a confrontation. 'Castles have always been used to secure allies, though – dukes or archbishops who would repay you by fighting for you.'

In the semi-darkness, he shook his head. 'This is simply how things used to be done. But princes are useless administrators.'

'Hey!'

'I was not talking about you.' She could hear the smile in his voice.

'I think you need allies, Heinrich. That is all.'

He contracted his jaw. 'First and foremost, I need to prove I am not weak. Those lands were extorted from the crown during my minority.'

She drew closer, laying her hand on his arm. 'Adalbert is recovering them for you, is he not?'

'He is. The moment they are returned to me, I build fortresses on them to mark them as mine, beyond dispute.'

'Those lands still need to be administered though,' she added cautiously.

'Rest assured they are.' He turned to face her. 'I give them to capable men; bishops or *ministeriales* devoted to the Salian dynasty rather than their own kin.'

She placed her hand in his palm and locked fingers with him. 'I enjoy when we have this kind of political chat, overlord to prince – about anything other than the implications of our love. It feels good.'

His fingers squeezed her knuckles. 'It is time you heard my ideas from me, rather than the pope or our "friend" Ildebrando.'

She kissed him on the forehead. 'Please continue.'

Drawing their joined hands to his lips, he kissed the back of her palm.

'To strengthen my power, I need excellent administrators. *Ministeriales*, intelligent people of no means, who owe their power to me, are the safest choice.' The candlelight shone on his fingers, lending a honey hue to his imperial cameo ring. 'But the best administrators remain the bishops, as we both know. This is why I entrust them with most of the lands I recover for the crown, and why I cannot stop nominating them – no matter what Rome says.'

She had heard Pope Alexander's view so many times that she could not hold her tongue. 'A bishop nominated by a king will be subject to too many temptations and struggle to be a good shepherd.'

'A bishop nominated by a king remains a man of God. With the added advantage that, given their inability to pass their lands on to their offspring, they are more likely to rule in the interest of the crown and the common people.'

A smile took over her whole face. 'So, after you become Holy Roman Emperor, all princes will be bishops?'

'I will need a few dukes to lead my armies, but I would have more bishops, yes – and some countesses.' He tickled her. 'Especially if they can double as admirals.'

'I am glad my future is safe, my overlord.' She tickled him back. Desire surged through her, but she pushed it to the back of her mind. She was enjoying the conversation too much.

The way he looked at her, he must have felt the same way. He rose, to put some physical distance between them.

'I was brought up by Anno, so I have seen the evil side of a bishop – that love of power for power's sake. That is also in the Roman cardinals. It is their darkest sin. I need a balance between them and the princes.'

She lit more candles. The scent of beeswax spread in the air. 'Judging by what happens in my lands, giving too much power to the bishops strengthens the cities. My mother thinks it is dangerous. Our nobility ends up feeling antagonised by the city grandees.'

It was a delicate subject. Heinrich had repeatedly upset the princes by giving preferential treatment to the Rhineland cities, especially Mainz.

'This is a concern from the last millennium,' he said with a shrug.

'The princes still behave as if Charlemagne was alive. The world has changed.' His eyes shone with excitement and there was the raw power of dreams in his voice. 'There has been no apocalypse, no antichrist. The world has not ended. There is shocking poverty, but there is also hope. It is time for new ideas, new buildings, new seeds to grow, new tools.'

His views went against everything she had been brought up to think. 'Who taught you all this?'

He poured a drop of wine into his cup. 'Adalbert used to conduct foolish experiments, like growing grapes in Bremen. But he is right, in life we need to try new things.'

'Is that why you called him back?'

He shared his cup with her. 'In part. I also learnt from my mother. People in Aquitaine have more hope. You cannot explain it all with a great climate. They have their problems too. But listen to their songs. Life is determined by how much you dare.'

He stroked her cheek. 'I also learn from you. You and your mother are builders: monasteries, castles, shelters. You want everyone in your lands to have a better life.'

Silence carried her surprise. Ildebrando and the great lords always cast Heinrich's political choices as proof of either his immaturity or utter evil. She could see now that they had twisted his vision and bravery into a sin. If only she could get her mother to see Heinrich as she saw him now, and to give him a chance.

She could make out his frame in the darkness, leaning against the window, stripes of moonlight across his hands.

'So, lady of Tuscany, it is not as evil when you hear it from the horse's mouth rather his enemies, is it?'

XLIV.

Anno arrived in robes as sumptuous as ever, a mixture of bafflement and anger spreading on his round face. He sat at his writing table, facing Adalbert. 'What do you want from me?' he growled under his white-streaked beard.

'Last year in Frankfurt we agreed to a truce, Anno. I hope it still stands.'

Grabbing a green glass bottle, probably Venetian, Anno poured some of its contents into a silver cup, which he pushed towards Adalbert. 'Go on.' The wrinkles around his eyes had become deeper.

Adalbert seized the goblet but did not taste its contents. 'I appreciate the difficulty of your position. You are caught between two fires: Ildebrando with his demands of loyalty to Rome, and the king who—'

'Two fires? You can add Siegfried of Mainz vying for primacy in Germany, Pier Damiani who is never completely in agreement with Ildebrando or the empress, and the empress herself, who loves me as much as she loves the plague...'

'You can understand the lady's reasons, surely?'

'Of course! But it does not help my predicament.'

From the sip he took, the wine was one of Anno's usual unimpressively bland whites. 'Sitting on the sidelines has advantages, Anno. One gains a different perspective,' he mused. 'I can see a way for you to climb back into the king's favour.'

Anno folded his arms behind his neck. 'I am all ears.'

He pushed the goblet aside and leaned forward. 'Help him divorce.'

Anno's brow creased, and his bull frame tensed. 'Are you joking?'

'It is a tricky balancing act, as you are the kingdom's arch-chancellor for Italy, however—'

Anno stood up, towering over him. 'It has nothing to do with the kingdom.' He banged his fist on the table. Something in his expression changed, as if a sudden thought had altered his perspective. He sighed. 'I am being blackmailed, Adalbert,' he whispered, as if the walls had ears. They were in Archbishop Siegfried's residence, after all.

'Ildebrando?' he enquired in a similarly hushed tone.

A nod. 'He has been breathing down my neck on and off over the years.' Another sigh. 'This last trip to Rome has been no different. His message is clear.'

'What is he threatening you with?'

He slipped back in his chair while he pondered how much to share. 'I will lose my seat's pre-eminence to...' his chin pointed towards the door, an obvious hint at his rival Siegfried, 'if I fall out of line.'

Anno was being honest, that was good. Now he needed to shake him out of his fears. 'You have Pier Damiani's trust. Have you confided in him?'

A shrug of his shoulders. 'It would be pointless.'

Adalbert rowed back to his initial topic. 'So, amongst other things, you are blackmailed on the subject of the king's marriage. Why is Ildebrando so fixated on it?'

'The Holy Spear, perhaps?'

Intriguing. 'He does not want the king lording over the Church like his father and the Saxon emperors did?'

'When Ildebrando visits me and starts dropping hints of simony, I do not exactly ask him what is going through his mind.'

'Perhaps you should, Anno. The imperial cross and the Holy Spear sit in your cathedral's treasury when the king is not using them. You suspect the Spear to be the reason for Ildebrando's hostility to the king. You may leverage that. Besides, Cologne being the relics' home should also help keep you above Siegfried.'

Now he had his attention. Anno sat down in a throne-like carved chair. 'What do you want to know exactly?'

Adalbert sat on a bench opposite him. 'Why do you think he is so desperate to keep our king married to Savoy?'

Anno scratched his head. 'I cannot answer that specifically. But I know that, after her discovery of the Holy Blood, Ildebrando's determination to oppose marriages between the Salians and Beatrice of Tuscany's offspring intensified.'

'So, ensuring the Spear and the Blood do not end up in the hands of the same dynasty could have been Ildebrando's chief motive.'

Anno had no inkling of Charlemagne's prophecy, but his nod signalled that the conjecture still made sense in his mind.

'It is possible, Adalbert. And Godefroy of Lotharingia has the Blood now, although I hear it has been moved to Orval,' he said, a conspiratorial twinkle in his eye. 'Perhaps he would be more amenable than his mother-in-law? Or could he pressure her to be amenable? He is the man of the household now. I suspect it would be an expensive transaction, buying it off him, but it may be worth it.'

'You know our king. Relics are not his thing.'

'How much does he want that divorce? The combination of those relics could scare Ildebrando into submission.' He grinned. 'You have not heard this idea from me, my Bremen friend. I need to keep a low profile on this, for the reasons I have outlined.'

'Of course.'

He rose. 'It has been a pleasure to talk to you, Adalbert. It reminds me of the old days. I am needed elsewhere.'

Adalbert remained in Anno's study, thinking the conversation over. He had found some answers, and they felt right. But they engendered more questions.

Godefroy would name a high price, a price Heinrich may be unwilling to pay. He had made it clear several times that he did not believe in relics. Would he be willing to gamble precious crown lands or the silver of the royal treasure on a relic? Maybe it would be best to focus his efforts on rational arguments and rational people: the pope and the Abbot of Cluny.

XLV.

Mainz, 26 May 1070

A fresh breeze from the Rhine relieved the heat in the audience chamber of the Archbishop of Mainz. Outside, boatmen were shouting at each other as wares from Lotharingia, Italy, Burgundy, and the East were being loaded and unloaded. It was another trading day on the mighty river.

'Thank you for making the time to meet me, Adalbert.' Empress Agnes, in light-coloured silk garments and a white veil, rose from her chair.

'Your message was such an unexpected pleasure.'

'I am delighted that you are back at court; my son needs you more than ever. Rome is not impressed with Liutpold and these new advisors he surrounds himself with.'

'It is good to be back. It looks like our fortunes are changing at the same time.'

'Indeed. Will you come with me to meet Siegfried? He was in the Holy Land when I was banished, and I have not seen him since.'

'I thought you had asked him to visit Charlemagne's library in Jerusalem and look for relics for you?'

'Precisely. I funded the expedition, and it feels as if he has been avoiding me ever since.'

'What about the co-leaders of the pilgrimage?' All of them owed their bishoprics to Agnes. 'Gunther of Bamberg has passed away, but have you tried Willem of Utrecht? He is loyal to Heinrich.'

'Willem seems wary, as if he thinks they have wronged me in some way but does not want to give Siegfried away.'

'Interesting. Let's see what Siegfried has to say.'

The Archbishop of Mainz looked like he had seen a ghost when they entered the room, and the ghost was not Adalbert.

Agnes went on the offensive. 'Has my son not informed you of my arrival?'

'No, Empress.' He bowed. 'What refreshments can I offer you?'

He went to the door to look for his chamberlain.

'We will not be long. Our paths have not met in a while; I just need to collect from you what you found in Charlemagne's library in Jerusalem. Adalbert will help me carry it.'

Siegfried scratched his beard. 'It has been a long time, and although I made notes, I do not recall to perfection—'

'I recall to perfection that you wrote a letter to me from Bamberg, before Bishop Gunther's death, signed by you, Gunther and Willem. You said you had found something that you would only give to me in person.'

'Perhaps we got ahead of ourselves. The experience of physically being in the Holy Land does that to you—'

'What had you discovered?'

Adalbert did not remember her so determined. 'Nothing major, only rumours and a scroll.'

She pressed. 'Where is the scroll then?'

'It is a long story.'

'I have time.' She sat down.

Siegfried did the same, seeming more and more uneasy. 'Our letter to you was... intercepted.'

She glared at him. 'Was it?'

'I received a visit... from Anno. He was on his way to Rome, to arrange the pope's approval for the king's marriage. He showed me a request with Ildebrando di Soana's seal.' He cleared his voice. 'It demanded that I surrender the scroll to Anno, who would bring it to him in Rome.'

Adalbert took the revelations in. Of course, Agnes did not know that Anno had been blackmailed all along, and there was no point in telling her, now or later.

The realisation of the extent of Siegfried's betrayal of her trust incensed her. 'Are you telling me that I funded your mission, just for you to hand your discoveries to the archdeacon? This is unforgivable!'

'I needed to think about my spiritual salvation.'

'Oh, I agree wholeheartedly! Betraying your patron takes you a long way on the path to salvation!' she hissed. 'Well, you will answer to God for this!'

'The archdeacon said that his discovery of our message to you was a sign from God—'

'You are not that naïve!' Her tone cut like a knife. 'As you have "surrendered" my scroll, will you at least tell me what the text said?'

'We cannot read Hebrew and did not trust anyone in Jerusalem to translate it for us. We know it spoke about the Holy Blood.'

Agnes rose, nodding to Adalbert to follow her.

Siegfried attempted an apology. 'I trust the respective abbots and abbesses will have made you aware that since my return I have made donations to your favourite monasteries of Fruttuaria, Quedlinburg, and Farfa.'

Silence.

He cleared his throat. 'My donations are intended to compensate you for the financial loss you incurred by sponsoring my pilgrimage.'

'There is no atonement for treason, Siegfried. Whatever you found was mine. I told you where to look.'

'You did, indeed.'

'I raised you from Abbot of Fulda to the second archbishopric in the kingdom. This is how you repay my trust.'

'I am eternally grateful for the trust you placed in me. But as you know, Mainz lost the right to crown the kings to Cologne. The archdeacon—'

'Promised to help you redress that, I am sure.' Agnes's voice dripped with sarcasm. 'Have you asked Anno if he has made promises to him too?'

Adalbert could have sworn that his Mainz colleague blushed.

'I did not think you so gullible, Siegfried.' And with that, they left.

They walked back to her lodgings. A servant had prepared a jug of fresh white wine mixed with water. She offered Adalbert some.

'I do not want to sound gloomy, but if Ildebrando has the scroll, we may as well consider it lost,' he said. 'Hopefully, it contained nothing of major significance.'

'I think it did. It mentioned the Holy Blood.' He noticed the exhaustion in her frown lines. She must have travelled from Rome at great speed, maybe to meet her son before he changed his mind.

'Is it worth writing to Willem, as he seemed more loyal?'

'I will try to meet him. But he does not speak Hebrew, so he will not know what the scroll said either.' She rubbed her face with her hands and sighed. 'I will deal with this later. I need to prepare for meeting my son.'

He placed his hand on her shoulder. 'If he invited you here, he must feel ready to welcome you back into his life. At least if my first meeting with him is anything to go by.'

'I hope you are right. I am so tense I cannot pray. Five years at his age... it is a lifetime.' Her voice quivered. 'I do not know how I will find him.'

'He has grown. The lanky boy with a spotty face has turned into a handsome young man, with his grandfather Emperor Conrad's steely determination.'

'I hope he has also developed some political sense, learnt from last summer's debacle. Five years ago, I tried to speak the voice of reason, and he held that against me.'

He tried to drag her away from unpleasant memories. 'Do you hold grudges?'

'I have asked myself the same question.'

'Have you sought Pier Damiani's guidance? He is your confessor, and he saw Heinrich last summer.'

She nodded. 'He instructed me to read the parable of the prodigal son.'

'That is exactly my advice.' The room smelled of roses and he thought of Mary. 'Also, pray to the heavenly mother, to help you make peace with your son.

XLVI.

Heinrich had prepared the beginning of his speech. 'At times I was unfair to you, Mother. I will not lay all the blame on Anno and Adalbert.'

The first emotion he read on her face was surprise, followed, perhaps, by pride. 'I appreciate your words, Heinrich. In fact, they fill me with joy. What has changed?'

'I have grown. I have learnt you were right, on a lot of things.'

'For example, on Matilde?'

Good, she was laying the path open for him. 'For example.'

'What happened with her, Heinrich?'

Truth was the best strategy. 'I never thought I could love a woman, but I can.'

She tested his motives. 'She could make your Italian politics a complete success.'

'It has nothing to do with that.' He looked for the right words to describe her. 'She is clever, she is beautiful, and she knows the loneliness of power. She is the only woman who can understand my life.'

'I agree, so much so that when you were children, I wanted your father to betroth you to her.'

Adalbert had said the same thing. 'I take it Father refused.'

'He loved the idea: Germany and Italy united again, like in the days of Charlemagne.'

'But?'

She let out a disconsolate sigh. 'Rome had too much to lose.'

'And *you* sided with the pope?'

'It was your father's decision, taken on the advice of Ildebrando di Soana.'

Just like Adalbert had said. 'And Father listened to him?'

'Where is she? I need to see her, my son.'

'Why?'

'To be sure that her feelings for you are as strong as yours for her, if I am to bless this love.' He must have looked unconvinced, because she added, 'I also need to speak to her on behalf of her mother.'

He sneered. 'And of the pope, I am sure.'

'The pope should be left out of this – Ildebrando even more so.' She reassured him. 'I am completely on your side. But I need to talk to her.'

'I will bring her to you after you answer another question.'

'Go on.'

'Last year you sided with Rome against my divorce. Would you back me on it now that I am settling on a woman you respect?'

'Ildebrando will turn your request into an opportunity to damage you.'

'Perhaps you could speak to Pier Damiani, or the pope?'

'I will try. But it does not mean I will succeed.'

§

Despite the caring tone, something about the empress's demeanour felt different from that of the friend who regularly visited her mother in Canossa. Seated in her chair, she was examining her. 'I understand Godefroy is not treating you right.'

Matilde needed to get the measure of Agnes as the mother of her lover, rather than as her mother's confidante. She chose a guarded reply. 'I am forever grateful to the king for the pain he has spared me.'

The empress looked away, at the summer rain pouring down on the fields. 'I had a nightmare the night before giving birth to Heinrich. I dreamt I was delivering him in blood. I always wondered what that meant. I think I know now. You and my son both carry Charlemagne's blood.'

The nightmare must have been unsettling, but the conclusion seemed far-fetched to Matilde. 'Forgive my impertinence, but other princes can boast a drop or two of his blood.'

Agnes shrugged off her remark. 'You are the largest landholder in the empire. If you marry my son, Italy and Germany will effectively be reunited. A boy born of you two would be a proper heir to Charlemagne – a considerable threat to the Church's independence.' Matilde remained silent and Agnes continued. 'But you need to deal with your enemies, Godefroy *in primis*. He will fight to keep you married to him.'

She gripped the arms of her chair. 'I am sure he can negotiate another wife for himself.'

The empress eyed her. 'There is too much at stake. Ildebrando will always back your husband against Heinrich.'

'Ildebrando is not the pope.'

Agnes's expression did not lighten. 'This is something you should discuss with your mother. She needs you to meet her in Italy – without my son.'

The request made her feel guilty. She attempted to justify herself. 'I do not want to fall back into my husband's claws. Could you relate that to her?'

Agnes's voice softened, but the command in it was even more obvious. 'Beatrice is not asking this lightly.'

'What does she need to talk to me about?' She needed the certainty that her mother was in good health.

'She will explain when you see her.'

On one hand, the reply reassured her. If health had been involved, Agnes would have said so. On the other hand, it reiterated Beatrice's urgency. Matilde did not want to be apart from Heinrich for the three weeks it took to ride to Mantova and back, but she needed to provide an answer that encouraged her mother somehow, when Agnes reported it to her.

'I have pleaded with the Holy Father for a divorce, given my marriage contract was breached. If he grants me that grace, I will ask Heinrich for an escort and ride to Italy immediately.'

Agnes did not seem pleased at all. 'My son has to stay out of this, for his sake and yours.'

At that precise moment, a guard knocked to announce the king. From the doorway, Heinrich eyed them both with some concern, but asked no questions.

XLVII.

Riding alongside Vinicia on the old Roman road heading north from Mainz, Matilde could not dispel the feeling that the empress had left something unsaid.

'Is that Aachen?' Vinicia asked.

Ahead of them, the unmistakable walls of Charlemagne's capital had come into view, surging above the green mantle of trees.

They followed the bodyguards Heinrich had provided for them, spurring their mounts on for the last stretch through the forests of the Eifel. Lampo was enjoying being back on the road and pearly sweat was gathering on his coat.

The trees' canopy finished abruptly against the walls of the palace. Attendants immediately materialised to take care of the horses. Their men went off to the armoury to drop their weapons, and an eager steward showed Matilde and Vinicia to their lodgings.

Charlemagne's residence was so vast there was no chance of her bumping into anyone from Heinrich's inner circle unless she wanted to.

Still, she asked to be lodged in the wing of the imperial palace directly facing the woods.

When she had taken leave of Berta in Goslar, she had mentioned the possibility of re-joining the court in Aachen, if circumstances permitted.

But she did not feel ready to meet her. Things had gone too far with Heinrich, and Berta did not deserve it.

She tried to dispel the guilt by refocusing on her unsettling conversation with Agnes, but struggled to concentrate, with Vinicia moving about to sort out her belongings.

'I am going for a walk.'

She made her way to the cathedral at the opposite end of the sprawling palace complex. The smell of beeswax and incense hit her as she stepped into the octagonal space where, since Charlemagne, the kings of Germany had been crowned at the altar of Mary.

It brought back memories of another day, a winter day, also lit by innumerable candles, also blessed by incense. She was ten, Emperor Heinz had just died, and Heinrich had been taken to Aachen and placed on Charlemagne's throne to be crowned. At five years old, he was barely aware of what was going on around him; Adelheid, instead, was crying for her little brother, a brother she had lost forever to gain a king.

She gazed up at the majestic dome, golden mosaic tesserae as the backdrop for the purple robes of a Christ enthroned, surrounded by the Elders of the Apocalypse, the embodiment of Charlemagne's belief in the sacrality of kingship.

Other memories gushed out. A younger version of her mother sitting on the front pew, pointing to the vault, holding her hand.

'There's a church in Ravenna that Charlemagne saw when he came to Italy. It was Christian, yet it was Roman, and it had a dome. He had never seen a dome before, and when he came home, he had one built here, by his favourite palace – a church that mirrored his soul, the church where he would one day be buried.'

They were complex ideas for a ten-year-old, but they had made the place special to her. 'When you do not know who you are and what you stand for, just come here, my girl. Go to Charlemagne's tomb and pray. He will make you strong.'

Had the ancestor's soul summoned her here, to remind her of who she was? She looked to her left. The emperor's tomb was right by the entrance, welcoming the worshippers. He had chosen, appropriately, a Roman sarcophagus. She brought her hand to her lips and placed a kiss on the white marble, asking him to watch over her.

Her gaze ran over the episodes of the story sculpted on the sarcophagus. It was of a pagan woman, forever young and forever beautiful, and somehow it felt so appropriate for an ancient goddess or nymph to be the womb preserving Charlemagne's body until the end of days.

The thought of wombs and women made her turn towards the altar of Mary. The green marble circle in front of it marked the place where kings and emperors would kneel before being crowned, under the watchful gaze of the mother of God.

It was between Sexte and None, and the cathedral was deserted.

She made for the circle, her steps resonating in the vast octagon. As she reached it, she hesitated for a moment, then she dropped to her knees on it.

She was not being irreverent, not in her heart. That was the spot where her brother could have been crowned; the spot where she, Matilde, could have claimed the imperial crown, rather than be destined for rape by Godefroy of Lotharingia.

She controlled the urge to cry. She had things to be grateful for. She had found Heinrich and hope. In that same spot, the man she loved had been crowned and robbed of his innocence but had also been reborn as the overlord who had saved her from Godefroy and a life worse than death.

With her fingertips, she caressed the green marble by her side. She turned towards her ancestor's tomb and made the sign of the cross. 'Charlemagne, make me strong. Give me the means to break my fate,' she whispered into the gold-encrusted vault, her hands joined in prayer so hard it hurt. 'Give us the means to break our fates.'

Someone stepped into the cathedral. Matilde rose from the spot and retraced her steps back through the nave, her gaze low. When she crossed paths with the worshipper, she recognised him. It was Heinrich's former regent, Adalbert of Bremen.

'I could not think of a more appropriate place to meet you, Countess,' he said, his chin pointing towards the coronation circle and a smile on his lips.

She smiled back and walked out, with a last glance at the marble sarcophagus.

XLVIII.

The night was warm and with only the trace of a cloud; summer was brewing its way in. The servants had moved a trestle to the solar, so that over dinner, the king and the countess could admire the stars. They ate simply; just bread and sausages, and some cheese from the Eifel, all washed down with a Burgundian red wine that Heinrich had received as a gift from the Archbishop of Bremen.

As they finished their food, Matilde disappeared into the room next door and came back holding a scroll with the papal seal. She had been dying to share the message with Heinrich. It was from Pope Alexander, and it hinted at her letter to Langerio and at her conversation with the envoy, promising to assess her situation.

He rolled it back, and his expression darkened. 'If you divorce, you will have to go back to Tuscany.'

'Perhaps it is time you agree on a date to be crowned emperor in Rome. It would be my duty to host you throughout the trip.'

He dismissed her words with an impatient wave of his hand. 'How can I leave? Rudolph is conspiring against me. Otto is swallowing up my lands in the Harz and rallying the Saxons into a rebellion. I told you all this!'

'I am sorry.'

'Come here.' He made her sit in his lap. Her physical proximity relaxed him, and he started showing her different clusters of stars. He pointed to his birth constellation, Scorpio. Then they talked about what the names of individual constellations meant.

'I hear the library at your castle of Canossa boasts some precious books... the Latin version of the masterpieces of the Arabs, the best astronomers on Earth, if my tutors were right.'

She teased him. 'Come to Italy with me and I shall let you read them.'

'Will your mother let me in?'

'If she lets me in. I am in as much trouble with her as you are.'

He traced her lips with his finger. 'Or you could bring those books as part of your dowry when you marry me.'

It was hard to reconcile this Heinrich, happy with a couple of astronomy books, with the power-hungry brat described by Ildebrando every time he visited or wrote. There was so much of him she simply did not know. 'Why do you like stars so much, Your Majesty?'

'Because I always feel like a prisoner; I am a prisoner forced on this imperial path my father prepared for me.'

It sounded familiar. 'We have become our roles.' She got up to refill his goblet.

He played with his cameo ring, as if the Roman eagle on it held all the answers. 'I am proud of my role. It is a privilege and a blessing. I just hate the compromises. Like the fact that a peasant can choose to marry the woman he wants, but I cannot, unless the pope says so.'

She kissed him on the cheek.

Sadness tinged his voice. He gazed upwards. 'When I look at the stars, I am free; they do not dictate how I have to live.' He emptied his goblet and rose. His thumbs ran over her cheek and her lips. 'The stars shine like your skin,' he whispered mischievously. 'I want to touch the stars.'

When she woke up, he was lying away from her. He looked distant, guilty almost, not the same man who had dined with her under the stars. 'There is something I have not told you.'

'What is it about?'

'I have made a plan to get rid of Otto. But it requires that I go back to Goslar.'

No point in running away from the truth. 'How long for?'

He drew her closer. 'It is hard to say. Someone accused him of treason. If I can get rid of him, I will strengthen my grip on Saxony, and it will become impossible for Rudolph and the Church to stop me.' He bent over to kiss her. 'I am tired of hiding you. I want you at my side all the time.'

'I am tired of hiding too. When are we leaving?'

His mouth lingered over her stomach, and his thumb on her nipples. 'I cannot take you with me this time, my queen. It is too dangerous. You will have to wait for me in Speyer.'

She tensed under his touch. How long had he been planning

this? He could at least have involved her in the decision about where she would stay.

She tried to turn the situation into an opportunity. 'If you allow me, I would like to ride to Italy while you are in Goslar – to bring my mother around.'

His voice took on an icy edge. 'I will not let Beatrice turn you against me.'

'Do you really think she could?'

'Better safe than sorry.'

She grabbed her chemise. He would be in Saxony for weeks, maybe months, with women throwing themselves at him every night, and she could not travel to see her mother. She tried to control her frustration. 'I could come, maybe not travel with you but be around if you need help. I can lead troops.'

He tickled her. 'I know you can, but your presence would be impossible to justify. Besides. I want to know that you are safe, at least, while I am at war.'

'How long will you be gone for?'

'I will leave in mid-July, after taking you to Speyer. I will entrust you to one of my best commanders. Godefroy will not touch you, I promise.'

She needed protection, of course, but she felt she was back in a gilded cage; the only difference was that this time the gaoler was the man she loved. She had to say something, although she needed to be careful not to part on bad terms.

'Thank you for protecting me—'

'I am not protecting *you*. I am protecting my own feelings. I do not want anyone to harm my woman.'

At least he was honest. She placed her head on his chest. His heartbeat, the living proof of his presence, reminded her that they would soon be apart. What he had done was wrong, but this was not the moment to bring it up.

She glanced upwards, her lips travelled from his chest to his neck and closed around his earlobe. 'Let's make the most of the time we have.'

XLIX.

Adalbert had asked his butler to bring his best Räuschling. It was from one of the vineyards Heinrich had assigned him as a parting gift.

Although at his age he had seen too much to get excited, he had felt a sense of triumph when the report had landed in his hands the previous evening. 'Your Majesty, I need to bring a certain matter to your immediate attention.'

Heinrich was carrying a small casket, which he placed on the table. 'I could do with some good news.'

He filled two goblets of the wine and passed one to the king, before handing two sheets of parchment to him. He pointed to the top sheet. 'It is the best piece of intelligence I have received in ages.'

Heinrich sat down to read, and Adalbert waited for him to finish.

One of their spies in Rome had intercepted a cyphered letter from Ildebrando. The messenger carrying it had been paid handsomely to reveal the name of the person it was destined for. Although they had not cracked the cypher, they finally had proof that the Tuscan monk was secretly colluding with Agnes's former protégé, Duke Rudolph.

Heinrich put the letter aside, on top of another recent report on Rudolph's movements. 'You have been discreet in the past, Adalbert.' He opened the casket he had brought with him. 'I am courting a lady at the moment. Can you help me choose a gift for her?'

If the king's reaction had not been surprising enough, the content of the casket stunned him. 'This is—'

'Yes, Adalbert, this is the Aquitanian gold, part of my mother's dowry, which you and Anno confiscated after Kaiserwerth.'

'I hope the lady will appreciate how much one of these pieces is worth.'

'She is no peasant, Adalbert.' He sat down with the casket, put it on a table and started going through the contents.

Despite his eagerness to press on with the political discussion, Adalbert was intrigued by the king's liaison – especially as for once he seemed seriously besotted with a woman. He just hoped that this mysterious noblewoman was not married. But first things first. 'About Ildebrando,' he said as he studied the pieces Heinrich was placing in front of him.

'Carry on, I am listening.'

'We know who takes his correspondence to Rudolph out of the Lateran and how. We need to intercept it all.'

Heinrich kept taking necklaces and rings and earrings and pearl-encrusted combs out of the casket, admiring them against the sunlight flooding through the window. 'What is the point unless you can crack their cyphers?'

'Those two are plotting against you, my lord: maybe a rebellion of the princes, maybe your assassination. It is serious. We need to give it the highest priority.'

Heinrich was studying a sapphire. 'I agree it is serious. But we cannot stop them, can we?'

Adalbert locked eyes with him. 'We cannot stop them, true. But we can pander to their individual interests, to break their alliance.' He picked up a ruby necklace. 'This may be too precious for your conquest.'

Heinrich examined the piece and put it in his pocket. 'She deserves it more than my mother, who raised that snake to the dukedom, and possibly to her bed.'

Adalbert did not comment on the baseless allegation. Although it had been naïve of him not to expect the Kaiserwerth conspirators to poison the king against his mother, he found it appalling.

Heinrich handed him the open casket and the key. 'Look after it for me. I am off to say goodbye to my lady before the war. Officially I am hunting.'

That was highly unusual. Was the young king so in love that he underestimated the danger he was in? 'In the meantime, I will put some of the best brains in the chancery to work cracking the cypher.'

Heinrich, at the door, turned. 'Do not stop at the letters. Pull your strings. I want every movement of Rudolph's tracked and documented.'

'We cannot spy on him constantly, my lord. He will realise it very quickly.'

'That is precisely what I want. The dog has to smell me and fear me.'

'I cannot help wondering if the lady is someone I should know.'

Heinrich's smile was imperscrutable. 'We will speak more on this when the time is right. I may need your help.'

L.

Margravine Beatrice closed her eyes for a second, not sure what to pray for anymore. Perhaps God had decided to teach her the humility that, according to her confessors, she had always lacked. Turning away from Agnes, she directed her gaze to the drawn sword of the archangel Michael that had comforted her at her lowest points.

'I pay for my sins,' were the only words she could muster.

Her fears had been confirmed. Matilde had allowed the protection of Heinrich the Salian, the son of her brother and father's murderer, to turn into a scandalous affair.

Waves of anger surged through her, wiping away the guilt. This was the same stubborn Matilde who had been willing to risk her honour with Rolando. 'How could she put her reputation at stake, her life even, to be in her overlord's bed for a week or two?'

'Their relationship has already lasted a few months,' said Agnes, guarded. 'They deserve credit for their feelings – even if their actions are sinful.'

'Love is not her only motive. As long as your son protects her from Godefroy, she will be at his beck and call.'

'You know her better than me, although your words do not seem to describe the Matilde I know,' Agnes said. 'All I can say is that my son is deeply in love. He would marry her if he could.' She checked her friend's expression. 'I know it hurts.'

It did hurt. 'It is not only about their relationship, Agnes.' She tried to still her thoughts. 'It is about the danger they are in.'

'Because of the prophecy?'

'The moment Ildebrando finds out about them—'

'Ildebrando may like to believe in Charlemagne's prophecy, but he has no more proof that Charlemagne ever uttered it than any of us do. Adalbert to this day is convinced that Conrad made the prophecy up. Although I think he is wrong about that.'

The small key-shaped pendant in her gold necklace brushed

against Beatrice's skin. She let out a tired laugh. 'He is most certainly wrong about that.'

Her fingers grasped the small golden key in her necklace. The wooden statue of Saint Michael was on the trestle. Her friend's gaze glued on her as she turned it upside down and inserted the key in the small hole, turning it until she heard the click.

Her fingers felt their way inside it to reach for the objects. Pieces of vellum, with Charlemagne's seal, more precious than all the gold in Rome and Constantinople, more valuable than Heinrich's relics and his silver mines put together.

She had been a young bride when Emperor Conrad had entrusted them to her care. He had crossed the river Enza on his horse, to spend some time with her, and check that Bonifacio was treating her well, as he had promised to do in Nijmegen.

Gliding over the memories, she turned to Agnes. 'Years before your marriage, Conrad came to hold court in Parma, and he gave me these.'

The vellum hung between them for a moment. Agnes grasped the sheets and unfolded the smaller one, her fingers mildly shaking. 'Is it what I think it is?'

Beatrice's index finger pointed to the seal at the end, the consonants KRLS outside a diamond shape. 'Charlemagne could not write, so he stamped it with his seal.'

Dear son,

In AD 804 the tomb of a saint was found in Mantova and its contents showed me the meaning of my earthly life in the great book of providence. A text was buried with the objects, a fragile sheet of papyrus, which I read with the help of the Bishop of Rome, Leo.

To preserve it for posterity, we had it copied on a solid sheet of vellum and inserted it before the word of John in my personal Gospel, which I asked you to read the moment I exhale my last. The text contains a prophecy which has guided me in my last years and consoles me as I prepare to face the Lord.

A church is being built in Mantova, dedicated to Andrew, the fisher of men. It will house the relics buried in the tomb. As for the prophecy, when your turn comes to leave your body behind, find a new guardian for these words. Their era will be ushered by the faith of one of our blood, when a new Leo sits on the throne of Saint Peter.

Your father, Emperor Karolus

Agnes unfolded the second sheet. The historiated initial of a rising eagle, symbol of John the Evangelist, proved it came from Charlemagne's gospel.

Man of posterity who finds this tomb, know that these bones are the remains of Longinus, soldier of Rome, who served across Our Sea in the days of Emperor Tiberius. Buried with me are my spear and the remains of the Holy Blood I spilled with it, the blood of Jesus who in his mercy healed my eyes, opening them to the light.

If you read this, the word of Christ has silenced the tongues of the Roman gods, a man by the name of Leo is the shepherd of your Church and an old man from the lands beyond the Rhine sits on the throne of Caesar.

Bring my words and these objects to the new Caesar. Say to him that even though God has taken so many of his sons, his line will grow stronger. Generation after generation, like his blood, his empire will grow old and weaken, until the dawn of a new millennium.

A thousand years from the destruction of Solomon's Temple, a new shoot shall come forth from his stump, and a branch shall grow out of his roots.

A child will be born, the Rhineland's Caesar's blood through the mother and through the father, partaking of the mastiff and the eagle. He will be the Caesar's true heir and overtake him in greatness. Anointed through the blood of our Lord, made invincible by the Holy Spear, he will hold the keys to heaven and earth.

Amen.

LI.

Agnes's face had turned the colour of ash. 'This is more than we were ever told - more than I can absorb.'

'I felt the same when Conrad gave it to me. It is actually two prophecies in one: Charlemagne's enshrines Longinus like a reliquary of words.'

'You are the custodian named by Charlemagne. Conrad gave you this text, and a few years later my husband's cousin became pope and took the name Leo, and you discovered the Blood.'

'The realisation shook me. And then there is the prophecy itself. Longinus predicted the existence of Charlemagne and that the relics would be discovered during his reign. It has all come true. Even the name of the pope of those days!'

'He predicts the arrival of a new Charlemagne, half lion, half mastiff.'

'The eagle could represent my bloodline or your husband's. The mastiff is on the Canossa coat of arms. Initially, I thought the new Charlemagne was Federico.'

'Did you tell Bonifacio?'

'No. Conrad made me promise not to reveal it until the time was right, and the time never was. I only told Pope Leo, when he came to Mantova to worship the Holy Blood. I felt like I had to, as he was mentioned in it.'

'What did he say?'

'Like Conrad, he urged me not to show this to anyone - not your husband, not Bonifacio. He warned me against the darkness in the soul of warriors.'

Agnes handed the vellum back to her. 'Do you think he might have told Ildebrando? He was his assistant in those days.'

'Pope Leo said he would treat my revelation as protected by the secret of Confession. Besides, a warrior pope like him was not the kind to dread a stronger empire. A new Charlemagne did not scare him.'

Agnes weighed her words. 'But it will scare Ildebrando, it will terrify him. The Canossa mastiff and the Salian eagle. If he gets his hands on this, he will want to destroy our children, to avoid being crushed.'

'You understand why I could never reveal this prophecy. Bonifacio, your husband, Ildebrando, others in the Church, Gottfried... Everyone would have tried to twist history into the shape that suited them and destroy someone else in the process.'

Agnes watched her placed the scroll back in the statue. 'Have you told Matilde?'

'I will, before I die. If she proves worthy of her lineage.'

Agnes squeezed her hand. 'You surely see that their relationship is a sign.'

Beatrice withdrew her hand. 'Matilde is the last legitimate descendant of Charlemagne. She will not spend her days as an adulterer.'

'I am not saying that, Beatrice. Let's suppose for a moment that Heinrich is serious about her and she is serious about him, and they both secure a divorce.'

Beatrice grabbed a golden crucifix from the trestle. 'I swear this on Bonifacio's bones. My daughter will not marry a Salian.'

'Heinrich is also my son, and I have always stood by you.'

'I thought you wanted to protect our children from Ildebrando's plots?'

'We can protect them by pulling them apart or by bringing them together, making them stronger than his intrigues.'

There was silence. It filled the room. Beatrice felt the tears running down her face.

Agnes wrapped her arms around her. 'Conrad was a Salian, but you loved him. This gift he made you, it proves he saw you like a daughter. What would he say to you right now, if he could speak?'

Beatrice turned towards her Saint Michael.

Agnes adjusted her veil tenderly. 'He would bless the union, don't you think?'

Beatrice wiped her eyes in silence, confronting her personal abyss. Her chin trembled.

Her friend's voice reached her. 'I will not press you further on that. But as you said earlier, our children are in danger. It is one thousand years since the destruction of the Temple of Jerusalem. They need to be told what they have entered into, unknowingly, and what they could enter into if—'

'Don't you think I know?' She turned to face her. 'I often wonder if Ildebrando would even kill, for God.'

LII.

Rome, 20 June 1070

Blanking Ildebrando, Pier Damiani addressed the pope directly. 'Holy Father, you know that I serve the Church by not siding with anyone but my conscience.'

'I do.'

If anything, Pier's determination to protect the Church by remaining outside its political machinery had intensified, to the point that, recently, he had placed the cardinal ring in his hands, pleading to be stripped of a title he had never sought.

'So here is my question to you both.' Pier's gaze darted from the pope to Ildebrando. 'What is the point of a marriage contract with a clause of non-consummation?'

As expected, Ildebrando got defensive. 'You are not naïve, Pier. The point in this case is the union between the extensive lands and titles of the houses of Tuscany and Lotharingia.' He turned to Pope Alexander. 'The lady Matilde may live like a nun, but she will be the most powerful woman in Christendom. Instead of crying at your feet, Holy Father, she should be grateful for the opportunity. There are far worse destinies.'

She had not cried at his feet. She had denounced a rape and a breach of her contract, which brought dishonour on Godefroy whichever way they looked at it.

Pier spoke before he could. 'Would God consider this marriage a sacrament? And anyhow, the contract has been breached. The Church should show some compassion.'

'Compassion?' Ildebrando's dark eyes were burning like lit coals. 'The Church needs protection!'

He stopped him right there. 'I am the bishop of Rome. The crucial value of the alliance does not escape me. What I ask, Ildebrando, is that you come up with a way to keep it together without this marriage.'

The archdeacon snapped. 'Beatrice has always had you wrapped around her finger.'

For once, Pier lost his patience. He banged his fist on the table. 'You are talking to your superior, Ildebrando!'

'I am sorry,' he backtracked, surprised by Pier's strength of feeling.

Pope Alexander pressed on. 'The margravine has been Rome's most loyal and bravest champion for decades. If I must choose between backing her or her son-in-law, my choice is made.'

Ildebrando fired a fresh challenge. 'Has young Godefroy not been loyal to the Church? We need his support – troops.'

Fear never worked as a deterrent with Pier. He half smiled. 'I agree with our Holy Father. Gottfried was my friend, and were he here today, he would call his son's behaviour dishonourable.' His bushy eyebrows arched in defiance as he leaned towards Ildebrando. 'Can you trust someone willing to hurt a defenceless woman – a coward – to defend Rome?'

Pier was playing the antagonist out of belief, but that left room for Pope Alexander to sound like the voice of reason.

'Pier is right. What do we know of this duke? He has been brought up across the Alps, far from here, far from the influence of his father; and his own bishop, Theodoric of Verdun, has reservations on his personality.'

Pier kept nodding. 'The protection of Rome cannot be gambled on unknowns. Right now, we do not have a sense of how far he is willing to go for our cause. But we know how far Beatrice and Matilde would go.'

'Would you leave the defence of Rome to two women?' Ildebrando shrieked.

Pope Alexander tried to soothe him. 'Pier is simply saying that Beatrice has never failed us, and she is on our doorstep. If the Normans turn up at the gates tomorrow, would you send for Godefroy in Lotharingia or for her?'

Pier locked eyes with Ildebrando. 'We fight, brother, because we want what is best for the Church. We should protect Matilde. Perhaps you could remind Godefroy that he has Beatrice to thank for inheriting his father's duchy?'

He bowed. 'As you wish.'

'Thank you, both, for your concern. Ildebrando, please hold off on reprimanding Godefroy. If he realises that Matilde has sought our help, he could turn on her. The account I received from her confessor is... troubling.'

'A young woman who has shown willing to give her life for Rome should not die at the hands of a violent husband.' Disgust and worry fused in Pier's voice.

'And what do you propose, exactly?' Ildebrando roared. 'We cannot send her to a cloister. If we do, the German crown will reabsorb her father's rights – they will be on Rome's doorstep.'

'King Heinrich acknowledged her rights years ago, so in her lifetime that should not be a problem,' he replied. 'We could dissolve the marriage on grounds of breach of contract and then influence her choice of a new alliance.'

Pier nodded vigorously. 'She is a young woman of rare intelligence and reputation – and beautiful. There will be a scramble for her hand. If she agrees to a marriage without non-consummation clauses, her dynasty could protect Rome in the next generation.'

That was too much for Ildebrando. 'The alliance between Lotharingia and Tuscany has been one of the Church's greatest diplomatic achievements. I will not tolerate its dissolution!'

'Why?'

Ildebrando gave Pope Alexander the answer he had been dreading. 'She will inherit the Holy Blood and is a Carolingian. We need to prevent her from fulfilling the prophecy.'

The pope and Pier exchanged glances, uncomfortable as always, when Ildebrando brought up the relics. 'Godefroy is of Carolingian lineage, but that does not seem to trouble you,' said Pier eventually.

'I thought I could control him – through the clause.'

Pier's bushy eyebrows arched. 'Now you know you cannot.'

'Do not worry about him. Of course, he believes he can use Beatrice's relics to lay claim to the imperial title, but she has already outsmarted him.'

How could such a fine intellect become so obsessed? 'There is a political reality much broader than the reach of those relics, Ildebrando,' he said.

Pier echoed his views. 'You say Emperor Conrad has made a pact with the devil? You are the victim of that devil, Ildebrando! A prophecy that could be a figment of Emperor Conrad's imagination is driving your actions and your decisions. This has to stop.'

The pope gave a slow but firm nod of agreement. 'You need to see your confessor, Ildebrando.'

The archdeacon stormed off.

§

From the Lateran, Ildebrando crossed through the old fora, walking swiftly to avoid the beggars and petty criminals sheltering between the crumbling buildings. He climbed Capitol Hill and made his way across Piazza Navona to the church of Santa Maria dei Martiri, a grandiose former Roman temple, whose majestic dome was rumoured to have been the architectural achievement of a pagan emperor.

The interior of the dark old basilica gave him relief from the heat. If only he could tell them what he knew, what he feared. But neither Pier nor Pope Alexander would understand.

At other times, the sunlight streaming from the oculus in the middle of the vault reminded him of the grace of God. Today it irritated him. So did the icon of Mary above the altar and the porphyry basin behind it, the resting place of cartloads of relics from the catacombs.

He was too angry to pray. He continued on to Saint Peter's.

His curly-haired, round-bellied cousin Francesco greeted him at the door of his mansion. He was a wealthy merchant, the owner of a few storehouses along the river. 'I have to run. A couple of boats just arrived from Ostia, bringing goods from Amalfi.'

Ildebrando walked up to his room. Since his return to Rome as the assistant of Pope Leo, he had always kept a room in the Pierleoni household. It was where he escaped to collect his thoughts, and where he kept his few belongings.

They were safer here than in his apartment in the Lateran. Thieves preferred coins to relics, and the Pierleoni's house was well guarded as they needed to protect their merchandise and their earnings. An old chest contained his family memories, and a shelf was laden with his most precious books. They were mainly religious texts, but there were also some translations of Greek historians, and some books in Hebrew.

He had never disclosed his knowledge of Hebrew to his

superiors. It might give out the wrong impression and hamper his progression through the ecclesiastical ranks. But his uncle Baruch had taught him how to read the mysterious characters, and Giovanni Graziano, his first real master, had deepened his knowledge of the Hebrew language.

It had strengthened their bond, a bond made in the blood of the Holy Land, the blood that could come back to haunt them both and prevent them from fulfilling their mission of restoring the greatness of the Church.

Christians still held the Jews responsible for the Crucifixion, and although Jesus himself had been a son of Israel, they would never accept a Jew on the Holy Seat.

That bond had made him a natural choice as Giovanni's secretary when he had briefly become Pope Gregorius VI and was the reason why he could not abandon him after his deposition.

To repay this devotion, on his deathbed in Cologne, Giovanni had gifted to Ildebrando his most loved possession; his Hebrew books, one of which he was particularly attached to. It was a book of prophecies. Often, in dark moments, Ildebrando had opened the brown leather-bound volume at random, and God had guided his hand, bestowing enlightenment upon him.

God had guided him in other ways, such as when his agents had intercepted the letter from Siegfried and his pilgrimage colleagues to the empress, enabling him to secure the scroll they had found in Charlemagne's library in Jerusalem. Appropriately, that scroll was now an additional page in the middle of Giovanni's volume.

He flicked through the sheets and admired it, as he often did. It was an annotated drawing, a map of the old city, revealing the hiding place of a Holy Chalice. He had no means to go to Jerusalem and verify its truthfulness. He had no ships. His power was built on intrigue, not armies.

At least he had beaten the empress to it. Agnes had no knowledge of Hebrew, but she would have relied on her friend Beatrice's translators in Canossa. All hell would have broken loose if she had shared the map with her son. By laying his hands on a different vessel of the Blood of Our Lord, Heinrich the Salian would have become the child of the prophecy.

The contours of the City of God on the map softened as he returned, soothed, to the present. Urgent matters required his attention. He needed to understand the seriousness of the rift between Matilde and her husband, and work with Beatrice to protect the Holy Blood from her son-in-law's claws.

LIII.

'Otto of Nordheim refuses to come to the ordeal unless you issue him a safe-conduct. He is making allegations that you are engineering his murder.'

Heinrich threw his seal in the air and caught it, laughing. 'Why would I stain my hands, when he does not stand a chance in combat against Egeno?'

Adalbert felt he had to insist. 'That is precisely why we should honour his request.'

'Your job is to secure my divorce. Stay out of this.'

Liutpold's scheme was either naïve or stupid, and Adalbert needed to convey that to Heinrich without offending his pride. 'What is your true plan?'

'Strip Otto of his lands and issue a ban against him.'

'My lord—'

Heinrich put his leather jerkin on. 'I have to draw the line somewhere.'

'I agree you should draw the line. But we need to tread carefully, to avoid falling right into Otto's trap.'

Heinrich fastened the strings of his jerkin. 'Enough of Otto. I need your advice on a thorny matter. Remember the lady I was courting in Mainz?'

Adalbert's lips relaxed into a smile. 'I remember the jewels we chose for her.'

'The lady is married.'

Perhaps it was good news. It might bring home the pointlessness of divorcing Berta. 'We both know how much adultery goes on at court,' he replied, matter-of-factly.

Heinrich filled two goblets. 'Given my recent run-in with Pier Damiani, I need to keep a low profile. But her family is well-connected in Rome and she might secure a divorce.'

'As a churchman, I should encourage this option.' He looked at the monarch. 'We have had this conversation before. It is wiser for a king to keep unmarried concubines.'

Heinrich did not react.

The wine was a light red, pleasant. He had another question for the king. 'Given the circumstances, shall we pause the diplomacy around your divorce?'

'No. Speed it up, rather.'

'Before you go, I would like to put forward a suggestion that may bring Otto to his knees, quickly and with limited bloodshed.'

'I am all ears.'

'Have you considered travelling to Saxony with the Holy Spear?'

Heinrich slipped his hunting gloves on, with a crease of his brow. 'I am fighting a civil war. I need military or political advice.'

Adalbert was not deterred. 'That is precisely what I am offering.'

'The Spear is just a symbol. In Magdeburg there are rumours it is a fraud; that it belonged to Saint Maurice and had nothing to do with Jesus.'

'I heard the story too. Yet Otto the Great won all his decisive battles with the Spear at the front of his armies—'

Heinrich shook his head. 'Otto the Great was a seasoned soldier. I am relatively untested in the field.'

'His grandson, the third Otto, was younger than you when he marched on Rome with the Spear. But he conquered it.'

The king ruffled his curls with his gloved hand. 'What is your point?'

'I do not believe in relics. Power comes from prayer and action. But the Spear... its presence fills soldiers with hope and belief; it terrifies the enemy's armies. And you are about to fight the Saxons—'

'Who used to worship a spear, Woden's spear, before Charlemagne forced them to convert.'

'Oh, they still worship it, my lord. I know my people. Just walk through a hamlet after dark at midsummer; you will see some interesting rituals being performed. You show them a spear, they see a manifestation of Woden. Place it at the front of your army and they may just lay down their weapons and drop to their knees. It would be the end of Otto.'

Heinrich shook his head. 'You of all people used to teach me that the king of Germany is Christ's vicar on Earth. I am not going to war as anything else.'

'The Spear does not only fascinate peasant pagans, my lord. It gives sleepless nights to superstitious clergymen in Rome too – Ildebrando to name one.'

After raising his head with interest, Heinrich laughed. 'You are trying every potential avenue to have the Spear removed from Anno's jurisdiction.'

'It has not crossed my mind. However, the Spear has certainly been rusting in Cologne for too long.'

'Hold the thought of using it to scare Ildebrando. I need to deal with the Saxons first. I am not going against them as the reincarnation of Woden; I am going to go as the devout son of Mary, the protectress of Speyer and the Salians. I will be the wronged Jesus, suffering an unjust fate, and Otto of Nordheim will be my Judas.'

Adalbert conceded defeat. 'Your dramatisation of the struggle is as good as mine, or perhaps even better, my lord.'

He finished what was left of his wine. Pity that Heinrich had not listened to his suggestion. Innocent blood would be pointlessly spilled on the fields of Saxony. All he could do was pray for a quick royal victory. The king's next journey, hopefully, would be to Rome – with the Spear.

LIV.

In his cell in Castel Sant'Angelo, Ildebrando was trying to make sense of the latest intelligence reports.

Agnes had left Rome but had not discussed her plans with Pier Damiani – or she had done so under the secret of Confession. She had been sighted in Mainz, where she had met her son for the first time in five years. That was not necessarily remarkable, but Heinrich's whereabouts in recent weeks had been more erratic than normal, often shrouded in secrecy. On several occasions he had disappeared from court or the army, with just a few bodyguards for company.

Despite the tight net of his informers, there were worrying gaps in the reports of Matilde of Canossa's movements: she had left Goslar, reappeared in Berstadt, and then vanished again.

Then there was the matter of her divorce request. Only by keeping her married to Lotharingia he could limit the power of the Salians.

The duke's behaviour worried him. Beatrice and Theodoric's fears for the Holy Blood were well founded. His stern letter to Godefroy, ordering him to leave the relics alone or risk his enmity, should do the trick – for now.

But his attack on Matilde proved that he had a mind of his own and wanted to start a dynasty. He was more stupid than the Salian but no less dangerous.

He went for a walk along the battlements to clear his thoughts. The Tiber was shining below the fortress of Castel Sant'Angelo, a silvery water snake glittering with the light of spring. But the distraction was short-lived. He needed to understand what was going on in the Canossa heiress's life.

Her repeated appearances at court troubled him. The Salian had visited her apartment a couple of times, to play chess, and had spent time with her at banquets. They had even spotted riding together.

Was he becoming obsessed with her? He feared it for a moment. She was only a woman, a pawn in a game bigger than her. There was nothing abnormal about what had been reported to him, but when it came to the Salian threat his mind could not rest.

To keep his sanity, he decided to put his concerns aside and dedicate the morning to the theological treatise he was writing. He walked back to his study but sat at a different table and unrolled a few scrolls, all numbered and inscribed with a heading.

His superior would disagree with some of their content, but he was a mortal too, and the next pope might look upon things differently.

He stretched his fingers to rid them of cramps. It was time for the Church to be bold and shake off the fetters that had tied it to a mortal emperor since the days of Charlemagne.

It was time to come out in the open and proclaim the independence of the Holy Roman Church from the Holy Roman Empire. With pride he studied the headings he had prepared.

a.   *The Roman pontiff alone can depose or reinstate bishops.*
b.   *That he alone may use the imperial insignia.*
c.   *That of the pope alone all princes shall kiss the feet.*
d.   *That it may be permitted to him to depose emperors.*
e.   *That he himself may be judged by no one.*

He felt drawn to the first one. He dipped a quill in the ink pot and started to elaborate his thoughts. *The emperor is not the master of the Church, but the first of her servants,* he wrote. Time to turn the young Salian into one.

LV.

From the open shutters, Matilde could almost smell the ripe barley in the fields, painted a pale gold by the full moon. It was the middle of August and the night was hot. Her chemise was sticking to her skin, and she was grateful for the light breeze and the cool stone under her bare feet. It grounded her, helping her shrug off her anguish.

Heinrich was still in Saxony. It was the first time they had been apart for so long, and the uncertainty was tough. For the last few nights, the image of the peasant girl who had blushed offering flowers to the king, back in the spring, had haunted her dreams.

Kings and great lords thought nothing of being faithful to their women, and he had made no promises before leaving. Always the voice of wisdom, Vinicia kept saying that men were different from women and could easily separate feelings from bodily actions. She had to hope she was right.

Even more than his likely unfaithfulness, she resented the fetters of clandestinity. She could go horse riding, and one of her bodyguards was practising sword fighting with her once or twice a week. But she was hiding in someone else's mansion, doing her best not to be noticed.

It had been bearable with Heinrich around, and her mind distracted by making plans to see him. His absence had made her look at her life under a new light.

And then there was the other, deeper reason for her anxiety. She had not bled for almost seven weeks. After the morning when he had broached the subject, they had never discussed pregnancy again. She regretted it now.

The part of her desperate to erase the memories of her past saw the possibility as a new beginning. The rational part worried about what it might mean for her life. There were genuine dangers: Godefroy's likely retaliation; the scandal if the news reached Rome; even Heinrich's reaction.

Sure, he had said he wanted a child of her womb, but that had been two months ago, and God only knew if the mission to Saxony had changed anything in the way he felt about her, and the dangerousness of their relationship.

She paced the room until the physical exhaustion became stronger than the worry on her mind. She had just managed to slumber again when she was pulled back to reality.

Someone was in her bed, lying next to her. She could not see in the dark but was sure it was a man. She reached for the dagger she had kept under her pillow since the night of Godefroy's assault.

'It is good to see you, my queen.'

'Heinrich, you scared me!'

He silenced her with a kiss and his fingers rushed through the laces of her chemise. He took her with such passion she could feel he meant his words. She was dizzy with happiness, relief, and sheer desire.

She ran her fingers through his curls. 'How was the mission?'

He drew her head to his chest. 'It has turned into an all-out war.'

'That is terrible! Please tell me it is over?' It had to be, or he would not be back.

'It is not over.'

'Can I help in any way? I have no influence this side of the Alps yet, but my mother does.'

'It is between me and the Saxons but thank you for offering.'

'I realise I sound a bit disconcerted.' She was still digesting his news. 'I do not want you to die on a battlefield, that is all.'

He kissed her fingers. 'I do not want to die either. Sadly, war is part of a king's job.'

Overjoyed as she was to see him, she struggled to explain why he had come back. 'Is there a truce?'

'We are marching to plunder his wife's lands in Westphalia. I took a detour to see you.' He reached for his helmet, put it on her head and drew her face to him, her lips to his. 'I missed you, my warrior queen – more than I have ever missed anybody.'

'It is good to hear.' She curled up to him and took the helmet off to return his kiss more comfortably.

He rolled on top of her again. 'I will need a couple of days in your bed before I re-join the army, my love. I have not seen a woman in four weeks.'

His words filled her with joy, the certainty of his love smudged the edges of her fear – that he might not be so pleased with her other news. She would tell him in the morning.

When she woke up, he was lying alongside her, tenderly tracing the outline of her breasts.

'I have something to tell you, Heinrich.'

'I am listening.'

'I missed my flux.'

He sat up, locked eyes with her. 'Are you sure?'

'I am sure. I am tired, also, and I often have nausea in the morning.'

His lips stretched in a smile that she could not decipher. 'Are you telling me you are carrying my child?'

'It is possible.'

'We should see my physician.'

Plain neutral words, but they filled her with dread. Women normally waited until the fourth month, when the baby quickened, unless they needed herbs to bring about a miscarriage.

'Is it not too early to see a physician?'

XLVI.

Speyer, 16 August 1070

'It is not too early, not in this case. We need to be sure as soon as we can.'

'We cannot be sure until the baby quickens.' She needed to know if she was alone in this. Ignore the nausea and face the truth, like a warrior on the battlefield. 'But my body is changing where it is expected to change.' Her heart leapt against her ribcage. 'I understand this makes me a problem for the crown.'

'A problem?' He held her face between his hands and kissed her. 'This is the best day of my life!'

He bent forward to brush her womb with his lips. 'Now that you are bearing my child, you are truly my queen.'

Only she was not his queen. 'Heinrich, you have no idea how happy carrying your baby makes me. After what I suffered, knowing that the seed in my womb is yours and not his—'

His gaze was intent. 'But?'

'Our child will be born in sin.' As she spoke, she caught a glimpse of her own nudity in the mirror on the wall. Naked, like Eve, and a sinner.

His left palm spread across her womb like a shield. 'This baby will not be born a bastard. We should learn some of Rome's tricks.'

'If Ildebrando finds out about this, and that you are the father, we will be excommunicated.' She donned her chemise.

He made her sit in his lap. 'This is why we need to learn their tricks. You cannot hide the pregnancy, but I can hide my paternity, until the time is right.'

Of course, he had to.

He read the fleeting sadness on her face. 'I am sorry, but I see no other way. We need to secure our divorces. Pope Alexander is well-disposed towards you, seize the opportunity.'

He was right on that front, the window of opportunity lay open. His case was more complex. 'What about your divorce?'

'My mother should be back in Rome by now, she can speed up

the pace of her diplomacy. And Adalbert can discreetly sound out the less hostile amongst the princes.' He squeezed her hand. 'The moment we are free, I will use my prerogative as head of the German Church to authorise my own marriage. Adalbert will perform the ceremony and legitimise the baby. Rome will be left with a fait accompli.'

He meant well, but it was a dangerous political step. 'Rome will view it as insubordination, like when my mother married Gottfried without your father's permission.'

'It is a perfect analogy. And we both know my father could not undo the marriage.'

She shifted in his lap. 'Heinrich, this could jeopardise your imperial coronation.'

He shrugged her fear off. 'My right to the imperial crown is a blood right. They can delay things but cannot take away what is mine.'

Was he just dreaming the impossible? Rome could not be seen to condone their sin; and they had not even tackled the subject of Godefroy.

Heinrich slipped on his undergarments and sat at her writing table, pulling a strip of parchment out of her ivory box. He reached for the inkpot. 'I am writing to my mother now; there is no time to lose.'

The mention of Agnes made her think of Beatrice. The empress would worry about the scandal but held no grudges against Matilde's bloodline. But her mother... How would she feel when she found out that the blood of the man who had killed her husband and son would flow in her grandchild's veins? Her heart shrank in sorrow. She needed to soften the blow, somehow. 'I need to tell my mother too – in person.'

'Summon her here.' He sealed the inkpot.

'Her health is too poor at this moment for such a demanding trip.'

Heinrich poured the wax on his scroll. 'Well, you cannot put my baby at risk.'

'This news will be... hurtful for her.'

He squeezed her hand. 'You are a queen in all but name now. You may be carrying my heir. You have a duty to the crown.'

'Winning my mother over is important for the crown too.'

He pulled her back from her thoughts, drew her to him, and nuzzled her ear. Despite the danger they were now in, he seemed more determined than ever. 'We will placate the margravine, do not worry about that. But I am re-joining the army tomorrow. I need my woman.'

In no time they were both on the floor, exploring every inch of each other's skin with their lips and fingers. She led him inside her, adjusting her hips to welcome him, inviting him to take charge.

As her body started to tingle, she wondered whether Heinrich was in love with her, or with the challenge their love represented. The excitement of the ultimate rebellion against the Church, the risk of losing everything put on the scale against the drunken feeling of absolute power over Christendom... No other woman, younger, prettier, better at sex, could give him that.

Then she felt guilty. She had no right to doubt him, not anymore. She had to get used to what love was, to what it meant. She abandoned herself to the pleasure her man's body was giving her.

XLVII.

Speyer, 10 September 1070

The sun had risen to midday. Matilde closed the shutters to keep the light out. Heinrich was still asleep. He had come all the way from Saxony, where his troops were plundering Otto's lands, changing horses and riding through the night, with Cuno and two guards as his only companions. Kissing his forehead, grateful that he was there and safe, she tiptoed out of the room to check if any messages had arrived.

Her letter had probably just arrived in Canossa. She had waited until she was exactly two months late before writing to her mother, to avoid breaking her heart over a false pregnancy. Happiness did not have to be so hard to share.

She still regretted not being able to deliver the news in person. As a ruler, Heinrich's demand that she did not leave Germany while carrying his potential heir was understandable. But her mother would be thinking about a husband coming home with an arrow in his chest, and a healthy young boy poisoned on his way to Florence.

Matilde knelt by her Madonna and prayed, a mother praying to a mother – for her mother, and her child.

When she returned to the chamber, Heinrich was up and dressed and the light was streaming through the open window. A parchment was unrolled on the table in front of him and he was applying his seal to another.

'I have convinced your cousin Welf to divorce Otto's daughter and marry Judith of Flanders,' he said. 'I will tie him to our cause in Bavaria and in Lotharingia.'

'It is a good move.' Welf was related to her father, and Judith to her mother.

'I have also made progress on your mother's front.' He handed her the scroll he had been working on.

She read aloud. '*Therefore, I am returning to Beatrice of Lotharingia, Margravine of Tuscany, all the goods and castles that my most illustrious father Emperor Heinz confiscated at the height of his dispute with her—'* She gazed at him. 'Oh, Heinrich, this so generous! But you did not have to.'

He finger-kissed her lips from across the table. 'Will it ease her pain at our union?'

'You are returning to her some of the most valuable lands and castles in the empire. It will not ease her pain, but it will prove to her that you respect her.' She went through the names of the fiefs he had listed one more time, moved by his decision. 'She will be delighted.'

He gave a light shrug. 'She is the rightful owner of these lands. Anyhow, you will inherit them one day, so they will come back into my possession through our marriage.' He winked. 'It is just a diplomatic ruse to win over my future mother-in-law.'

Outside the window, the slender towers of the Kaiserdom, across the square, filled her line of sight.

The majestic building had been the impossible dream of Emperor Conrad. The son of an obscure count who had managed to become Holy Roman Emperor, Conrad had wanted for his dynasty a cathedral that could compete in glory with Aachen and Cluny.

Dedicated to Mary like Aachen, the Kaiserdom fulfilled his ambition. It was the largest cathedral in the Western empire, and only Constantinople could boast bigger churches.

A smile touched her lips as she realised that Conrad's grandson had inherited his visionary spirit.

Heinrich followed her gaze, standing behind her, inhaling the rose oil scent in her hair. As his beard brushed against her cheeks, she thought, with tenderness and pride, that becoming a father to their child was completing his transformation from boy to man. He pointed to the towers. 'Let us go there.'

'I am unwell. You go.'

It was an excuse, and he knew it. Conrad had laid the first stone, but most of the work had been undertaken after his death, by Heinrich's father, the man who had destroyed the male line of her family. He insisted. 'I want you to come.'

'Why?'

He placed a protective hand on her womb. 'One day, I will be buried here, and if you marry me so will you, and our children. I will not take you to my father's tomb, I respect your feelings. But we will visit the tomb of Grandfather Conrad.'

At moments like this, memories of Federico and her father cut through her like knives. Had she betrayed them? She could not picture herself buried in that crypt. It was hard to extricate Conrad's actions from his maleficent son.

'I can pray for your grandfather; he loved my mother like a daughter,' she conceded.

Entering through a side door, she followed him along the nave to the main altar. There was a marble sepulchre in front of it, and the carving indicated that it was Emperor Conrad's resting place.

Heinrich knelt, crossed himself and prayed – something she had never seen him do in private before.

She thought, for the first time, that if the founder of the Salian line had not arranged Beatrice and Bonifacio's marriage, Matilde herself would not have been born. Heinrich's grandfather had created her family, and his father had destroyed it. But she had survived. Was she an expression of Conrad's will? Was her baby an expression of Conrad's will? She made the sign of the cross and checked on Heinrich.

He was still immersed in prayer, his gaze on the Roman marble of the emperor's tomb. She touched his elbow. 'What are you praying for?'

'Conrad loved your mother and my father. Maybe he can intercede for us. I want the baby to be born as mine.'

She squeezed his hand. 'It is in God's hands, Heinrich.'

'I know.' He got to his feet. 'But my mother used to tell me how happy and proud my father had been at my birth. If I had a son with Berta, I would feel no pride.'

Matilde instinctively touched her womb. Heinrich had not visited Berta's bed since conceiving their baby daughter, but unless the divorce came quickly, he could not avoid her forever.

Should Berta bear Heinrich a son before her divorce was finalised, it would become impossible for Heinrich to pass the empire to Matilde's child. Or the German princes might play the two children against each other, in a civil war.

Despite her own worry, she tried to soften him. Berta was a victim in all this, a pawn just as they all were. So was Heinrich's little daughter. 'Berta's children are innocent—'

'So are my two bastards, and I am providing for them. But, in my heart, only our children are truly mine.'

Most princes had children outside wedlock – her own father had left behind a few offspring, who had been given discreet roles in their army or household. Ildebrando used every opportunity to gossip about Heinrich's bastards, making it sound like there was a string of them rather than a couple.

So, his mention of these children should have been a relief. Instead, it was unsettling. Why had he never mentioned these other offspring to her before? Did he not even deem them worthy of a passing reference?

'What is wrong, Matilde?'

'Nothing.'

He held her shoulders protectively. 'Let us pray to grandfather together, for your safe delivery and for this baby to be born healthy and sit on my throne.' He knelt on the stone floor once more.

Tenderness swept her fears away. After over a decade on the throne, it was easy to forget that the king of the Germans was not yet twenty. He had ruled with ruthlessness, at times with a cynicism beyond his years, but somehow he had managed to cling to a kind of purity.

Doomed as it may have been, his attempt to refuse a loveless arranged marriage, defying centuries of convention, was a shining example of that.

So many times, she had heard her mother praise the bravery of Emperor Conrad. His grandson had clearly inherited his fearless spirit. He was ready to challenge heaven and earth for what he believed in. The princes and the Roman Church had damned him for showing the quality that most befitted a king – the courage to want what was right.

Kneeling next to him, she let the stillness of the church give her the peace she needed. She prayed to Conrad, that he would help bring her mother around and help her move on from the pain and death in her past. She prayed that he would help Heinrich be a good father to the one child he wanted, in breach of all rules of God and men.

LXVIII.

Lotharingia, 15 September 1070

The sun was rising on the pale outline of the abbey of Remiremont. The conversation with the ambitious Abbess Gisela, a cousin of Beatrice's who had asked for the king's intercession in settling a dispute, had gone well. Heinrich had flattered her by offering to Remiremont the status of imperial abbey, reporting to him, rather than to a distant pope. His proposal had been received with interest.

Given her kinship, including Matilde in the negotiation had seemed natural, and had given them a plausible excuse to travel there together. Besides, although officially a monastic house, Remiremont was more of a retreat from the world for virtuous highborn ladies. As such, it was a perfectly honourable place for a woman of Matilde's standing to stay while accompanying her overlord on a diplomatic mission – and a safe place for her to await his return.

He spurred his horse on and rode off in the morning light. He hated leaving her, but he tried to snap out of his dark mood.

His small and well-armed troop joined the larger one that had been waiting in the woods by the Roman road to Trier. The group headed north, coasting the bank of the Moselle.

Heinrich needed to make sure the content of his message was clear to Godefroy of Lotharingia.

Before midday they reached the castle of Bar. The drawbridge was lowered. In the courtyard, there were a couple of dozen heavily armed Lotharingians, who knelt to the king and paid homage. The numbers seemed even.

Heinrich and about ten of his men left their horses in the care of the other half of their group. The captain of Godefroy's soldiers came forward. 'The duke is waiting for you in the chapel. He requests that you leave your men outside, as he has done with his.'

'That is fair,' said Heinrich, nodding to his men to position themselves opposite the ducal guards. 'Provided my captain has the opportunity to verify your claim.'

A sentinel opened the door, and Heinrich's captain inspected the dimly lit interior. 'It is as they say, my lord.'

Heinrich stepped in and closed the door.

Godefroy was sitting in the front pew before the altar. He turned around but did not get to his feet to pay homage. 'I have received your message,' he sneered. 'About your new court whore.'

'I pay you to be a cuckold.'

'Oh, you do. Between men, have you tried ripping her clothes with her precious sword when you are on top of her? The way she squeals—'

Heinrich punched him in the face and sent him sprawling.

Godefroy rose to his knees and wiped the blood from his cracked lip. 'I will keep her dowry as payment for her services to you.' His nostrils flared with anger. 'Even her precious relics. I will seize them from Orval.'

He despised Godefroy's greed. 'Suit yourself. She has plenty more. Let's finish this business.'

'Are the land deeds ready?'

'The chancery is working on them. I am assigning to the child the lands I mentioned in my letter; they are yours to administer until he or she is out of minority.'

'I will double-check the deeds against your letter.'

'Sure. As for dates... Listen and memorise. You were at court in Merseburg in late May, and Matilde was in Berta's household in Goslar. You and her spent some time together after you left court.' It was plausible. Berta had been in confinement and no-one was checking on Matilde's movements.

Godefroy, his right hand on his lip, nodded. 'When am I "becoming" a father?'

'Around Lent.'

He got to his feet. 'I see. She acted all fussy with me, but she opened her legs to you pretty fast.'

Heinrich hit him again. 'Never, ever talk about *my* woman that way.'

This time, Godefroy did not lose his balance. This was his chance to hit back. In the corner of his eye, Heinrich saw the duke's hand clasp around his dagger.

'Murder in a church? Are you willing to stoop so low? I kill people for much less than a bad thought, Godefroy of Lotharingia.'

The duke's fingers loosened on the dagger.

Heinrich got to the door, then stopped and turned. 'As I said, I am making provisions for the child's future and that way you will expand your land holdings, until the child is out of minority. But if you do not behave like a good vassal to his overlord, I will make sure that he inherits all your possessions much sooner.'

LIX.

Bishop Theodoric of Verdun was moving around the cloisters at a slower pace and seemed to have shrunk a bit since last time. His deep greenish eyes, always full of life, looked out of place on his wrinkly face.

'Your Majesty, your visit spares my ageing limbs the long ride to Speyer.' He pointed to the stick he was now using.

'I do not require demonstrations of your loyalty,' Heinrich replied, but he was wary.

Theodoric had been an unwavering supporter ever since his coronation. But he had been the lead celebrant of Matilde's wedding, and in recent weeks he had written letter after letter to the king, pleading for a meeting. Had Godefroy set him up?

Theodoric lowered himself on a bench, relying on his hands and the stick for support. 'I needed to see you because I have promised an old friend, Beatrice of Tuscany, to bring up a confidential matter on her behalf.'

He summoned a polite smile. 'Of course. What does she require of me?'

Theodoric played with the pommel of his stick. 'She is hoping you may be willing to offer her daughter Matilde military protection, to enable her to travel to Italy.'

Heinrich decided not to beat around the bush. 'You are aware of the countess's estrangement from her husband?'

Theodoric cleared his throat. 'I am aware that you are relying on her as an advisor on the Italian situation, and on Lotharingia.'

'Her views are valuable.'

'She is a remarkable young woman. It is very generous of Your Majesty to protect her, although you will need to ensure you do not alienate the duke.'

Heinrich dissimulated with the usual ease. 'I actually met with him yesterday and assigned him more lands. I hope this reassures you.'

Theodoric tapped the stick on the floor a few times. He was probably trying to work out how Beatrice would feel about that. 'If I may, you should give her mother's suggestion some consideration. The moment the countess is safely delivered to Italy, she becomes the margravine's responsibility. You would be relieved of the embarrassment of mediating on what is a domestic issue between Lotharingia and Tuscany.'

'I cannot send Countess Matilde to Italy - for political reasons, of which it is premature to explain.' To close the conversation, he set his gaze on the last withered rose petals scattered by the wind.

'Your Majesty—'

'The margravine will understand my reasons soon.'

Theodoric bowed, conceding defeat. 'The margravine would be grateful for your assistance in another delicate matter, which involves me as well.'

'Of course.'

'Countess Matilde's dowry includes some precious relics that she brought from Italy.'

Godefroy's threat was still fresh in his mind. 'The Holy Blood?'

'The duke has already attempted to raid the abbey of Orval, where the relics are kept. If the marriage fails, he may try again. I have made Archdeacon Ildebrando aware of my concerns.'

Interesting piece of information. 'Why would the archdeacon care?'

'He is devoted to those relics. He has issued stern warnings to the duke. But he will not be able to stop a Lotharingian army.' He let out a sigh.

Heinrich had no desire to provoke Godefroy further - not until Matilde's divorce had come through. But Theodoric was precious to him, and those relics seemed to have a power of their own, which it might be useful to exploit.

'Theodoric, the Salian house is indebted to you.' He kissed the ring on the bishop's bony finger. 'I cannot send an army to protect Orval, but I could facilitate the relics' discreet removal.'

Theodoric's wrinkles were blurred by his sudden excitement.

Heinrich held the bishop's right hand between his. 'Please make any plan you see fit with the margravine. You will have a safe-conduct through my lands, and an armed escort if needed. My only request is that you keep Ildebrando out of your plans.'

Theodoric did not seem too bothered by the last request. 'God has given you a noble soul, my son.'

Heinrich offered the bishop his arm and helped him rise. If the lands he had reassigned her were not enough, the return of the Holy Blood should prove to Beatrice that he was a worthy match for her daughter.

Could it also become the weapon with which to annihilate Ildebrando? He thought about Adalbert's words on the Holy Spear. His path to victory seemed somewhat strewn with relics, and he did not need to believe in them to harness their power.

LX.

Speyer, 25 September 1070

Cuno knocked at the door of his master's chamber. It was late, approaching Vespers, and Heinrich had just dispatched the last petitioner of the day. 'You have an unexpected visitor, my lord. The empress is here.'

He placed the document he was reading and his seal in the ivory writing box. 'Let her in and leave us.'

She pulled her cloak about her. There were a couple of free chairs, but she did not even sit down. 'I came as soon as I could. There is no time to lose.'

'You should be in Rome pleading for my divorce.'

She did not fall into the trap of his confrontational attitude. 'What will you do?'

'Adalbert is working on my divorce, as I am hoping you will be. As for hers, the pope sounds well-disposed.'

'My son, I wish nothing for you more than happiness with Matilde. But you are both running a mortal risk.'

'I have bought Godefroy's silence with a few pieces of land.'

'It is not Godefroy I worry about. How will the pope react when he discovers that the only female prince of the empire, a married woman whose soul had been in his care, is pregnant with your child? He could excommunicate you both.'

'I take it your mission to soften him did not go too well.'

'I take it being careful with her did not cross your mind.'

The space between them filled with silence.

Eventually, he challenged her. 'What Rome views as sin is my God-given right.'

The room was not well-lit at this hour, and it was hard to read her expression. 'It is not just about the adultery; a child born of you and Matilde is a threat to the Church—'

He finished her sentence. 'If she bears me a boy, a Salian will literally rule in the Church's back garden.'

'Well, I am glad Beatrice has not heard you. She fears your interest in Matilde is politically motivated.'

'When you stop in Canossa on your way back, you can reassure her on my behalf.'

She let out a sigh. 'Heinrich, we need to talk without fighting. There is more than meets the eye. All the Salian brides have Carolingian ancestry: Gisela, myself, Berta... But Matilde's bloodline is the noblest. Her mother descends from a legitimate male grandchild of Charlemagne.'

He had no time for history lessons. 'I have a kingdom to rule—'

'If you care about your kingdom, you will listen to me.'

'I am listening.'

'When you went to Mantova with your regents, did you see the relics of the Holy Blood?'

'I was too busy.'

She sighed. 'It was an important moment when Beatrice found them. They are our Saviour's most precious relics. Your father feared it made her family the chosen one, anointed to continue Charlemagne's mission.'

He could not stop tapping the table with his index finger, irritated.

It did not deter her. 'That made her daughters an ideal match for the Salians; only Ildebrando was completely opposed to it.'

Adalbert's revelations were taking on a new light. 'The mighty Ildebrando fears a marriage between me and Matilde because her mother found some relics?'

'Through her husband and children her relics may end up in the hands of someone he cannot control: you.'

He sat back at the table, placing the candles between them. 'He cannot control Godefroy either! And Godefroy is obsessed with those objects.'

She drew a deep breath. 'It is time to lay a few things out in the open.'

'Go on.'

'When he neared the end, Conrad saw your father alone. He revealed to him a secret; a prophecy uttered by Charlemagne, and passed down from emperor to emperor, even after the Carolingian dynasty ran out.'

He needed her to focus on their immediate priority. 'This is not relevant.'

She ignored his comment. 'According to the prophecy, Charlemagne's blood will be reunited in the body of a child – a child anointed through the blood of Christ... destined to rule over the whole of Christendom, and to win battles with a holy spear.'

'Unless you manage to shift some people's views in Rome quickly enough, Mother, your prophecy will not apply to this child – he will be born a bastard.'

'So was Charlemagne. His parents married after his birth.'

'A remarkable coincidence.'

'Precisely, Heinrich.' Her tone grew more urgent. 'If your child is a boy, just think; the circumstances of his birth will mirror Charlemagne's, Charlemagne's blood will be reunited in him; he will inherit the Holy Blood from his mother and the Holy Spear from you. He will be the anointed one, the *Vicar Christi*, literally and figuratively.'

Had she just handed him the solution to his problems? 'He could rule over Church and empire...'

'In theory, yes.' Her expression changed. 'Unless Ildebrando stops you.'

'Does he know?'

'He said so to Beatrice – and that it is the real reason he will never let you marry Matilde.'

LXI.

They kissed the moment Vinicia disappeared into the adjoining room. He made her sit in his lap, his hand on her womb.

'How did it go?' Matilde asked.

'My mother is terrified.'

'Your mother?' She had been referring to his meeting with Godefroy.

'She came to see me. She is terrified of Ildebrando di Soana.' Heinrich played with the pearls in her hair, but his mind seemed elsewhere. 'What do you know about the Holy Blood relics?'

'My mother believes they are the most powerful relics in Christendom. Your father wanted them, and my mother made them part of my dowry, rather than hers, to meet Gottfried's demands without provoking your father.'

'Did Ildebrando negotiate your marriage contract?'

'He did.'

He took hold of her hand. 'Matilde, I do not believe in relics. Their only power is the fear they can instil. But maybe we can exploit that fear.'

'Godefroy has them now. Although I know my mother was planning to move them to Orval when I left Lotharingia.'

'They are in Orval.'

'How do you know?'

'Theodoric of Verdun told me. He asked to see me, so I dropped by on the way back from meeting Godefroy.'

'I am glad. That was always my mother's plan. She and Theodoric built the abbey as a safe place for them. Godefroy cannot touch them unless Theodoric agrees to it.' She was struck by a different thought. 'Why did he need to see you?'

'Your mother made a request through him: that I provide you with an escort to go to Italy.'

Matilde's heart sank. If Beatrice had been willing to swallow her pride and ask for Heinrich's help, she must be desperate to speak to her. 'Why did you not tell me?'

'I have just arrived. I was going to.' Heinrich undid the top string of her gown. 'Anyway, your mother would not ask if she knew of your state.'

'You could have left it to me to explain that I cannot go. I may be pregnant, but I can still handle my correspondence!'

He put a finger to her lips. 'You are so attractive when you are angry.'

'I am serious.'

'I did not want her request to upset you, as it clearly as. Our priority should be your health and the baby's.'

She went silent.

'I have offered Theodoric all the men he needs to escort the relic back to your mother, if she so wishes. I hope it will soften her towards... us.'

Matilde considered the idea for a second. 'It might help.'

'Although, that was before my mother told me about the prophecy.'

'Charlemagne's prophecy?'

His brow creased. 'Did you know?'

'Of course, I did. I never mentioned it because I cannot take it seriously. It could so easily have been made up! But my mother believes in it staunchly, and so does Ildebrando.'

'That is what attracted my interest. Everything about this alleged prophecy suited my grandfather's agenda. I cannot believe intelligent people choose not to see that. But if we can turn Ildebrando's credulousness to our advantage—'

Her heart quickened. 'How?'

'I am Theodoric's overlord; I could demand the Holy Blood from him.'

'No.'

'Why not?'

'If my mother misreads your actions and your motives, she will never forgive you or me...'

He put his finger to her lips. 'Fine, for now. If Ildebrando denies us our divorces or tries to excommunicate us, we may need to reconsider. With the Blood and the Spear, we could blackmail him.'

'We should not go down to his level. I will lose the Holy Father's trust if we do.'

He ran his palm along her stomach. 'My love, your only concern should be your wellbeing and the baby's. Leave the rest to me.'

How could he even say that? Since she had told him about the pregnancy, there had been so many little signs that he had stopped seeing her as an equal, and they were building up. And they had not even discussed his confrontation with her husband.

'How did it go with Godefroy?'

'He will oblige, and you are safe. That reminds me...' He rose and vanished into the anteroom. She could hear him call out to his guards. Footsteps climbed the stairs, and he reappeared in the doorway. He was holding a sheathed sword.

'I thought it was time for you to get a new one, with no bad memories attached.'

'Did he... tell you?'

He nodded. Seeing the turmoil on her face, and her fight to control her tears, he was swift to change the subject, as if eager to protect her from her own memories. 'The hilt is silver and engraved with roses. I thought it suited you.'

She grasped the sword from his hands, trembling. 'You do not know what this means to me.'

His face was full of light. 'I think I do.' He drove her face close to his and traced her lips with his fingers. 'You are safe now. I will look after you forever.'

She placed the sword against the wall and wrapped her arms around him, her head on his chest. 'Thank you.'

Tears of relief filled her eyes. The memories of Godefroy's attack would stay with her forever, but she could leave the pain in the past and build herself a future. With her new sword, he was helping her turn that page, restoring her dignity.

He stroked her hair, holding her tight, then lifted her face and wiped the tears from her cheeks. 'It has been too long.' He kissed her on the mouth, hungrily.

It had been too long, and it felt like the first time all over again, only better.

LXII.

Rome, 1 October 1070

The afternoon heat was receding as Ildebrando stepped into the papal apartment on his daily visit to his superior.

'I have news that will put your mind at ease,' said Pope Alexander.

'Good news?'

'Our views on it may differ. Godefroy of Lotharingia informs me that Matilde is with child.'

Ildebrando checked his understanding. 'With child?'

His mind raced through the reports he had received. They had lived estranged, although Godefroy had been at court twice in the spring. Maybe she had been forced into the act more than once?

Pope Alexander echoed his suspicion. 'After the attack she denounced to Langerio and Pieter, perhaps there have been others.' His voice had a slight tremor in it as he delivered his conclusion. 'She would not have surrendered willingly.'

Ildebrando slipped into a chair as his mind evaluated the new situation. 'The past is in the past. We need to look at the big picture. As long as the pregnancy does not go to Godefroy's head—'

'My concern is Matilde.'

'You know how strong her sense of duty is; she will make her child her priority. If it is a boy, God may have secured the Church a new defender in the next generation.'

Guido, the pope's chamberlain, came in to light some candles. The sun would set soon and was lending its ochre tone to a tuft of light cirri.

The Holy Father was staring at him. 'Ildebrando, you are not my confessor, but let me say this to you. I have no experience of women, but I have heard a lot about love and fear as a confessor. In this matter, I will listen to my conscience.'

He waited for Guido to leave and then his words came out, calm and firm, unexpected. 'Now that there is a child, I will allow her to divorce.'

'You cannot be serious.'

'I am. The child will inherit, bringing together the transalpine Lotharingian duchies and the old kingdom of Italy. Although formally he will be the overlord, Heinrich will be controlled by the Lotharingians. It is a good power balance. It gives the Church the independence we want.'

Ildebrando swallowed. Controlling Godefroy would be a tough task, but much less of a risk for the Church than having a divorced Matilde, free to contract a new marriage. No point in bringing up the prophecy, the pope would rubbish his concerns.

The Holy Father's voice filled his silence. 'Her offspring will be a great contender to Heinrich's legitimate heir, if he ever has any. She can raise her child close to us, so we can strengthen the alliance between Tuscany, Lotharingia, and the Church for the next generation.'

Intriguing as his superior's thinking was, it had plenty of flaws. 'What if the child is a girl? Or dies? Many infants do not make it to adulthood. Let her have two or three boys and then she can come back.'

'It is time to put an end to her suffering.'

'Does the Salian know?'

'Why does it matter?'

'Matilde is spending too much time with her overlord for my taste. And we know how depraved he is.'

His superior received the insinuation unperturbed. 'I know Matilde's soul. She holds the Salians responsible for the death of her father and would never manage more than civil politeness through gritted teeth to one.'

'She has been at court since early spring!'

'She is in the queen's household, as you would expect of a lady of her standing. I truly do not understand your concern.'

'She is at court without her husband.'

'Her violent husband.'

Even that did not shake his unease. 'Does the king know about her pregnancy?'

'He must. Godefroy informs me that he has granted him additional lands, to be assigned to the child, if it is a boy, when he comes of age.'

'Why would the Salian do that?'

This time, the Holy Father looked taken aback for a moment. 'Perhaps he is trying to keep Godefroy on his side. He knows what a threat this child could be to his future.'

'Hmm, it all seems too rushed. The child may be a girl.'

'Maybe he was not bluffing when he told Pieter he is getting closer to Godefroy. Regardless, I will write to Matilde, and tell her I am reassessing her situation.'

'As you wish.'

Ildebrando went to his study on the opposite end of the Triclinium, ignoring the mosaic emperor on its walls. He penned a brief note to Theodoric of Verdun, alerting him of the need to strengthen the defences of Orval, and a summons to Beatrice to meet him in southern Tuscany.

The war was about to enter a new phase. The Church may be about to defeat the Salians, but the possibility of starting his own dynasty could go to Godefroy's head. And if the Holy Father went through with his plans for Matilde, it would only make things worse. They needed to be ready.

Ripping a small piece of vellum from the roll, he wrote a cyphered letter to Bert, the spy who had infiltrated himself in the Goslar palace. He asked for a full report on Heinrich's movements. Perhaps he was obsessed with him, but better to be sure that his meetings with Matilde were innocent.

LXIII.

Canossa, 11 October 1070

Beatrice broke the seal of the message from Theodoric of Verdun and glanced over it. After his decision to return the lands that she had lost at the height of her fight with his father, this offer to help Theodoric confirmed Heinrich's eagerness to ingratiate himself to her. But she was not born yesterday. His motive was obvious.

Her first feeling, on opening Matilde's letter, had been raw anger. After burying a father and a brother, after the years of struggle they had endured to ensure that Bonifacio's rights were passed to her, she had become the lover of Emperor Heinz's son, and, throwing common sense to the wind, had allowed him to get her pregnant. Beatrice almost regretted stopping her from going off to a life of obscurity with Rolando.

Anger had faded into guilt. For two weeks she had fasted and made penance for the sin of ambition, that had driven her to listen to Ildebrando and commit her daughter to Lotharingia, unleashing the unbearable outcome she was now faced with.

Her gaze caught the tip of Saint Michael's sword. Wrapping herself in her shawl, and closing the door to keep the heat in, she made her way outside.

As she pushed open the sculpted door of Sant'Apollinare, her thoughts wandered to a time that felt too distant to belong to her: that banquet in the imperial palace of Nijmegen, when Conrad had introduced her to Bonifacio. Her betrothed was much older and, being famed as a warrior, probably rough. She had dreaded the meeting.

'He will worship the earth you walk on,' Conrad had teased her. As always, he had proved a remarkable judge of men. She had been happier than most brides she knew.

The memory of Bonifacio's last hours, instead, was always with her, as raw as ever. His spring morning journey to the swamps of San Martino, by the Po riverside, for one of his beloved magnificent hunting parties... the lack of a goodbye, as they had been fighting and she was busy with the children's Latin preceptor... his guards bringing him back on an improvised stretcher with an arrow in his chest, their faces signalling that he was beyond hope.

Grey hair glued to his sweaty forehead, his face turning towards the sound of her voice, his hand tentatively reaching for hers. She had had him carried to their bed so he could die with dignity.

Already, he could not speak, but his glassy eyes were desperate to utter the name of his murderer. He had managed a nod, and it had been all she needed. Only one man in Christendom had the means and the motive to plot his assassination. She had held his hand, whispering that, despite the bitterness of recent years, she still loved him, promising that she would not rest until justice was done.

She had kept her promise, too numb for fear, rising, a woman against the emperor. She was still that woman, and she would fight for justice until her last breath, even if Matilde decided to throw away her life.

Her knees were hurting, so she did not kneel by the altar. God in his mercy would understand. Her hands joined in prayer, finding strength in pressing one palm against the other.

At times like this, she missed the comfort of a tomb, and regretted not laying Bonifacio to rest in the crypt of Sant'Apollinare with his ancestors. As she aged, it would become harder for her to visit his sepulchre at the feet of the archangel of justice in his beloved chapel in Mantova.

Thoughts of Mantova pulled her back to the present, to Theodoric's letter. According to Matilde, Godefroy had agreed to pass as the father of the child, but she could imagine his fury. Hopefully, the funds she had entrusted to the Count of Chiny had bought enough soldiers to protect Orval in the immediate. But the relics could not remain under Godefroy's jurisdiction.

Should she take up Heinrich's offer? It made sense, yet she could not bear the idea of entrusting the Holy Blood to Emperor Heinz's son, even temporarily. The young king's charm did not blind her. He had a cynical streak, and although Agnes swore that he did not believe in relics, the temptation of seizing such a precious object may prove too strong.

No, Heinrich would not touch the Blood. She would rather rely on Ildebrando, who had just asked for an urgent meeting.

If only she could convince him to divorce Matilde and Godefroy, for the Holy Blood's sake. The marriage contract would be voided, and the relics returned to her, for now.

She heard footsteps on the stairs and the outside light poured into the nave. From the doorway, Agnes made her way to the altar, listless and determined at the same time.

On their children's relationship, they agreed to disagree.

Agnes saw it as a sign from God, a love that should be supported into marriage and the fulfilment of the prophecy.

Beatrice was not ready for that. To her, what mattered was protecting Matilde from scandal and excommunication. Acceptance of the rest would, maybe, come in time – when holding a grandson in her arms.

'I have something else to tell you,' Agnes said. 'I saw Archbishop Siegfried.'

'Was he a bit less evasive in person?'

'Less evasive, but more disappointing. He had found something in Charlemagne's library in Jerusalem but was blackmailed into giving it to someone else.'

'Someone we know?'

'Ildebrando.'

All roads were leading to him. Establish the facts, first. 'Do you know what he found?'

'A map.'

Beatrice took in the news. 'If I know Ildebrando, it has disappeared in the catacombs or some secret vault in the Lateran, and we will never hear of it again.'

Agnes smiled, a smile almost like Conrad's. 'Archbishops have a tendency to underestimate women. I took a detour after talking to Siegfried. I have met Willem of Utrecht.'

Willem had co-led the pilgrimage. 'To what avail?'

'He is a loyal, more grateful man. He has made a copy of the map and given it to me. But it is in Hebrew.'

Some of the fire of her youth was still alive in her, and Agnes had just stoked it. She could barely feel the gout pain in her knees. 'Brother Aesculapius, my librarian... He can translate it for us.'

§

'God is working through the female bloodlines,' said Beatrice as she led Agnes to the library.

It had taken less than a day for Brother Aesculapius to produce a quick and dirty translation, although it was likely to take a lot longer for him to produce a map of equivalent quality to Willem's copy.

'What does the translation say?'

The monk, his arms folded, explained with a scholar's calm demeanour. 'It is a map of Jerusalem, as we suspected, and it leads to the hiding place of a chalice.'

'A chalice?'

'A chalice in which, if the legends have captured a fragment of truth, a man called Joseph collected blood from Jesus's wounds when washing his body for burial.'

Agnes brought her hand to her mouth. 'What an incredible find that would be! Could I ask...' She turned towards Beatrice, who read her mind.

'Brother Aesculapius, if you could prepare a Latin equivalent of this map, the empress and I would be most grateful.'

'Of course, my lady.'

They stepped out into the autumn light. 'I suppose we have enough to deal with at the moment,' said Agnes. 'But I am so glad I went to see Willem of Utrecht now.'

'Do you trust him never to give this secret away?'

Agnes nodded. 'I do.'

'Then we have another advantage over Ildebrando. Once again, like with the prophecy, we know what he knows, and he does not know what we know.'

LXIV.

Glimpsing his own image in a window pane, Pope Alexander realised his hair had gone completely white over the summer, and his wrinkles seemed deeper. How long did he have to finish the work of the Lord on this earth?

They had all aged with worry; the empress looked gaunt, with a grey halo under her eyes.

Pointing to a seat by the hearth, he proceeded without further ado.

'God be thanked for Adalbert's return to court. The quality of your son's advisors has clearly deteriorated in recent months.'

'I welcome your concern. It is exceedingly difficult to influence Heinrich from afar.'

Grateful for her directness, he placed a reassuring hand on her forearm. 'I appreciate that, my daughter. I am not trying to lay the blame on you. How did you trip to Germany go?'

'It broadened my perspective, Holy Father. This is why I would like to discuss a delicate matter with you.'

'You can count on my discretion, as always.'

She clutched the ends of her shawl. 'I feel that part of the problem with Heinrich is that he does not have a wife capable of exerting a strong emotional and political influence on him.'

No point in denying that.

Agnes continued. 'I care deeply for Berta. She has a heart of gold and I am sure she is a wonderful mother. But I fear she and Heinrich are too different. And she is not gifted with a political mind.'

He thought for a moment. 'I do not disagree with your judgement, Agnes.'

She straightened her back, as if emboldened by his words. 'I have come to think that their divorce would be the lesser evil, if we could find for him a wife who can match him in intelligence and power – someone he could grow to trust.'

'All my years as a confessor have taught me that trust can only develop out of a loving relationship. As far as we know, your son has experienced lust, but not love.'

Agnes spoke with renewed emphasis. 'If we encouraged him to marry a woman he could grow to love, and who is trusted by the Church – like they trusted me, when I was put forth to marry his father – it would be the best solution for his soul. And politically.'

She had a point. The previous year, while they had all got hung up on Heinrich's scandalous behaviour, Pier alone had put his hand in the king's wound. Why had he let Ildebrando's argument sway him? It had been a flawed decision – he could see it now. A year on, Rome's priority should adjust, to address the root of the problem.

'The right wife could counteract the wicked influence of his new advisors.' He paced the room. 'We need to identify someone he can love body and soul, or he will keep straying.'

Agnes graced him with the most charming smile. 'So, you can help?'

He pointed to his white hair. 'If time is on my side.'

'In his great wisdom, the Holy Father appreciates that an annulment is much easier before a son is born.'

He laid a reassuring hand on her shoulder. 'Germany is in enough of a mess as it is. But as you may know, I am trying to free Matilde from her marriage vows now.'

'Thank you for that.'

He looked at a cloud chasing the sun in the blue sky as if it held the answer to his concerns. 'After I free Matilde, who was married for the good of the Church, it will become much easier for me to release Heinrich, whose marriage does not benefit Rome. Give me time, my daughter.'

Agnes kissed the *anulus piscatoris*. 'I knew I could count on you, Father.'

'Agnes, I need to impress a point on you. Releasing your son from his marriage would be *much* easier for me if he stops nominating bishops and interfering with the Church's politics.'

His stark warning took her by surprise. 'I will do my utmost to bring him to reason, Holy Father.'

'Good.'

She fidgeted with her hands in her lap. 'I beg your forgiveness if this comes across a bit forceful, but how soon do you think you can start working on his release?'

'Matilde is coming to Italy after the birth. Once she is here, I will pronounce her freedom. Then I will start working on Heinrich's case.'

Guido had returned and started to lay plates, cheeses, and apples on his writing table.

'I hope my beloved daughter will join me for my simple lunch.' He pointed to the spread. 'The food will be plain, as befits an ascetic old man, but the view will repay you.'

§

It was Terce when Agnes took her leave. The whole of Rome was shining below Pope Alexander's window bathed in a pink gold haze. The roofs and belltowers and crumbling monuments of the eternal city reminded him of his place in history. Being the successor of Saint Peter did not make him infallible. All he knew in his heart was that peace should be the priority of any man of God.

Even if Ildebrando's obsessive devotion proved right, even if Conrad had not fabricated Charlemagne's prophecy, freeing Heinrich felt as right as freeing Matilde.

He sometimes wondered why everybody was so dismissive of the young king. He had shown some emotional instability, but was that so surprising considering he had lost his father young and had been held hostage by the princes for three years? Despite the wounds of his past, he was maturing into a decent warrior and a competent ruler. He should be given a chance.

With the right wife at this side, his energy could be channelled into something positive for God.

LXV.

Adelheid had obviously inherited Agnes's beauty, even though it was a gift she had reserved for God. The blonde locks had either been shorn or hidden under her veil. She welcomed Matilde with open arms. 'God be thanked! How long has it been, fifteen years?'

Matilde gave Lampo a reassuring stroke before handing him over to an attendant.

Adelheid stroked him too. 'You still like good horses, I see. Maybe we should go hunting!'

'That would be wonderful,' Matilde said, unsure whether to inform Adelheid of her condition immediately or wait. 'Thank you for allowing me to stay.'

'This is a crown abbey. I could not refuse my brother. Besides, I still have your letter from the spring. I am so glad of the chance to spend time with you!' She took Matilde's hand like in the old days and led her along the path to the guest quarters. 'I have allocated you the royal apartment, as it is free. That means not just your servant but also your guards can remain close to you.'

'That is so kind of you.'

'I shall see you in my dining room before Vespers. There was a fire at the church recently. I need to speak to the masons.' She produced a bunch of scrolls from under her mantle. 'These arrived for you from Italy.'

Matilde clutched the scrolls. 'Thank you.'

After quickly examining the rooms, she sat on a chair covered in soft wolfskins to take her boots off. Heinrich had decided that she should travel to Saxony in a different convoy from him.

'Otto could lay traps for me at any point. I do not want to put you and the baby at risk. I shall see you in Quedlinburg.'

From his messages, he was about a day's ride away. She missed him greatly. The nausea had subsided and although the mantle was doing a good job of hiding her condition, she had started to show, and that made her feel exposed.

The first of the scrolls Adelheid had handed to her had the papal seal. Matilde had not heard from the Holy Father since the summer. She opened it with trembling hands.

My beloved daughter in God,

Your husband informs me of your condition. Mindful of the wrongs you have suffered, and shared through Pieter, I am inviting you to Italy with your child as soon as you are out of confinement. That will enable you, your mother, and I, to discuss the most appropriate future for you.

She drew the scroll to her heart, melting into tears of release. She dreaded the idea of parting from Heinrich for a few months. But the pope was coming around. That was all that mattered.

The images of their last meeting in Rome, when she had begged him to save her from her marriage, no longer hurt. Her destiny would go full circle. She put the letter in her writing box, away from prying eyes.

The other scroll had the Tuscany seal. She braced herself for Beatrice's onslaught of anger or misery.

§

'To what do I owe the pleasure?' asked Adelheid as Heinrich entered her elegantly appointed scriptorium.

He accepted some sweets from a novice and then ordered her to leave them. Her raised eyebrow warned him that she did not like her brother overstepping. Quedlinburg was her territory.

He played with her seal. 'I am here to check on Countess Matilde.'

She snatched the seal back. 'She only arrived yesterday.' Her gaze searched him for clues of whether he knew. 'I was a bit surprised by your letter. What brings you both here? Some alliance

I am unaware of?'

'You could call it that.'

Adelheid studied her brother. 'This abbey is home to highborn ladies who wish to retire from the world—'

'Matilde's retirement from the world is temporary.'

'Can you explain the situation to me? I need to know what I am committing myself to.'

'Matilde is expecting.'

Surprise took over Adelheid's face. 'Why is she here then? Away from Lotharingia, from her husband...' The words died in her mouth.

Heinrich stretched his lips in a smile. 'I think you can put two and two together, sister. I need you to take care of her now.'

'How could you do this to her! She is not one of your...'

'Whores? No, she is not one of them.'

She laid accusing eyes on him. 'How do you explain your actions, then?'

'I did not force her into this, Adelheid. I am surprised by how badly you think of me.'

'Someone like Matilde puts her honour above everything else.'

'Indeed, and actually I also care about her honour – much more than you may think.'

Scepticism was all over her face.

He insisted. 'She is the lady I mentioned to you in May.'

'The one you said you would marry if only you could?'

'In our hearts, we are man and wife.'

Adelheid sighed. 'You cannot stay here Heinrich, only Matilde can.'

'I will not stay. I have a war to fight. But she needs a safe place to deliver the baby.'

'We have helped ladies in that kind of trouble before.'

Heinrich kissed his sister's ring. 'When the war allows me, I will visit her in the royal apartment. I will be discreet.'

LXVI.

Vinicia, in the main courtyard, was carrying two baskets brimming with leaves and roots and late berries. Heinrich recognised silvery sprigs of sage and wrinkly rosehips.

'I am harvesting as many medicinal plants as I can before the first snow. The midwife will need all the help she can get when the time arrives,' she explained.

'How is the countess faring?'

Vinicia produced a key from her tunic's pocket. 'If Your Majesty wishes to leave me to my herbs, I am sure my lady is about to feel much better.'

'It is good to see you,' he said as he entered. Thinking it was Vinicia, Matilde had not lifted her head from her reading.

'Heinrich!'

He squeezed her tight, his lips brushing her hair. 'Let me feel that you are real.'

She kissed him with longing. 'You are tense. Did something happen during the journey?'

He gave a light shrug. 'We were ambushed, it was not pleasant.'

'I am so glad nothing happened to you,' she said on his chest.

His arms wrapped around her even tighter. 'That divorce cannot come soon enough. The moment my son is legitimised, nobody will dare rise against our dynasty.'

Matilde shifted in his embrace. It was going to take time, patience, and respect to train her to see herself as a Salian. She pulled away to face him. 'How will you feel if this baby is a girl?'

His finger traced the profile of her bump. 'A girl is easier to legitimise, and it would be simpler for me to pass the empire to a son you bear me after we marry. But a part of me, the part that always wants to challenge everything, wants a boy now.'

'As long as you do not end up having a boy from Berta first.'

He looked at his feet, as if she had caught him out. He had been under serious pressure to visit Berta's bed. Liutpold was bringing up the subject at least once a week. 'I am doing my best to avoid that.' He felt tears pushing through, the same tears he had cried five years earlier, when he had first been told to marry Berta or lose the empire.

'I know.' With a smile, Matilde pointed to a scroll on her writing table. 'I have good news. Pope Alexander has summoned me to Italy as soon as I am out of confinement, to discuss my future.'

He swore through gritted teeth. 'Let us go for a walk.' He preceded her to the door.

They crossed out of the portcullis in silence and walked down the steps excavated into the rock the abbey was perched on. The last flowers were drying in the crisp, sunny air. But the beauty of their surroundings did not ease his tension. He struggled to focus.

'You cannot expect me to jump with joy,' he snapped. 'The pope may be ready to receive you, but have you thought of the baby? You cannot take a newborn all the way to Italy, for God's sake!'

A cloud of disappointment passed over her face. 'Heinrich, it means a lot to me that you do not want me to go. But the Holy Father has set his heart on releasing me. We need to seize the opportunity.'

She was right on that, but he had to make her see where her priorities should lie. 'Wait until the summer. The baby will be stronger.'

'Pope Alexander is not getting any younger. God only knows who will succeed him. He is our only hope.'

Those were urgent and well-intended words, but he would not let them sway him. 'I do not like being cornered, Matilde, especially not on this.'

They had reached the bottom of the steps. She changed the subject, perhaps to defuse the tension. 'How is the war going?'

She did not know what that simple question meant to him. No-one cared about how a king felt, people only cared about what they could get out of him. Her words filled him with the certainty of her love.

Taking her hand, he led her to a wooded expanse nearby. 'I am more worried about Rudolph than about the war with Otto right now. There's so much intrigue going on.' He paused, unable to look at her. 'I cannot believe my mother was in love with that snake.'

'It must be German propaganda against her.'

Undoubtedly, she meant her words, but he could not make peace with the rumours. He clenched his jaw. 'I will never know unless I ask her.'

Matilde caressed his cheek and squeezed his hand. 'We all make mistakes.'

They sat on a fallen chestnut tree trunk. The air was heavy with the scent of autumn. He held her tight.

'I hope you are right. Anyhow, she needs to stop travelling up and down the Alps every month. Ildebrando has spies.'

'She must be worried. I try not to think about what would happen if they found out.'

He gave a shrug. 'Rudolph would get the empire, Godefroy would get your lands, and we would be excommunicated.'

Suddenly, she pulled herself up.

'What is wrong, Matilde?'

She turned sideways on the tree trunk, so she was facing him, and drove his hands under her mantle, to her womb. 'Keep your hands here.'

Heinrich waited. Eventually, he felt a light, soft movement, as if one of her organs were suddenly pushing against her skin. 'Is it... the baby?'

'Shh.'

Soon, he felt the same light pressure against Matilde's skin. 'I love you both,' he whispered. He drew her to him and gave her a hungry kiss.

'Heinrich, the serfs come here for wood. What if they see us?'

He struggled to draw away from her. 'Let's go inside.'

A young woodcutter moved away from the pile of cut logs behind one of the oak trees, where he had been hiding. The moment the king and the countess disappeared, he walked away from the abbey.

LXVII.

It was good to be back in Goslar, especially in autumn, when the Rammelsberg slopes turned into a mosaic of russets and golds. You could hardly tell it had been five years. In the king's chamber, the ivory chessboard was on the same small table in the solar, and the tapestries with hunting scenes covering the walls were still some precious Gent pieces bought by Agnes as a young bride.

A young manservant cleared what was left of the pork and the pigeons and placed a tray laden with cheese and dates on the embroidered cloth. Adalbert still remembered the day he had first bitten into a date. They were a southern delicacy and Agnes had brought them from Aquitaine.

He raised the cup of lovely-smelling Burgundian to Heinrich. Even the goblets, exquisite Venetian, looked familiar. 'My prayers have been answered. You have made it back from your expeditions safe and sound.'

Heinrich toasted and invited him to sit by the window and enjoy the mild October sunshine.

'We shall speak about Otto in due course. There is another matter I need to discuss with you.'

'Of course, my lord. What is it about?'

'In the summer you told me that Ildebrando had talked my father out of a marriage with Tuscany – and that my mother was best placed to explain why.' His lips smiled but not his eyes. 'Well, I have asked her.'

Conscious of being in treacherous waters, Adalbert trod carefully. 'I am glad you took that step. I was oath-bound to her, henceforth—'

'Your loyalty is a credit. I simply want to know what you make of Charlemagne's prophecy, now that you are free to discuss it.'

The wine tasted mellower with relief. 'My opinion on the subject is quite fluid. I am agnostic when it comes to relics, as you know.'

The king refilled the glass goblets. 'Despite several marriages between members of the bloodline, the new Charlemagne has not materialised.'

Adalbert admired the wine through the chalice. 'True, but only the most recent marriages could fulfil the prophecy. Charlemagne's heir's anointment with the blood of Jesus would not have been possible in your grandfather's days, for example. The Holy Blood had disappeared from the face of the earth.'

'How unfortunate that it was re-discovered by Margravine Beatrice.'

Adalbert took a sip. 'Your mother and I were not as troubled by the news as your father – the right marriage for you would still make a Salian the child of the prophecy. Only such a prospect proved a bit too... unsettling for Ildebrando.'

'The Holy Blood is a pile of blood-stained sand. You cannot anoint a child with it.' Heinrich placed his cup on the trestle and warmed his hands by the fire. 'The archdeacon's credulousness never ceases to amaze me.'

'Our archdeacon prefers metaphorical to literal readings, clearly.'

Heinrich turned towards him. 'If Charlemagne really had been a prophet, which I find hard to believe, don't you think he would have put his prediction into writing, cast it in stone, rather than just speak it?'

'The lack of a written record is the reason I suggested it may be your grandfather's invention.'

'What did Father say to that?'

'That I lacked faith.' He gave a light shrug. 'That Longinus himself had hidden the Holy Blood and it had already been found once, precisely in the days of Charlemagne, in that same town of Mantova where Beatrice found it – before being lost again.'

'His point being?'

'His point being that the text of the prophecy could also have been hidden in the same way – hence it could still be out there somewhere.'

Heinrich picked up the king chess piece. 'Let us look at things from Ildebrando's perspective. He went through the trouble of doing and undoing marriages, on the basis of allegations that a dead emperor uttered a prophecy?'

Adalbert smiled. 'He does not lack faith, does he?' He pushed the queen to the middle of the chessboard. 'Undoubtedly he also dreaded the hard reality: if you married Matilde of Tuscany, your successor would control two thirds of Charlemagne's empire.'

Heinrich placed the king back on the chessboard, facing a bishop piece. 'We should produce an ancient-looking piece of vellum inscribed with the prophecy – make his fears come true.'

Adalbert eyed his former pupil. 'What would he have to fear? You and the countess have both been married according to his needs.'

'The Holy Blood is in Lotharingia now. I am on good terms with Theodoric of Verdun. Let us suppose for a moment that I manage to intercept it.' His lips turned upwards in a smile. 'My mother is of the bloodline; I have the Spear. In that scenario, I become the child of the prophecy...'

Here was Conrad's grandson, fearless, devilish possibly. Adalbert shook his head, intrigued and anxious. 'I would not play with fire, my lord.'

LXVIII.

'Why are you here? You could blow your cover.'

Bert bowed to Ildebrando. 'I did consider it, my lord. But on balance I decided to come. I have a woodcutter working for us in Quedlinburg. He delivers logs to the kitchens and helps the convent's labourers when they do repairs.'

As if that could dispel his irritation. Woodcutters were low level informers, easy to recruit. Bert was his main man in Saxony, not someone he could replace easily. 'I hope he is a worthy source.'

The spy nodded. 'He is reliable, and what he reported, in my view, needed your immediate attention.'

'Let's hear it.'

'The king is in Goslar, but visits Quedlinburg regularly.'

'He is close to his sister.'

'The gossip in the kitchens is that the abbess has a guest, a noblewoman who is spending time in prayer away from the world – the wife of the Duke of Lotharingia.'

'There is nothing strange in that,' he said, more to himself than to Bert. A pregnant noblewoman wishing to prepare spiritually for the birth in the peace of a convent, especially if the husband was violent and they lived estranged... yes, it was a sensible choice.

'I said the same to the woodcutter. But I also instructed him to keep an eye on things. He had noticed nothing unusual until about two weeks ago. What he witnessed... You are best placed to draw the conclusions... Once I relate the facts, I hope you will understand my decision to report in person.'

'Speak.'

'The king and the duke's wife went for a walk in the woods outside the monastery. In the beginning, they were tense with each other, maybe fighting. Then he held her hands, held her in his arms, she touched his face, and after a while she drove his hand to her womb, and he kissed her in... a lustful manner.'

Ildebrando had hired Bert precisely because embellishing the truth was not one of his talents. Even without enhancements, there was enough to ruin both the Salian and Matilde – if he decided that her ruin could benefit the Church.

'You did well to come, Bert.' Despite his turmoil, he smiled. 'Now you need to lie low. Do you know Rome? Go to the Schola Saxonum. After the Norman conquest, hardly anyone comes from England; they will have a free bed for you. Worship at Santo Spirito with the Saxon pilgrims for a few days. Then, unless you hear from me, return to Goslar.'

Leaving the brown circular walls of Castel Sant'Angelo behind, Ildebrando crossed the bridge. He would take a detour, walk to the Lateran through the Capitol, taking in the view of Rome from the top.

The day was muggy. Sheep grazed on the ruins of the Caesars' hill, as usual. He avoided a begging widow feeding a child at her breast, under an umbrella pine, and kept looking ahead, skirting broken columns and crumbling brickwork.

When he reached the summit, he spun around, full circle. The pope's palace of the Lateran on one side, Saint Peter on the other, across the silver ribbon of the Tiber – emblems of what he had sworn to protect.

His breath was shallow with anxiety, but his resolve was as strong as it had ever been. Christianity was in danger, and he had to take the situation into his own hands.

When, years earlier, he had revealed to Pope Alexander that he was aware of Charlemagne's prophecy, a secret passed down from pope to pope since the days of Conrad, his admission had been met with coldness.

'I do not know who shared this information with you, but your soul should receive it with purity.' The hazel in Pope Alexander's eyes had darkened. 'God is not in the habit of predicting our future or improving our present. He works through the goodness of our heart.'

Ildebrando had tried to object, but the Holy Father had waved an admonishing finger at him, his forehead furrowed with lines of exasperation.

'Behind prophecies and relics there is always an interested party, a lord, a bishop, or a monastery trying to enrich their pockets, or in the best case, their people,' his superior had concluded, with typical

Lombard stubbornness. 'We follow our Lord through His symbols – the other way round is heresy.'

The threat had cornered him.

Five years ago, Ildebrando had tried to resume the conversation by bringing him the scroll found by Archbishop Siegfried in Jerusalem. That had also failed.

'I cannot consider a document in an un-Christian language,' had been his excuse. Sometimes it was hard to get into his head that Aramaic had been the language of God. The Lombards always preferred to think of Him as speaking Latin.

That was the past. He was at an allegorical crossroad. Terror at the prospect that the prophecy might be about to come true contended in his mind with the thrill of having gained knowledge that could destroy the Salian. The child in Matilde's womb was Charlemagne's blood, but she and her royal lover were ripe for excommunication. That could deprive them of all power and influence, and of their relics, voiding the prophecy.

He walked down the other side of the hill, finding his way through the crowded alleys. His pace was faster now; he was eager to get in front of his superiors and lay things in the open. His best option was to act like Bert, and simply report the facts. They were earth-shattering enough.

§

Ildebrando looked around the chamber. 'Where is Pier?'

'In Anagni, resolving a dispute.'

'It is probably a sign from God. I need to discuss something with you alone.'

Curiosity was not one of Pope Alexander's sins, but something about Ildebrando's countenance made him alert. 'Sit down.'

'I received an intelligence report from Germany. You will not like it.'

He waited for the archdeacon to continue.

Ildebrando enjoyed setting the scene. 'A trusted acquaintance at the German court has seen Heinrich head out of Goslar with only his chamberlain Cuno and a couple of bodyguards.'

'So?'

'He has followed them. They have gone to Quedlinburg.'

Pope Alexander unfolded his icon, making it clear he had no time for gossip. 'His sister is the abbess.'

'Adelheid has a guest: our friend Matilde of Canossa is staying at Quedlinburg.'

'I am aware of that.' Matilde had written she was on her way to Quedlinburg. 'Abbess Adelheid is perfectly capable of hosting Matilde and her brother at the same time...'

'It is not that simple. Adelheid hosts Matilde, who in turns hosts the king.' There was a pause, probably for effect. 'The Salian devil has turned a holy monastery into a... a brothel!'

The pope sighed, exasperated by Ildebrando's tendency to see scandal everywhere. 'I am not interested in conjecture. Are there any facts in this report you received?'

'A witness saw Heinrich and Matilde kissing lustfully and all over each other in the woods outside the abbey.'

The breath died in his throat. 'It cannot be, Ildebrando. She is pregnant.'

'Indeed. It was my first thought too. Heinrich is depraved, but even I cannot imagine him choosing a visibly pregnant woman as his sexual interest.'

The pope remained silent; trying to find an anchor in the gaze of the Madonna in his icon.

Ildebrando made eye contact with him. 'I can draw only one conclusion, and I am sure you will agree with me. She is an adulterer, and Heinrich fathered her child.' Was there a hint of gloating in his countenance?

Pope Alexander kept his expression as neutral as he could. If the allegations proved true, he could not save Matilde. 'This is a damning claim, Ildebrando. How reliable is your source?'

'Someone rode all the way from Goslar to report this sighting to me.'

'Let's separate the facts from the conclusion. Your source, this man who has come to Rome, has not witnessed the facts he describes?'

'No. But his source is reliable.'

'Still, I cannot base my judgement on second-hand gossip.' Especially if the judgement in question involved excommunication.

'Besides, Godefroy is acknowledging the child.'

'The duke's position is a mystery I am trying to unravel. But you have no reason for doubting the reports.'

'As I said, even if I accept the reports as true, we need to draw a line between fact and conjecture.'

Ildebrando lost it. 'Surely you can see that the facts I described are incriminating enough. And it is the Salians we are dealing with! The grandfather made a pact with the devil, the father was born on Judas's day, that boy *is* the devil incarnate.'

'I would not disturb the devil for an analogy, Ildebrando.'

The other was relentless, a dog with a bone. 'Well, your priority is protecting the Holy Roman Church. Heinrich is the antichrist... bringing about the end of the world!'

'Are you going to bring up the prophecy now, and their relics?'

The archdeacon paled, his expression numbed, until he found an angle from which to unleash another attack. 'Don't you feel sick at the idea of that devil fornicating with your innocent Matilde, lustfully debasing her once pure flesh?'

This was too much. He wished he could punch him. He took a deep breath instead. 'You are better than me at diplomacy, Ildebrando, but you have lived in monasteries and in the papal administration. As a priest, and as a bishop, I have confessed for decades.' He paused to let his words sink in. 'In confession you put your hand in the wounds in people's hearts.'

Ildebrando eyed him in disbelief. 'You cannot defend two sinners!'

'What you are reporting is shocking. I am examining my conscience, as you should. We are God's humble servants, and we have not always operated in accordance with His will.' He grabbed the cross hanging from his neck. 'We forced her into a marriage she hates. We let him be pushed into a marriage he hates. We gave them similar fates. Young, beautiful, powerful in everything but powerless in love, and surrounded by people who manoeuvre them like pawns.'

'Are you turning me into the guilty party?'

'I am not, Ildebrando. But we have created a situation where they have become each other's most natural support.'

'Now we need to deal with the biggest scandal in the history of the Church,' he stoked.

'Do *we*? There is no "we" this time, Ildebrando. *I* am the successor of Peter.' He could feel his self-belief return, like embers still glowing. 'I will pray to our Holy Mother for advice. The Church has survived worse moments than this. Remember the year Rome had three more or less worthy individuals squabbling to be pope?'

Ildebrando stormed out. Allusions to the days of Giovanni Graziano's deposition always made him petulant. But it was a slight consolation.

Pope Alexander was shaken by the events, more than he would ever admit. He grounded himself in humility before the icon of the Virgin Mary, with her eyes full of stars. He prayed for forgiveness, for his intellectual arrogance, and his decision to sacrifice Matilde to Rome's interest.

He also prayed for the young king. For over a decade, the Church had left him in the hands of awful political advisors in the unspoken hope that he would self-destruct. That the boy, now a man, had survived all those years and held on to his throne was a miracle.

Maybe it was a sign from God, a sign he should heed.

Eyes closed, he slowed his breath to still his mind and search his feelings with detachment: to recognise them, name them, overcome them.

When he opened them again, the image of the starry-eyed Madonna and her Child loomed even more poignantly. For a moment, the mother of God's smile faded into Matilde's.

Was Heinrich sincere in his feelings for her, or had he played a game of seducing someone he saw as the Church's favourite princess? The suspicion thickened his guilt for the part he had played in her ruin by forcing her to honour the contract.

Then he remembered Agnes's recent visit, and her words. Instead of simply pleading for his divorce, she had insisted on his need for a different woman. Her description of this woman's qualities sounded very much like Matilde's. Did she know, or at least suspect?

If Heinrich's feelings were genuine, the path ahead was clear. The Church should forgive both and try to patch their sins up with a reparatory marriage. He had to move carefully and swiftly. He was not getting any younger, and the Saviour could call him to His side at any moment.

God the Father, allowing events to unfold as they did, was showing that protecting Matilde and Heinrich was one with protecting the Church.

Ildebrando, though, would argue the opposite was true. If the archdeacon succeeded him, or managed to influence his successor, his fears would destroy the Church as he tried to save it.

One step at a time. First, he needed to conduct his own investigation of the facts. Inhaling the comforting smell of parchment, he penned a message to Empress Agnes. Beatrice was constantly ill, but he wrote that she gave audience to his nephew, the Bishop of Lucca. He wrote to him next.

His last letter was to Hugh of Cluny. As the head of the Cluniac order, he was Ildebrando's superior, so he had the spiritual power to challenge his views. He also happened to be Heinrich's godfather.

LXIX.

Rome, 1 November 1070

As Agnes knelt to kiss his ring, the pope placed his right hand on her head. 'I absolve you of any sins you committed out of maternal love.' She glanced upwards, surprised. 'Sit down, my daughter. It is going to be a long afternoon.'

She obeyed him.

'Last time we spoke you kept saying your son needed a different woman.'

Agnes remained composed, hands in her lap. 'I thought we agreed, Holy Father.'

He fastened his gaze on her. 'It is time to be straight with each other, Agnes.'

She shifted around as if the oak chair had suddenly become uncomfortable.

He kept his expression neutral. 'The personality of the woman you described to me as Heinrich's ideal wife sounded very much like the daughter of your friend Beatrice of Canossa.'

She looked like she had been struck by lightning, yet she came up with a perfect diplomatic reply. 'Matilde is an exemplary ruler and woman.'

'There is a lot we can agree and disagree on, my daughter. But as I said, it is now time for the truth.' His gaze dug deeper into hers, the gaze of the judge, not of the confessor. 'When you came to see me, did you know that your son had started a relationship with Matilde?'

An answer, any answer, could damn Heinrich, and she knew it. She chose well, once again – she chose silence.

He continued. 'I love Matilde like a daughter. I want to protect her. Others may not feel so tender towards her sin.' He made a deliberate pause. 'She is an adulterer, and so is your son.'

'Holy Father—'

'I am not angry with you, Agnes. You are a mother. You tried to protect him. You thought that a marriage would save them.' He felt as broken as she did. 'Nobody in this room is without sin. I allowed Matilde's marriage to Godefroy, even though she desperately asked me to save her. I know he raped her.' That never stopped feeling like a personal defeat.

She must have noticed it, as she raised her head. 'Are you saying you forgive her?'

'The Church cannot forgive her so easily, although as her confessor I can.' He looked for a moment at the Roman roofs outside his window. 'I could bring myself to forgive Heinrich. He is not a clean soul like Matilde, but if he genuinely loves her, maybe this could be his redemption.'

Her eyes glistened at the unexpected opportunity, and she clung on to it, like a drowning man to a floating log. 'This is my hope too, Holy Father.'

'Hugh of Cluny will be here in three days' time. He, rather than Ildebrando, will be my advisor in this matter.'

He straightened in his chair, making his expression sterner. 'One last question, my daughter, and I expect nothing but the truth from you.'

'Yes, Your Holiness.'

'Is Heinrich the father?'

§

Sitting on a bench in the Triclinium Hall, Ildebrando seethed as he glanced over the new report from Bert. The dalliance continued. The Salian was still in Goslar, and visiting Quedlinburg every week, staying overnight. Security around the royal apartment was tight. An attempt to be hired as a helper in the stables had failed.

What was it going to take to open Pope Alexander's eyes? He felt nothing but anger for his superior's stubborn handling of the situation.

Slipping the report into his robe, he checked the time on the sundial in the courtyard. He had seen Agnes arrive earlier in the day. It was her third visit to the pope in a week. Something was going on, but during their afternoon meetings his superior was keeping his thoughts and plans well-guarded. The lack of trust was insulting, considering Pope Alexander owed the Holy Seat to him, and to his influence of the cardinals.

Although he owed obedience, Ildebrando was not going to let a weak successor of Peter damage the Church's interests, and those required him to eradicate the threat of the prophecy.

Pope Alexander was dismissing Bert's reports as mere deductions. But although the paternity could not be proved, the liaison could be - and it should be sufficient ground for excommunicating the adulterers.

He would give his superior another month to change his mind; in the meantime, he had to lay the foundations for an alternative plan.

He baulked at the prospect of eliminating Matilde. He had never thought much of the girl, but Beatrice was the only prince he truly trusted to defend the Church and the relics, and after her son's untimely death, losing her daughter could kill her.

Dispatching Heinrich posed obvious challenges. When at court, like all kings, he had servants tasting his food and drink. Manoeuvring Rudolph of Swabia into rebelling against him would take longer but was a safer route. The latest letters from the duke were encouraging in that respect.

The other option was acting on the child. Could Matilde be poisoned to miscarry? For that, he would need to place a perpetrator in her service, someone who could fool her devoted Vinicia. It might be more sensible to wait for the birth. Matilde could still miscarry or have a stillbirth.

If she delivered the bastard, and it turned out to be a boy, the Salian would face an uphill struggle to legitimise the product of a double adultery - a struggle Ildebrando was sure to make even harder, with every legal weapon at this disposal.

He needed to talk to Godefroy, get the truth out of him first. The price he would surely name for denouncing his wife's adultery was a price Ildebrando could not pay. It was clear as daylight now that Godefroy should not be trusted near the Holy Blood. Besides, if he had kept to his non-consummation clause, they would not be in this nightmare.

With so many babies dying in their first year, disposing of a child in an unsuspicious manner was often easier than disposing of an adult ruler. Bert needed to find someone intelligent enough to do that job cleanly.

Whichever option he went for, his immediate priority had to be quashing the dalliance. He would write to Rudolph, order him to pressure Heinrich to visit his marriage bed. If Queen Berta delivered him a boy, his bastard would remain such.

He checked the sundial again, and the firm footsteps of a tall man on the marble and mosaic floor made him turn. It was his superior, Hugh of Cluny. A bitter taste spread in his mouth as he realised the pope had outmanoeuvred him. But he had to follow protocol. He kissed the abbot's ring. 'What brings you to Rome, Father?'

'A summons from our beloved shepherd. God be with you, Ildebrando.'

'Perhaps I can be of assistance.'

Hugh eluded his trap elegantly. 'This is a job for my conscience. To quote Pope Gelasius, at the hour of death, priests have to render an account for the souls of kings.'

It was unwise to press any further. The abbot's not-too-veiled rebuke made it clear that he agreed with Pier Damiani's view – that keeping the king married against his will had been a mistake. 'I bow to your wisdom,' he conceded, between gritted teeth.

LXX.

Goslar, late November 1070

Rudolph of Rheinfelden was sitting by the hearth, dressed in silks and furs to keep the chill of out of his bones. His hands were gloved.

'I need to talk to you, as a caring and concerned member of your family.'

He always alluded to their family connections with relish, while Heinrich could feel his blood curl.

Rudolph had aged, was going bald, and the drinking and meat-eating showed in his rounded belly, but his deep, dark eyes, his strong cheekbones, his charming manner, were still there. He had cut a dashing figure in his youth, when a lonely young empress needed a shoulder to cry on.

By the end of the regency, he had secured the duchy of Swabia, and a Salian princess in marriage – although poor Tilda had died almost immediately, barely thirteen. Then he had negotiated himself a marriage to Berta's sister.

Heinrich repressed his disgust, steadying himself with Matilde's persuasion that his mother was innocent. Until his intelligence officers cracked his cyphered correspondence with Ildebrando, he had to play along. 'Speak.'

Rudolph's tone became conspiratorial. 'It pains me to tell you this, but you are in extreme danger, my lord. Your lack of a legitimate heir is causing... concern amongst the princes.'

Heinrich's face was bereft of any expression. 'Things are about to change.'

Rudolph lowered his voice to a whisper, his gloved hands over his knees. 'Unfortunately, the princes are aware that you are not visiting your wife.'

Heinrich was being played, and he knew it. The rumour, if there was one, would have been started by Berta's sister, rather than the princes.

Rudolph insisted. 'I fear the princes may decide to make their own plans for the empire's stability.'

His face was blank. 'You can reassure your noble friends. Is there anything else you want to discuss with me?'

'Nothing else, my lord.'

The moon was shining, the same moon that must be watching over Matilde in Quedlinburg right now.

The moment the duke was out of the door, Heinrich threw a goblet on the floor, then a couple of ancient Latin history codes from the Fulda library. The wine stained the precious parchment pages – a couple of years of hard work for a skilled copyist.

'Bitch!' he shouted. 'Little, stupid, insignificant bitch!'

He called on Cuno to bring him fresh wine, and then dismissed him. He drank in silence, alone. Then he pushed the goblet aside and headed for Berta's apartment.

§

Matilde had clearly impressed her taste on the royal apartment. Colourful Flemish tapestries covered the walls of the main chamber, and elegantly carved chairs had been placed by the hearth. Heinrich took his rain-soaked mantle off and placed it by the fire to dry. Vinicia offered him some warming wine laced with nutmeg and cloves.

'How is she?'

'She is struggling to sleep.'

'Is it normal?' He had never slept in the same room as Berta during her pregnancy, so he had no idea.

'It is at this stage; it is nothing to worry about, Your Majesty.'

A rustle of silk and wool announced Matilde's arrival. She was wearing a pale green gown with pointed sleeves. Vinicia had adapted it to her changing shape, so her state was not visible. They moved to a bench by the hearth.

'How is life here in Quedlinburg?'

'Adelheid has been wonderful. For the first time in years, it feels like I have a sister.' She was beaming, and her wrists were scented with sandalwood oil. 'My mother wrote to me.'

'What did she say?'

'She congratulates me and "the father." She asked me to visit her in Canossa, so she might see her grandchild.'

Heinrich's hand closed tightly around hers. 'Has she accepted me?'

She returned the squeeze. 'She has found the strength to make peace with the past somehow.'

'The mighty Beatrice is temporarily on my side? My mother must have worked some magic on her.'

'Your mother or your actions – those lands in Lotharingia mean a lot to her. Or your offer to help Theodoric...'

Her happiness made him feel even worse.

She sensed his unease. 'What is it?'

The rain outside filled the silence between them.

He lowered his gaze for a moment, readying himself to meet hers. 'I am sorry, Matilde. If you hate me, I understand. I had to do it.'

'Do what?'

'What I avoided doing for all these months.'

She reached for him, but he gently pushed her away. He stiffened. 'You may not believe me, but I had to get drunk before... seeing her.'

'Why now?' There was a quiver in her voice.

'Rudolph says the princes are conspiring against me, because I am making no progress on the dynastic front.'

'Heinrich—'

'Let me speak. I have never asked anybody for forgiveness since becoming king. But I am asking you now.'

'From what you say, you were cornered.' There was sadness, not anger in her eyes.

'It seemed the safest thing to do. Go once, so the gossip that I have restarted working on the succession spreads, and they all leave me alone for a while—'

'Heinrich, I forgive you.'

'I knew you would. But even that makes me feel unworthy. You do not deserve this.' He hesitated. 'It may sound out of place coming from me, but I was proud of being faithful to you.'

She smiled through her sadness. 'I am not angry with you, Heinrich.'

'Can I kiss you? I will understand if you say no.'

'You can kiss me, and you can make love to me, to undo the memories of last night.'

He brought the inside of her wrist to his lips and worked his way up her arm. 'I was too drunk. I do not have memories.'

When he woke up the next morning, one of her fingers was twirling his curls. He smiled to her. 'What are you thinking?'

'Nothing can break us. I will not let it happen to us.'

'I will not either.' He kissed her on the lips and between her breasts. 'I cannot stay. I was meant to be in Goslar, but I could not bear to be away from you after what happened.'

'When will you be back?'

'Tomorrow evening, if I can, or the day after.' He slipped his undergarments on.

'How are you feeling, physically? Vinicia says you are struggling to sleep.'

'I am, a bit.'

He traced her bump with his finger, eyeing her mischievously. 'Is my baby getting too big?'

'Maybe. Maybe I also miss you. I slept better last night with you here.'

'You are putting me under pressure to come back soon. King Heinrich does not like to be under pressure, you should know that by now...'

She stood on her toes to kiss him.

LXXI.

Adalbert sensed the king's dark mood the moment he entered his chamber.

'It is time Ildebrando pays for his decades of meddling in the crown's affairs.'

'I concur fully. But I suggest we hold off on any concrete plans until I have secured your divorce. The Abbot of Cluny has been surprisingly receptive to my approaches.'

Heinrich downed the contents of his goblet and wiped his mouth with the cuff of his sleeve. 'Really? Good. You are the one who taught me about divide and rule. We shall apply that to Rome. We will remain on the good side of my godfather, and we will court the pope. I need his support more than ever...'

Adalbert had to ask. 'Why more than ever?'

'Because I will divorce Berta and marry his protégée Matilde of Canossa, like my father wanted.'

Adalbert was stunned. In the silence, Heinrich filled and downed another cup of wine. His drinking was becoming a concern. A king could not afford clouded judgement.

'Now that would be an interesting development,' he said and raised the obvious hurdle. 'If only she was not married to one of your princes.'

Heinrich shrugged. 'This is why we need to secure the Holy Father's support.'

'Countess Matilde may be relieved to be rid of a husband she loathes. Your recent reallocation of her mother's dowry lands may help as well. But given the recent history... what makes you think the mighty Beatrice will accept the offer?'

Heinrich's tone was detached, his gaze assured. 'Things have gone too far for the margravine to oppose the marriage.'

'Despite the margravine's dislike of her stepson, I would not count on that.'

Heinrich fiddled with the base of his goblet and eyed Adalbert.

'Matilde is the highborn lady I was courting in the summer.'

'This summer just finished?'

The Salian smiled one of his undecipherable smiles. 'The child is mine.'

Adalbert had seen his fair share of scandal at court, but there were unspoken boundaries. In terms of impropriety, this one beat all the affairs he had heard of in a lifetime.

The woman pregnant with the king's bastard was the wife of a duke, and the closest thing Pope Alexander had to a daughter. Had he not been worried for his pupil, Adalbert would have laughed at the irony of it all.

Yet, looking beyond the scandal, the match retained all the undeniable positives of when he had first aired it at court, and more.

Beautiful Matilde was as highborn as her overlord, and the largest landowner in the empire. Heinrich had tested the lady's conceiving ability and was satisfied she could provide heirs to the crown. She was an experienced ruler, diplomat, and had even dabbled with the military. She would be perfectly equipped to take over the reins of the kingdom if her consort had to go to war.

It was the best marriage the Salian dynasty could make – and the most dangerous.

He started by highlighting the positives. 'A marriage to the beautiful lady of Canossa would give the crown a much-needed boost. It could even end the war with Saxony. The whole of Germany would submit in earnest.'

'I am glad we agree.' Heinrich's imperial cameo ring reverberated with the rusty light of the flames in the hearth. 'Beatrice will be forced to accept it, to shield her daughter from the scandal. We just need to convince Pope Alexander that this match is in the Church's interest.'

Adalbert shook his head. 'Ildebrando would rather push his superior off the Holy Seat with his bare hands than agree to this. And although Pope Alexander has pleasantly come into his own, Ildebrando remains the puppet master. He has made him pope; he can unmake him.'

'On what grounds would he depose Pope Alexander, when as you say he has not set a foot wrong?'

'Oh, he can come up with something. He probably has a list of potential replacements ready. There is always a submissive archbishop or abbot eager to sit on Saint Peter's throne.'

'I disagree with your reading this time, Adalbert. It would be an incredibly dangerous route for him to take. Cadalus has never officially given up his claim... Ildebrando would be opening Pandora's box.'

'He is the belligerent type.'

'Then we will give him a belligerent response. You said if I marched on Rome with the Holy Spear God would be at my side?'

He had been unwilling to use the spear to end a civil war but would use it to undo his divorce and marry the woman he loved. Adalbert had a duty to make the king appreciate the implications of such a course of action.

'Ildebrando may see that as his opportunity to cast himself as a martyr. Besides, do you trust your court to support your endeavour?'

'Obviously not Rudolph.'

'The prize is dazzling. It is the ultimate prize – but at the greatest risk.'

A flash of anger crossed the king's eyes. 'All my life has been a bloody compromise. I will not budge on this.'

Ermelinde, the love of his youth... Adalbert had budged – and had lived to regret it. Heinrich might be brave, crazy, in love, or all three, but he was trying to do what he thought was right. He deserved his help. 'We have to tread carefully. Where is the countess now?'

'She is Quedlinburg, with my sister. She gives birth in early February.'

'We do not have much time, my lord.'

'This is why I need to cast myself as Pope Alexander's prodigal son.'

LXXII.

'I have spent the night thinking about your predicament, my lord.'

Heinrich handed the sword back to his trainer and dismissed him. He took his leather jerkin off, slipped into a wool and silk tunic and joined Adalbert who was warming his extremities by the fire.

'Hugh of Cluny is somewhat receptive on the subject of your divorce. This gives me hope that Pier might be persuaded.'

'If Pier and Hugh support me, Ildebrando may struggle to exert his influence on the other cardinals. This may free the pope's hand.'

'I agree with you. But that does not solve the problem of the countess's married status.'

'The Holy Father has indicated a willingness to grant her a divorce.'

'I am relieved.' Adalbert fiddled with his seal. 'So, as long as your paternity remains unknown, both divorces are achievable. The real challenge will be negotiating your union. In my view, the only solution is to leave Rome with a fait accompli. I will marry you in secret the moment you are both free.'

Heinrich's eyes glinted with satisfaction. 'I knew I could count on you, Adalbert. But are you comfortable with the risk? When all the facts are known, Ildebrando will make sure you join us on the excommunication list for marrying two sinners.'

In truth, the prospect amused him. 'I do not have many years left to put up with his games – and I am not worried about my soul. However, we need to consider other risks.' He did not expect his suggestion to be received lightly. 'It may be advisable for you to delay legitimising the child.'

Heinrich's expression hardened. 'I will not have my son passed off as Godefroy's.'

Adalbert played with his episcopal ring. 'It may be a temporary price to pay, my lord. The child would still live with the countess, of course. Legitimisation could be timed to coincide with at a moment when Ildebrando's grip on the cardinals is weakened – or when he passes away.'

'What about the risks to succession? If this child is a boy and Matilde bears me other boys after I marry her, I may end up with two sons fighting over the crown.'

'Indeed. However, I recommend that we deal with problems in order of urgency. The countess's pregnancy is too scandalous... if you allow me to say so. Your role of head of the German Church will be questioned immediately, in many quarters.'

'I will confess to Abbot Hugh, and to the pope if I have to. All sinners are entitled to seek absolution.'

'Do not underestimate the alliance between Ildebrando and Duke Rudolph.'

'I will not.' He pointed to the food that had been laid on a trestle by the fire. 'We can instil fear in his superstitious soul. He thinks he has taken care of everything. Beatrice found the Holy Blood, but being a woman, cannot be the new Charlemagne; her only son is dead; her daughter was married with a clause of non-consummation.' He took a swig of the red in his goblet. 'Through marriage to Matilde I will own the Blood and the Spear.'

'Given the reach of his influence, he can ensure you are denied the imperial coronation.'

'Even if he denies me the imperial title, Matilde's pregnancy changes everything. My son by her fulfils the prophecy, and even Ildebrando's fine grasp of theology will not allow him to allege that an innocent child is tainted by his father's sins.'

'I am intrigued. You said you do not believe in the prophecy.'

There was a twinkle in the king's eye. 'This is not about believing; it is about exploiting it. The moment you marry us, I will legitimise my son and announce the birth of the new Charlemagne.'

Adalbert felt a pang of unease. 'Ildebrando will fight back. He could argue that the offspring of a double adultery is unsuited to rule over the Church – that he is more antichrist than Charlemagne. He will claim you are morally unfit to head the German Church. He will endorse Rudolph. We need to consider the princes.'

'I will beat Ildebrando at his game,' Heinrich replied as if he had not heard him. He flicked through the pages of a code of gospels in the Rheinland style, distractedly lingering over the image of Saint John's in a star-studded toga. 'Ildebrando will be defeated by his own fears of a prophecy which may never even have been uttered.'

Adalbert looked on, drawn to the elegance of the images and the richness of the blue background. 'He could turn that against you, my lord – challenge you to produce evidence.'

'If the papal chancery fabricated a donation of the city of Rome by Constantine, why can't my chancery forge a little piece of writing, provide him proof that his worst nightmare has come true?'

He swallowed, uneasy. 'I would feel more at ease if you marched on Rome with the Spear, like previous emperors.'

Heinrich laughed. 'I did not mean to scare you, Adalbert. Let us start from the beginning by exploring the option of securing an agreement on my divorce directly from the pope, without the cardinals, without a synod.'

Sweat dried on Adalbert's forehead. 'This is what Abbot Hugh has suggested. It would expose you to less manoeuvring.'

Heinrich closed the book. 'I like your plan. But we will need to raise the stakes, Adalbert – and soon.'

A.D. 1071

LXXIII.

Gudrun, the midwife, was a Saxon woman with long blonde hair streaked with grey. She had successfully delivered several children of the local nobility, and this was why Adelheid had sent for her.

A quick look at Matilde and she asked Heinrich to wait outside. 'I love you,' he whispered, letting go of her hand and kissing her forehead, acting as if he had not noticed her fear.

He sat on a coffer in the anteroom. He could not focus on the colourful tapestries covering the wall. The midwife came out almost immediately. He shared his worry. 'We thought she would give birth in two or three weeks. Why is she in labour now?'

Gudrun was aware she was speaking to a powerful man, although his identity had not been revealed to her. But she held his gaze. 'In general, it is not a good sign.'

Heinrich swallowed.

Her gaze stayed on him as the news sank in. 'Now, my lord, about the mother...'

'Yes?'

'It is going to be a difficult delivery. In these kinds of cases, I need guidance from the husband. Sometimes I have to choose between saving the baby or the mother.'

On that he had no doubts. 'Save the mother.'

'God bless you, my lord.'

Something that looked like gratitude softened her features. He had surprised her, clearly. Men of all classes chose the child, and he would have done exactly that with Berta. Women were child-bearing tools, and sometimes their fate was to perish in the process. But Matilde was more than that. He could not lose her.

From the open door, he could see Vinicia helping Matilde. 'Keep walking,' she was repeating in her ears. 'It will help the baby shift down.'

Her hair was glued to her head and when the next wave of

contractions shook her, she dropped to her knees in pain.

Gudrun's hand seized hers, reassuring. 'It will be painful, but you will make it out of here alive.'

'And the baby, will the baby make it?'

Gudrun met her gaze, her grip of Matilde's hand probably tightening. 'The baby is in the hands of God. You need to save your energy for the birth now.'

The last thing he saw before Vinicia closed the door was Gudrun grabbing her by the shoulders to stop her from falling.

§

The labour lasted a few hours. Heinrich, waiting outside, felt numb. Even when Pier Damiani had shattered his hopes of divorce, he had not felt so powerless.

The images on the tapestries had become dark and hazy, and from that he knew that night was setting in. He lit some candles and slumped back on the coffer, hunched against the wall.

Vinicia came to sit next to him. 'Cry with me now, Your Majesty. When you go in to see her, you will have to be strong. We will all have to be strong.'

'Thank you,' were the first words that crossed his mind.

She mustered a smile out of her sadness, opened her arms and invited him to place his head on her shoulder. He could not cry. Vinicia's chest was heaving with her sobs. Then, finding some strength deep within her, she wiped her eyes and left to assist Gudrun.

When Heinrich was called in, the midwife met him by the door. 'The herbs I have given her will make her sleep. She has lost a lot of blood. She needs rest.' No mention of the baby.

From the bed where she was lying, Matilde saw him enter. 'I'm sorry I failed you,' she muttered. Her face was ashen.

He took his imperial cameo ring off and placed it on her middle finger. 'You cannot fail me.' He stroked her hair. 'Now you will sleep, and I will hold you.'

He looked around the room and she noticed it. 'Do you want to see... our daughter?'

He squeezed her hand. 'Sure. What shall we call her? She is our first child. She needs to have a name.'

Between sobs, she said. 'Could we... call her Beatrice?'

'Of course.'

Gudrun was standing in a dark corner of the room. Next to her was a little bundle covered by a blanket. He lifted it and looked rapidly at the baby. He wished he had the strength to kiss her tiny fingers and her forehead.

'She is beautiful, Matilde. We will remember her beauty.' His voice was shaking.

Matilde was crying quietly.

He tried to think of something to say to ease her pain. 'Adelheid will call a priest, and tomorrow morning we will have a funeral for her, my love. We will put her to rest here in Quedlinburg, so Adelheid can take flowers to her grave and pray for her – until the time is right to move her to Speyer. There, Conrad will watch over her.'

Vinicia, against the opposite wall, was nodding encouragingly.

He kissed Matilde's hand. 'Both your mother and mine had losses like this. We will get through this. As soon as you are recovered, we will try for another baby.'

The midwife whispered to him. 'The herbs are starting to work; she is about to fall asleep.'

Matilde's breathing became more regular, and he hoped she would find some peace in her slumber. 'Can you both wait outside?'

Vinicia and Gudrun left. He checked that Matilde was still asleep. Then he turned to the wall and dropped to his knees. He wished he could scream his anger and his fear, like he had done that afternoon in Kaiserwerth. Instead, all he could do was cry.

LXXIV.

Beatrice of Canossa was warming her hands by a brazier, under the watchful eye of the Queen of Sheba in her unfinished tapestry, when Ildebrando di Soana was admitted to her study.

'This visit reminds me of another.'

'We have met in Canossa many times.'

She poured the monk a small goblet of white wine, and one for herself. She was mildly shaking but determined not to let him see her fear. This time, she was not going to fail her daughter.

'I am referring to that winter day when you came and convinced me to re-marry. Please, have a seat.'

Seats were ready for them by a well-stocked fire.

'Your marriage to the duke had its drawbacks, but it was a good idea. It saved your life and your daughter's.'

She let herself sink into her chair, as smoothly as her illness allowed.

Although her pregnancy had ended in tragedy, Ildebrando was probably itching to bring up Matilde's sins. She had to tread carefully. 'You and I could not predict that one day young Godefroy would go against his father's will,' she said.

He studied her in hostile silence.

She pressed on. 'Just like we could not imagine him becoming a threat to the Holy Blood. Yet he has.' She joined her hands in her lap. 'You must get the same reports as me from Theodoric – that Godefroy continues to hover around Orval with armed men.'

The silence stretched. Through half-closed eyes, Ildebrando seemed to be weighing her motives.

She did not let it deter her. 'These relics cannot fall into the hands of the Salian, the son of the man who exterminated my family.' She paused for effect. 'But neither should they fall into the hands of anyone else who may misuse them for personal and political advancement.'

'I cannot disagree.'

'Ildebrando.' She called his name gently, in a reassuring display of female submissiveness. 'There are many sinners in this story, and I certainly cannot cast the first stone. But I need to humbly say this: by violating his marriage contract and the will of his father, Godefroy has violated the will of the Holy Roman Church.'

More silence.

'The idea of passing these relics on to his own flesh and blood stokes his lust. We cannot allow such a weak man near the relics. I am no theologian, but weakness is a door to sin.'

He rose from his chair, as if surprised by her conclusion. He warmed his hands over the flames for a while. 'What do you propose?'

'I believe that the Holy Blood can only be safe here, in my care, away from Lotharingia and away from Germany. Theodoric shares my view.'

Ildebrando paced the room. 'The latest developments make it imperative for us to look at the future of the relics.' He nodded, as if to himself. 'I will order Godefroy to surrender the relics to you. He will not disobey me.'

'May God reward you for looking after our Saviour's blood.' She kissed his ring.

Her flattery did not work. 'I hear your daughter is coming to Italy.'

'She is taking up the Holy Father's offer of spiritual guidance.'

'It is a grave mistake,' he commented sternly.

'I pray that, through the Holy Father's wisdom, God will enlighten her soul,' she said diplomatically.

'So do I.'

She needed to steer the conversation away from Matilde and her sins. 'I would welcome your guidance in a different but equally important matter – the rule to be adopted by our monastery of Sant'Apollinare, here in Canossa.'

'Of course, I have strong views on the subject.'

Thank God for that.

LXXV.

'Red suits you, you remind me of roses in May.' Heinrich pointed to her wool gown. 'Even the deepest sorrow cannot tarnish your beauty.' He grasped her ruby necklace between his fingers. 'Good that you are wearing my gift.'

'It is a way to be with you when you are not around.'

He kissed her. 'You still have time to change your mind. You do not have to rush back just because the pope says so.'

She buried her face in his chest. 'Heinrich, please do not make it harder than it is. I am doing this for us.'

'Are you?' For a moment he sounded accusatory. 'Securing your divorce is crucial. But you could stay here a bit longer and try for another baby first.'

'Then you would say I have to stay until the birth.' As had already happened.

'What is so wrong about wanting the woman I love close to me?'

She kept him focused on the goal. 'This is a sacrifice we are making for a future together. Unless you have changed your mind about that—'

He silenced her with another kiss. 'You are the redeeming grace of my life.'

She swallowed to bottle up her tears, touched by his sudden intensity. 'And you of mine.'

'Come.' He took hold of her hand and started leading her towards the stables. He pushed the doors open and pointed in the direction of a white stallion. 'He is fast and strong. He has served me well against Otto. You can use it for war against me, if you wish, and he will not disappoint you.'

Weiss was his favourite mount, the one he trusted on the battlefield. She stroked his mane, and the animal seemed to recognise her and relaxed. 'Heinrich—'

'If I cannot be with you, at least my Weiss will.'

'He and Lampo will become friends.'

They walked back to the courtyard. 'When will you get your dowry back from Godefroy?'

'I do not know nor care. I will discuss it with my mother and the pope. He can request it on my behalf when the time is right.'

'You should care. Your mother never took up my offer to escort the relics to her. But she should demand them back from Godefroy.'

'You are insistent,' she teased him. 'Maybe she has already asked.'

He squeezed her in his arms. 'There is something we have to do before leaving.'

She followed him to the wooden cross under the fig tree in the abbey cemetery. The snow had hardened, as if it wanted to shield her baby from the sadness of the world. She cried for her little girl until she ran out of tears, leaning against the majestic tree.

He stood behind her, holding her shoulders through it. 'We are stronger than this, Matilde. Fate will not beat us,' he whispered.

They walked back, holding each other's hand. The afternoon was giving way to a stormy evening.

He wrapped her in his mantle to shelter her from the icy wind. 'I am sorry I have not come at all these last few weeks.'

She was not going to pretend it had not hurt her. 'What happened?'

'Otto, as usual. There were a lot of little skirmishes, and the negotiations—'

'I understand.' He was a man and a king; he had not been present when Berta had delivered their daughter, so she should count herself blessed. Of course, he had no idea of what pain a woman went through with a stillbirth. Thank God for Vinicia or she would have died of sorrow.

'I was hoping to finish him off, but it did not work out.'

She feared to ask the next question. 'So what will you do next?'

Heinrich's jaw tensed. 'I am no longer the boy he kidnapped in Kaiserwerth. Your cousin Welf is trying to help us to a truce. We shall see.' At lease he was not offering false hopes. 'Our love has to be stronger than this war, Matilde.'

His words did not dispel her worry. 'If Godefroy returns those relics to my mother, I will ask her to send them to you. They may help you win the war faster.'

His smile was bittersweet. 'Your mother will never accept, and it is fine. I will prove my worth to you. I will win the war with my own means.'

'I know your worth already.'

His kiss was intense. 'I hope you'll still feel the same way after... a few months apart,' he said, holding her waist between his hands. 'I wanted to take you as far as Tirol. Because of this war, I cannot. But at least thanks to Welf I have an excuse to ride with you to Augsburg.'

'You are riding with me to Augsburg?' Her heart filled with something akin to joy.

'I want to make the most of the time we have.'

They made it back indoors, and he helped her take her cloak off. The moment she stepped into the bedroom, he drew her to him and nuzzled her ear. 'I believe forty days have passed.'

Suddenly, he sounded like he had moved on, and put Beatrice's death behind him. Hurtful as the thought was, she pushed the tears back and gave in to his kisses. He was right. It might be their last chance to be together in months. He lifted her in his arms and onto the bed. 'I am hungry for you.'

He started undoing the laces of her gown, but soon lost patience. He got hold of her underdress, lifted it, swiftly lowered his hose, and found his way inside her. He paused for a moment, kissed her tenderly, his hands exploring her breasts and the soft curve of her hip, as if he had longed for her skin in those weeks apart.

She could sense love in the urgency of his need, although she wished he would give her a little more tenderness.

'You will cross the Alps with a part of me,' he whispered. 'We will make things right.'

LXXVI.

Carpineti, 5 April 1071

Beatrice's wrinkles were deeper, and the last streaks of blonde had gone from her hair. She seemed to no longer bother with dye. Pulling away from the tapestry she was working on, she motioned for Matilde to come in and put her arms around her.

It was too soon for words. They sat down in chairs in the embrasure, soaking in the golden late afternoon light, close but distant, like animals studying each other.

Beatrice's hands were almost ethereal, fingers interlaced on the blue fabric of her gown. 'I am building an abbey for her, in Frassinoro.' Her voice had a hint of restrained warmth.

Matilde nodded, unable to speak for a moment.

Her mother's right hand squeezed hers. 'The foundations are almost complete. The site is so beautiful, like a terrace overlooking the city of Modena.'

'Let us go tomorrow.'

'Do not run away from the pain, Matilde. Stillbirths are common, but the first is the hardest. Tell me about her if you can.'

She summoned her strength. Every word uttered made the loss more real. 'Heinrich asked Adelheid to have her buried under a fig tree.' The tears swelled inside her like a river. 'He said the only fitting place for her was the Garden of Eden.' She swallowed. 'At least Adelheid will pray for her every day.'

Beatrice drew her into her arms. 'This turn of events may be God's way of saving you and Heinrich from political ruin, but there is no joy in the death of a baby.'

Matilde's tears became sobs. Hearing Heinrich's name spoken while she was so far from him hurt more than she had imagined.

Either incognito or officially, he had promised he would make plans to see her as soon as he was done with Otto. Realistically it might be months, and although she did not regret coming to Italy, the separation made the loss of her baby cut deeper.

During their travel to Augsburg, he had made love to her every night. Another pregnancy would just put them in more danger with Rome, but she had never stopped him.

The part of her that felt guilty about losing their daughter was desperate for a fresh start. Perhaps he felt the same, or perhaps it had been his way of making sure she would not go off with someone else.

She had discovered he was jealous. He had quarrelled with one bodyguard he had assigned to her escort because, in his opinion, he had eyed her with too much interest.

She had also become jealous. During the last stages of the pregnancy, she had felt strong and powerful, his love and his queen in all but name, carrying his heir.

Now her womb was scarred and barren, and the day they would be reunited was in the hands of God. When she had arrived in Verona, her period had started, and it had been like parting from him again.

Her mother's fingers running through her tresses brought her back to the present. 'There is something you need to know.' Beatrice leaned back against her chair. 'You were in the advanced stages of pregnancy and Agnes and I did not want to put you in more distress.'

Matilde glanced towards her mother.

'Ildebrando found out, somehow.'

'Found out what?'

'That Heinrich was the father.'

'Why were we not excommunicated?'

'He tried to excommunicate Heinrich. Thankfully, Pope Alexander refused.'

'What about me?'

'Well, given the pope said no to excommunicating Heinrich, he knew it would be pointless.' She reached for her walking stick, propping herself on it to rise. 'There is more. Agnes did some good work. She persuaded the Holy Father, Hugh, and Pier that you falling for each other was a sign from God. They agreed that your love should be tested and if not found wanting—'

'Were we so close to being granted our wish?'

Beatrice rested her back against the tapestry-covered wall, her skin even paler against the bright reds, golds, and greens of the threads.

'There was, there still is, agreement in principle on the divorces. A marriage will take significantly longer to negotiate. The pope and Pier see the benefits of the union for your and Heinrich's souls, but Ildebrando is doing his best to persuade them that the political negatives outweigh the spiritual positives.'

'Would Charlemagne's prophecy be one of the negatives?'

'Of course.'

Matilde joined her by the wall. 'Ildebrando seems such a strong man. Yet his actions are ruled by a someone's claim about Charlemagne uttering a prophecy... With no proof whatsoever!'

Beatrice said nothing.

'Is there anything we can do to persuade him to agree to... the marriage?' Matilde blushed as she asked. 'Perhaps through your ownership of the Holy Blood relics, you could exert some pressure?'

Her mother stiffened and looked away – she had not forgiven Heinrich, that much was clear. The silence filled with guilt and her mind with the image of Federico's cross on the road to Lucca. Her sins felt heavier on her heart.

'I am sorry for the pain my actions caused.'

'It is good to have you back...' Her mother smiled with wet eyes. 'When you were in Germany, I sent a message through Agnes, that you should come and meet me.'

Another apology was in order. 'I am sorry I let you down. Heinrich was too worried the journey may put the baby at risk.'

'I understand his point of view, as a lover and as a dynast.' Beatrice's hands closed on the pommel of the stick. 'With hindsight, it is probably better that you did not come. He may have held the loss against you. In these things the woman always picks up the blame.'

'What did you want to tell me?'

There was a knock at the door.

'My dear Matilde, I thank God you made it home safely,' Agnes said.

She seemed to be overcome by some emotion. She exchanged glances with Beatrice, who seemed confused as to what she meant. Eventually, slowly, she handed a scroll to Matilde. 'I have a letter for you, from my son.'

LXXVII.

Carpineti, 6 April 1071

Matilde entered her mother's chamber and slumped into a chair. The spring light was a painful reminder that she was alive, that she had to live through this. All night she had tried to bury Heinrich's letter in some deep recess of her mind. He had never kept from her that he had been cornered to visit Berta's bed, but had never brought the subject back afterwards.

Yet, considering the time it took for letters between Germany and Italy, and that his letter had travelled to his mother in Rome before being delivered to her, it was clear he had known about Berta's pregnancy while he was riding with Matilde to Augsburg. How could he keep it from her?

Beatrice placed a kiss on her cheek. 'It has been an awful blow. But time will not stand still.' Her voice was warm. She pushed a chair across the room to sit opposite her daughter. 'Things could still work out, even if it seems impossible right now.'

Matilde's jaw contracted. Sure, the child could be another girl for Berta, and even make it easier for him to build a case for repudiation. Or may not survive – although after what she had suffered, she could not bring herself to wish that for Berta.

That things could still work out was not the point. The point was that Heinrich had betrayed her trust, intentionally, and for days, maybe weeks. She was not just sad; she was angry. Wounded pride rescued her from the rawness of her pain. 'I cannot afford hope, Mamma.'

'Let me give you some hope.'

Matilde stared at her blankly.

Beatrice took a key from her gown's inner pocket. 'This opens something very precious. There are only two copies.' She placed it in her palm. 'One is now yours.'

Matilde studied the small metal object between her fingers.

Her mother pointed to the wooden statue of Saint Michael on the trestle. 'It is time you know why this sculpture follows me everywhere.'

Matilde crossed the room. She had always known there was a secret drawer at the bottom of the statue, full of mementoes of Beatrice's father. She inserted the key in the lock. It clicked.

She rummaged through the objects inside, until her finger met a warm greasy shape – vellum, folded. Two pieces, joined. 'These are not your father's, are they?'

Beatrice had risen from her chair and joined her. 'These,' she said, her index finger touching the rich texture of the parchment, 'belonged to Charlemagne.'

For a second, Matilde stopped breathing. She spread the vellum, her fingers shaking as she began to read. Charlemagne's words, framing Longinus's.

The elegant Caroline script that prefigured her future was strangely comforting, and so was the finality of the seal. Charlemagne's blood ran purest in her veins, her mother had always said. She remembered a tomb in Aachen, a marble urn sculpted with the tale of a woman. It was all making sense now.

But how had these texts ended up in Saint Michael's statue in Canossa?

'Conrad,' said Beatrice, as if reading her mind.

'He chose you... over his son?'

'He saw through him, in his final years.' Her voice trembled with pride. 'He could not give me the empire, so he made me its custodian.'

Matilde folded the vellum, thinking of her prayers to Conrad, not long ago, in Speyer. She had certainty now that he would have blessed her union with Heinrich. But even he could not save his grandson from himself.

The strip of parchment felt heavier, thicker, in her hand. She handed it to her mother. 'Just yesterday I was saying that, without a text, the prophecy has no foundation.'

The light in her mother's eyes was something she had not seen in a long time. 'These small pieces of sheepskin change everything.' She caressed the folded vellum. 'They make everything fall into place, the blood of Charlemagne and the Holy Blood. They are the keystone.'

It was almost too much to take in. Yet she needed to piece the mosaic together now. 'Who knows about this?'

'Conrad's instructions were clear. I could share the "legend", the rumour, with your father if I so wished, like he had done with his son, and with Rome. The text, however, had to remain secret. He warned me against the darkness in the souls of warriors.'

'What about Federico?'

Her mother's voice grew hoarse, and she placed the parchment on the trestle, as if it had suddenly become irrelevant. 'I was waiting for him to come of age and marry,' her chin wobbled, 'to tell him he could be the father of the child of the prophecy.'

'Did you ever—'

'You will be its next guardian. So, yes, I meant to tell you sooner.' She drew a sigh. 'My faith in the relic was shaken when Federico was taken.' Her hand reached for the stick, for support. 'The events of last summer taught me that the prophecy had other ways of fulfilling itself. They proved that it was time for you to know.'

'I see.' At least she had not deliberately excluded her from the knowledge. But in all likelihood her mother's first choice of confidante had been someone else. 'Agnes knows, does she not?'

'Only since last summer.'

Matilde dreaded to ask the next question. 'Did she tell Heinrich?' She could not bear the idea of him knowing before her – and keeping it from her... If he had been capable of concealing Berta's pregnancy from her, why not this? A knot formed in her gut. All his plots to secure the Holy Blood were suddenly bathed in a sinister light.

Her mother placed her hand on her cheek. 'Of course not! We know he is not ready.'

'Good. Keep it that way, please, until he proves he is a man.'

Beatrice placed her stick against the wall and hugged her. 'I will not tell him, and Agnes will not either. It will be your responsibility, one day, if you feel it is the right thing to do.'

Matilde shook her head vigorously, resisting the urge to cry. 'That day will never come.'

Her mother's weakened body exuded strength now, the strength of pride and purpose. Her eyes, even her skin glowed.

'It will be no consolation to you now, but hopefully one day it will be. He has the Holy Spear. Yet, the purest blood of Charlemagne runs through your veins. You are heir to the Holy

Blood relics, and to the text of the prophecy. With this text, *you*, a woman, can become the most powerful leader in Christendom, more powerful than Heinrich, if so you wish.'

'You were in the same situation, Mamma. But you were always at the mercy of men.'

'I should have been braver – trusted myself more.' There was a tear in her mother's eyes. 'I cannot undo what I have done to you, but I can teach you what I have learnt.'

LXXVIII.

Aachen, 15 May 1071

Heinrich was in bed with a palace maid when Cuno announced the empress. The chamberlain helped the girl collect her clothes before showing her the door, with a dry: 'You know the way.'

Then he scattered some lavender flowers in the fire to scent the room, poured Heinrich fresh water from a jug and handed him his undergarments. He slipped them on, dragged himself to his washing table, rinsed his face in the bowl of scented water, and donned his silken tunic. He gestured to let his mother in.

'I came as soon as the Alpine passes were practicable,' she said.

He formally kissed her hand to conceal his wine breath.

'Pope Alexander feels for you,' she was saying.

'No-one in Rome feels for me.' His head was hurting.

She insisted. 'If Berta's child turns out to be another girl, you will have the beginning of a repudiation case... The nobility will start grumbling – just like they did before I had you.'

'Rudolph will stand by his wife's sister, surely.'

'The majority will back you. That is all that matters.'

'What about your Roman friends?'

'If the princes shift, Pier says the Church will follow, whatever Ildebrando may say.'

Heinrich burst into bitter laughter. 'I very much doubt it.'

She tried to comfort him. 'We need to put our trust in Pope Alexander and Pier.'

'Too many "ifs", Mother.' He spread the shutters open. The sun was reaching midday on the sundial in the courtyard. 'I need to see Adalbert. You are welcome to dine with me on my return.'

She glared. 'Can it not wait until tomorrow? I have travelled three weeks to see you.'

He snapped. 'Your protégé is plotting to take my kingdom from me, and Adalbert is trying to stop him.'

'I thought Otto was your enemy.'

'Let us say I was forced to make choices. Otto has become the scapegoat because I cannot touch your Rudolph.'

She did not to take his bait. 'Why can you not touch Rudolph?'

'You live in Rome, Mother. You must know he has slipped into old Gottfried's shoes. He is Ildebrando's new best friend.'

She considered his words. 'They see eye to eye on the election of bishops.'

He laughed bitterly. 'You can defend him as much as you like. It will not change the facts. Rudolph sees eye to eye with all my enemies.'

He did not sway her. 'He writes to me regularly.'

'I am sure he does.'

Her features tensed this time. 'He always acts like he is on your side—'

'You said it, Mother, he *acts*. Adalbert brought me proof that he is conspiring with Ildebrando against me.'

'It cannot be! He owes me his duchy.'

Heinrich sneered. 'Well, gratitude is not his forte. He owes you his duchy, he buried your daughter within a year, and no questions were asked. But I am putting the pieces together. Adalbert thinks they have joined forces with Otto too. We just need conclusive evidence.' He bit his lip. 'And I hope Adalbert lives long enough. He is ill.'

His mother gaped and made the sign of the cross. 'He made no mention of his health in his letters. Please tell him that he is in my prayers.' Her defences suddenly crumbled. 'I will always be grateful for the way he took care of you when I could not.'

§

As he had promised, he came back for dinner. Talking to Adalbert had calmed him, and he was determined to stop taking his anger out on his mother. She had come to help, after all. He waited in silence for Cuno to finish carving their pork and pour them wine before leaving them alone.

She joined her hands.

'You can say your prayers, if you wish,' he said, as he waited to

- 273 -

tuck into his food.

She said her grace, shock all over her face. He could guess what she was thinking. What would Ildebrando do with the information that the head of the German Church had lost faith in God's goodness?

He passed her some bread and asked casually, 'How is she, Mother?'

She lowered her gaze for a moment, as if preparing her answer. 'The timing could not have been worse. She is hurting. But she is a fighter.'

'I should have told her before she left. But she had just lost our baby, and I kept hoping Berta would miscarry.'

Agnes listened in silence.

'I wrote that letter you delivered to her the moment we parted. I wanted her to have it from me.'

'You have done right, my son.'

Heinrich clenched his jaw. 'She knew Rudolph had cornered me into visiting Berta – she said she had forgiven me for that.'

'I am sure she did.'

He stared into his goblet. 'It has been two months. She has yet to reply.'

'The distance makes it awfully hard—'

'I said exactly that to her. I assured her that nothing has changed in my heart. But all I got was silence.'

She put her hand over his arm to comfort him. 'Sometimes love hurts, and when it does, silence becomes your shield.'

'Will you visit her on the way back?'

'Of course. I will be their guest, as usual.'

'Please tell her I am sorry.'

'Being a woman, I can see why she feels so hurt.' Her voice was soft, concerned. 'Being your mother, I know you meant well. I will do what I can.'

LXXIX.

For the first time in her life, Matilde was not looking forward to seeing Pope Alexander. Since returning to Italy, she had postponed the visit twice.

Her former spiritual guide was perfectly entitled to voice his disappointment in her actions, of course. Being shamed for her sins would have been bearable, had it been a means to an end. She could not bring herself to face him because she felt betrayed, humiliated. Even the pope had known of Berta's pregnancy before her.

'Our love has to be stronger... it will be tested,' Heinrich had said when they had parted in Augsburg. Empty words. His feelings for her had not even been strong enough to know that she deserved the truth, and that she could take it.

Instead of seeing that the roots of love were in truth, when she was at her lowest, when she had needed him most, he had hidden behind lies and excuses.

Would her pain make her sins a little lighter in the eyes of the Holy Father? Or was he going to condemn her for her stupidity? She did not know.

Perhaps she deserved to pay. God had punished her for her adultery, by denying her a living child. Now He was punishing her for blindly trusting Heinrich, by showing her how ill-placed that trust had been.

She could not afford to imagine a future with Heinrich because it all depended on the outcome of Berta's pregnancy. But even if the queen delivered a girl and Heinrich secured repudiation, could they ever be together the way they had been? Or would the wounds of his dishonesty deface the beauty of their relationship?

Memories of Heinrich making love to her on the way to Augsburg, his fingertips running along her skin, his voice in her ears, his body inside hers, it all filled her mind. Why had he been so determined to get her with child, when he surely already knew about Berta?

Had it been his way to hang on to hope against all odds? To have her pregnant at almost the same time as Berta, so if God chose to bless Matilde but not Berta with a son he could revert to their initial plan with no delay? Or had it been his way to avoid the need to tell her truth, filling their time together with sex rather than words?

Thoughts for another day. The pope would be more interested in understanding what had driven her to sin, and to betray his trust in her.

To gather her wits, she studied the mosaic floor, in which pagan imagery mixed with angels and saints' faces. Amongst the dozens of figures on the floor, the eye of a pale mythical bird with a halo around her head stared into hers, a phoenix.

Perhaps it was a sign – she owed it to herself and her lineage to rise from the ashes. But the phoenix had a light to fly toward, and she had none in her life.

The noise of creaky hinges announced that it was her turn. Guido let her in, closed the door gently behind them and left, almost on tiptoe.

Kissing the ring, dropping to her knees, she mustered all the dignity she had left. 'Forgive me, Father, I am a sinner.'

He seized her hand. 'We all are.' His tone was firm but warm.

She glanced upwards. Her mother was concerned that his health may be failing, but at first sight his face had not changed much. The eyebrows were whiter and bushier perhaps, and the wrinkles around his eyes had dug deeper into his skin. His vigour, as he gestured for her to rise, seemed unchanged.

'I have not summoned you to Confession, my daughter, although you may confess, if you wish.'

'I wish so,' she blushed. 'It will not undo my sin, but I hope it will help you understand why I sinned.'

'Good, help me understand.' They were standing, as if matters needed to be cleared before she could be invited to sit down and fully welcomed – still, his gaze was open. 'From the letters you wrote, I gather you must have felt very lonely and scared in Lotharingia.'

The images of that night of terror crowded her mind: her

defencelessness, her sword used against her, the cruel laughter in her ears. 'Godefroy would have killed me unless I gave in. Perhaps even if I gave in, after I had given him an heir.'

'Is it why you went to the king?'

'My plan was to put myself under the protection of the Bishop of Augsburg. But I met the king on the way.' She wished the veil would cover her cheeks, as her blushing was so intense. 'He gave me shelter and support.'

The memories of those beautiful early days with Heinrich, after the horror, brought tears to her eyes.

He pretended not to notice. 'His offer of help, in itself, was noble.'

'He risked a lot to protect me.'

'Did he say he loved you?'

'Yes.'

'Did you love him?'

She nodded. 'I am ready to do penance for my gullibility – for trusting his words. I cannot make honest penance for my actions with the king – or my feelings for him.'

'I will not ask you to.'

'Why not?' She could not believe her ears.

He winced. 'As your confessor, I sense that you gave yourself to this young man in search of some purity after your ordeal.'

It was true, but she would not lay an unworthy claim to innocence. 'As my confessor, I admit to you that I did not surrender to the king's approaches merely to forget what I suffered.'

'What drove you to it then?'

'The belief that he loved me, and my feelings for him.'

His lips relaxed into a half smile. He clearly appreciated her honesty. 'What do you think drove him to you?'

'I have asked myself that question many times. He had a... reputation, but I hoped he loved me. I am not so sure anymore.' Perhaps her mother was right that the loss of her baby was making her see everything in a negative light. 'If he had loved me, he would have been man enough not to withhold the truth from me.'

'Perhaps he was afraid of losing you.' He reached for her hand and squeezed it. 'The empress swears he was ready to move heaven and earth to marry you.'

'With all due respect, Holy Father, the empress lives in Rome and her guess is as good as ours.'

Pope Alexander weighed his reply. 'Your loss has punished you enough. You are absolved of your sins. Please do make peace with the past.'

'It is harder than I thought. He has wounded our love, our trust. Now he is trapped in his marriage... If only I had my daughter...' The tears in her mouth, the contrast between the salt of the sea when she had dreamt of freedom on the Tyrrhenian Sea and the salt of her pain as she longed for her baby, and a love and trust that may only have been an illusion. She burst into sobs.

He held her in his arms, let her weep on his golden cross. 'Wounds take time to heal. Heed my words: God will show you a future when you make peace with the past.'

'I have lost the man I love, and I am married to the man who abused me. How can there be peace in my heart?'

'I will help you divorce. We just need to negotiate a few hurdles.' He raised his hand to bless her.

LXXX.

Beatrice's face remained a mask as Duke Godefroy kissed her hand in the throne hall. 'To what do I owe your presence?'

He grimaced. 'You do not sound too thrilled to see your son-in-law.'

After what he had done to Matilde, she despised him too much to indulge in pleasantries. Besides, she had the measure of his little games. 'I reserve my judgement until I am clear on the purpose of your visit.'

'You signed a contract with my father. I am here to reclaim what is mine.'

She raised her chin. 'My daughter is not here.' He had been stupid enough to cross the Alps with a small army, and Beatrice, alerted of his arrival, had dispatched Matilde off to Lucca.

'I will find her wherever she is.' He grinned. 'I always get what is mine, eventually.'

Beatrice felt like spitting in his face. 'Then why are you wasting your time with me?'

'Because I hope you can be reasonable.'

'I am reasonable.'

'Good.' He edged closer. 'You played quite a horrible game last year, with your friend Theodoric.'

She replied in turn. 'If you refer to Orval, it was not a game. Both Theodoric and I are accountable to Ildebrando di Soana and the Holy Father.'

'Is your daughter accountable to Ildebrando di Soana for her behaviour?'

'Why should she be?'

'Because she is a whore.'

She did not flinch. Her voice hardened. 'A man who rapes his wife cannot cast the first stone.'

'A man has a right to his wife's body.' His lips twisted into a nasty smile.

Beatrice felt ready to strangle him. 'Not if that is explicitly excluded from their marriage contract.'

She could tell he did not feel the slightest guilt. 'You will make sure my wife comes back to me.'

'It is not for me to decide.'

He laughed, too loudly. Then, even at the cost of his personal humiliation, he dealt Beatrice what he clearly expected to be a lethal blow. 'You may not know this, but your perfect daughter shunned her honest marriage bed to get knocked up by her boy king.'

Beatrice breathed deeply to control her nerves.

'What would Ildebrando do if he knew? He would denounce her to the pope and the pope would have to act, no matter how much he owes you. Would you like to see your daughter excommunicated – lose everything you have worked for all your life; your castles, your relics?'

Beatrice sat down and eyed him coldly. 'I was right not to trust you, Godefroy.'

'What do you mean?'

'I have taken precautions against your dishonesty.'

'Such as?'

Her gaze shifted to the tapestry of the Queen of Sheba in the opposite corner of the room.

'Do you want the Orval relics, or do you want Matilde?'

The laughter, again. 'The relics and Matilde both belong to me. Read the contract you signed.'

'You have broken that contract, Godefroy.'

He placed his hands on his belt and puffed his chest out. 'Ildebrando will back me once he knows what your daughter did.'

She challenged him again. 'He already knows you tried to snatch the relics from Orval. Do you really think he will be more concerned about you keeping your wife than about the Holy Blood's safety? Right now, the contract is an obstacle in his path.'

He bared his teeth. 'I am riding to Rome to tell him what she did.'

'Ildebrando knows everything that goes on in Christendom, Godefroy. Spare yourself the time and the humiliation.'

He whitened, with shock, presumably. She nodded to the guards at the door. 'I am finished.'

They opened the door and escorted the duke out.

Beatrice slumped onto the cushions on the throne, grateful to be alone. She felt physically sick. Her hands clung to the lionheads carved on the arms of the chair, and she whispered prayers to cleanse herself of the cruelty and twistedness of her stepson.

She would do whatever was needed to keep Matilde away from him for as long as she lived, and even that would not atone for allowing the marriage to go ahead in the first place.

§

It was chilly in the library, even at the height of summer, and Beatrice wrapped her shawl around her chest. Agnes did the same. She had stopped on her way back from Germany.

Brother Aesculapius was standing by a table flooded with afternoon light. A large sheet of vellum was spread in front of him, held in place by four stones. Pots of various colours were aligned to the right of the parchment: green from malachite, white from chalk, blue from the indigo plant, cochineal, and rust reds, sepia black, and his precious saffron yellow.

Giovanni, their most skilled copyist, brush in hand, was putting the finishing touches to one of the wall towers of Temple Mount.

'After Brother Aesculapius finished with your scroll, I asked him to resume a job I had left unfinished after Bonifacio's death.'

'What job?'

'Going through all the descriptions of Jerusalem we could find, in Greek and Hebrew texts scattered across Christendom, and make a copy of them for the Canossa library.'

'I am glad the translation inspired you to do so,' said Agnes.

'Brother Aesculapius suggested that the descriptions could be turned into a map, which should be combined with yours. So, if one of us ever manages to go to Jerusalem, we will have all the information possible at our fingertips.'

Beaming, the librarian pointed to young Giovanni's work. 'It is coming together,' he said. His fingers and nails were stained with goldleaf.

'It is a precious piece of work,' acknowledged Agnes, 'and beautiful.'

Beatrice mustered a smile. 'This research is the most rewarding part of my life at the moment.' Her fingers stroked the wooden cover of a volume from Iona Bonifacio had purchased for her so long ago. 'It brings back precious memories of happier days.'

Bonifacio used to dream of leading an army to Jerusalem and laying it at her feet. He had started planning a crossing, and building a fleet in Pomposa, the abbey by the Adriatic Sea where their confessor Guido was teaching angels to sing.

'Where is Matilde?' the empress asked.

'In Lucca and still hurting. At least Bishop Anselmo will offer her some spiritual comfort.'

'A stillbirth is tough to recover from,' said Agnes. 'It being her first pregnancy makes it worse.'

Beatrice decided to open her heart to her friend. 'I have often heard of women troubled to the point of illness after a birth, even a successful one. I think in addition to grieving for her loss, she may suffer from that. She is in a dark cloud, and the cloud is devouring her.'

Agnes pondered her words. 'The circumstances of this stillbirth are also quite... exceptional. Being apart from Heinrich, and the blow of Berta's pregnancy.'

'You are right. I think the news killed something inside her. And having Godefroy hovering around here will not help either. It renews her fears. He is going to Rome, and I have asked Ildebrando to dispatch him back to Lotharingia. Feeling safe may help her heal.'

'I hope you succeed.' Agnes hugged her. 'You said you were going to tell her about the prophecy? Did that give her some comfort?'

'Not as much as I hoped. She understands its implications, rationally, but it does not seem to matter to her.'

LXXXI.

Lucca, 20 June 1071

The Lucca noblemen repeated their oath of loyalty on their knees before taking their leave. Bishop Anselmo led them out of the throne hall to the nearby cathedral of San Martino. They would take Mass together to thank the Lord for the fruitful meeting. Matilde had made her excuses and stayed behind. She was not feeling ready to take Communion.

The room was sweltering, and she wished she could remove her veil. Her stay in Lucca had come about by accident. On her way back from seeing the pope, an urgent message from her mother had reached her there: Godefroy had crossed the Alps headed for Canossa and she should stay put until sent for, while Beatrice dealt with him. She could have been stuck in a far worse place than Lucca.

Bishop Anselmo, a gentle young man of admirable learning, was a perfect host and had helped her transform her stay into an opportunity to assert her role as the city's future overlord and meet with the city greats.

Besides, since her return from Germany, her mother had handed her the responsibility for Florentine affairs; so she had used her stay in nearby Lucca to seek an update from the lord of Florence, Count Guido. His envoy was due any moment, with a report on the city's revenues.

Going beyond politics, the family palazzo in Lucca was one of her favourite residences. The walls of the throne hall were covered with tapestries of exquisite Flemish craftmanship, a treasure from her mother's dowry. A marble statue of a Roman emperor, found amongst rubble behind the amphitheatre, took place of honour between the two thrones. She walked around it, admiring the detail of the armour, and the flawless recreation of the human form.

The doors creaked open, and the ushers let the envoy in. She slipped back in her throne. If she dealt with him swiftly, she could retire to her apartment to rest during the worst of the heat.

The envoy, on his knees, seemed to hesitate before lowering the hood of his short summer cloak. Matilde waited until he lifted his head. The eyes that looked into hers were eyes she had never forgotten.

Even from the throne, she could see Rolando blushing. 'I apologise if my arrival is unsettling. Martino is unwell, and the count chose me as messenger.'

If the guard at the door could hear the conversation, or considered anything about it unusual, she could not tell.

'I am not upset, I am surprised.' The sentinel's expression had not changed, but better to be safe than sorry. 'Wait outside,' she ordered him.

As the door closed, Matilde took in the man kneeling in front of her throne. He was even more handsome that she remembered. The set of his face had broadened with age, and so had his shoulders. He must be unbeatable with a sword in his hand.

'How is life treating you?'

'I have done well under Count Guido.' She recognised in his gaze the depth and gentleness she had carried in her heart all those years. His well-cut summer linen tunic confirmed his words. 'He says a soldier who can write is a rarity. He is entrusting me with important missions, like this one.' He passed a hand over his hair. 'He is a good man.'

'The Lord of Florence is lucky to have you.' She mustered a casual smile. 'Do you have a wife yet?'

He nodded.

She managed to sound detached. 'Children?'

Again, he blushed. 'One... and another on the way.'

Perhaps her nod came a little too quickly. 'I am happy for you. You deserve a good family.'

'So do you.'

She laughed. 'Noble people operate differently, as you know.'

'Of course. I have learnt it the hard way.'

She did not avoid his gaze. This man had suffered for her. Life had given her a chance to see him again and ask for his forgiveness.

'I am sorry,' she said in one breath, stepping off the dais to be level with him. 'I have been sorry every day of the last six years for... what they did to you.'

His eyes shone with the same intensity that had bewitched her.

'It was not your fault.'

'What did they do to you?'

As he smiled, the first lines showed in his brow. 'I healed, and it does not matter. My actions were my choice. I have no regrets.' Typical Rolando, too dignified to linger on his pain. 'How is married life?'

'I left my husband,' she said, with as much indifference as she could. This was not the time to think of Godefroy riding to Canossa and hovering around her lands.

Surprise mixed with pride in his face. 'You have always been brave.'

Brave, he had said, as if speaking a magic spell. His words re-awakened feelings buried deep inside her, reminding her of who she truly was, before her loss, before her marriage. Brave.

'Do you remember where the bishop's stables are?'

He nodded. 'I just left my horse there.'

'Go there and wait for me.'

She did not allow herself to think – it would prevent her from acting. Hurrying to her apartment, slipping on her riding hose and tunic, she made her way to the stables. Rolando was feeding his mount and whispering to him.

She chose a mare recommended by the bishop for her docility. He came over to check her saddle and stirrups, like in the old days.

'Ride behind me,' she said.

They followed a trail into the thick growth of cypresses, oaks, and olives outside the city walls, spurring their horses into the late afternoon sun. The vegetation thickened as they moved deeper into the wood. Matilde pulled on the reins to stop her mare so Rolando could catch up. She dismounted, and he did the same.

'Is it cold in Canossa still?' he asked.

'It has been a cold spring.'

'I miss it.'

Guilt gripped her. Rolando's old father was still carrying the shame of his son's banishment. In all probability, she walked past him most days, but she had become blind to his existence.

When had she stopped noticing other people's feelings and needs?

'I will take care of your father until the end of his days; you have my word.' It was the least she could do.

'Will she let you do it?'

She, her mother. 'She will.' With everything that had happened since, her innocent love for Rolando had most certainly paled into insignificance in Beatrice's mind. 'You should ask Count Guido to send you to Canossa next time – instead of Martino.'

'Seriously?'

'Seriously.' Although she had suggested the ride, she struggled for something to say. 'Thank you for coming.'

'Thank you for the opportunity to spend time with you.'

Considerate and caring as he had always been. The word "time" rang in her ears, and found its way to her head, where it coupled with "brave". She stopped and turned. 'I should have been braver with you, back then.'

She lifted her arm, and her finger slowly traced his cheek. Rolando's hand closed on hers and time stood still. In the end, he squeezed it and drew it to his lips. He let go, nervously ruffling his hair. 'I apologise, I am just too happy to see you again.'

'So am I. Fate may never give us another chance.'

'Another chance?'

When she realised how he could read her words, she rushed to clarify. 'I do not want to tempt you – or be tempted by you. We should go back.'

He studied her. 'Have you ever loved, Matilde?'

She nodded.

'Did he deserve you?'

She shook her head.

His finger followed the outline of her nose, as if she were an ancient goddess or a Madonna to worship in awe. 'I love my family, but when I see you, I still wish God made me highborn.'

'God has a debt to you,' she said. 'To us, actually. They judged us and punished us when we were innocent.'

As her word sank in, his arms closed around her and his fingers traced the back of her neck under her tresses. 'All these years I have dreamt of this,' he whispered.

She hugged him, savouring the feeling of her body against his, of their heartbeats joining.

He held her face between his hands, and his lips brushed hers softly. 'I hope God can forgive me.'

She would never find anyone like this again, not in her world.

Once in her life, she wanted to kiss him like the lover he could have been. And this time, it should not be Rolando who paid the price.

'This is my sin, not yours,' she said. Her mouth sought his, and could not let go, each kiss a bite of paradise. 'Thank you for teaching me to fight... and for trusting me... and for never betraying my trust.'

He held her tightly as if she could disappear, his lips all over her face, her neck, the inside of her wrists.

Was it lust she was feeling, or love? Or a dark desire to get back at Heinrich, even though he would never know? All she could tell was that both her body and his were quickly approaching the brink of a precipice, of another sin that she would have happily committed, but did not want Rolando to commit, because he deserved better.

She pulled away. 'I will not turn you into a lesser man than you are. I love you because you have dignity.'

He nodded, understanding. Unlike Heinrich, he did not need sex with a woman to prove that he owned her heart, or part of it. 'There are many ways to love. I will always be there for you, in war, and in peace.'

LXXXII.

The abbot and chief librarian remained seated at a table in the light-filled scriptorium of Nonantola, flicking in wonder through the pages of a precious manuscript Beatrice was lending them to copy, as Matilde took leave.

She had been in Nonantola for two weeks, hoping that readings and spiritual exercises would help her to make sense of her mother's revelations on Charlemagne's prophecy. She had timed her retreat to coincide with the likely arrival of the news of the royal birth, in the hope it would cushion the blow. She kept fluctuating between pain and hope.

The terracotta walls seemed an extension of the autumn leaves, as she made her way to the cloisters where her visitor was waiting.

The thick dark hair and well-built frame of Archbishop Guiberto of Ravenna were easily recognisable from afar. He walked to meet her. She had always felt uneasy in his presence, and it was no different this time.

'Cousin,' he said, ceremoniously kissing her hand.

The words lingered in the air, probably a deliberate reminder of what could have been. Hailing from a cadet line of her paternal family, Guiberto had lost out when Beatrice had succeeded in claiming Bonifacio's and Federico's rights on Matilde's behalf.

Denied the Canossa inheritance, he had carved an ecclesiastic career for himself, with remarkable results.

After joining Empress Agnes's service during her regency, he had made friends amongst the top echelons of the German clergy, and advanced to the prestigious archbishopric of Ravenna at surprising speed.

Although their paths had never crossed when she was at court, Heinrich held him in high esteem. Yet Beatrice mistrusted him. 'Never forget that he is where he is because of his ambition, not because of his vocation.' He had given plenty of proof of that.

'What brings you here?' she asked, foregoing the customary kiss of the archbishop's ring.

'I could ask the same of you. This is an imperial abbey.'

'I need not remind you of my family ties with Nonantola.' Destroyed by the Hungarians, the abbey had been rebuilt thanks to substantial donations from her mother.

'I see marriage has not tamed you,' he said.

Matilde unwillingly blushed. Despite her hatred of Godefroy, she resented the knowledge that her reputation was being smeared in high places.

Guiberto relished his little victory and smiled. 'What a pity that fate has played out the way it has. I bet you would much rather have retired to a convent than married the Duke of Lotharingia. If only your mother had not been too scared to promote your male relations.'

She had no patience for his pathetic games. 'Are you disappointed in your lot as a prince of the Church?'

Everyone knew that Guiberto had lovers, and she was ready to throw it in his face, if he continued with his provocations.

'Let me tell you what brings me here, my lady cousin. I visited Denis of Piacenza and the dear bishop has asked me to deliver you a letter from our overlord.' He frowned mockingly. 'The king is concerned that your mother might filter your correspondence.'

'My mother does not filter my correspondence.'

'Maybe not—' Guiberto's eyes tightened. He was obviously relishing the conversation. 'But I am glad I can be of service. Perhaps our overlord is hoping for your support in the resolution of the Milan crisis, which your mother may find difficult to offer.'

She had no intention of getting into a political conversation with Guiberto.

'Where is this letter you mention?' If it contained news about the royal birth, better face reality.

Guiberto took a scroll out of his pocket. 'I have been warned it is cyphered – not that I would ever—'

She grabbed the scroll and headed for her apartment in the guests' quarter, leaving Guiberto in the cloisters.

After confessing Berta's pregnancy, Heinrich had written a few letters. She had not replied to them, she had even left one unopened. Hope, ironically, had been one of the reasons behind her lack of reply. Silence could make him realise the suffering he had caused and teach him the value of honesty.

Pain had been another. She could not bear to hear news of Berta's pregnancy when every day she was waking up to an empty womb, and the despair of barrenness.

There was a third reason. 'I will prove my worth to you,' he had said to her in Augsburg when he already knew about Berta. Well, this was his opportunity to prove his worth. She needed to know that he was man enough to fight for her trust, for their love.

His tortuous theory that Beatrice might intercept his letter, if he had really entertained it, did not bode well. It was a childish blame game, a refusal to confront the fact that his behaviour had broken her heart.

The scroll between her fingers felt heavy. Coming a month or so after Berta was expected to give birth, this letter could spell the end of all their dreams or give their love a lifeline. Should she open it? He had gone to so much trouble to make sure it reached her, perhaps she should. Her fingers trembled as she broke the seal.

My beloved,

I failed you by not telling you about Berta's pregnancy, and that caused you incredible pain. There is no point in repeating that it was not my intention to hurt you. I simply judged that our loss was still too raw, and that the news would have killed you. It may have not killed you, but it has killed our love, and this I regret every day.

When God took our baby from us, we wondered if He may have been against our love and punished us for our sins. But God has now taken Berta's son too, after barely a day.

The likes of Ildebrando are probably saying my sins are so dark that God has to keep punishing me. To me, this new death proves that God did not condemn us. God has no preference for my lawful wife over the woman I love.

I hope that this turn of events gives you a chance to reconsider my behaviour and whether I do deserve to be excluded from your life. I hope you will find in your heart the strength to forgive me and look to the future we can have together.

The political climate is getting darker, and right now is not a good moment for me to canvass for repudiation. Perhaps I have made some errors. I know Rudolph would turn on me immediately. I need to win this war first.

But Adalbert is ready to resume his job. If Berta continues to fail to produce an heir to the crown – and I will make sure she does – that day will come. That day I will want you by my side, if you can forgive me and grant me that honour.

Heinrich

LXXXIII.

Merseburg, a month earlier

Traditionally, the appointment of the archbishop of Milan was a royal prerogative, and one the Milanese themselves proudly defended. In the eyes of the city's nobility and a large part of the population, their archbishop was not inferior to the Roman pope; they saw their diocese as equal to Rome and independent from it, and they took pride in having their own separate liturgy.

In recent years, an extremist religious movement going under the name "Patarines" had made friends in high places and challenged the archbishop's authority. The Roman Church had nurtured their seditiousness in the name of purity. Pier Damiani and the Milan-born Pope Alexander had supported their crusade against married priests and continued to have a soft spot for them. But their true ally in Rome was Ildebrando.

For years, their leader, the former knight Erlembardo, had been the archdeacon's dearest friend, steadily supplied with gold from Roman coffers and blessed papal banners.

Thank God Archbishop Wido, who had held the seat since the days of Heinrich's father, was a man of steady loyalties. Unjustly banished by the Patarines, he had stood by his oath to the Salians at the price of exile.

The young deacon kneeling at Heinrich's feet was Wido's envoy. Solidly built, hazel eyes, straight nose, and a gentle-looking face. Heinrich had forgotten his name the moment it has been uttered. He focused on the message, rather than the messenger.

'Your Majesty, sadly, our Archbishop Wido's health is ailing. He believes Our Father is about to call him to Him.'

'I am sorry to hear it.'

'My master Wido is not concerned for his soul. He is troubled by the knowledge that Erlembardo intends to defy your right to nominate his successor. He is already suborning the populace. This is why he has sent me to you.'

'What can I do to help him?'

The deacon presented a small wooden box. 'Being sound of mind, my master Wido is secretly resigning, returning to you the ring and staff that he received from your father. He hopes this will give you time to nominate his successor, foiling Erlembardo's schemes.'

Heinrich was aware of the stares of his advisors. Erlembardo and his thugs had overstepped and should be taught a lesson. And the idea of stoking Ildebrando was hard to resist. Besides, given the choice, he would rather lead an army to Milan than back to Saxony.

The young man had acted bravely, crossing the Alps at the risk of his own life to deliver a message that Ildebrando's henchmen would have stopped at nothing to delay.

Carefully avoiding Adalbert's eye, he addressed the deacon. 'Your master speaks highly of you in this letter.'

'I am grateful for kind words from a master I cherish with all my heart.'

'What is fear for you, deacon?'

The young man, still on his knees, blushed faintly. 'I try to act so I do not give myself too much time to think, Your Majesty.'

He liked the answer. For him too, this was time to act. 'You can keep the staff and the ring; they are now yours.' He gestured for the deacon to stand. 'I shall need all the brave men I can muster, if I want to win Milan back. Go back as my archbishop, and challenge whomever they choose to elect.'

He still could not remember the deacon's name, but it would come back to him soon enough.

§

Adalbert had asked to have a word in private. 'Your Majesty, had you been pre-warned about Wido's resignation?'

He poured him some wine. 'I had not. But appointing the Archbishop of Milan is my prerogative.'

Of course, Adalbert was going to be uncomfortable with his approach. But he was tired of delays and wrangling. The appearance of the deacon, probably no older than him, and ready to risk his life for what he believed in, had been a sign.

'You acted within your rights, yet your decision to appoint the new archbishop will not be well received in Rome.'

'It is time to grab the bull by the horns.' He removed his coronet.

Adalbert's features were taut. 'I speak the truth to you now, like I spoke the truth to your mother when she pleaded with me to vote for Antipope Cadalus.'

'Go ahead.'

'Naming the Milanese archbishop, without the slightest act of spiritual deference to Rome, will damage your position there. At other times, you could afford this. At this moment, when your mother and Abbot Hugh are putting your divorce back on the Lateran's table, you need all the goodwill you can get from Rome.'

'Liutpold says our Italian politics have been passive for too long.'

Adalbert had not touched his wine. 'Liutpold does not know about your matrimonial projects. This stance with Milan has the potential to damage the countess's position too. It delays your imperial coronation, which makes Lotharingia more important to Rome. It may stall her divorce.'

He had not thought of that. But perhaps Adalbert had not understood his plan completely. 'This crisis gives us the opportunity to weaken Ildebrando, Adalbert. Milan is one of the sources of his power over the cardinals.'

'Do you want to—'

'Go to Milan.'

'I urge you to reconsider. The only way you will enter the city of Milan is by force.'

'This is the warning we keep receiving from Duke Rudolph – what Ildebrando wants us to believe.'

'I struggle to see a good justification for attacking Milan. Unless you are willing to blow everything you and the countess are working towards.'

Heinrich remained silent, his eyes firmly set on the snake of the Rhine shining outside the window.

Adalbert's voice had a ring of surprise at his own conclusion. 'Do you see this as an opportunity to go to Italy and work things through with the countess?'

He did not agree nor deny. Despite her silence, he had cast his pride aside and written to Matilde as soon as he had buried his son.

Adalbert did not know. She must have received his letter by now. If he met her face to face, even once, she would know how much he still cared. And dangerous as it might be, they could resume their relationship. Milan was not too far from Mantova; he could visit her.

Adalbert pressed on. 'The best way to achieve your desired outcome with her is to ingratiate yourself to Pope Alexander.'

'On my mother's advice, I have asked for his spiritual guidance on the matter of the dissolution of my marriage.'

The answer was evasive and they both knew it. He hated to admit it, but Adalbert was right. He had misjudged; his desire to settle scores with Ildebrando had blinded him to the pope's closeness to the Patarines. He had to backtrack a little, be sweet to the Holy Father until he had blessed his divorce, and Matilde's.

'We will put the idea of a military attack on Milan on hold for now,' he conceded. 'However, we need to extirpate the Patarine movement once and for all, or it will remain a thorn in the empire's side,' he warned, without looking the archbishop in the eye.

His haste to see Matilde had led him to commit a faux pas with the pope that would have the opposite effect: delay their reunion. All his hopes rested on his letter now. He had written it with all the love he still felt for her. If that did not bring them closer, he did not know what would.

LXXXIV.

Nonantola, 2 October 1071

Matilde retreated to her room. The flames spread the scent of lavender, keeping the autumn at bay. She re-read Heinrich's letter. His intensity enveloped her, as if he were physically next to her, wrapping her in his mantle, in his arms.

There was no heir, and his present, their present, could be re-opened, could blossom into a future. They were both in a decent position to free themselves from the yokes of their marriages. Perhaps God had really meant for them to be together. She just needed to write a loving letter back, and the last six months could be wiped off. Only they could not.

She lay on the bed, staring at the ceiling, trying to name and make sense of the feelings in her heart. There was hope, and there was relief, but they were mixed with resentment, and it was not the resentment for his dishonesty in Augsburg.

In light of his letter, she was willing to give him the benefit of the doubt for his silence; perhaps he had truly misjudged. But the resentment was still there, and it came from a place of deeper loss, of deeper betrayal.

How could he even consider picking up his quill and writing to her when his baby had just been buried? He should have been by his child's grave, he should have been comforting his wife, no matter how little he felt for her.

Despite the depth of her guilt, Matilde ripped a sheet of vellum and started writing to Berta. She could not confess her sins, especially now that she would be in so much pain. But she needed to reach out to her.

Dear Berta,

I write to you, like to a sister, who having recently suffered the same loss you are suffering can understand the pain in your heart.

I pray to God that your body may heal fast, and your soul too.

I know the sleepless nights, when you wake in your chamber and feel guilty and failed because you could not snatch from death the baby you are expected to deliver and nurture.

I pray for the soul of your baby, and I pray that God may look upon you with favour, granting you grace after this loss.

I hope your little Adelheid is well and healthy and her little arms and smiling face bring you the joy you deserve.

As I am too far to pay a visit, I am sending you a manuscript from the Nonantola library, whose words have been of comfort to me in my grief, as I hope they will be to you.

You have been nothing but kind to me, and I hope we will meet again in some not too distant future, when we are both healed.

She placed the quill back in the inkpot, waiting for her message to dry. Despite their different personalities and their different ambitions, right now her life and Berta's did not feel that dissimilar.

How long had it taken Heinrich to put their daughter's death behind him? Had he shoved her out of his mind the moment he had turned his back to her snow-dusted cross in Quedlinburg? She placed her hands over her womb and cried.

The letter to Heinrich could wait until tomorrow. It was time to go back to Canossa.

§

Her mother came to meet her in the courtyard, looking distressed. 'I have news, from Milan – worrying news.'

'What happened?' Matilde asked, handing her horse to an attendant.

'Heinrich has nominated the new Archbishop of Milan, one of old Wido's deacons, without discussing it with Pope Alexander – or anyone.'

That could not be. Why would he risk alienating Rome when the outcome of Berta's pregnancy handed him the opportunity to undo his marriage? 'Rome will see it as an outright provocation,' she said, still incredulous.

'Perhaps it is,' said her mother, gloomily. 'And his misjudgement could have heavy consequences for you.'

'How could he not have seen that?' Tears of irritation filled her eyes. His letter may have spoken of forgiveness and love and a future together, but his reckless and insensitive actions were the undoing of his words.

'Adalbert would never have encouraged such a childish course of action,' said Beatrice. 'It must be this Liutpold's doing.'

'Surely Heinrich has been on the throne long enough to see when the advice he receives is stupid.'

The moment she snapped her anger turned to sorrow. Had she remained at his side, perhaps she could have influenced him positively, from behind the scenes. She shrugged the thought before it took hold. Coming to Italy was a choice she had made in the best interest of both of them – to secure their future together, and to become his queen as soon as possible.

And now that their future was within hand's reach, he had smashed it into a thousand pieces like precious glass.

LXXXV.

Canossa, 20 October 1071

Ildebrando di Soana was casting a distracted look at the tapestry of the Queen of Sheba when Beatrice arrived in a flurry of gowns, deliberately late.

His downturned lips bore a trace of anguish. 'I bring upsetting news,' he began. He paused, as if postponing the utterance delayed the finality of his words. 'The Byzantines were slaughtered by the Turks at Manzikert.'

Beatrice made the sign of the cross, quivering at the thought of the savage bloodletting. The Constantinople Church had clashed heavily with Rome about fifteen years earlier, and the schism had never been recomposed, but theological difference paled into insignificance in the light of the news. 'Whatever the recent past, our Eastern brothers need our prayers right now.'

Ildebrando nodded. 'We have lost the most powerful Christian army, our bastion against the Infidels, the guardians of the roads to Jerusalem.' There was a slight tremor to his voice. 'Our beloved Mother Church... is under attack from all directions: the Turks in Jerusalem, the Germans in Milan, the Norman snakes wherever they can squeeze themselves into...'

In all their dealings, she had never seen him so visibly troubled.

He sighed. 'I sometimes wonder if the Church will survive my lifetime.'

'Shall we pray, Ildebrando?'

Slowly, he assimilated her invite. 'With pleasure, Sister Beatrice.' He knelt by her statue of Saint Michael, and she joined him. 'Let us pray for justice, for God's justice.'

For the first time in their decades of knowing each other, she could feel a heart under the shield of his arrogance and faith. The litanies seemed to help him. His pallor lessened and his lips straightened, the lines around his eyes becoming less visible.

After making the sign of the cross, he offered his arm to help her rise.

'Now, let us hear the matter you wished you discuss.'

'Godefroy stopped here in early summer, on his way to you in Rome. I thought he would give up and accept his lot. Instead, he has taken up residence in my lands and is refusing to leave without my daughter.'

Ildebrando dropped the pretence. 'I have persuaded him to do so.'

Suddenly they were enemies again, playing a game of chess that could have lethal consequences for a third absent person. 'Can I ask why?'

'The Salian has not been crowned, nor shown himself worthy of the imperial title. I thought it premature to rely on him to defend Rome.'

Beatrice had to be careful not to open her flank to his attack. 'I appreciate the immediate military benefits to Rome of the continuation of the alliance, but we cannot ignore his behaviour.'

He rose so he could look down on her. 'You have my word that nothing will happen to your daughter, or the relics.'

'How can you give your word when he has already betrayed his commitment to the Church by breaching the contract?'

'Slowly, I am bringing him to reason.'

She propped herself up to a standing position. 'Godefroy may have made promises to you. But he will not keep them. Besides, I urge you to consider the needs of Matilde's soul. The marriage has wounded her, and rather than resuming it she is ready to drop her inheritance and retire to a convent, away from temptation of the flesh.'

He arched an eyebrow. 'She is more suited to war in the service of God than a convent.'

'I agree with you. She would not shy away from going to battle in the name of God. She could place the Holy Blood at the front of her army when fighting for Rome, if only Godefroy returned it.'

His lips smiled, but his eyes did not. 'As I promised, I have ordered him to restore the relics to you. He will comply. In return, he demands his wife back. I cannot explicitly deny him that, not until the relics are here and the imperial coronation resolved.'

Beatrice pursed her lips, trying to keep her anger from boiling over. Had he done a deal with Godefroy, agreed to let him have Matilde as the price for the return of the relics? Surely, he would not go that low. And if he did, his superior would never agree.

'I will die at the Holy Father's feet rather than put my daughter through this,' she snapped.

He cast a murderous glance in her direction. 'As you said, it will be the Holy Father's decision.' His mouth was twisted as he kept churning thoughts. 'You must have heard the news from Germany.'

She lowered herself back in her seat, adjusting the wolfskins. 'I am so sorry for the poor young queen. I have sent my condolences through her mother.'

'Sorry? We should be grateful to God. The queen has proven that she can deliver boys. Her position is secured.'

So that was the true reason he was backing Godefroy again. It was not to have a defender for Rome. It was to stall her divorce until the day Berta delivered a living heir to the crown, trapping Heinrich in his marriage.

She had to take the positive, the reassurance that he actually did not care if Matilde remained estranged from Godefroy, as long as there was a marriage on paper. 'I am sure we will hear of a new royal pregnancy soon,' she replied coldly. 'In the meantime, I urge you to focus Godefroy on the return of the Holy Blood, with no conditions attached.'

A.D. 1072

LXXXVI.

What change a year brought. The only thing in common was the snow. It enveloped everything, including Matilde's pain, softening it, for now. Snow would be her daughter's blanket, keeping her little body safe under the dark earth. By now, she would have been smiling, walking, saying her first words. Instead, before Christmas, Matilde had written to Adelheid, asking her to scatter dried rose petals on her grave on her birthday.

Theologians did not believe that babies could go to heaven, as they had not been baptised. But she could not think of her daughter being anywhere else.

She had not heard from Heinrich after she had replied to his letter in the autumn, other than for the customary Christmas wishes penned by the royal chancery. She had been hard on him and she knew it, but the hardness had come from a need of her soul – to see him rise to the challenge, her challenge.

She ached to hear him express sorrow for his dead children and to see him fight for her forgiveness, for her love. She yearned for proof that there was still more to Heinrich than the selfish short-sighted brat who had blown up her chances of divorce for the sake of appointing an archbishop in Milan; or the coward who had hidden the truth from her; or the father who could bury a child and then another and just move on, his heart barely scratched by the pain around him.

She had hoped the one-year anniversary could be the turning point, the moment the loss of their daughter confronted him in all its starkness, forcing him to grieve; the moment he found words of love for the innocent child they had buried together. But no words had come from him. Had he even remembered, spared a thought, for the child under the fig tree?

The flakes were landing slowly, whitening the valley below.

Her cheeks were streaked with tears that would not stop flowing.

It was not meant to end like this. Her memories were buffeting like a raging wing. Heinrich holding her and comforting her when she had escaped from Godefroy... Their first night in Goslar... Heinrich making love to her in Speyer when they had found out she was pregnant... The king who had risked his throne to love her and start a dynasty with her.

What had happened to that man, to that king? With hindsight, the political errors had started earlier than Milan. His conflict with Otto, according to her mother, had had a dubious start. Milan had only been the next book in the poem of his downfall. Because it felt like a downfall.

Would things have turned out different, had she stayed by his side? Could she have stopped him from clashing with Pope Alexander? From stupidly jeopardising her divorce to settle scores with Ildebrando? Could she have persuaded him to seek a rapprochement with Otto? Perhaps.

Perhaps her lot as a queen would have been to shield him from his many demons.

Shields... Swords. After being raised to fight and to lead, would she have been happy just whispering suggestions into his ear, as a reassuring power behind the throne, even when she could see things more clearly than he, or his advisors, did? Her mother had struggled with that fate.

The sword he had made for her was hanging on her wall. She had never loved him as deeply as she had the day he had given it to her. Why? Because that day, through his choice of gift, she had felt he knew her soul, the way knights and ladies in poems knew each other's souls.

She trembled as she touched the tip of the sword. Suddenly, her offer to retire to a nunnery felt like the betrayal of a higher destiny God had called her to; a destiny Heinrich himself had sensed in her, at the height of his love.

'Charlemagne's blood is meant to rule, not to obey,' she whispered as she dried her cheek.

The death of her child had made her feel barren and unworthy, and so had the failure of her love. The heartache had devoured her soul, blinding her to the meaning of her mother's revelation.

God had not handed her the text of Charlemagne's prophecy, the Holy Blood, and the right to fulfil a destiny higher than the Holy Roman Emperor, just for her to rule by the sidelines.

She whispered another prayer for her child, and a prayer for Heinrich, that he may find again the beauty in his soul. She had lost her man. But in doing so she had found her future.

Outside, it was still snowing.

LXXXVII.

Goslar, 2 March 1072

Adalbert hated being bed-ridden and unable to receive his king properly. His servant arranged the cushions to help him sit upright and, at his nod, disappeared into the anteroom.

He was sure he would not see another spring. At least he had made it to Goslar, where the court would be until Easter. Other than in his palace in Bremen, he could not think of a better place to die.

He had fought his illness with all he had for over a year, keeping it secret at first. He did not want to leave his king in the midst of a civil war, with a treacherous court, and no-one to trust. But his body had had enough of the fight.

'My mother sends her regards.' Heinrich handed him a letter from Agnes and pulled up a chair to sit by the side of the bed.

Adalbert smiled, remembering an enchanting young lady who had arrived at court with a flurry of liveliness and dreaminess, and those unforgettable rosebud lips. 'Any word from our empress brings me solace.' He reached out his bony hand but did not break the seal.

Instead, he glanced at Heinrich. 'I am grateful she is still here to support you after I am gone.'

The king looked surprised. 'Anno never trusted her, but you did. Were you ever lovers, Adalbert, after my father's death? You can tell me now.'

He shook his head. 'There was merely the trust of kindred spirits. Not many people could understand her Aquitanian soul in this rigid Nordic court. We bonded when I comforted her after your father banned jesters from their wedding banquet.'

Heinrich giggled for a moment. 'That sounds very much like you.'

'In truth, I would have seized my chance if she had shown me that kind of interest. But our relationship was always honourable.'

'Thank you for the truth.'

Adalbert placed the scroll by his side and adjusted the pillows behind his back to see more of the chamber.

His Ghent tapestries, his ivory writing box, his jewellery coffer, his silver-hilted sword, and his collection of precious goblets: alabaster, rock crystal, silver, Venetian glass... So many earthly treasures to cherish for a little longer and then dispose of.

Arranged neatly on two sturdy tables were a selection of his manuscripts – works of the ancients and religious works, appropriate reading for a bishop, and his selection of maps of the Scandinavian lands and the islands of the northern ocean.

The love poetry was all stored away in the painted coffer with the Goseck coat of arms, in his chamber in Bremen.

His gaze surveyed all his possessions and came to rest on the young king, who had just thanked him "for the truth."

Like all kings, truth was what he would need most, and would struggle to find, so truth should be his parting gift.

He took as deep a breath as he could and smiled. 'It is time for my last life lessons to you. Then, like a pachyderm, I will ask to die alone.'

Heinrich stoked the fire, probably to master his feelings. A weak late-winter light was pouring in through the window; only two weeks and it would change to the rosy hue of spring if he could live to see it.

He stretched his cramp-ridden hands on the silk and wool sheet. 'Your father was my master. I honoured him by taking care of you. But there is a lot of your grandfather in you.' Lovingly, he took in the features of the young man facing him; his gaze, the way he furrowed his brow. 'Your grandfather was fearless, always ready to challenge his fate, and to challenge others. I have tried to nurture that in you.'

Heinrich kissed the archbishop's ring. 'You have taught me all I know.'

'My time with you has been short, and, understandably, it has taken you some time to trust me after Kaiserwerth. I have taught you what I could. And I have loved you like a son.'

A tear trickled down Heinrich's cheek. He did not wipe it.

Adalbert grasped up a key from the table next to his headboard and handed it to Heinrich.

'This opens my writing box. I have made a will, of which you will be the executor as well as the main beneficiary. I would like you to keep any volumes from this room you may wish to read, and my collection of maps of the northern end of the world.'

'It will be my honour.'

'I have other books in my palace in Bremen, some relics, some jewels, and my cellar, of course. Although it is your prerogative to assign them, I would love it if you kept the vineyards you gave me, and drank to me once a year.' His lips relaxed into a tight smile. 'Maybe I have made you too much like me.'

Heinrich's face twisted for a moment, but he managed to turn his sadness into a smile.

Adalbert took a small sip from the cup between his hands, smelling the earthy cloves and orange peel.

'I would like to recommend one person to you, as someone you can trust with your life.'

'I would heed your advice.'

'Young Gottschalk of Aachen... He studied at Saint Jude... You may have heard some of his poetry.'

Heinrich remembered him. 'His writing is superb.'

Adalbert reached for a wet cloth and wiped his forehead to relieve the fever. 'His mother was an Aquitanian maid from your mother's following.'

'Really? How did he end up at Saint Jude?'

Adalbert's palms spread on the cool bed cover. 'The maid became pregnant outside wedlock. The empress, although very displeased, felt she had to cover up the scandal.' He mustered a smile. 'To this day your mother does not know. He is my son.'

The surprise came and vanished. 'I am honoured by your trust.'

He wiped more sweat from his forehead. 'Gottschalk has known since last summer. He has sworn he will look after you when I am gone.'

'I will treat him like a brother.'

Adalbert went silent, to gather fresh energy. He was holding on to life, breathing into life, with the determination of someone who knew his mission was not over.

'Counsellors come and go, and often pursue their own interests. Two people you can always count on: your mother, and the lady Matilde. You have broken her heart, but she has not retaliated. This shows she is a woman of great integrity.'

He coughed for a few moments, slipping back along the cushions. 'When her mother is gone, you will have an ally in her. If fate is on your side, when this war is over, she will become more than an ally again.'

Heinrich did not comment.

Adalbert overcame another fit of coughing. 'There is a letter from Otto in my writing box. It has just arrived. He has agreed to make peace.'

Heinrich seized his hand. 'I could not ask for better news from you. You have my deepest gratitude for trying until the end. I hope this allows you to go in peace.'

Adalbert had no time for gratitude, time was running out. 'You will be under no illusion, and rightly so – you always have to watch him and Rudolph. They both want your crown. Divide and conquer, all you can do is keep playing them against each other.'

'I will.'

Heinrich had expelled Rudolph from court, accusing him of conspiring against him, but he would have to reach an agreement with him, for the kingdom's sake.

Adalbert closed his eyes, gathering sparkles of energy from somewhere deep within. 'Amongst your bishops, trust Theodoric of Verdun and Altwin of Brixen. Everyone else is pursuing their own interests. Anno is blackmailed by Ildebrando, and his Saxon nephews are siding with Otto.' His voice weakened. 'The empress tells me something is wrong with Siegfried of Mainz too.'

'I will heed your warnings.' Heinrich's throat sounded tight. He took a golden cross, part of Agnes's dowry, out of a pouch on the table. 'This is for you. You would honour me immensely if you wore it for your last journey.'

'It will make the journey sweeter.' For a moment, the film of tears made the cross shine brighter. 'Speaking of crosses, speaking of Rome...' His energy was fading. 'You have inherited Conrad's courage, and his right to rule over the Church as Holy Roman Emperor, and the Holy Spear. But Rome has spent two decades demolishing the sacrality of kingship...'

The king placed the cross in his hand. 'I will fight for my right, always.'

Adalbert, exhausted, nodded. It was time to take leave of his young master and find God. He raised his hand. Slowly, he gestured the sign of the cross on Heinrich's face. 'I bless you one last time... with the power given to me by the Omnipotent.'

Heinrich forced a smile. 'You have truly blessed me, Adalbert. You taught me that you cannot love God without loving life. I will take your teaching to my own grave.'

LXXXVIII.

Rome, 10 March 1072

After Pope Alexander had excommunicated Godifredo of Milan, on the day of the Epiphany, in the presence of a papal legate, the Patarines had engineered the election of Atto as their archbishop. But the populace and Milanese nobility had risen immediately, renewing their loyalty to King Heinrich and forcing Atto to renounce his oath.

In her attempt to mediate, the empress had tried justifying her son's actions and she and Pope Alexander had ended up fighting. Today, though, he was sorry for her.

The orange trees in the middle of the atrium of the Lateran palace were in bloom, but the news he had just received was going to make Agnes feel like she was alone in the midst of a winter storm.

'It is better if you hear this from me, my daughter. Pier has left us.' Despite the depth of his faith, the utterance made him feel lonely and weak.

Bringing a hand to her mouth, she began to weep. 'How?'

He held her in his arms for a moment. 'God was merciful to him. He passed away after a brief illness, while visiting his homeland of Faenza. The monks at Santa Maria degli Angeli are already reporting miracles.'

'Mary and her angels will be honoured to have him.' Her voice wobbled.

'I know how hard this is for you, and that you need a few moments to recollect.' He did not normally admit women into his personal chapel, but Agnes right now needed to be in God's arms, under God's gaze. He showed her inside. 'Let's pray for Pier's soul, and for his guidance from heaven.'

Prayer worked its usual miracle. She recovered her composure, although not her serenity. She was too politically aware not to see the dangers of the situation.

'We need to talk about what Pier's passing means for your son.'

'Of course, Holy Father.' She dried her cheeks. 'Pier's charisma made him an ideal mediator between Rome and Germany. Now—'

'Now your son has dug himself into a deep hole. We owe it to Pier's soul to lend him a hand.'

'Thank you for your generosity, Holy Father. My son has committed serious errors of judgement in his handling of Milan.'

She was trying to apologise, and he had promised Pier he would be kind to her. He offered her the truth. 'I need to impress the seriousness of the Milan crisis upon you. Ildebrando says excommunicating Godifredo is not enough. He is urging me to use the anathema against your son.'

Agnes almost choked. 'Excommunication seems too high a price for his political crimes.'

'I agree with you. Pier would be urging us not to close our hearts to your son's suffering.'

'My son is suffering more than he even realises.' She lowered her gaze, despondent, probably missing Pier's paternal presence. 'Last year, he was visibly maturing, as a man and as a king. With hindsight, a lot of it was down to Matilde's influence.'

He killed the argument before she could fully formulate it. 'I cannot encourage her back into your son's arms, Agnes – for political and moral reasons. I hear he has gone back to his lustful ways.'

Agnes bowed. 'We know how much temptation is thrown at a young king; but he loves her, and she is far away and giving him the cold shoulder.'

Pope Alexander waved impatiently. 'There is a lot in your son's life I feel sorry for, but the way he conducts his love life is despicable.'

Agnes blushed.

'Going back to his political misjudgements, please tell him that while for the moment I will not excommunicate him, I cannot and will not compromise on Milan. Until he backtracks on Archbishop Godifredo and stops nominating bishops elsewhere, he can also forget about his divorce.'

'I will relay your message... however I feel I need to manage your expectations. My son is dealing not with one but with two major crises in Germany—'

'Oh, yes, I hear he has turned on Duke Rudolph.' Ildebrando had shared the news that Heinrich had thrown his brother-in-law

312

out of court. 'Why does he keep on going from crisis to crisis, in your view?'

'Adalbert blames it on the advisors he is surrounding himself with – incompetent, who depend on him for advancement and enrichment.'

He softened his tone. 'It is becoming a real problem, Agnes. Pier's loss makes it imperative that your son rises to his responsibilities.'

'What do you suggest?'

'Duke Rudolph has asked for Rome's help. I cannot send Ildebrando to Germany, a clash with your son is guaranteed. After we celebrate Easter, I will need you to go and broker a peace between Rudolph and your son.' Fear flashed across her face. 'Hugh of Cluny will join you,' he added, to strengthen her resolve.

'I pray Pier will watch over us from heaven; we need a miracle.' She bowed, clearly doubting her ability to recompose the crisis.

He placed his arm on her shoulders. 'He will, and I will be with you in prayer.'

'There is also the war with Otto.'

He smiled. 'You are right, we need two miracles... Three if we add Milan.'

If Pier, from heaven, could not touch Heinrich's heart, no-one could.

LXXXIX.

Beatrice pushed the scroll aside and muttered a prayer.

Another piece of her youth had been spirited away by time. In her memories, Adalbert was still the handsome knight revelling at her engagement in Nijmegen, before accepting his fate of third-born son and taking his vows.

At times she still wondered how she had managed not to succumb to his charming ways. Eyes like a cloudless southern sky, intelligent, educated, elegant – he had broken so many hearts with so much ease. Some people should not be allowed to turn to dust.

She was in her fifty-third year, and the people she had known that had made it past their prime had started to wither and fall like leaves.

The walls of her Roman palazzo regained the solidity of reality, and Agnes's voice pulled her back to the present.

'On his deathbed, he left my son the gift of peace with Otto.' She dabbed her eyes. 'It is unjust that he goes now, after his months of tireless negotiation, when he could finally reap the reward.'

'I think he would say this is the best moment to go,' said Beatrice, embracing her friend. 'From heaven, his soul will look down over the fields of Saxony and see peace this Easter.'

'As if losing Pier was not enough,' Agnes let out, embracing her back. Two women who had fought for decades for their standing in a man's world, and their most trusted allies were deserting them, one after the other. 'Let's pray that Pope Alexander is preserved for us,' said Beatrice with a shiver. 'Or our children will end up at Ildebrando's mercy.'

The recent deaths were not only a blow to Heinrich. Adalbert's backing of Matilde's divorce amongst the German princes would have provided a solid stalwart against Ildebrando's intrigues, just like Pier Damiani's charisma could have done.

Agnes turned to her. 'How is Matilde?'

'Physically she is safe. Ildebrando has accepted that she is only returning to Godefroy over my dead body.'

'Good. And how is her soul?'

She gave a light shrug. 'Heinrich remains a deep wound. I think she has wrapped it up in bandages and soldiers on. But in other ways I think the cloud is lifting. She is trying to find the true meaning of her life.'

'I am glad. I will see how I find him when I go to Germany after Easter. I don't think he will ever forget her.'

Beatrice felt cold, as if an icy wind had snapped into the room. 'She has suffered enough, Agnes. Now that she is finally healing, I do not want you to encourage him.'

The empress's eyes glistened with urgency. 'But the prophecy! The spear and the blood, the eagle and the hound... They were meant for each other!'

Beatrice thought again of Adalbert: so much effort, so much devotion, how much of it repaid? No-one knew God's way. 'If that is their destiny, God will guide them to each other again. But we should not push them.'

'You are wiser than me, as usual. In the last year I have often found myself thanking God for the promise I made to you – not to tell Heinrich the full truth about the prophecy.'

The mere prospect filled Beatrice with dread. 'Thank God we decided that way. Given how he has handled himself in the last year, God knows what he could have done with the knowledge.'

Agnes let out a sigh. 'Oh, Beatrice, I still cannot believe that my son blew his opportunity to be happy as a man and stronger as a ruler.'

Neither could she. 'It was hard for me to bless her union with Heinrich, Agnes, but I had come around to it. I had started imagining her crowned after you on the steps of Saint Peter.' She had never before admitted that to Agnes.

Her friend's expression filled with gratitude, and she kissed her on the cheek. 'Nothing would have made me happier, Beatrice.'

She dried a tear. 'Our children have to find their way to fulfil their destiny.'

315

XC.

Pope Alexander was on his knees by the icon of the Virgin in his private chapel. He nodded for Matilde to join him. She dropped onto the green and red mosaic floor next to him, and wove her voice with his, reciting the *Ave maris stella*, entreating Mary to loosen the chains of the guilty, and send forth light to guide the blind, help them find their way.

She still struggled to look at babies without bursting into tears, so she was grateful to pray by an image of the Madonna not holding the child. With her jewel-studded veil and ringed hands, this Mary was a princess like her, a sister she could pour her heart out to. Even their gowns were the same colour.

She prayed to her to bless her conversation with Pope Alexander, to shine light on her path.

At the end of the hymn, making the sign of the cross, they turned away from the soft gaze of the blue-cloaked Madonna of the seas.

'Father.' She addressed him like in the old days, omitting the adjective "Holy," 'I need your spiritual guidance.'

'Of course.'

'I believe you are aware of all the prophecies being whispered, about the birth of a new Charlemagne.'

He arched an eyebrow. 'I do not want you fooled by these dubious claims,' he warned.

His scepticism felt good – a sign that there had been no ulterior motive when he had refused to help her pull out of her marriage three years earlier. She adjusted her veil so he could see her eyes and trust her words.

'I am here with my mother's blessing. The prophecy was not just a figment of Conrad's imagination. She has proof.'

His upturned lips betrayed a mixture of interest and surprise. 'That is quite a claim,' he said, showing her out of the church and into his private scriptorium. 'What proof exactly?'

'Years ago, Emperor Conrad gave her a parchment sheet with

the text of the prophecy and Charlemagne's seal.'

Seated at his table, he glanced up, and his expression darkened.

Still standing, with her hands on one of the carved chairs, she continued. 'Conrad swore her to secrecy, and she kept her oath. But when I returned from Germany, she decided I should know.'

He motioned for her to join him at the table.

Matilde took his cue. 'I will inherit responsibility for the prophecy from her. My first act as the prophecy's custodian is to share my knowledge with you – under confession.'

'You can begin.'

She pulled a folded sheet out of her pocket. 'I will need you to read it and then burn it.'

'Of course.'

His face betrayed no emotion other than interest as he ran over the text. Then he went to the nearest brazier and watched the flames devour the vellum.

She joined him there. He was studying the image of Saint Peter the fisherman on his ring, as if to gather his thoughts. Then he looked up. 'Thank you for coming to me with this. I am proud of you – for your honesty, and your courage.'

She smiled.

He did not smile back. 'Your mother and Emperor Conrad did right – the existence of the text should remain a secret. Too many people, on both sides of the struggle, would be ready to exploit it for their ends.'

'You have answered my question – the time is not yet right.'

He took her hand between his. 'Two people above all should never know: Ildebrando and King Heinrich.'

At the mention of her former lover, Matilde inadvertently blushed.

He noticed it. 'How are you feeling about him now?'

She did not mind his directness. 'He wrote to me, after...' She could not bring herself to combine the words "death" and "baby" in one sentence, even someone else's baby.

He understood. 'And?'

'It does not matter. He threw everything to the wind with the Milan debacle.'

His gaze was on her, and it was gentle. 'Agnes thinks he did not realise what that would mean for you.'

'Trapping me in my marriage? Maybe not. But he did not really fight for me after that. Even at the anniversary of our loss... I hoped it would trigger something in him. But he did not even write.'

He glanced at his Mary icon, swiftly, as if for guidance from a mother. 'I can judge his political actions, as they speak for themselves. It is hard to judge his feelings for you without hearing his side of the story.'

'Maybe.' Was her trust so broken that she could not bring herself to see Heinrich's point of view? What made it worse what that she still missed his warmth, his touch, the texture of his skin.

Pope Alexander's voice remained neutral. 'He has no living heir yet. This prophecy you have shared with me... the implications if you two married... You could start the most powerful dynasty in history—'

Matilde shook her head. She could not afford to dream and have her heart broken again. 'As you said, he cannot be trusted with this knowledge.' She spoke a bit too hastily, to shrug the temptation off.

'I suppose I hate seeing all his promise and talent go to waste.'

Her lips trembled, although she managed not to cry.

'At least yours will not.' He reached for her hand and squeezed it. 'You have suffered deeply, Matilde, at the hands of your husband, for the loss of your child and for the man you gave your heart to. But maybe God has called you to a destiny higher than Heinrich's, and higher than earthly love.'

'I am done with earthly love.' She raised her chin, suddenly defiant. She had come to Rome to seek guidance on the prophecy and had ended up talking about her love life; so be it. She expanded on her point, softening the edges of her argument. 'One thing I know for sure: if and when I manage to free myself from my yoke, I will not marry again, Father.'

He looked concerned. 'It may prove difficult. Besides, I am sure your mother will involve you in the choice and negotiate a good husband for you next time.'

'I do not want to be a subject to anyone. I have seen what it has done to my mother, and what it has done to me. I want to rule like men do.'

His expression was blank as he digested her words. He rose, and paced the room, stopping by her side. 'From the first moment I met

318

you as a young girl I believed that you had a great destiny, yet I was unable to perceive what God wants for you. I doubted myself, I saw your sex as an obstacle, and that made me weak at times when it came to steering you on your path.' His tone was warm and affectionate now. 'That text we burned reinforces my belief. You are going to be more than its guardian.'

She met his gaze. 'I dared to think the same, as I... mourned. This is what I wanted to discuss with you. Could the prophecy refer to a woman?'

He paused. 'Charlemagne did not specify the sex of the child. You were trained in the use of arms like any noble boy. You have led fleets. The emblems mentioned in the prophecy could refer to your parents just as much as to you and Heinrich.'

She raised the other obvious hurdle. 'My father is not of Carolingian descent, at least as far as we know...'

Pope Alexander insisted. 'As far as we know, you have said it. God has His ways.'

He most certainly did.

The Holy Father placed a hand on her shoulder. 'As your confessor, I ask you now, is my suggestion that you might be Charlemagne's heir what you hoped to hear from me today?'

'It is. But I know what the Church thinks of the role of women. Does my lack of humility disappoint you?'

'I think it proves you worthy. God has an unusual design for you, and you are heeding His call.'

The Madonna of the Sea, with her arms free of babies, had heard her prayer, showed her the light. 'Father, the scars I bear... I do not know if they will ever heal. But you are what your pain makes you.'

'The *Via Crucis* leads to the Resurrection, my daughter.' His smile was broad now, and open.

Suddenly, her resurrection felt within hand's reach.

He gazed at his fisherman's ring again. 'Alas, I feel in the fulfilment of your destiny I acted like a real successor to Saint Peter. I failed you, numerous times, before the cockerel sang. Then I must ask you, Matilde, do you forgive me?'

She smiled, her heart filling with the starry blessing of the Madonna of the Sea. The sea healed her wound with memories... A day on the Tyrrhenian, at the mouth of the Tiber, the taste of salt on her lips. Freedom, hope, hope of freedom.

She dared to tease the Holy Father. 'If I do, what will you do next?'

'I know not how many more years on this earth God will grant me, and be warned that we will have to proceed in steps negotiate hurdles, such as undoing your marriage...'

'But?'

'But you are the anointed one, and it is my duty to support you so that this prophecy might be fulfilled, and revealed to Christendom, when the time is right.'

'Then, Father, my answer is yes.'

-THE END -

HISTORICAL DICTIONARY OF MAIN CHARACTERS

Adalbert, Archbishop of Bremen (1000-1072). Co-regent (with Anno of Cologne) during the last years of King Heinrich's minority, he retained an influential role afterwards. He had been one of Emperor Heinrich III closest advisors, and there were rumours that he had refused to become Pope.

Adelheid, Abbess of Quedlinburg (1045-1096). King Heinrich's eldest sister, she was destined for the cloisters and was made Abbess of Gandersheim in 1061 and of Quedlinburg in 1063.

Agnes of Poitou, Holy Roman Empress (1025-1077). Widow of Emperor Heinrich III, she was regent for her son King Heinrich between 1056 and 1062. After the coup of Kaiserwerth she lost the regency to Anno. She moved to Rome in 1065 and lived there until her death.
She was held in high esteem by the Church and was often tasked with challenging diplomatic missions to influence her son's policies. She hailed from the ducal house of Aquitaine.

Anno, Archbishop of Cologne (1010-1075). During King Heinrich's minority he orchestrated the young king's kidnapping to end Empress Agnes's regency. He then became co-regent with Adalbert of Bremen. As Archbishop of Cologne, he was officially head of the German Church, directly responsible to Rome.

(Pope) Alexander (1010-1073). Anselmo da Baggio had been Bishop of Lucca before his election to the Holy Seat, and therefore technically a subject of Beatrice of Tuscany. He was her daughter Matilde's confessor.

Beatrice of Bar-Lotharingia, Margravine of Tuscany (1020-1076). Adopted by Emperor Conrad, King Heinrich's grandfather, she was given in marriage to Bonifacio of Tuscany, the greatest warrior and largest landowner in the empire.

After her husband was killed, possibly on Emperor Heinrich's orders, she agreed to a union with her kinsman Gottfried of Lower Lotharingia. Her only son Federico, Bonifacio's heir, died mysteriously at fourteen, as he was coming of age. Her third-born Matilde was the only one of her children to make it into adulthood. Beatrice was tireless in her defence of her former Bishop Anselmo da Baggio, elected to the Holy Seat as Pope Alexander II, against the challenge mounted by Cadalus of Parma.

Thanks to her political marriage, her diplomatic ties with the German princes, and Rome's support she achieved the (almost) impossible: securing the right of a daughter to succeed a father as margrave and count.

Benno, Bishop of Osnabruck (1020-1088). After a pilgrimage to the Holy Land at barely twenty, Benno became a teacher at the Benedictine school of Goslar in Saxony and, shortly after, was made headmaster of the cathedral school at Hildesheim by Heinrich III. Soon he was appointed imperial architect. He retained his role when King Heinrich IV came of age and was responsible for the construction of many of his castles.

Berta of Savoy, Queen of Germany (1051-1087). Betrothed to King Heinrich of Germany as a toddler, she married him in Trier at fifteen. She suffered public humiliation when three years later her husband attempted to divorce her, claiming he could not bring himself to consummate the marriage. Although his request was denied and they ended up having children, Heinrich continued to keep lovers and she is likely to have been an unhappy wife.

Cadalus, Bishop of Parma (1010-1072). Chosen as antipope by the Roman nobility and the German court, to oppose the appointment of Anselmo da Baggio by the Roman cardinals, he continued to consider himself the legitimate Pope, even after the synod of Mantova proclaimed his opponent.

Cuno, royal chamberlain. Possibly an unfree servant, sources refer to him as Heinrich's trusted chamberlain and one of his childhood teachers.

Godefroy, Duke of Lower Lotharingia (1040-1076). He married Matilde of Canossa in late 1069, just as he inherited his father's duchy. The marriage failed almost immediately. Matilde escaped to Italy in 1071 and never returned.

Gottfried the Bearded, Margrave of Tuscany and Duke of Lower Lotharingia (997-1069). He rebelled against Emperor Heinrich, who stripped him of his title of Duchy of Lower Lotharingia, in favour of Frederique of Luxembourg. He managed to become Margrave of Tuscany by secretly marrying his kinswoman Beatrice. The union, negotiated by Ildebrando di Soana, angered the emperor who exiled Beatrice and her daughter Matilde to Germany.
After moving to Italy, he started meddling in papal elections and managed to get his cadet brother elected to the Holy Seat in obscure circumstances.

Guiberto of Correggio, Archbishop of Ravenna (1029-1100). A cousin of Matilde of Canossa, after a brilliant career that saw him nominated chancellor for Italy during Empress Agnes's regency, he supported Cadalus. That cost him his place. He continued to cultivate his connections in Germany and eventually, in 1072, Heinrich made him Archbishop of Ravenna.

Heinrich the Salian, King of Germany, future **Holy Roman Emperor** (1050-1106). Crowned king at his father's death, Heinrich was left in the care of his mother until age eleven. After the coup of Kaiserwerth, his education became the responsibility of Adalbert of Bremen and Anno of Cologne. His relationship with his mother remained difficult even after he came of age.
He is one of the most controversial Holy Roman emperors. Officially head of the German and Lombard churches, he fought hard to retain the right to invest his bishops. The clash with Rome over the appointment of bishops, known as the Investiture Controversy, developed into a fully- fledged crisis when Heinrich decided to invest the new Archbishop of Milan. In 1070 he also let himself be dragged into a series of intrigues that resulted in a civil war in Saxony.

Hugh of Semur, Abbot of Cluny (1024-1109). Firstborn of the Loire count Dalmatius, he asked to enter Cluny while still a child, defying his father's will. Impressed by the strength of his faith, Abbot Odilo allowed him to take his vows at fourteen. At Odilo's passing, his brethren voted for twenty-five-year-old Hugh as their new abbot.

He would become one of the longest serving and most influential leaders of the Cluny order. He mediated tirelessly between his godson King Heinrich and Rome. He built the third abbey church at Cluny, the largest structure in Europe for many centuries.

Matilde of Canossa (1046-1115). Third-born of Margrave Bonifacio of Tuscany and the Lotharingia princess Beatrice of Bar, Matilde was destined for the cloisters. The premature death of her brother and elder sister made her heiress to her father's vast domains.

As a child she accompanied her mother into exile in Germany where she spent a year in the imperial household and attended King Heinrich's coronation in Aachen.

Married against her will to her distant cousin Godefroy of Lotharingia, she accused him of rape, abandoned him and made her way back to her lands. She lived estranged from her husband and gradually took over the reins of power from her mother.

Ildebrando di Soana (1015-1085). From the hamlet of Soana near Grosseto, Ildebrando studied in Rome as a youth. Among his masters was the erudite Giovanni Graziano, the future Pope Gregory VI. When the latter was deposed by Emperor Heinrich III and exiled to Germany, Ildebrando followed him to Cologne.

In Cluny in 1048 he met Bruno of Toul, who was about to become Pope Leo IX. He went to Rome with him and became one of the most influential figures in the Curia. He engineered a few papal elections. He was also in charge of Rome's diplomacy, negotiating alliances and marriages to suit the reformist Church.

Otto of Nordheim, Duke of Bavaria (1020-1083). Appointed Duke of Bavaria by Agnes in 1061, the following year he played a crucial role in the coup against her. He was behind the temporary banishment of Adalbert of Hamburg-Bremen in 1066. He was one of the best military commanders in the kingdom.

In 1070 he was accused of being involved in a plot to murder the king. Heinrich decreed that Otto should submit to trial by combat at Goslar, but after being refused a safe-conduct he declined to appear. He was deprived of Bavaria, while his Saxon estates were plundered.

Pier Damiani (1007-1072). Poor and orphaned, he managed to become one of the most celebrated teachers of his age, but in 1035 he gave everything away to become an itinerant monk and a hermit. His charisma proved a double-edged sword and Rome soon required his services. A passionate reformer, he was put in charge of complex diplomatic missions between Rome and Germany, including, in his late years, King Heinrich's divorce. He was a friend of Pope Alexander and was Empress Agnes's confessor. He did not always see eye to eye with Ildebrando and tried to exert a restraining influence on him.

Rudolph, Duke of Swabia (1025-1080). Briefly married to Heinrich's middle sister Matilda, unproven rumours claim that he was Empress Agnes's lover. In 1066, as Heinrich married Berta, Rudolph married her sister Adelaide, becoming brother-in-law to the king twice over. It is difficult to work out his exact role in the Saxon rebellion, but he is likely to have been allied on and off with Otto of Nordheim.

Theodoric, Bishop of Verdun (d. 1089). Bishop from 1045, he was loyal to King Heinrich's father and then to Heinrich, who held him in high esteem. There seems to have been some genuine affection between the king and the bishop. Theodoric was also close to Beatrice.

AUTHOR'S NOTE

The Middle Ages lacks proper historiography. What it offers in abundance is chronicles and propaganda. You could argue that the eleventh century is the first age of fake news.

The extant accounts of the lives, motives, and actions of Countess Matilde of Canossa, King Heinrich of Germany, their mothers, and the great figures of the Roman Church in the 3rd quarter of the eleventh century are irrecoverable, buried under so many contradictory and highly polarised retellings. My novel is a creative attempt to tie up those loose ends. It is an Ariadne's thread in a maze of lies.

Apart from Matilde's lover Rolando and her maid Vinicia all the novel's characters are historical. So are the political events and the settings. But the plot is fiction.

I first came across the historical characters of Heinrich of Germany, Ildebrando di Soana and Matilde of Canossa as a child. Later on, while studying the period, I was fascinated by the unusual number of women who seem to have played leading roles in eleventh century imperial politics.

By a combination of fate and tenacity, Matilde of Canossa, her mother Margravine Beatrice and Empress Agnes, managed to hold on to positions of exceptional power in a male-dominated era. The Church, which officially, in the words of Humbert of Silva Candida, was misogynistic to the point of denying women the right to speak inside a religious building, held all of them in high esteem.

The true trailblazer, though, was Countess Matilde. Probably the first woman to lead armies since Roman times, she ruled for most of her life without a husband. Roman sourced depict her a pious woman denied her wish to retire to the cloisters and forced to rule against her deepest wishes, whereas German chroniclers suggest that she was lustful and even the pope's lover. The words of her contemporary are too polarised to draw any conclusion, so I have chosen to base my judgement of her on the facts. Her lifelong political involvement is proof, in my view, that there was much more to her than a series of fatal coincidences that brought her to inherit her father's titles and lands. Matilde stayed in power, fought for her power, with too much passion and determination.

Deciphering Heinrich IV of Germany is equally difficult. We have documents, even irrefutable papal sources like Pier Damiani, casting him as a priest-king. He was legally the head of the German Church and displayed a lifelong devotion to the Virgin Mary. But since his ill-fated attempt to divorce his wife at eighteen, Roman and Saxon sources have taken turns depicting him as some sort of mediaeval Jim Morrison, precipitating further and further into excess and debauchery. Emperor Heinrich IV may have been a tyrant, a mediaeval *poèt maudit* or an angel. Thanks to mediaeval chronicles, we will just never know.

If we try to extrapolate the bare facts from the sources, we know that Matilde and Heinrich shared important formative experiences. They spent a year together during their childhood in Germany, were both brought up by exceptionally powerful mothers, and both lost their fathers at an early age.

They were also both married against their will in the same years and fought against their fates with stubborn determination. Matilde was sent across the Alps just after Heinrich had been denied his divorce.

Heinrich's movements since his coronation at five are abundantly documented in German chronicles such as the *Res Gestae Imperii*, whereas Matilde's whereabouts before she inherits her lands in 1076 are poorly documented. But as an illustrious imperial heiress, countess and margravine, and distantly related to both king and queen, she is likely to have spent time at court in 1070 and 1071. Subsequent history and documents reveal a bond that would not have been natural between strangers. In surviving letters, King Heinrich claimed to trust Matilde and her mother above all other princes.

No source indicates that their dealings in 1070-71 went beyond the customary feudal relationship. Also, no sources suggest that Matilde's stillborn daughter may have been a lovechild. But we know that Matilde ran away from her husband and escaped to Italy, at personal risk, as soon as possible after the birth.

I was also puzzled by the Church's determination to keep both Matilde and Heinrich in marriages against their will, and that drove me to wonder if one reason for it may have been to keep them from marrying each other.

King and countess were related within the forbidden degree, and would have required a Church dispensation to marry, but when it suited the Roman agenda, realpolitik would prevail and such dispensation would be granted. Dispensation was given for Matilde's marriage to Godefroy, and her mother's marriage to Gottfried.

An alliance between Tuscany and Germany would have consolidated the crown and brought peace to the Holy Roman Empire, yet I have found no reference in the sources to suggest that such a marriage had ever been touted.

This brings us to Ildebrando di Soana. The all-seeing archdeacon, in charge of Church diplomacy and intelligence, personally negotiated Matilde's marriage and strongly opposed both her divorce and Heinrich's. It is unlikely he would have backed their union, as he would have deemed it a threat to the Church. Reuniting Northern and Central Italy to Germany would have recreated the status quo of the days of Charlemagne, and Ildebrando would not have wanted that. Could there have been other, deeper reasons? This is where I took some liberty.

Mediaeval devotion is marked by an obsessive fascination with relics. We know that Heinrich had inherited the Holy Spear. He had an inscription added to it, stating that a nail hammered into the blade was a relic from the Crucifixion.

The mysterious weapon, bought at huge cost by one of his predecessors, seemed to have talismanic powers. The moment it landed in imperial hands in the tenth century coincides with the end of the most dramatic period of the dark ages. The Holy Spear's obsession stretches throughout German history all the way to the Third Reich and would have made a good Indiana Jones story. Could Ildebrando's hostility to Heinrich be at least partially explained by a fear of his relics?

As for Matilde, we know she had relics of her own that made her fit to be a military leader and turned her femininity into a negligible consideration. Her mother had been involved in the rediscovery of the Holy Blood relics (which remain in Mantova to this day). These relics first came to light in the age of Charlemagne. With access to a relic of such power, it would become plausible for

Ildebrando to see her daughter Matilde as an alternative leader to Heinrich, or as a minimum as the most unsuitable wife for him.

Historians remark that all three Salian kings married women of Carolingian lineage, as if this legitimised their power. Matilde, related to Heinrich through his Carolingian grandmother Gisela, also belonged to the Carolingian bloodline. Was there something explosive in the union of Carolingian blood and Crucifixion relics, something that persuaded Ildebrando that she could never become empress?

I have tried to "connect the dots" by inventing the prophecy of the child of Charlemagne. Prophecies were another great mediaeval political tool. The millenarist impulse has always relied on stories of a miraculous child being born and bringing about a Golden Age. Virgil's *IV Eclogue* stretches its fascination all the way to Dante in the XIV century, so it is plausible that similar prophecies on the restoration of the empire may have been uttered by powerful rulers.

To my knowledge Charlemagne (and Emperor Conrad) never made such claims, but they would have been perfectly credible in the cultural climate in which these rulers operated. The Faustian Emperor Conrad, rumoured to have made a pact with the devil to secure the empire for his dynasty, seems a particularly attractive candidate.

The tapestry of eleventh century continental politics continued to be defined by Matilde, Ildebrando, and Heinrich in the successive decades of the eleventh century. It will form the subject of my next book, in which the king and countess meet again, in vastly different circumstances.

Every end is a beginning.

Read on for the opening of:

THE ROAD TO CANOSSA

PROLOGUE

Rome, 22 April 1073

Avoiding the usual gangs of beggars and petty criminals sheltering under the crumbling walls of the Circus Maximus, Cardinal Ildebrando di Soana climbed towards the convent perched on the top of the Aventino hill. The bald, long-limbed brother at the gate greeted him with the customary *benedicite*, and Ildebrando hurried along the familiar cypress-lined path to the domed Basilica of Santa Maria. Before setting foot inside, he turned to glimpse the Vatican hill across the Tiber. *May he rest in peace.*

From the distance of the Aventino, Pope Alexander's death felt like a bad dream. Only, it was not. The holy warrior Pope Leo, the even holier hermit Pier Damiani, Pope Stephanus, Pope Nicholas, now Pope Alexander – the names were like beads in a prayer chain, their feet no longer treading the earth. God had taken them all, orphaned His Church.

Ildebrando's heart was heavy as he stepped into the peace of the nave. In the Byzantine icon hung behind the plain marble altar, the pale palm of the Mother of God was spread open in greeting, her holy gaze radiating comfort under her jewelled veil.

On his knees, whispering a hymn, he revisited the options. The abbot of Montecassino was well-meaning, but was he too indecisive? Cardinal Hugo Candidus was experienced and shrewd – maybe too shrewd. The rumours that he may be tainted with simony, the trade in divine offices, were hard to ignore. The young archbishop of Ravenna was bright but too eager to please the German crown.

Ildebrando was aching with fear. If only he could stay forever in the peace of Santa Maria, instead of joining the other cardinals gathered in San Pietro in Vincoli for the election of the new pope. If only he could prolong this moment of uncertainty, rather than recommend an appointment he could come to regret.

The silence was broken by some commotion outside, perhaps a tussle between beggars. The smoke of the candles was making his eyes burn. *Time to go.* A shiver ran through him, as if Mary's fingers had touched his cheek in maternal blessing. Light flooded the worn marble floor as the side door sprang open.

'He is here!' shouted Cardinal Hugo Candidus, stooping through the low entrance, his long beard flowing sideways as he neared in the semi-darkness. When the cardinal kissed his sandals, Ildebrando jerked back. Then he saw the thin line of men trickling in through the side door: priests, monks, deacons. They headed for the transept; they knelt in a circle around Ildebrando.

The door swung closed, yet the commotion outside neared and intensified. Those were not the screams of a gang; it was a choir of voices, repeating the same words, over and over. Light blazed in. The door opened a second time. The rugged faces of the people of Rome, his people, filled the spaces between the columns. Local tradesmen, paupers in rags, even children... one after the other, they dropped to their knees, keeping a respectful distance, hands joined in prayer.

A withered candle-seller of the Lateran nodded to a stocky guard, and to a young deacon with a broad, honest face who had arrived with Hugo Candidus. Without a word, they lifted Ildebrando onto their shoulders. One last time, he searched Mary's painted gaze. *Guide me.*

Hugo Candidus opened the front door. The light painted yellow strokes on the marble floor. Ildebrando walked through it. In the narthex, a crowd of Roman plebs were singing hymns, shouting his name so loud that God in the heavenly spheres would hear it. 'Ildebrando *papa.*'

The Holy Spirit was descending upon him, but in his case the tongues of fire of the Scriptures were not the beacon of God's grace and light; within the fire of his personal Pentecost was the cold torment of guilt. The afternoon sky above him was almost too blue. More faces, more arms; it was no longer three men carrying him. It felt like a multitude. Turning his neck, he recognised the cone pines and the ruins of Nero's golden palace, halfway up the Colle Oppio. They were taking him to the place he had been avoiding all morning.

He felt powerless, with no will, no thoughts. The April air carried orange blossoms. Before long, they were climbing the steps of San Pietro in Vincoli. They came to a halt and knelt, to put him down as gently as they could muster.

Standing on his two feet was a relief. The bronze doors opened. Ildebrando crossed the threshold. One by one, the cardinals rose, embraced him, and kissed his feet.

Hugo Candidus was last. 'God has spoken through the people of Rome, by acclamation.' His deep Burgundian-accented voice filled the nave. 'He has chosen you, Cardinal Ildebrando di Soana, to succeed Pope Alexander.'

It could not be. It should not be. Ildebrando's heart was closed by fear, his mind engulfed by flames – God's tongues of fire, or Satan's, he could not tell yet. 'I thank you and the other *porporati* for the honour, which I am bound to refuse.'

Hugo Candidus and the Cardinal of Palestrina exchanged a quick glance, brows furrowed. They had expected his reticence. 'We urge you to reconsider,' they said in unison.

Ildebrando climbed the few steps to the altar so they could all see him. 'Brothers, colleagues, you are aware of the unsurmountable barrier I am facing.' As he began his explanation, his resolve came back. God would expect him to speak the truth. 'Accepting power from the people of Rome breaks the rules I have fought to establish and to preserve – under the holy Pope Leo, and our beloved Pope Alexander. It would be no different from accepting an investiture by the Roman *signori*.'

The *porporati* roared their disagreement. He silenced them with his hand.

Hugo Candidus seized his raised hand and held it between his. 'Brother Ildebrando, God has many ways of speaking His will. He may blow it into the souls of the cardinals or choose to give us a sign through external events.'

His words were greeted with rapturous applause.

Hugo Candidus let the clapping die out and continued. 'We, *porporati*, cardinals of the Holy Roman Church, have heard God's will in the voice of the people. This makes your election legal, within the terms of our constitution.'

'It does not, and we all know it.'

To escape temptation, Ildebrando stormed through the nave,

forcing the cardinals to give way like the sea before Moses. He did not look back. The biggest test of his will was waiting on the other side of the bronze doors: the humble people of Rome crammed onto the steps of the porch – the sinners who saw him as their hope of redemption, who loved him and whom he loved back. *Do not succumb to love and vanity. Your duty is to God.*

He pushed the doors open. The cheers were deafening. Taking a deep breath to conceal the doubts creasing his soul, he dispensed blessings on the crowd.

Two soldiers from Pope Alexander's personal guard, people he trusted, stood to the left of the doorway. 'Escort me to the Lateran.'

If they had an opinion, they were too concerned for his safety to voice it; they hurried him down the steps of San Pietro and through the back roads at the bottom of Colle Oppio, freer of crowds.

On the doorstep of the vestibule of the papal palace, he thanked them and dismissed them. They shrank to the size of an ink dot and vanished into the distance. The afternoon light was thickening and darkening over the hills.

Stepping inside, he rushed up the steps of Pilate's Staircase to Pope Alexander's study. The small, sturdy door closed behind him. He dropped to his knees on the cold, uneven mosaic floor, breathing hard. His olive-skinned hand clutched the cross hanging from his neck. The feelings that had overwhelmed him turned into words, spoken aloud. 'Why me, my Lord?'

Hugo Candidus was right; it had been a call from God. But why had God called him, Ildebrando, the champion of orthodoxy, in such an unorthodox way? Was He testing the depth of his faith?

The full moon replaced the sunset and whitened the roofs, framed by the marble window of the papal study. Images crowded his mind, and with the images came the understanding of God's plan. He, Cardinal Ildebrando di Soana, was not an innocent soul, but he could fight. The flames of his Pentecost would never burn pure – but burn they would, bringing about the change Christendom needed. Barely two decades had passed since Humbert of Silva Candida had dared to proclaim that there was nothing sacred about a king. Now the Roman Church was rising from its ashes. It was time for the final battle.

Darkness descended into the room. Ildebrando lit a few candles and sat at his predecessor's writing table. Grabbing a quill from the writing box, he unrolled a fresh sheet of parchment. Slowly, he traced the letters of a name that came to him from the abyss of his heart, from the sacred and dangerous place where faith meets doubt. He watched the ink dry on the parchment.

He, Ildebrando di Soana, would become Pope Gregorius. It meant 'guardian' in Greek. No name seemed more appropriate for the man called to ferry Saint Peter's bishopric to salvation. He, Ildebrando di Soana, would be like the raging of the east wind, buffeting the earth with violent blasts, swiping away everything that stood in the way of God's will. He dipped the quill in the ink. For his inaugural letter, he would quote from Jeremiah:

'See, I have set you this day over nations and over kingdoms, to pluck up and break down, to destroy and to overthrow, to build and to plant.'

A.D. 1073

I.

Rome, late May 1073

'The Holy Father will see you in the Council Hall,' said the stern-faced chamberlain. 'I shall check if he is ready.'

The bronze doors were grandiose, decorated with gilded crosses and eagles Their hinges creaked, as he disappeared inside the room.

Matilde sat down to wait and adjusted her pale silk veil. She took a deep breath – to calm her wits and strengthen her resolve.

The antechamber's floor was covered in polychrome stone tesserae, and the walls in marble slabs. Elegant in a very Roman way. Not that it mattered.

Ildebrando di Soana had been enthroned at terce the previous afternoon, in the Lateran Basilica, the official seat of the bishop of Rome since the days of Constantine. A clear sky had blessed the coronation; the incense emanating from precious golden holders had mixed with the scent of the first roses of the year, but all throughout the ceremony Matilde's attention had been elsewhere, curled around thoughts of today, of what to say, and how – to compel him to listen, and give her back her life.

Over the years, as the head of the papal diplomacy, Ildebrando had cast aside the Christian virtue of compassion with surprising ease to further the power of the Church. Matilde had been one of his pawns, betrothed at eight to Duke Godefroy of Lotharingia, and later forced to marry him to secure military support for the Eternal City. Now, at twenty-seven, for the first time, she could glimpse an opportunity to escape Ildebrando's chessboard. She had to seize it.

The gilded eagles on the bronze doors spoke of Rome, of law, of justice. She had not ceased fighting for justice after the bishop of Verdun had pronounced her a wedded wife, turning her into the property of Godefroy of Lotharingia. Piece by piece, she had come so close to dismantling the political edifice that had caged her.

Few princes of the Church would view marital rape as a crime. Pope Alexander, though, had trusted her. When she had fled her husband, he had not allowed political considerations to obfuscate his judgement. But a month ago – a month that felt like a lifetime – he had joined his predecessors in their everlasting sleep under the vault of Saint Peter's.

The gentle smile of the late pope vanished from her mind's eyes. The shining shapes of the burnished eagles evoked strength. She would need all her strength to persuade Ildebrando di Soana to complete his predecessor's work. The odds were stacked against her, but now was the time to try, while he felt blessed by God's will and while he needed political support for his anomalous election. *My Lord do not let him bring up the other matter.* Her mouth dried at the prospect.

Inside the room, steps approached; the eagles came forward and sideways as the bronze doors opened. Matilde did not need to cross the threshold to notice the change.

Pope Alexander had been a brave and humble man. There was no humility on the face and in the garments of the man sitting on a mosaic-encrusted throne, raised on a dais, under the Council Hall's famed gilded wooden ceiling. The red robe with a gold-embroidered hem imitated the clothes of an ancient Roman emperor.

Joining her palms in prayer, she knelt at the feet of the throne. 'Father,' she said in a whisper, unable to address him as 'Holy', a word that in her heart belonged to Pope Alexander alone. 'Thank you for making time for me.' She kept her head bowed, submissive, for now. 'My mother sends heartfelt apologies.'

'Another bout of her gout?'

'I am afraid so.'

His right hand, covered in a gem-studded glove, blessed her from the distance. 'Rise, daughter. We have a lot to talk about.'

Standing alone in the middle of the room made her feel exposed. That was the effect he wanted to achieve, surely, to weaken his opponents before they could deal him any blow. Before confronting him, she visualised an imaginary shield. 'Holy Father,' she managed to address him, 'you would be aware of the progress made by our beloved Pope Alexander towards the dissolution of my marriage.'

Ildebrando's eyes were black darts. 'You should pray, daughter. Prayer will remind you of your duty to support the Holy Roman Church through your union with Lotharingia.'

Three years after escaping Godefroy's claws, she still had nightmares. She would not endure being raped over and over for the good of Rome. Surely Jesus would not demand that of her. She suppressed a bout of nausea. *Ildebrando senses fear like a dog*, her mother had warned her. *Never cry, never break in front of him.* But she had to stop him.

'Father—'

'You should not interrupt me, daughter.'

For once, she was grateful for the veil she was wearing; it concealed the anger that must be chasing fear off her face, and her urge to hit him.

Clenching the ruby-encrusted cross on his chest, he let out a deep sigh. 'Prayer teaches me the limits of my faith. It shows me the way, the *Via Dolorosa* the Lord has called me to walk.' He paced the dais. 'The Church is under attack from all sides: the Normans south of Rome lifting their heads, and across the Alps, the wretched king of the Germans insultingly appointing bishops as if he had some God-given right.' A piercing glance, as if to search the recesses of her soul.

Her cheeks blazed. She bowed her head to hide her unease with a display of humility. As she did so, she glimpsed his feet, clad in magnificent golden slippers – probably not suited to walking a *Via Dolorosa* in Jesus's footsteps.

He kept talking. 'Worse even is that since the Infidels slaughtered the Byzantines at Manzikert, the inland road to Jerusalem is closed.' Thank God the conversation had moved on from Heinrich of Germany, although she struggled to fathom what the events in the Eastern Mediterranean had to do with her divorce. Besides, going to Jerusalem was not completely impossible. Pisa, a city she loosely ruled over, was growing rich, transporting pilgrims and goods to the East and back.

'God in his mercy has kept the sea route open,' she offered.

The golden slippers stilled. 'The sea route is not enough,' he sentenced. 'The Holy Roman Church needs a champion.'

Her breath died in her throat. Godefroy's father had held the title of Sword of Saint Peter. After his death, the honour had remained vacant, because Ildebrando, despite his determination to keep Lotharingia and Tuscany united against the power of the German king, mistrusted Godefroy and his motives. What had changed?

Her heart was pounding at the thought of her estranged husband commanding armies in the Roman countryside, physically near her. Ildebrando was studying her, his brow slightly arched. Then the smile came, as unsettling as his gaze. 'I am paying you a compliment, daughter. Pope Alexander was right: God has carved a unique path for you. *You* can become the most glorious Christian leader, now that your father-in-law is in the arms of Our Lord.'

'I?'

He stepped off the dais, down to her level. He was shorter than her and not someone who enjoyed feeling diminished, so the action startled her.

'Yes, you. Six years ago, you joined your father-in-law's expedition against the Normans in the *Campagna*. And you were barely an adult when you helped him rescue Pope Alexander from the Germans' claws, leading his fleet.'

She was surprised he even remembered. Ildebrando had never acknowledged her as anything more than a dynastic pawn.

'In both instances, Our Lord blessed you with victory. These are signs I cannot ignore. Despite your sex, He believes in you. So, you, of all princes, should support my holy mission.' He was still smiling. 'We will sail a fleet to the Holy Land, convert the Turks, and restore Jerusalem to the Christians.'

The East had been at peace for a couple of decades, and the Turks seemed to tolerate Christian pilgrims, but would they welcome a foreign fleet with open arms? Eyeing him under the veil, she gathered her thoughts. *If you highlight the dangers, he might decide you are a weak woman and call on Godefroy.*

'I am deeply grateful, Holy Father, for the honour you are paying me. Regrettably, an expedition of such magnitude requires funding on a scale—'

'Pisa is the mightiest sea power in the Western Mediterranean; their bishop is your vassal. Apply pressure and you will have a magnificent fleet ready to sail before the summer is over.'

She swallowed, looking for the right words to explain. 'The Pisans use their galleys for trade. They would rebel rather than lend them to me – or demand compensation commensurate to the riskiness of the expedition.'

The moment of complicity was over. With an impatient shrug, he slipped back on his throne on the dais. 'Will you tell the Lord that He is beyond your means?'

'Of course not.' She could not afford a straight refusal. 'I am trying to convey the complexity of such a mission... I fear—'

'You should not fear.' His voice dropped to a whisper. 'Last year, I secured the return of your dowry from your husband. So, your mother has her Holy Blood relics back – ready to be placed in the service of God.'

'I do not think I understand.'

'We will carry the Holy Blood at the head of your army.'

'The Sacred Vessels? My mother will never part from them again.'

His eyes reduced to slits, he glanced at her with a slightly amused expression. 'She will – to protect you.'

Finally, the reason he was offering a woman the leadership of the expedition was clear. *It is not my skill he wants; it is my relics.* The realisation was sobering. She was being charmed by a snake, by the glare of a basilisk. Time to steer the conversation back to her divorce plea.

He did not give her the chance. 'I hear you are not taking Communion.'

Unspoken between them, the sin that made it impossible for her to take Communion hung in the air in all its magnitude. For a moment, everything in the room was still, including her heart. Was he about to corner her into remaining married to Godefroy. Or excommunicate her? The silence dragged on, heavy.

She managed to find words. 'Not every day. My humble comfort is prayer.'

The strange smile reappeared on his lips. 'When you search your heart in prayer, consider this. A mission to Jerusalem would atone for all your sins in the eyes of God and allow me to pronounce you free of your marriage.'

II.

Rome, late May 1073

'The relics are mine.' Seated, Margravine Beatrice looked even smaller than she was, although queen-like in her green gown cut out of magnificent cloth from the East. 'I will not give them up.' Her unwavering determination did not reassure Matilde. 'I cannot afford to anger him, Mamma.'

Beatrice's bony fingers clasped the precious Byzantine hand fan on the side table next to her chair. 'Oh, you can.'

The peacock feathers of the fan moved back and forth. Their rhythmic movement did not soothe Matilde's mind. 'He will use the past against me.'

'He will not.'

'What makes you say that?'

The fan stilled. Behind the green and blue plumage, her mother's eyes shone like two stars, winter-cold with resolve. 'He is desperate for my relics. So let him bring up your sins. I will tell him I cannot in all conscience entrust what is left of Jesus's Holy Blood to a sinner.'

Matilde's cheeks were burning with shame, as they always did when her mother alluded to her adulterous relationship with King Heinrich of Germany; a relationship Ildebrando had uncovered, and would not hesitate to use against her, if pushed.

'If you condemn my sins, you are giving Ildebrando an incentive to—'

'Denounce you?' There was a hint of amusement in Beatrice's tone. 'He wants to go to Jerusalem. The Normans are breathing down his neck. Does he trust Godefroy? No. Would he ask King Heinrich of Germany to become the Sword of Saint Peter? Never.' Beatrice gave her a knowing look. 'If Rome needs protection, we remain his safest bet.'

'We are two women.'

She placed the fan in her lap. 'He invited you to lead his expedition, so your sex does not bother him – at least, not enough.'

A maidservant announced the arrival of Heinrich's mother, Empress Agnes. Her palazzo was also in the Lateran neighbourhood, so she visited frequently when they were in Rome. She slipped into the seat opposite her best friend Beatrice. 'Nine years, and I still struggle with Rome's heat,' she complained. Pearls of sweat shone on her forehead. She removed her veil, revealing her thick tresses, a deep blonde, barely streaked with grey.

The maidservant poured Agnes lemon-scented water from a jug into a green-hued Venetian glass cup. Matilde found a third chair by the wall. When the two mighty ladies met, she preferred to respectfully listen, fading into the background.

Beatrice was too curious for preambles. 'So, Agnes, how did your audience with our new Holy Father go?'

'It was most extraordinary.' The empress sipped her water. Her health was still good, and she looked younger than her fifty years. The skin on her hand was as white as her ring's cameo. 'Although he refused to reverse Pope Alexander's excommunication of Heinrich's advisors—'

'You asked him to consider that?' For once, Beatrice sounded surprised. 'Do you regret endorsing Pope Alexander's actions?'

'Most certainly not.' Agnes shook her head. 'Pope Alexander weighed two options: excommunicating either my son or my son's counsellors. I backed the lesser of two evils.'

'The lesser evil based on what we knew at the time,' commented Beatrice.

Agnes sighed. 'No choice of pope could be more disastrous for Heinrich.'

'So, what made the meeting extraordinary?'

At Beatrice's direct question, the empress leaned forward, gripping the carved sides of her wooden chair. 'He made no mention of striking Heinrich with the anathema – none at all.' Her cheeks now seemed rosy with excitement rather than heat. 'And... he is thinking of crowning him emperor!'

'Any conditions?' Beatrice frowned, doubtful.

Only that Heinrich rids himself of his excommunicated advisors, which seems reasonable.'

The flapping of Beatrice's fan was the only noise in the room. 'Surprising words,' she said eventually. 'I read them as a sign of desperation.'

'Ildebrando admitted he feels uneasy about the unusual circumstances of his election.' Agnes lifted her tresses to let fresh air cool the back of her neck.

'Uneasy or not, he has accepted it.' Beatrice rested the fan in her lap. 'And now he is becoming accustomed to the luxurious padding of the Holy See, he has no intention of leaving it.'

'I agree.' Agnes accepted a strawberry from a bowl the maid was passing around. 'He is offering my son an olive branch to strike a deal with him.'

'Heinrich turns a blind eye to Ildebrando's "illegal" election; Ildebrando forgets the past and crowns him Holy Roman Emperor. *Tabula rasa*, on both sides.'

'It just seems too good to be true,' mused Agnes. Her eyes wandered around the room before settling on Matilde. 'My dear, how did your audience with Ildebrando go?'

Beatrice spoke first. 'He sets an impossible condition for her divorce.'

Matilde explained, 'He wants me to take him on an expedition to Jerusalem—'

Beatrice snapped her fan in her lap. 'He dreams of placing the relics of the Holy Blood at the front of his troops. Dreams. I will not lend them to him.'

An unreadable thought flashed across Agnes's face. 'Hold your ground and you may get your wish, Matilde.' Her smile was as warm as her voice. 'Heinrich will not ratify the papal election overnight. In the interim, Ildebrando needs military support—'

'Precisely,' Beatrice fanned herself again. 'Speaking of your son, Agnes... Have you appraised him on your conversation with Ildebrando?'

'Not yet,' the empress replied. 'Since backing the advisors' excommunication, all I have received from him is insults.'

'He has been far more pleasant towards me,' said Beatrice. 'He wrote to thank me for supporting him against Otto of Nordheim.'

At the mention of the disgraced Saxon duke, Agnes started to play with the cameo of her imperial ring, as if to soothe her mind. 'Otto of Nordheim's rebellion is yet another reason Heinrich should dispense with his advisors in earnest. My son is the head of the German Church. Consorting with excommunicated—'

'Otto will not use theology against your son.' Beatrice shook her head. 'He is a man of action – a soldier.'

'Once a snake, always a snake,' Agnes hissed, leaving her ring alone. Was she thinking of the distant spring day when Otto of Nordheim had kidnapped his eleven-year-old king, damaging the relationship between mother and son beyond repair? Her face betrayed no emotion. 'We need to remain focused on our goal. The prospect of an imperial coronation may spur Heinrich into constructive action.'

Beatrice followed her train of thought. 'An imperial coronation would strengthen Heinrich against Otto and the Saxons.'

'Indeed.' Agnes fidgeted. 'Although Ildebrando's sudden willingness to crown him makes me nervous.' Her gaze shifted to Matilde. 'What did you make of his clothes?'

'They are a statement: that he is the only true emperor,' she replied.

'I interpreted them in the same way,' said Agnes, her gaze firmly on Matilde. 'And that made his other proposal even more surprising: he wants me to join him and you on the expedition to Jerusalem.'

Matilde shivered, and in her shiver were both fear and anticipation. Her mother clutched the sides of her chair. 'You!' She sounded angry with Agnes.

'I told him I am too old, Beatrice. He replied that I am a sinner, my son is a sinner, and that I should go to Jerusalem to ask the Lord to intercede for him.'

'He is blackmailing you, just as he is blackmailing Matilde, telling her the expedition would atone for her sins.'

Ignoring the fire on her cheeks, Matilde tried to make her point. 'Mamma, I need a divorce—'

'I won't let you go.'

'It is not up to you, or me,' said Agnes. 'Heinrich is her overlord—'

'Heinrich should stay out of this.'

Two pairs of eyes dug into Matilde's. She hated that her personal feelings were so easy to read. She offered a political reason for not wanting him involved. 'Until the crisis between him and Rome is resolved, Heinrich cannot afford to put a foot wrong.'

Beatrice barely heard her. 'I have lost a son to Ildebrando di Soana's grand ideas. I will not lose a daughter too.' Her voice was steely with the determination born of distant suffering. 'What did you reply to him, Agnes?'

'That although I am honoured by his offer, I cannot leave until Saxony is pacified, and my son has received the imperial crown.'

Beatrice's frown eased. 'Good answer, my friend.'

'If Heinrich becomes the Sword of Saint Peter, the protector of Rome, Ildebrando will have obtained what he wants,' Matilde objected. 'He would be free to sail to the East.'

'Indeed,' conceded Beatrice. 'Only he will leave without the Holy Blood – and without you.'

'If I commit to the expedition, my divorce will become urgent for him, Mamma.'

Beatrice's tone shifted from angry to firm. 'There is no link between your divorce and the expedition. That is just what he wants you to think. Ildebrando will release you from your vows when it suits him.'

Agnes was looking at Matilde. Was there a hint of complicity in her gaze? Did she share her desire to go on a journey that seemed impossible for a woman? Before her mother could notice the exchange, the empress had turned the other way.

ABOUT THE AUTHOR

Since childhood, Lara Byrne has always been passionate about history and historical fiction. After reading for a PhD in literature and working day jobs in marketing, she has decided to take the leap and write the genre she loves.

Lotharingia is her debut novel. It is the product of two years of research, and two years of writing.

Lotharingia's sequel, entitled *The Road to Canossa.*, will be released in paperback in March 2023.

Have you enjoyed this book? If you could post a review on Amazon - or on any other platform/channel you regularly use, Lara would be so grateful!

For updates on the release of *The Road to Canossa* and Lara's research, writing and travelling, you can subscribe to her mailing list. All you need to do is visit her website:

www.larabyrneauthor.com

Lara is on:
Bookbub: @larafbyrne
Twitter: @larafbyrne

Printed in Great Britain
by Amazon